Juno Rushdan is the award-winning author of steamy, action-packed romantic thrillers that keep you on the edge of your seat. She writes about kick-ass heroes and strong heroines fighting for their lives as well as their happily-ever-afters. As a veteran air force intelligence officer, she uses her background supporting Special Forces to craft realistic stories that make you sweat and swoon. Juno currently lives in the DC area with her patient husband, two rambunctious kids and a spoiled rescue dog. To receive a FREE book from Juno, sign up for her newsletter at junorushdan.com/mailing-list. Also be sure to follow Juno on BookBub for the latest on sales at bit.ly/BookBubJuno

Julie Miller is an award-winning *USA TODAY* bestselling author of breathtaking romantic suspense— with a National Readers' Choice Award and a Daphne du Maurier Award, among other prizes. She has also earned an *RT Book Reviews* Career Achievement Award. For a complete list of her books, monthly newsletter and more, go to juliemiller.org

Discover more at millsandboon.co.uk

ROGUE CHRISTMAS OPERATION

JUNO RUSHDAN

K-9 PATROL

JULIE MILLER

MIX
Paper from
responsible sources
FSC
www.fsc.org
FSC C007454

This book is produced from independently certified FSC™
paper to ensure responsible forest management.

For more information visit: www.harpercollins.co.uk/green

Printed and Bound in Spain using 100% Renewable Electricity
at CPI Blackprint (Barcelona)

MILLS & BOON

First Published in Great Britain 2021
by Mills & Boon, an imprint of HarperCollins*Publishers* Ltd
1 London Bridge Street, London, SE1 9GF

www.harpercollins.co.uk

HarperCollins*Publishers*
1st Floor, Watermarque Building,
Ringsend Road, Dublin 4, Ireland

Rogue Christmas Operation © 2021 Juno Rushdan
K-9 Patrol © 2021 Julie Miller

ISBN: 978-0-263-28357-0

1021

ROGUE CHRISTMAS OPERATION

JUNO RUSHDAN

To my husband, thanks for being
my hero every single day.

Chapter One

Her rental car slid across the ice and swerved. Hope gripped the steering wheel tighter, regaining control.

The night was pitch-black. Storm clouds that threatened to unleash more freezing rain blocked out the moon. To her right, beyond the darkness, was a steep slope that led straight to Goode Mountain Lake. No streetlamps or guardrails were along the side of this godforsaken road—*the only road*—that led in and out of the insulated town of Benediction, Virginia. There were only the bright lights from the SUV behind her.

High beams blared into her sedan. She glanced up at the rearview mirror. The light reflected was blinding.

Raising a palm to shield her eyes, she squinted against the harsh glare, but her car swerved once again. Hope put both hands back on the wheel as her heart drummed faster.

The dark two-lane road was slicker than she'd anticipated tonight from the rain earlier and the dropping temperature. She needed to slow down, but the driver behind her picked up speed, riding her bumper.

Misgivings stirred in her gut, crawling through her like worms beneath her skin, but she ignored them. She had to do this. For her sister, Faith. For her own peace of mind. She had to keep going until she made it inside Benediction, got answers about Faith's death.

No matter the cost.

Steeling her nerves, Hope tapped the accelerator. Just enough to get some distance between her and the SUV.

Nothing was going to stop her.

Raindrops hit the windshield and pounded the roof in a frenetic beat, ratcheting up her tension. She winced as she turned on the wipers. The downpour only obscured her visibility and made the road even more treacherous.

Wiper blades whisked aside the rain from the windshield, giving her a spotty view.

Headlights from an oncoming vehicle ahead pierced the darkness. A car had left Benediction. In the distance, she barely made out the lights from the lampposts marking the electric security fence surrounding the restricted town.

She checked the rearview mirror.

The SUV roared up behind her, too close on her tail. She touched the brakes to back him off, but the vehicle tapped her bumper.

She jolted forward in the seat, holding tight on to the steering wheel. Heart racing, she accelerated. A little farther and she'd make it.

The rain picked up, the torrent battering the car. Anything past sixty feet was erased by the deluge. Headlights from the vehicle that had left Benediction were no longer visible.

The SUV rammed her again. The steering wheel jerked in her hand as the back end of her car fishtailed. She forced herself not to struggle against it. Steering in the opposite direction would only make things worse.

Hope flicked a glance at the hazard button on her dash. She could hit it, slow down, stop the car and turn back to Goode, the neighboring town. Turn away from Benediction. Give up her search for the truth.

She'd been warned. That's what everyone wanted. For her to leave it all alone. To go back to California and bury her head in the sand.

But then a murderer would go free.

She had failed her sister once. Not again. She swallowed past the ball of anxiety in her throat. *You can do this.*

The SUV zoomed up alongside her, sending a new wave of fear crashing through her. What was he doing?

No sooner had the thought crossed her mind than the SUV swerved sharply. The front end slammed into her side of the car, propelling it into a wild slide toward the edge.

Hope panicked, hitting the brakes. The wheels locked. Her vehicle lost traction and went into a skid. Everything was happening so fast. Too fast.

Spinning out of control, her car missed a large tree and slid over the edge of the slope. A high-pitched cry escaped her lips. Dirt and rocks spit up. She tried to straighten the steering wheel and pumped the brakes. Her car fishtailed, clipped a tree and went airborne.

The sedan flipped. Rolled end over end down the gradient. Metal crunched and groaned around her.

Hope's seat belt jerked hard across her body, cutting off her oxygen for a second.

The airbag deployed like a hot fist, knocking her head back against the seat. Dust and chemicals saturated the air.

Her lungs seized as a scream lodged in her throat.

The car slammed to a stop with the impact of crashing into a brick wall. Her skull smashed into something hard.

A riot of pain flared…everywhere. In her head, chest, bones—even her teeth hurt.

Her vision blurred. Not that it mattered. She couldn't see past the airbag, which was the size of a large beach ball in her face.

Hope pushed on the light fabric, and the airbag deflated. Coughing, she wiped at the wetness coming from her nose with the back of her hand. Blood. Her nose was bleeding.

She switched on the interior light and pushed the deflated airbag out of her way.

The headlights were still on.

Water.

The car was in the lake. Beneath the water, or at least half of it. The weight of the engine pitched the front end forward, so that the car was almost pointing straight down. She looked back at the rear window. Rain and darkness.

Water was starting to seep inside the vehicle. The foot well was filling up as water rushed in. Faster and faster.

Hope pressed the button to release the seat belt. But nothing happened. It was stuck, jammed tight. She yanked on the belt, trying again, tugging and pushing. Praying.

Oh, God. She was trapped.

Icy water rose past her hips to her waist. Shockingly cold. Her toes were already growing numb, and she was shivering. She had to get out. Now!

Her purse floated up on the passenger's side. If she reached it, got to the Swiss Army knife inside, she could cut herself free.

She extended her hand in the water. Her bag was inches from her fingertips. She stretched out as much as she could, straining her arm muscles. A pang wrenched through her chest, her eyes tearing at the intense pain, but she didn't stop. She kept reaching for her purse. Almost had it. The bag was so close—she needed to stretch a hair farther, but the seat belt had her pinned.

The car shifted, still moving. Down and down it sank. The car tipped to the side, and water carried her purse away, out of reach.

No, no, no. It's not supposed to happen like this.

Pressure built in her ears, making her head pound. The headlights flickered and died. Then the interior light blinked off. Everything went black.

I'm going to die. In this cold, dark lake without ever learning the truth.

This was a mistake.

She screamed, venting her grief and rage, until her lungs were empty.

Faith. You deserve justice.

Even if the seat belt was useless, Hope had to try. She got back to work on getting the hell out of there. With her last breath she'd fight to get free.

Tugging harder, she pushed on the seat-belt release again as a surge of water wrapped its icy arms around her chest.

"WHAT IN THE HELL?" Gage Graham said aloud to himself, slowing down his truck.

An SUV had just run a car off the road right in front of him, wheeled a U-turn, and the driver was hightailing it from the scene.

In his thirty years, he'd seen a lot of insane stuff, most of it horrible, but nothing quite so bizarre.

Gage tried to make out the license plate number of the SUV, but it was impossible in the dark with the raging storm.

It burned him to the bone to let such a vicious piece of work get away, but he didn't have much choice. The driver of the sedan might be hurt or worse.

He pulled to the opposite side of the road and stopped at an angle with his headlights pointed in the area where the car had gone over the side. Switching on his high beams, the lights illuminated the area well enough for him to get a decent look at the situation.

The car had gone into Goode Mountain Lake. A fifteen-thousand-acre reservoir. The whole front end was submerged, and the rest was quickly sinking. It'd only take minutes, maybe five, tops, for the entire car to fill up with water. By his count, more than sixty seconds had already lapsed since the car went off the road.

Calling 911 was pointless. Goode was twenty-five miles away, and first responders wouldn't make it in time.

As for the residents of Benediction, they didn't respond to anything outside its gates. One of the many iron-clad rules. Most of the road was considered no-man's land. Luckily for the driver of the car in the lake, he wasn't a typical inhabitant and believed if a rule couldn't be broken, there was usually a way to bend it.

Gage pulled his Sig Sauer P220 from the ankle holster and stowed it in the glove box. After switching on his hazard lights, he jumped out of the car.

Icy-cold rain pelted down on him like tiny daggers, soaking most of his clothes. He only had on a down puffer vest over his turtleneck, since he hadn't planned on being exposed to the elements. The weather had turned from bad to nasty with the inbound winter storm that was going to drop an estimated foot of snow tomorrow. The temperature had already dipped into the thirties, but it wasn't below freezing yet.

He hustled around to the back and popped open the door to the under-bed storage compartment. Fished out a flare from his emergency roadside kit.

The last thing he needed was a passerby sideswiping his truck, exacerbating the situation, because they didn't see his hazard lights until it was too late.

Gusts of wet wind lashed his face and stung his eyes, but he'd been through much worse. This paled in comparison to what he'd endured in the CIA. Besides, he'd take cold rain over sand in his eyes any day.

With the flare lit, he tossed it a few feet away in the direction of oncoming traffic. He grabbed the flashlight—a floating, waterproof one that was impact resistant and could be used as a weapon in a pinch. He slammed the trunk closed and took off for the embankment.

A patch of ice had him slipping on the road but didn't take him down thanks to the traction on the soles of his thermo tactical boots. He made his way along the slope. Moved quickly but carefully over the slick grass.

There wasn't a second to lose. The smashed-in trunk of the sedan slipped underwater.

He dived into the lake.

Although he'd braced himself for the cold, the brutal chill of the water was startling. A jolt of pain ripped through his whole body, but he didn't stop swimming.

Diving deeper, he swam to the driver's door and shone his flashlight inside.

A woman was trapped behind the steering wheel. She

gasped for her last breath of air as the water inside the car overtook her completely, and then she was under.

She moved her head, her dark hair flowing in the water, and looked at him. Terrified, pretty and about to drown if he didn't get her out. She pointed to her seat belt and yanked at it.

The belt was stuck.

Gage tried the door handle. Locked. He tapped the window, gesturing for her to unlock it.

She glanced down and hit the button. The lock disengaged, and he pulled on the handle as she pushed. But it didn't budge.

Doors didn't jam when submerged, but they became very heavy due to the pressure exerted by the water pushing it toward the car. It'd be nearly impossible to open until the car completely filled with water. Then the pressure would be in equilibrium, but she didn't have that kind of time to wait.

Gage slammed the hard case of the flashlight against the window. He swung again, and the glass held. Blunt force wouldn't work.

Too bad she hadn't rolled down the window before the car had lost power. The windshield was a spiderweb of cracks. From the inside of the car, it could be kicked out. Trying to do the reverse, from the outside in, wouldn't work.

He was almost out of air. His lungs strained for oxygen.

Gage pointed to his chest and then up.

She pressed her palms to the glass. Her eyes were wide with panic as she shook her head. For him not to go? That she couldn't hold her breath for a minute longer?

Either way, it'd serve no one if they both drowned. Still, something in his chest squeezed at what he had to do next.

He had to leave her.

Chapter Two

Hope shook her head, desperate for the man not to leave. Help had come. The stranger from Benediction had stopped his car. Had dared to jump into the lake against the odds. Tried and failed to open the door. Only to abandon her.

She banged on the window, frantic. *Please! Don't go!*

He held up one finger. Then he turned and kicked off the car with his feet. He swam away through the darkness, leaving her behind and taking the light with him.

No! Hope screamed the word in her mind.

She yanked at the seat belt. Kicked the dash. Pounded at the glass. It was no use.

The car sank deeper, leveling out. The pressure popped her ears, and she was now dizzy.

Her lungs began burning, starved for oxygen. Fear inundated her. No matter how hard she fought to get loose, she was helpless. Probably ten, twenty feet from the surface, but it might as well have been twenty miles.

Was this all a lost cause?

He'd warned her, told her not to do this. *Mark my words, you'll end up dead, just like Faith, if you don't let this go*, he had said to her.

Desperate for the sweet taste of oxygen, she clutched at her throat. Her lungs ached like they were on the verge of exploding. The weight of the water, the strain of holding her breath hurt so much.

She couldn't fight the urge any longer. The impulse was as instinctual as it was overpowering, even though she knew it would it mean the end, but there was no stopping the inevitable. She gasped and sucked in water.

Excruciating pain mixed with blinding panic as her lungs filled. She flailed like a madwoman. Frantic to get out.

Something brushed her head. She reached up and grabbed it. Smooth leather in her hand.

Her purse.

Hope struggled to unzip it. Her hands were shaking so badly. She gagged and choked.

God, oh, God. She was drowning.

A bolt of agony and sheer terror went straight through her. But a sense of calm quickly followed as everything slowed and faded.

Suddenly, she wasn't afraid to die anymore.

Soon, she'd see Faith again.

GAGE POPPED TO the surface. The torrential rain pounded against his face. He sucked in a few deep breaths, easing his lungs while he thought of a way to quickly get the woman out. Teeth chattering, he shed his soaked-through down-filled vest and heavy wool turtleneck, leaving his long-sleeved thermal undershirt while keeping a grip on the flashlight.

His knife. He could use it to get her out.

He took another breath, the deepest, longest one he could hold, and dived back under.

Before he'd left the woman, he had held up one finger to the car window, letting her know he wouldn't abandon her. All he needed was a minute and then he'd be back.

Hang on.

The car had settled into the muck at the bottom close to shore. He swam to the driver's side and cast the light inside.

Her arms were floating up by her purse, and her eyes were closed. She was no longer conscious.

Damn it. He'd taken too long.

Gage dug into his left boot, his fingers numb from the frosty water, and pulled out his Venom double-action knife. It had a lightning-fast release button, but he didn't need the four-inch blade yet. He angled the handle at the window. On the end of the knife was a pommel designed to break glass, though he'd never used the feature prior to today and for a moment had forgotten it was even there.

One hard tap pierced the window, fracturing the glass. A second tap and the pane shattered.

Gage hit the button on the side of the knife, releasing the blade. First, he cut the shoulder strap, followed by the one across her lap. He shoved the knife back in his boot, grabbed her purse and let go of the flashlight.

Taking care not to hit her head on the door frame, he pulled the woman from the car. The flashlight was floating to the surface, the beam of light providing a guide.

The cold pressed in on him from all sides, icy teeth sinking into his skin, deeper to his bones. He pushed off the car with both feet for a boost, but it wasn't nearly enough. Keeping one arm wrapped around the woman's chest, he swam with one arm, pulling at the water, scissoring his legs with all his might.

Blood pounded in his head along with his thundering heartbeat. His lungs screamed for oxygen, the cold knotting his muscles. Every cell in his body burned from the cold.

He clawed his way through the water, following the light. They were close. *So close.*

Slowing down wasn't an option even as his lungs ached and heaviness set into his limbs.

Darkness danced on the edge of his vision. He was growing tired, but he ignored the fatigue. It was only a product of the cold. He ran six miles a day, lifted weights, stayed in peak condition since he'd been disgraced and disavowed from the Agency. There was no doubt in his mind that he had the strength to make it to the surface.

He was not going to let this woman die. *Keep going. Don't stop.*

The flashlight was right there, and then he broke the surface.

"Uh!" He raked in rejuvenating air as he also sucked droplets of water into his heaving lungs.

Relief whooshed through him, but he was nowhere near done. He pushed onward, doing a sidestroke while ensuring her head stayed above water until he reached dirt. His body ached from the exertion, and the chill spearing through him only made it worse. He wanted to rest for a moment, but the rush of adrenaline kept him moving. If he was going to save her, he had to act quickly.

Panting, Gage hauled the woman up onto the muddy bank and into the brightness from the headlights. Her face was pale, nose bloody and her lips had turned blue. Getting her breathing was paramount, and getting her warm would be equally important.

The freezing rain hadn't let up. It was coming down hard at a vicious angle, making his next task even more difficult.

He rose on his knees beside the woman and began chest compressions. The heel of one hand on the center of her chest, the other hand on top of the first, and he used his entire upper body, not just his arms, to push. Counted to thirty.

No response from her.

Come on.

He tilted her head back and pried her lips apart. Pinching her nostrils closed gently in case her nose was broken, he sealed his mouth over hers, wasting no time. He blew life-giving breaths into her. Two, long and steady

Still nothing. He resumed chest compressions, pushing even harder this time. "Breathe for me. Come on!"

The woman jerked and pushed him away with a force-ful cough.

Gage rolled her onto her side, swept her hair back from her face and helped her expel the brackish water. Those first few breaths must've felt like fire. He rubbed her back and her arm, encouraging her while she wheezed and sputtered.

Once she finished hacking up the liquid, she dug her palms into the mud and rolled her upper body off the ground. She looked him over. Brilliant eyes took in his face as her lips quivered, body shaking, chest rising and falling in the desperate rhythm of the utterly spent.

Gage exhaled hard himself, white puffs of breath leaving his mouth.

"Thank you," she said, still gulping air. Her soft voice was barely audible over the pounding rain. "You…okay?"

Gage was fairly sure he was the one who should've been asking that question. She'd nearly died but was concerned about his welfare. That told him plenty about this woman despite the fact that he didn't know her name.

"I'm fine." He pressed two fingers to her carotid artery. Her pulse was slow and thready. He had to warm her up. Frigid water lowered a person's body temperature faster than air. Hypothermia was already setting in. At least she was conscious and talking. "I've got to get you out of this rain. Can you make it up the embankment to my truck?" he asked, sliding his hand up to cup her cheek. Her soft skin was like ice.

It registered to him on some level the gesture was too forward, too intimate between strangers, and at the same time, the impulse to comfort her after saving her life was as natural as breathing.

She nodded weakly, though she didn't look as if she even had the strength to stand, much less walk uphill.

The wool jacket she wore would be burdensome on the climb, and it was only transferring heat away from her body at this point. "Better to toss the jacket than lug it," he said, teeth chattering. "Don't worry, the truck will be warm."

She reached for the zipper, but from the way her body shook, he doubted she could mange it. He pulled down the zipper for her and peeled the sodden wool jacket off.

Refusing to give in to his own fatigue, he grabbed her purse, cupped her arm and helped her up to her feet.

She swayed and staggered forward two steps before her legs gave out from underneath her. Gage caught her, expecting her lack of coordination and the fragility of her limbs.

Nearly dying took a lot out of a person. He'd know better than most exactly how much.

He lifted her, putting her slender body across his shoulders in a fireman's carry. She went limp on him. Soaking wet, she was heavier than she looked. Not to mention the added drag from his own wet jeans weighing him down, but in this position, he was capable of carrying a grown man almost double her size.

Lurching into motion, he began scrambling up the slick ground. The embankment was slippery and rocky, but he made decent progress, even if it wasn't as fast as he would've liked.

Grunting with effort, using the last reserves of his strength, he climbed to the top.

He caught his breath and then hurried around the front of the parked truck and opened the passenger door. The cabin was toasty from the heat he'd left running, and he welcomed the rush of warmth that escaped. Carefully, he set her down on the seat.

Once he closed the door, he ran to the driver's side. He hopped in and turned the heat up full blast, angling all the vents toward her. On the console between the seats he spotted a zip-up hoodie he'd taken off the other day and forgotten in the car. Just what she needed.

"This will help." He handed her his lightweight jacket and set her purse down. "Better if you take off your wet shirt first." When she hesitated, he added, "You'll get warmer faster that way."

"Y-you're n-n-not try-trying to get me…naked?" Her words slurred, which was a bad sign, but he gave her points for the humor, considering.

"I'm positive." Though staring at her pretty face, the idea of seeing this woman unclothed—*under different circumstances*—was unquestionably appealing. "Promise not to look." He turned toward his window.

She had on a simple pullover sweater. No buttons. No zippers. As long as she was able to lift her arms, she shouldn't have a problem.

Glimpsing her reflection in the glass, he watched her for a split second to be sure she was all right before lowering his eyes. He was nothing if not a man of his word.

"I'm Gage, by the way." He deliberately neglected to mention his last name. Force of habit. Secrets were his constant companion, but she'd learn his surname soon enough where they were going. "And you are?"

"Hope." Hard to miss that she'd done likewise with a similar omission, but her purse was on the console and he was willing to bet two forms of ID were inside.

"Any idea who ran you off the road or why?" The sound of the zipper trying to close was his cue. He shifted, facing her. "Need an assist?"

She nodded. "C-can't feel f-fingers, t-toes."

Keeping his gaze on her face, he got the zipper closed for her.

She pulled the hood up over her head and settled back in the seat like she was ready to close her eyes and fall into a deep sleep.

Another bad sign.

Questions would have to wait for now, but eventually he'd get answers. No chance he was going to let the bastard who'd run her off the road get away with it.

He backed the truck up, spun the wheel, turning them ninety degrees, and shifted to Drive. Benediction was ten minutes down the road. A quick and easy ride.

Getting her through the gate was a different story.

Benediction was a closed town, with strict travel and residency restrictions. No unauthorized personnel were allowed. Only assigned government or military personnel and grandfathered-in residents who kept the town running with the essentials—diner, grocery, pub, auto shop, tailor, one-school

K-12, nondenominational church, funeral home/crematorium and the clinic. Special dispensation was granted on a case-by-case basis only to relatives of residents.

They rode in silence with the blasting fan from the heater on high, static noise in the background. The patches of black ice on the road were the worst at night and early morning. He'd only ventured out to go to Goode and stock up on essential supplies that weren't available in Benediction before the storm hit. None of which he'd gotten and all of which he needed.

The rain eased from a downpour, turning into a relentless drizzle. The bright lights of the front gate cut through the darkness as they approached. By daring to go a little faster on the road, it had taken them less than eight minutes. He slowly pulled up to the guardhouse, mentally kicking his brain into gear for some quick thinking and smooth talk.

Gage glanced at Hope. Eyes half-open, she was still shivering, and her breathing was a bit shallow. The tremors racking her body hadn't improved. Didn't help that she was stuck in drenched clothes from the waist down and soaked shoes.

A predicament he understood all too well. The steady shudder running through him had his hands shaking on the wheel.

"Pull the hood back. The guard will need to see how bad you are to let you in," he said, bringing the car to a stop under the overhead canopy.

Hope slid her hand up and pushed the hood down to her neck.

"For the next two minutes, say as little as possible until I get you through the gate." That shouldn't be too hard, with her suffering from the effects of hypothermia and fatigue.

Two US Army soldiers came out of the heated guardhouse. Sidearms were holstered on their hips. Pepper spray was clipped to the other side of their belts. Gage knew from witnessing an incident with his mouthy teenage nephew who'd gotten drunk and belligerent one night that they also carried handcuffs in a side utility pocket.

Gage rolled down his window. The specialist checked the underside of the truck with an inspection mirror while the corporal came up to his window.

Benediction was small, population 250, including the rotation of military personnel and government contractors. The guards working the gate got to know faces, names, and make and model of vehicles fast.

In turn, Gage made it his business to learn as much as he could about everyone.

"Corporal Livingston," Gage said.

"Evening, Mr. Graham. Surprised you're back…" Livingston stopped short, studying him with a wide-eyed gaze. The kid was a baby. Couldn't have been more than twenty-two years old. "What happened, sir?"

"Car accident. A few miles down. This woman was run off the road." Gage indicated his passenger, and the corporal peered inside the truck. "Her car went into the lake. If I hadn't gotten her out, she would've drowned. I need to take her to the clinic inside."

Corporal Livingston shook his head. "You know the rules. I can't let her in."

"She needs immediate medical attention."

Specialist Porter finished checking the undercarriage and was now inspecting the truck bed.

"You'll have to take her to the hospital in Goode, sir," Corporal Livingston said.

"Perhaps you missed the word *immediate*. She won't make it to the next town. Look at her."

Livingston's hard gaze shifted from Gage to Hope but didn't soften. He took a flashlight off his hip and shone it inside, getting a better look.

"You've got no choice," Gage said. "You have to let her get medical treatment unless you want her death on your conscience. Either hypothermia or pulmonary edema will kill her before we make it to Goode." Gage believed that deep in his gut. "Never mind the fact that I might not make it there myself. There has to be some kind of exception for a medical emergency."

Conflict twisted the young man's features. "I can call my sergeant. See what he thinks."

The specialist finished in the back and came up along the passenger door.

Gage sighed. "In the twenty minutes you'll take regurgitating what I just explained to your superior, who can't see firsthand the dire state this woman is in, and going back and forth, debating, I'll need medical attention, too. You want to be responsible for two deaths in one night?"

The specialist climbed up on the running board, casting his flashlight on Hope. "Oh, man, Corporal Livingston. She looks really bad. Maybe you should let her in."

Porter was new, had been in Benediction less than two months and hadn't had a full dose of the isolationist Kool-Aid yet. All positives in Gage's book.

"It'll be my butt on the line," Livingston snapped. "Not yours."

"I didn't save her only to watch her die in my truck because you're worried about getting a slap on the wrist," Gage said. "Let us go straight to the clinic and get her checked out. You'll be hailed a hero after the doctor and I speak to your superior."

Livingston lowered his eyes and rubbed his forehead. "If anything goes wrong, you understand it might be grounds to have you kicked out of Benediction permanently?"

Gage was aware he had to watch his every step. This town was the best haven, where he was hiding in plain sight. If he were ever forced to leave, it would mean he'd have to go back on the run. Then his days would be numbered, but saving Hope's life was worth the risk.

"I understand," Gage said.

"All right, but Specialist Porter will follow you and provide an escort. I need to see her ID for the report."

Thank goodness, sanity prevailed.

Gage turned toward the console and reached for her purse,
but it was gone.

"L-l-ost…lake," Hope said.

Easy enough for Gage to chalk it up to him being mistaken. Perhaps he had forgotten her purse on the bank or had
dropped it in the water during the swim. A lot had happened
quickly. His had brain misfired more than once from the cold.

But he knew better. After eight years with the CIA, he
didn't make rookie mistakes.

Hope's purse wasn't lost. She was lying.

Her gaze bounced up, and those sparkling green eyes met
his. She looked frightfully fragile and impossibly tough all
at once—a beautiful contradiction.

A person's life could pivot in a second—with a single
word, the smallest choice that might not feel like any choice
at all. Destiny often whispered a promise or a warning. All
you had to do was listen. Gage was listening right now.

This woman is trouble.

He attracted trouble—was attracted to it, same difference. Basic magnetism, like a lodestone to iron. There was
no changing his nature, what compelled him, any more than
one could alter the laws of physics.

At that moment, his gut was telling him that if he brought
Hope into Benediction, she was going to toss his house of
cards upside down.

Chapter Three

The past week of prying and pushing and, most recently, nearly dying had led to this moment. Nothing was going to stop Hope from getting inside Benediction now. If the soldier saw her ID, it'd take him thirty seconds to learn that she was on their blacklist and then he'd sooner let her freeze to death than allow her through the gate. Of that she was certain.

Gage might be her savior, but that didn't make him her ally. *Yet.*

Hope placed her shaking hand on top of his. "P-please." She only had the strength to utter the single word.

By plunging into the freezing lake twice, Gage had risked his own life to save her, a stranger. That meant he had guts *and* he was a good man. She prayed it would be enough.

For a split second his dark eyes narrowed, then they brightened in a way that warmed something inside her. Gage looked back at the soldier standing at the driver's side. "Her wallet was lost in the lake," he said, and relief loosened some of the tightness in her chest. "Let's get her to the clinic. Once she's warmed up and they examine her, she'll have to fill out forms with all the pertinent information. Specialist Porter can call you and pass along the details for a full report before your shift ends. Okay?"

The soldier nodded. "All right, sir, but I've got to let my sergeant know." He waved the other young man over, spoke to him a moment and sent him running toward a parked vehicle on the other side of the controlled entry point.

After the soldier ahead of them had started his car, the guard pushed a button and the long-arm barrier lifted.

Anticipation whispered through her in a dizzying rush from the top of her head down to her belly, perhaps even lower, but her legs had grown numb. The ringing inside her head was loud, shutting out everything else in that instant. No pain. No cold. No doubts.

Gage hit the gas, passing the gate, and they entered Benediction.

I'm in! I made it.

Hope's stomach flip-flopped, part exhilaration and part nerves. This was the farthest she'd ever been, but her battle was just getting started.

A parcel of land covered with evergreens was a buffer zone between the gate and the town. From the outside, it was impossible to get a clear look at Benediction, even with a telephoto lens, due to the trees. She had hired a local tour guide who specialized in the Goode Mountain area to take her out on the lake, so she could see the town from the water.

No luck on that front, either. There was a similar swath of dense trees on the other side of the electrified fence around the rear perimeter of the town. The only thing visible was the top floor of a building—steel and tinted privacy glass—and half of a sign for Nexcellogen Industries. Forget about renting a helicopter to do a fly-by to give her a chance to snap some photos from overhead. The town was protected by a strict no-fly zone. No pilot dared violate the statute for fear of having their license permanently suspended.

This town was hiding something. Hope knew in her bones it was the reason Faith was dead, even though she couldn't prove it.

Beyond the evergreen woodland, Gage drove through the tiny town, which was little more than a well-planned community. This was the one main road, she realized when they came to a large roundabout. At the center of it stood a fifty-foot tree decorated with luminous multicolored lights and a crystal star on the top. The Christmas tree made the creepy town almost look normal.

A street lined with shops was off to one side of the main road. Twinkling white lights had been strung up in rows.

On the other side of the road were homes decorated for the holidays. Town houses and a variety of one and two-story homes within walking distance to the shops.

After they took the second turn out of the roundabout, staying on the main road, they passed a large park with a playground, a school and a church.

The one building that stood out like a sore thumb, set apart from everything else, was the sprawling three-story Nexcellogen research facility, where Faith had worked as a scientist.

In a few short minutes, she spotted a small volunteer fire station and the clinic.

The soldier parked his car in a row of spots across from the building. Gage stopped the car beneath the emergency entrance's awning, near a lone ambulance awash in eerie sallow light, before running around to the passenger side.

He opened the door. "I'll help you inside."

She scooted off the edge of the seat and slid, more so than climbed, down. Gage drew her from the step rail. He scooped her into his arms without letting her feet touch the ground and *helped* her into the clinic by carrying her through the automatic doors.

If she hadn't been drained to exhaustion and needed his assistance, she would've protested, but she didn't even have the energy to enjoy it, either. Where the man got the herculean strength to lift her after everything else that he'd already done was a wonder.

He wasn't a large guy. Six feet tall with the hard, honed body of an athlete. Or a man of action. Impossible to miss, since his sodden thermal top hugged the curve of his muscles. And he was handsome, as in make-your-jaw-drop-and-forget-your-name kind of gorgeous.

The automatic double doors whooshed closed behind them. She squinted against the bright fluorescent lights as Gage carried her into the clinic. The soldier was right by their side.

A woman in her late twenties, maybe early thirties, wearing scrubs, caught sight of them. "What happened, Gage?" She jumped to her feet behind the front desk and came around to meet them.

"Her car went into the lake. She took in a lot of water. Lost consciousness. She almost didn't make it."

Hope's heart clenched at how close she'd come to drowning in the lake, but she'd do it all again to get inside Benediction.

"She's an uncleared outsider," the soldier said, staying close on their heels.

The woman's gaze bounced from the armed guard back to Gage. "Follow me." She led them to an exam room, where she hurriedly grabbed a few foil blankets and spread one out on the exam table. "Set her here."

Gage laid her down.

"Hi, my name is Danielle. I'm the physician assistant on duty tonight." She draped another foil blanket on top of Hope and tossed one to Gage.

"I need her name for the report, and Corporal Livingston said that as soon as she's warm I'm to escort her back to the front gate."

Hope's stomach twisted in dread. She turned her head away from the young man and pulled the foil up to her chin.

"Do you expect her to walk twenty-five miles in the freezing rain all the way back to Goode?" Gage asked. "It'd be best, safest for her to leave in the morning."

"Not my problem, sir," the soldier said. "I've got my orders."

"I need both of you out of my examination room," Danielle said.

The two men turned toward the door.

"No." Hope reached out to Gage. "Stay." He'd proven himself an ally, for the time being, anyway, and the prospect of him walking out the door and her not seeing him again was too much to bear. It dawned on her that she couldn't accomplish the monumental task ahead without help from someone on the inside.

Gage came back to her bedside and took her hand in both of his. "I'll stay if you want," he said. The concern in his eyes calmed Hope with the sincerity she saw there.

The soldier hovered on the threshold. "If he stays, so do I, ma'am."

"I need to get you out of these wet clothes and examine you," Danielle said to Hope. Then her gaze dropped to their clasped hands, and she straightened with a look of distaste on her face. "That means both of you gentlemen will leave. Now."

Gage nodded to Danielle, and then he looked at Hope. "I won't go far. Promise." Unwavering sympathy resonated in his voice despite his chattering teeth.

"Doc has a clean set of sweats in the locker room," Danielle said. "Warm up and I'll check you out when I'm done with her."

"Okay," he said to Danielle, giving another nod but without taking his eyes from Hope's. He squeezed her hand once, and the dread that had been bubbling inside dissipated.

Gage ushered the guard from the room and closed the examination room door on his way out.

Danielle put a stethoscope to Hope's chest inside the zip-up sweater. "Take a deep breath as best you can," she said, and Hope drew in as much air as possible. "A few more for me." She moved the stethoscope around, listening. "Sounds good. What's your name?"

Hope considered lying. Something she should've done with Gage and would've if she'd been thinking clearly. Since he already knew her first name, it made little sense to lie to the PA. "Hope."

Danielle took out a small electronic device and clipped the gadget onto Hope's index finger. "This'll measure the oxygen level of your blood." She opened the drawer of a cart beside the bed and took out a pair of medical scissors. Danielle slipped off Hope's shoes and began cutting her jeans. "How do you know Gage?"

Hope tensed at the question. "I don't." The stutter from the cold had left her, but she was still chilled down to the bone.

"Hmm. Well, he seems sweet on you," Danielle said, a hint of something in her tone Hope couldn't quite pinpoint—it made her squirm.

Was it jealousy? Irritation?

Danielle was attractive, with deep-olive skin, keen eyes alight with curiosity and an athletic build. It wasn't hard to picture her with Gage.

"Why do you say that?" Hope asked, intrigued to hear the answer.

The woman shrugged. "The way he interacted with you. The blatant show of concern. He's got a big heart, but he doesn't wear it on his sleeve."

"It must be a rescuer-rescuee thing, I suppose." With the mounting hurdles she had to overcome, the last thing she needed standing in her way was a jealous girlfriend. "Are you two together?"

Danielle snickered, but the sound was forced. "If we were, my wife might have something to say about that. It's just odd seeing Gage take to a stranger. Or to anyone, for that matter." Danielle tossed the wet pieces of denim in the trash and threw a wool blanket on top of the foil one over Hope. "He's the oil in our water. Doesn't quite mix, but we don't mind him, either." She removed the device from Hope's finger and took her blood pressure.

"Like all the other government contractors here?" It was clear from the conversation at the gate that Gage wasn't military, but Hope needed to know his connection to Benediction and, more important, if he had any professional ties to Nexcellogen.

Taking off the blood pressure cuff, Danielle held her gaze. "No. The military and the contractors are a necessary evil. Benediction never would've been born without them. Gage is different. He's a resident. A townie, sort of. But what do you know about the government contractors here?"

"Nothing. I heard rumors in Goode, though." Rumors that came with stern warnings.

"Did those rumors bring you to Benediction?"

"No." Hope forced herself to maintain eye contact and reminded herself not to fidget. "I was run off the road."

Danielle looked at her closely, her gaze taking in every detail of Hope's face. "The one road in and out of Benediction. Tell me about your car accident."

"There isn't much to tell," Hope said, her blood suddenly running cold again. She struggled to avoid the woman's scrutiny. "Someone sideswiped me and sent my car over the embankment into the lake."

"No one finds that road unless they're looking for it." Danielle put her hand on Hope's shoulder. "One of the pledges I made as a medical professional is to hold in confidence the information shared in the course of practicing medicine. Anything you tell me in this examine room is between us."

In theory, that sounded lovely, but Hope had earned a degree in the harsh realities of life the hard way. Danielle could be on Nexcellogen's payroll, for all Hope knew. This town safeguarded the company's and the military's secrets and clearly was indebted, since Benediction wouldn't exist without them.

"I told you," Hope said. "There's nothing more to it."

Danielle pulled back and folded her arms. "Let me put it to you another way. I believe in and practice first, do no harm. I can tell that soldier out there that your vitals are sufficiently stable for you to be transported to Goode within the hour. Or I can recommend that you stay the night, which I honestly think would be best in your condition, as does

Gage. His opinion means something to me, but I need to be sure that your presence isn't going to do harm to anyone in my town. So, what's your story?"

Hope took a deep breath.

Trust was a precious commodity, and she wasn't about to invest one drop in this woman.

Chapter Four

Sighing with relief to be in dry clothes, Gage stuffed his wet things into a plastic bag and headed for the locker room door. He gritted his teeth at the icy sting from every step thanks to the soaked boots on his feet, but he'd have to tough it out until he got home.

He pulled the door open and rounded the corner, going back toward the front of the clinic. Hope had looked terrified at the prospect of him leaving her. Then again, Benediction could be a terrifying place for someone who didn't know how to navigate the endless land mines—some seen and others well hidden.

But one question kept repeating in his head. *What was she doing on that road to begin with?*

A military police patrol car pulled up out front behind Gage's truck. The blue and red flashing lights were on, but the siren was off. A minute later, the double doors of the clinic opened and in walked Staff Sergeant Burton.

Holding a clipboard in one hand, he removed his patrol cap with the other. He marched down the hall like a man on a mission, his thick-soled boots pounding against the linoleum floor until he reached the front desk.

Livingston had called his supervisor, which Gage had expected. He hadn't expected Burton to throw on a uniform and leave the comforts of his house, where he had a sleep-deprived wife and a four-month-old baby, to race over to the clinic.

"Where is she?" Burton asked the specialist.

Porter hiked a thumb at exam room two. "Inside with PA Varma."

Staff Sergeant Burton stormed over to the door and banged a fist against it.

Gage charged across the hall, bypassing the specialist, and came up alongside Burton as Danielle opened the door.

Burton didn't acknowledge Gage's presence with so much as a glance. "I need to speak to the woman in there."

"We were having a chat, but I'm starting to get dizzy from going in circles." Danielle stepped aside, letting him in.

"I'm Staff Sergeant Burton with the military police." He held up the clipboard in his hand, facing it out toward Hope. "Ma'am, is this you?"

Hope pursed her lips as all expression drained from her face.

Gage strode up to the bed and glanced at the front of the clipboard. There was a black-and-white picture of a woman standing at the gate next to her car, speaking to one of the guards. It was clear as day the image was of Hope and little point in her trying to deny it.

Specialist Porter joined them, taking a position next to the staff sergeant.

"Ma'am, is this you?" Burton asked again, his tone harsh, his expression hard as granite. "Are you Hope Fischer?"

"Fischer?" Danielle shot a worried glance in Hope's direction. "Are you related to Faith Fischer?" Her question reflected typical Benediction suspicion.

Everyone in town knew the name Faith Fischer. For the past ten days, the whole town had been abuzz about the scientist who had killed herself.

"Yes, that's me," Hope said, defiance lighting up her eyes. "Faith was my sister."

Burton handed Porter the clipboard. Then he took out his handcuffs, grabbed Hope's wrist and shackled her to the bed rail.

"What are you doing?" Hope yanked on the restraints.

"Is that really necessary?" Gage asked, meeting Hope's terrified gaze.

"Yes, sir, it is." Burton pivoted, facing him. "This

woman was never to be permitted past the gate. Under *any* circumstances."

"Now that I'm here, I'm not leaving without answers about Faith's death."

"That's where you're wrong, ma'am." Burton shifted his stony gaze back to Hope. "You'll leave as soon as you're medically cleared."

"My sister was murdered. Someone in this town knows why and covered it up."

Danielle rubbed her arms as if a chill had come over her and eased back toward the door.

"Not my area, ma'am. You already submitted a formal request for information, and it will take six to eight weeks to be processed, at which point you will be mailed a formal—"

"Two months," Hope scoffed, cutting off the staff sergeant. "That's ridiculous."

The time frame was generous considering the deliberate technological limitations in Benediction. No internet. No Wi-Fi. Cell phones didn't work, and forget about email. It was like living in the dark ages, which was exactly why Gage loved the town.

Made it the perfect place to hide out under the CIA's radar.

"That's the way it is," Staff Sergeant Burton said. "You won't stay in this town a moment longer than absolutely necessary."

Gage turned to ask Danielle for her medical opinion, but she had slipped out of the room. He stepped into the hallway and barely heard Danielle's voice. She was speaking to someone in a hushed tone. He crept down the hall and peeked around the corner at the front desk.

Danielle was on the phone, rubbing the nape of her neck. As she flicked a glance in his direction, Gage ducked back so she wouldn't spot him and strained to hear the one side of the conversation.

"She has questions," Danielle said. "Thinks her sister was

murdered." A short pause. "I don't know. What do you want me to do?"

Burton marched into the hallway, past Gage to the desk, and rapped on it with his knuckles, drawing her attention.

Danielle raised a finger at him. "Okay. If you think so. I'll take care of it. Get some sleep." She hung up the phone. "Yes, Staff Sergeant?"

"When can Ms. Fischer be discharged?" Burton asked.

"We're going to keep her overnight." Danielle folded her arms. "Ms. Fischer is at risk for complications such as hypoxic cerebral injury, acute respiratory distress, pulmonary damage secondary to aspiration and cardiac arrest. I'll have the doc look her over in the morning. If he clears her, she's all yours."

"Gage," Hope called for him. "Gage!"

He hurried back into her room. "Yeah, I'm still here."

"Can you bring me my purse from your truck?" Hope asked. "It's under the front seat."

"I thought you lost it, ma'am," Porter said, evidently more astute than he appeared.

Hope glanced at the specialist. "My wallet was lost. Not my purse."

Porter nodded with a confused look on his face, but he didn't ask any further questions.

"I'll grab it for you." Gage patted her shoulder and left the room. He crossed paths with Burton in the hallway.

"I need a word with you," the staff sergeant said.

"I'll be back in a minute, and then you can have as many words with me as you'd like." Gage kept moving, not waiting for a reply. He didn't want to leave Hope alone with soldiers any longer than he had to.

He ran to his truck and found her purse right where she'd said. Smart of her to hide it if her identity meant she might've been denied medical treatment.

A sleek silver sedan pulled up. Gage recognized it immediately. The vehicle belonged to Ian McCallister, head of security for Nexcellogen.

Had an emergency telephone tree been activated?

Not wanting to get tied up in a conversation, Gage headed back inside and didn't slow down until he was in the examination room. He handed the purse over to Hope, but Burton snatched it.

The staff sergeant unzipped the wet bag and took a quick look. "Sorry, ma'am. I have to check for a weapon." Once he was satisfied, he zipped it and gave her the purse.

Ian McCallister knocked on the door and strode into the room. Always polished and poised, he wore a crisp white shirt and dark slacks. His silver-flecked dark hair was coiffed, and the scruff of late-day stubble over his cheeks and jaw was the only thing to mar the perfection of his appearance. "Good evening, everyone." He turned to Burton. "Do we know who our visitor is?"

"Yes, sir. She's Faith Fischer's sister, Hope."

"Really?" Though the corners of McCallister's eyes crinkled in sympathy, his watchful gaze was appraising everything and everyone in the room. "I'm sorry for your loss and to hear about your accident on the road," he said to Hope.

Unlike other security chiefs Gage had encountered in the past, McCallister didn't have a bulldog personality or menacing persona, but he did have what could only be described as *presence*. That it factor better suited for public relations than his current line of work.

Single women in town fawned over him, along with some not so single. He was that guy other men wanted to be friends with, who paid for a round of drinks after bolstering you up instead of putting you down. He even started the Future Leaders Club at the school, which had impressive attendance because kids liked him, too.

"Thank you," Hope said. "But if you feel an ounce of

compassion for my situation, you'll explain to me why my sister's murder wasn't investigated."

McCallister clasped his hands in front of him. "The medical examiner looked at your sister's body. I'm afraid it was ruled a suicide."

"She didn't kill herself," Hope insisted.

"I can see you've been through a lot tonight." McCallister took a deep breath. "How long will our visitor be with us?"

"She'll stay overnight," Burton said.

"Perhaps we can talk in the morning, after you've had breakfast," McCallister said. "Give us a chance to allay your concerns."

"Once the doc discharges you, Ms. Fischer, we're escorting you to the front gate," Burton said.

"How am I supposed to get back to Goode?" Hope asked. "My rental car is in the lake."

"Specialist Porter," Burton said, looking at the young man. "Call a tow truck to have her rental car taken to the next town and make arrangements with a taxi company to have one waiting for her by 0900 sharp at the gate."

"Yes, sir."

"Don't ever *sir* me again, son. I work for a living."

"Yes, Staff Sergeant."

McCallister rolled his eyes at the exchange between the soldiers.

"Best of luck getting a taxi to show in the morning." Gage leveled his gaze on Burton. "The snow is going to start in the wee hours." It didn't snow often in Virginia, but when it did the snowfall could be heavy in this mountainous region, closing schools and shutting down the roads.

"Calling for a cab was merely a courtesy to Ms. Fischer," Burton said. "But taxi or no taxi, at 0900 she will be put out of Benediction."

"If the doctor clears her, you mean," Gage said.

Burton flashed a cold smile. "We'll see to it that he does. At 0900 Ms. Fischer *will* be at the gate."

"Rest assured, Ms. Fischer," McCallister said, "you will not be walking back to Goode. Ms. Lansing and I will both be here to oversee this process. I'm sure she'll want to offer her condolences personally."

Michelle Lansing was the director of Nexcellogen and the pseudo mayor of the town. Although she had no authority over the military troops or the townspeople, she ensured affairs between all parties remained smooth. She found ways to deepen relations by holding various events that everyone looked forward to—the Easter egg hunt, movie night in the park, the Fourth of July bash. That sort of thing. She was the thread weaving the town, the military and the company closer together into one cohesive group.

"I welcome a face-to-face chat with her," Hope said. "In the meantime, am I supposed to stay handcuffed to the bed all night?"

Burton took the clipboard from Porter and tucked it under his arm. "Yes. You are."

"Surely," McCallister said, "we can remove the handcuffs and allow Ms. Fischer to recuperate in comfort instead of treating her as though she were guilty of a crime."

"I have my orders," Burton said.

McCallister pulled the staff sergeant aside, but Gage was still within earshot. "Her sister just died. She's grieving. We need to show compassion. Besides, this isn't a good PR look for Nexcellogen. I can see the headlines now."

"Not my area," Burton snapped.

McCallister slipped his hands into his pocket. "Ms. Lansing won't be pleased to hear about this."

Burton shrugged. "She'll have to take it up with Captain Finley."

"What if I have to use the bathroom?" Hope asked, drawing everyone's attention.

"You have three choices, ma'am. One," Burton said, actually lifting a finger, "you can hold it. Two, you can soil yourself. Three, PA Varma can insert a catheter." He wagged his three fingers and it was all Gage could do not to sock the guy in the jaw. "I don't care which you choose. What's it going to be?"

Hope narrowed her eyes at him, not the least bit intimidated. "I'll hold it."

McCallister stepped forward. "On behalf of Nexcellogen, I apologize for this deplorable treatment."

"If you need to relieve yourself during the night," Danielle said, coming back into the room, "just press the call button. I can help you with a bedpan."

"Thank you," Hope said. "But I'm sure I'll be fine. I just need some peace and a few hours of sleep."

"Speaking of which." Danielle came closer, extending a medicine cup with two tiny pills and a small drink of water.

"What is it?" Hope asked.

"A sedative. It will help you sleep."

"No, thank you." Hope pulled the blanket up. "I don't take tranquilizers. I don't react well to them."

"Rest is the best thing for you right now." Danielle jiggled the medicine cup, causing the pills to rattle. "I have to insist."

"She's already handcuffed," Gage said, giving Danielle a warning glance to back off but keeping his tone even. "Forcing her to do one more thing that she doesn't want to do can't possibly be good for her. If she changes her mind, she can always use the call button."

"Mr. Graham is quite right," McCallister said.

Danielle nodded and stepped back as Burton gave Porter additional orders.

Gage leaned in toward Danielle. "Hey," he said low, "who were you talking to on the phone a minute ago?"

"Dr. Howland. I wanted to update him on our latest patient."

"Gage." Hope held out her hand. "Can you sit with me for a little until I fall asleep?"

"Let me run home, change my shoes and I'll stay as long as you'd like."

"No, Mr. Graham, you won't." Burton eyed him. "It's time we had those words." The staff sergeant gestured for him to go out into the hall.

"Actually, you should all leave," Danielle said. "Ms. Fischer has been through a traumatic experience. It's vital that she rests."

"Ms. Fischer," McCallister said, "get some rest. Ms. Lansing and I will see you in the morning."

Danielle shooed everyone from the room. "Light on or off?" Danielle asked Hope.

"On. Strange place. Handcuffed to the bed."

"I understand. I'll make sure no one else disturbs you. Try to get some sleep." Danielle closed the door behind her.

McCallister was already headed out the door. Once Danielle and Porter went back to the front, Burton turned on Gage.

"Captain Finley gave me orders that you are not to remain at the clinic."

Not only had Livingston called his supervisor, but apparently Burton had notified his own, as well. Finley must've called McCallister. Gage smothered his annoyance, not letting it leak into his expression.

"She would like to discuss the matter of you bringing an unauthorized, blacklisted person into the town," Burton said. "You're to be in her office in one hour, and she said not to come empty-handed."

The captain was referring to the package Gage owed her. It was on his list of essentials and was still sitting in Goode. "Tell her I'll be there in two hours."

"The captain said one."

Although it would've been satisfying to knock Burton's lights out, it also would've created more problems than it was worth. "I'm sure your boss doesn't want me getting hypothermia. My boots are wet and freezing, and in case you hadn't noticed my hands are still shaking." A fact he hated. "I'll be there in two hours." Gage still had to go to Goode and pick up his supplies, including the package Captain Finley was expecting.

He swallowed the bitter taste in his mouth from being at the beck and call of the captain, but that was the deal.

"It's your funeral," Burton said.

Gage clenched his hands and headed for the door. The sleek silver sedan was gone. McCallister probably couldn't wait to get back home.

In his truck, Gage tossed his bag of wet clothes in the back and fired up the engine. But instead of going straight home like he should've, he pulled off from under the awning and away from the doors, where Burton was watching him, and drove around to the side of the clinic. He backed up alongside the building, parking the car so it was shielded by an ambulance and killed the engine.

His thoughts kept circling back to Hope. Once the two soldiers left, he would sneak in and check on her. Make sure she'd be okay right for the night.

He stared at her window, the only lit room on that side of the building.

After a few minutes, two cars passed by, taking the service lane back to the main road. Burton and Porter were finally gone. Gage could only imagine how ticked off Captain Finley was going to be once Burton delivered his message.

Hope was major trouble, all right. Bringing her into Benediction had placed him in Finley's crosshairs, and she was a crack shot. Forgetting about Hope and washing his hands of this business was the smart play, but he'd gotten involved the moment he pulled her out of the lake and hustled her into town.

She had been caught in the wrong place at the wrong time

and had nearly died. That made him feel for her, especially since she only seemed to want answers about her sister.

Then there was the matter of Faith Fischer. Everyone believed the rumors about the scientist, swallowed the story that she had a nasty breakup with someone, withdrew from social situations, started spending all her free time alone and got depressed around the holidays.

Everyone except Gage. Something was off about the circumstances surrounding her death. Call it professional intuition. He was an expert when it came to death. How to cover one up, to make it disappear, to eliminate every trace from the scene.

At the CIA, that had been his job. His forte. He'd been assigned to a four-person team. Such a small word to describe the people who, over the years and through the close-call ordeals, had become his family. Their covert missions had been to carry out high-value target assassinations. Everyone had a specialty.

He was the cleaner.

Movement inside Hope's room pulled him from his thoughts. Gage straightened, leaning toward the steering wheel. A shadow darted up to the window and raised the blinds.

Hope.

She was free from the handcuffs.

How in the heck had she managed that?

Hope unlocked the window and raised it. Holding the two blankets around her shoulders so that they covered her body, she threw a leg over the side of the windowsill. A long, toned leg followed by the other one.

What in the hell was she doing?

She eased herself down from the sill, holding her purse and shoes. The second her bare feet hit the cold ground the distress on her face turned to shock. Gage could only imagine the pain she must've experienced in that instant. She hopped up, pulling the window closed.

He started the engine, and his headlights blinked on.

Hope's head snapped up, turning in his direction, and she froze. He shut off the lights and waved to her when she looked ready to bolt in the opposite direction.

She ran to the truck and climbed into the passenger's seat.

"You must really have a death wish," he said, "running around with no clothes on in this weather when your body is still fighting hypothermia."

"I need to get answers about what happened to Faith. Tonight. Once they kick me out in the morning, I'll never make it back inside Benediction. I'll never learn the truth."

"In this town, the truth won't set you free and it won't bring your sister back, but it might get you killed." He shifted in his seat toward her. "So, do you?"

Hope tensed. "Do I what?"

"Have a death wish?"

She blew out a heavy breath and lowered her head. "I can't live with not knowing who killed my sister and why."

Not knowing what happened to a loved one could drive a person insane. In his case, it had driven him to the CIA. His father had worked for the Agency. Went out on a mission and never came back. The circumstances had been classified.

Even after he joined, he never uncovered the specifics surrounding his father's death. The details had been above his pay grade.

Every day it ate away at him. A stinging, helpless feeling he wouldn't wish on his worst enemy.

"I won't let a murderer get away," Hope said. "Someone has to be held responsible."

Every person on his team's kill list had been human garbage, and eliminating them had been for the greater good, to make the world a safer place. Justice had been the cornerstone of each assignment.

If someone had taken the life of an innocent woman in Benediction, there was no way Gage could turn a blind eye to it and allow a killer to run loose in the town. His conscience wouldn't let him rest, and Hope looked determined not to stop until she got answers. Without his help, her endeavor could cost her life.

He looked around at the darkness, trying to figure something out. "What's your plan?"

"From here, I'm winging it." She rubbed her hands together, the sound reviving his sense of urgency. "What are you doing out here, sitting in the dark?"

He sensed her watching him and he wanted, no, needed to look at her but dreaded meeting her eyes. The fact that she had become the focal point of his need or dread in less than an hour knocked him off kilter. Left him unbalanced.

"I told you I wouldn't go far," he said. "If nothing else, I'm a man of my word. I always keep my promises." Gage looked at her, met that intense, piercing gaze, which was searching his as though she could see right through him—or wanted to.

He hadn't been *seen* in a long time, and the thought of it, like everything else about Hope, had a knot of terror tightening inside him and a strange elation unfurling.

Saving her life had roused his protective instincts, but it didn't explain or give a name to what he was feeling.

"Good to know," she said.

"They'll realize you're missing long before morning. I say you have a few hours until Danielle checks on you and reports that you're gone." Without knowing whom else Danielle had called, Hope might have even less than that.

She held her shaking hands up to the vent. "I'm not leaving this town until I find out what really happened to Faith."

"I have an idea that'll buy you time," Gage said, hoping like hell that it'd work. "But you'll need to do exactly what I tell you. Can you follow orders?"

Hope straightened in her seat. Her features hardened with

grim determination, and her eyes gleamed with a fierceness that warmed him but also worried him. "I'll do whatever it takes."

That was precisely what concerned him.

Chapter Five

Hope had neglected to confess she wasn't the best at following orders. The nature of her job required her to defy authority and toss out the rulebook. Two things that came effortlessly for her.

Gage turned on the truck's headlights and pulled off. They cleared the clinic, hitting the main road.

"Where are we going?" she asked, scooting down low in the seat to ensure that any passersby wouldn't see her.

"My place. You'll be safe there — for a while, anyway." The roads were empty as he went through the roundabout, taking the turn into the residential section of town. "But if they find you, they won't show an ounce of leniency."

Chilled inside and out, Hope leaned in closer to the vent, staying down low near the dashboard. That helped warm her, but her feet were blocks of ice.

They drove through the confines of the compact neighborhood to the far side. All the homes were built of brick, painted light gray. The lawns were small and shaded by decades-old trees. American flags hung from the eaves or mailboxes of every home.

Gage pushed a button on the remote clipped on the visor as he made a right turn into a driveway. The house was at the end of a cul-de-sac, tastefully decorated with white string lights and a brightly lit Santa's sleigh complete with reindeer adorning the front lawn. The door of a double garage opened in front of them. A gold SUV was parked inside, and a mountain bike hung on the wall.

"You don't live alone." The possibility of a wife or girlfriend hadn't occurred to her.

"No. I live with my stepsister, Claire, and her son, Jason. I stay in the apartment above the garage." He pulled in, parked and hit the remote-control button, lowering the garage door.

"So you're single?" she asked without thinking. Not that she regretted it. Clarity was a good thing.

"I am. No romantic attachments for me."

At the moment? Or ever? "Why?"

He was smart, brave and attractive. Had chosen to help her when others would've abandoned her. Everything about him was hard but appealing, from the expression on his face to his sculpted body.

"My life is complicated. It wouldn't be fair to ask someone to deal with my baggage." Before Hope had a chance to ask any further questions, he said, "Wait here for me. I'll only be a minute." Gage jumped out of the truck and made his way into the house.

The interior garage light went out, and the ensuing silence was unsettling. Would Gage tell his stepsister about her? Was he the type of man to keep secrets from those closest to him?

A shiver ran through her, more from the quiet and waiting than the cold. She missed the soothing heat blowing from the vents, but the truck cab stayed warm until Gage returned.

As promised, he'd only been gone a couple of minutes.

He came around to her side of the truck with clothes, shoes and a sealed Tupperware container full of food in his hands.

She opened the door and looked down at the floor, dreading the feel of the concrete against her bare feet.

"Don't worry." He thrust the bundle that he was holding into her arms. "You carry that stuff and I'll carry you," he said, as if reading her mind.

Her whole body softened in gratitude while her brain warned, *It'll be a mistake, a big, big mistake!*

In twenty-eight years, no man had ever carried her until Gage, a gorgeous, good citizen who was willing to lift her into his arms for a third time in one night. "You probably shouldn't. It's starting to become a habit and I might get used to it."

"I can think of a lot worse tendencies to get used to."

He had a point, but she needed to use better judgment. "I'm strong enough to walk."

"No doubt about that after your great escape from the clinic." His smile was crooked, playful and had her smiling in return.

It was so unlike her. She never let a sexy grin or an impressive body throw her off stride. Knew better than to be lured in by chivalry and charm. She stayed on track. Took whatever risks were necessary regardless of the danger. She'd do the same with Gage. He was her best option to get answers, but he was also a stranger. Still, something about him kept derailing her focus from the cold and death and had her thinking about ridiculous things, like how warm his eyes became when he smiled.

The way he'd fearlessly endangered himself to save her—twice. His refusal to cave under pressure from the military and willingness to hide her in his home. The selflessness that became more apparent with each of his actions, and that inclined her to trust him despite the fact that everyone in Benediction was a suspect she had to investigate.

Her instincts regarding him were dangerous.

Kindness was the best disguise when a person had something to hide. She couldn't drop her guard around him.

Not that she had any intention of sharing that. It was hard enough to admit to herself for some reason. "I can handle the cold ground for a little longer."

"No need." He plucked a pair of sweatpants and canvas sneakers from the pile in her hands. "You and Claire are about the same size. I think they'll fit."

She took the pants and shoes, setting the other stuff down. "Thanks."

Gage nodded and went to the front of the truck, putting his back to her, giving her privacy.

The lounge pants were tapered through the leg, fitting like snug pajamas, but they were warm. The sneakers would do, even if they were a little too loose on her feet.

She hopped out of the truck and closed the door gently. "Thank you."

He took the rest of the stuff from her. "Come on. It's this way."

With the two blankets from the hospital wrapped around her shoulders, she followed him. Gage led her through the side door of the garage and up a steep exterior staircase. Glancing behind her, she checked to be sure no neighbors spotted her.

At the landing, she had a clear view behind the house to a one-story building. It looked commercial, at least twice the square footage of any of the residences with plenty of parking in the area. Only an uninterrupted expanse of grass and a footpath ran between the two properties.

Gage quickly unlocked the door, ushering her inside, and switched on the lights. "Feel free to look around."

She took in the simple apartment, not that there was much to see. Three rooms consisting of an eat-in kitchen connected to a living room with a gas fireplace, bedroom with a queen-size bed and a full bathroom.

The walls were white and plain. No paintings, no pictures, not a single personal photograph. The furniture was well-worn and mismatched like pieces picked up from a rummage sale. Though she barely knew Gage, nothing in the apartment seemed to fit him. She imagined his taste would run toward brown leather and dark polished wood.

"How long have you lived here?" she asked, folding both blankets into a neat pile.

He set the container of food and other clothes on the kitchen counter. "Here in this apartment or here in Benediction?"

"Both."

"Well, the answer is one and the same. Nine months."

"What brought you to Benediction?"

He put the Tupperware container in the microwave, setting it for two minutes. "It's complicated."

That was fast becoming his favorite word, she noticed.

He crossed the room, going to the gas fireplace, and turned it on. "Claire has lupus. She had a bad flare-up around the time I needed a major change in my life. They weren't sure if she'd make it. I came and helped her out."

Hope had never met anyone firsthand who had the autoimmune disease, but she knew it was chronic and triggered the immune system to attack the body's healthy tissue. The disease could affect the skin and joints, cause organ damage. The severity and symptoms varied from person to person. "That was extraordinary of you to put your life on hold like that for her."

"Not really." Looking Hope straight in the eye, he said, "Please don't think I'm noble or anything close to it. Because I'm not."

The more she learned about him, the more *noble* became the perfect word to describe him. Along with modest and brave.

Why downplay his acts of kindness? Humility she understood, respected, but this self-denigration felt like deflection.

His brow creased, and a look of raw vulnerability flashed across his face as she considered him.

"Dumb luck brought Claire and me back together, and we both got something out of it." He held the stare for a beat longer, then he bent down and unlaced his boots. "She's doing much better now, can handle things on her own." Slipping the boots off, he gave a sigh of relief. He set them on the hearth. "Put yours next to mine to dry. Excuse me a sec. I'm dying to get something warm and dry on my feet." Gage went into the bedroom, leaving the door open.

Hope sat on the soft shag rug close to the fire, placing her shoes near his.

All this time, he'd put off his own needs without complaining while looking out for her at the entrance to Benediction, at the clinic, in the garage. Yet another example of how he came across as a good person at the core. Not just for show. Most of the men who had passed through her life had only helped her if they benefited in return.

The microwave beeped.

She was rising from the rug when he came back out wearing socks.

"I've got it. Stay seated and rest. Doc's orders." He tossed her a pair of wool socks.

She caught them and didn't waste a second trading them for the canvas sneakers.

He switched off the main overhead light, leaving the soft glow from the fire to illuminate the room. Her eyes softened and her shoulders relaxed in immediate response. She hadn't realized every muscle had been clenched.

Gage washed his hands and grabbed two spoons from a drawer and bowls from a cabinet. "I hope you're hungry and eat meat."

"I am and I do."

He took the container out of the microwave and removed the lid.

A heavenly aroma wafted through the room, making her stomach rumble. She hadn't realized she was hungry, but it had been hours since she'd last eaten. "That smells delicious."

"Claire is a good cook." He divided the food between the two bowls, then, coming closer, he handed her one along with a spoon and sat beside her in front of the fire.

The stew was thick, with chunks of meat and hearty vegetables bathed in a fragrant broth. The first slightly gamey bite told her it was venison, fixed with carrots, juniper berries, turnips and parsnips rather than potatoes. "This is wonderful. Claire isn't a good cook. She's excellent."

"Hits the spot, doesn't it?"

After almost dying, a ham sandwich would've been ambrosia, but the stew was truly tasty. She nodded to him and finished eating, letting the warmth of the food soak into her body.

"Need something to wash it down?" he asked.

"Yes, please."

He took her bowl from her and stood. "Water or brandy? I have the good stuff."

"Both." Her body had relaxed, but her mind still whirled with thoughts of Faith and the military police and what would happen if they found her. "On second thought, maybe I should stick to water. I only have a few hours before—"

"I promised to buy you time, and I will." Though he neglected to say how. He poured two waters and one brandy, leaving the bottle on the counter. "I'm a man of my word, remember?"

How could she forget? "I guess it's my turn to ask what's your plan."

"Leave that to me." He carried the three glasses to the rug and gave her a water and the brandy. "I want you to focus on resting and getting your strength back."

"No brandy for you?"

"I need a clear head if I'm going to ensure no one comes looking for you, but you should drink up. You've been through a lot tonight. I'm sure there's still too much adrenaline in your system. The sedative Danielle offered was probably a good idea, but I can understand you not wanting to take it. Not knowing how it might affect you. But the brandy will make it easier for you to relax. You'll be safe here."

She wasn't prepared to put her complete trust in him, but if Gage had wanted the military police to capture her and kick her out of town, he wouldn't have picked her up outside the clinic. It would've been a heck of a lot easier to simply report her. Whatever his motives for helping her, for now, they appeared aligned with her own.

Hope sipped the brandy. Smooth and warm, the amber liquid burst with complex flavors, relieving the vestige of tension in her chest. "The good stuff indeed."

"There's something I need to ask you," he said. "How did you get out of the handcuffs?"

"Let's just say that after being detained by authoritarian governments, taken hostage by a warlord and restrained by a local extremist group, I've learned how to get out of a pair of handcuffs."

The corner of his mouth hitched up in a half grin that was endearing and equally sexy. "You used something from your purse that the staff sergeant overlooked, right? It's the reason you asked me to get your handbag from the truck."

As a matter of fact, he was right. Her handy-dandy Swiss Army knife had a variety of features, including a handcuff key that had gotten her out of more than one pinch. Most people dismissed the multitool because of its glittery, jewel-tone case, not bothering to examine it further. "Thanks for the assist. Without it, I'd still be locked to the bed."

He drank his water. "Authoritarian governments, warlords and extremists. That's an impressive list."

"It comes with the professional territory."

"What profession might that be?"

"I'm a photojournalist." The equipment she used made her easy to spot in a crowd, and her images always drew unfriendly attention. Intimidation, imprisonment, even torture happened to those in her line of work sometimes. Hope had never experienced the extreme end of the spectrum, but she knew of others who had.

"Ah," he said with a touch of a smile on his lips. "That

explains the intrepid, won't-back-down air about you. I like a persistent woman who goes after what she wants."

His flattery was comforting in a way it shouldn't have been. A verbal stroke of her ego that made her smile. But it was more than that. There was such warmth to him she wanted to bask in.

She pulled her legs into her chest and rocked slightly, fighting the strange sense of ease that came over her in his presence. "I'm not intrepid." Though she did like the sound of it, almost as much as she enjoyed the idea of him thinking of her as such. "Merely stubborn." She'd learned the difference a long time ago.

Weren't they a pair? He wasn't *noble* and she wasn't *brave*.

Gage leaned in toward her, forcing her to meet his eyes, and everything inside her quieted. "I see real courage when I look at you. And determination. Most people don't have either. Their resolve is born out of fear. Unlike yours."

Not quite knowing how to respond to the best compliment she'd ever received, she looked away from him and sipped the brandy.

The fire provided the only light between them and continued to spread its warmth through the room. The heat eased the stiffness in her body.

A moment later, she found her voice. "Courage is admirable. My tenacity has often been called reckless."

"No doubt. Climbing out of the clinic's window barefoot without any pants on in this weather was reckless, but the truly brave always are. How can I fault you for that?" Gage got up, snatched a heavy blanket from the back of the sofa and dragged it around her until she was encased in a cocoon. "I have to go. Once you feel like sleeping, take the bed. I'll bunk on the sofa."

"Where are you going?"

"To run an important errand to get supplies. Then I have to go see Captain Finley."

"Who's that?"

"The one person in Benediction who can call off the military police."

Chapter Six

Sheriff Ryan Keller didn't think his night could get much worse. But every minute it slid farther downhill from *bad* to *wretched*.

Wearing a black turtleneck and jeans—instead of his uniform, since this was supposed to be his night off—he walked into the station and up to Deputy Owen Finnegan.

He stared at Finn's battered face, black eye and broken nose, and exhaled a string of expletives. "Did that kid do this to you?" Ryan asked, hiking his chin at a male, no older than eighteen, who was locked up in a holding cell, pacing back and forth like a rabid wolf ready to gnaw off a limb.

Finn lowered the ice pack from his bloody nose. "Kid? More like a doped-up punk."

"It took the two of us to subdue him," Deputy Dwight Travers said, pouring himself a cup of coffee.

Ryan took off his black wool beanie and traded it for the stiff ball cap he rarely wore. The front panel of the cap had white block letters that read *Sheriff*. Besides his cuffs and Glock holstered on his hip, the ball cap was the closest he was getting to an official uniform tonight. Tomorrow it'd be business as usual with his Stetson. "Good thing he didn't have a weapon."

"Still, he did a number on Finn," Dwight said.

"What's he on?" asked Aimee Newsome, his administrative assistant and the heart of the office. She kept things running smoothly and the station stocked, made sure he didn't miss anyone's birthday or anniversary.

Dwight stood next to Finn and put a hand on his shoulder. "Must be Zion."

That was the name of the latest and greatest drug on the

streets. There was always something new, but this stuff supposedly made a person feel invincible with no nasty hallucinations.

He'd read reports that it was fast becoming an epidemic in cities like Richmond, Virginia Beach, Arlington, DC.

This sort of thing wasn't expected to happen in a sleepy town where you had to drive two hours for soft-serve frozen yogurt. Granted, the preconceived notion that smaller equaled safer wasn't accurate. Crimes happened across geographical areas. People locked their houses and cars in Goode, but they didn't have junkie dens, meth labs and drug-related assaults there.

At least they weren't supposed to have them.

A long time ago, he'd made peace with the fact that he was stuck in Goode, caring for his ailing dad. Alzheimer's and cirrhosis were slowly eating away at him. Ryan loved his father and didn't mind the thankless task of playing nursemaid in the absence of the home care helper. He'd even convinced himself that he was lucky to have this suffocating job, but the only luck he had was the bad kind.

Now he had to deal with the cons of a big-city life with none of the perks on top of everything else.

Ryan rubbed the metal bump on his sternum under his sweater. A reminder attached to the chain around his neck that this was all his life would ever be.

"Now that I'm here, Dwight, take Finn over to the ER so he can be checked out."

The local tow truck came down the street, hauling a banged-up sky blue sedan. The front end and trunk had been partially crushed, the roof was crumpled and the driver's window was busted.

Ryan's hair stood on end. He knew that car. A rental that belonged to Hope Fischer. The woman hell-bent on getting answers about her dead sister. "Give me a sec," he said.

He shoved through the door and jogged across the street to where the truck waited at a traffic light.

"Hey, Zach, where did you get that car?"

"I pulled it out of Goode Lake on the road to Benediction."

Damn it. "Was it completely submerged?"

"May as well have been."

"What about the driver? Do you know what condition she's in? Is she alive?"

"They took her to the medical facility in Benediction for treatment. Can you believe that they let her in? That newcomer must have good mojo. If it had been one of us Goodies, we'd be dead on the side of the road."

The fact that she was receiving medical care meant she was alive. "I'll call over in the morning and see how she's doing."

"No need, Sheriff. I heard the MPs scheduled a taxi to pick her up tomorrow."

Then her condition wasn't serious. *Thank God.* Strangers never understood that it was best to stay away from Benediction. "All right." Ryan patted his door. "Thanks."

As the light changed, he crossed the street.

He'd give it forty-eight hours. If Hope Fischer wasn't back in Goode by then, he'd drive over to Benediction. His sheriff's badge wouldn't get him through the gate, but he'd raise hell until he knew that nothing fishy had happened to her.

SNOW FLURRIES HAD started falling earlier than the forecast had predicted. Luckily, Gage had made it to Goode, picked up the essentials he needed and returned before the snow started to stick.

He parked near the Benediction military police station. The unmarked building was within walking distance of the shops and diner but sat apart from everything else. Glancing at the clock, he saw he had two minutes to make it to Captain Erin Finley's office or he'd face her ire.

The CIA had taught him many harsh lessons, including

how to deal with someone who had a gun pointed at your head when you only had a knife.

Taking a deep breath, he prepared for battle. When it came to his personal situation, which was now compounded by the liability of protecting Hope, winning wasn't an option. The best he could hope for was a draw.

Keeping the MPs from conducting a manhunt in town to find Hope would be tricky at best, but the deception was necessary if she was going to stay in town to find answers about her sister's death. And it appeared she had every intention of doing so. Gage understood the feeling and would do likewise in her position.

The woman roused his protective instincts, and there was little he could do to fight nature. But what would he do if that impulse were pitted against his own sense of self-preservation?

In the next sixty seconds, he was going to find out.

Gage grabbed the box from the passenger's seat and hopped out of the truck.

Floodlights bathed the one-story building and surrounding area. At least one guard was always on duty inside. The contingent of MPs in town was small, ten enlisted plus Finley, and they were a tight crew.

As he approached the entrance, the soldier seated at the front desk spotted him and hurried over to assist.

The specialist held the door open for him. "Evening, Mr. Graham. She's waiting. You should hurry."

All the MPs were aware of Gage's regular deliveries, though he suspected none of them knew what they consisted of or had the gumption to question Finley.

Gage quickened his step down the short, narrow hall, passing the evidence room.

Finley's office door was closed.

He peered through the glass insert. Seated behind her desk in uniform, her blond hair in a tight, slick bun, she was working on her computer. No doubt she'd heard his footsteps approaching and was cognizant of his presence, but she didn't acknowledge him.

A silly show of power. Not that he blamed her for being miffed she was there later than normal on his account.

He rapped on the door, balancing the heavy box on his knee, and waited.

Lifting one hand from the keyboard, she beckoned to him to enter with a wave, still not looking away from her computer.

He strode in, his shoulders squared and his head held high. No slinking in like a dog with its tail between its legs for him. He plopped the box on the desk, causing the glass bottles inside to clatter, and took a seat.

"Cutting it down to the wire, aren't you?" Leaning back in her chair, she finally stopped typing and looked at him. Her amber eyes were cold as frostbite.

"Good evening to you, too, Captain Finley."

She drew her mouth tight in a sour expression and checked the contents of the box.

Ten pounds of imported gold-grade Wagyu steaks, hard-to-come-by bottles of Château Margaux and Lafite Rothschild, and a few hand-rolled Cuban cigars.

Residing in Benediction made it impossible to procure such high-end luxury items online. No internet was one thing. Package delivery companies didn't service the town, and Benediction wasn't a part of the regular postal system. Mail was routed through military channels for security purposes because no civilian postal carriers were allowed inside the town.

Life here was miserable for those unaccustomed to the constraints.

Even under *normal* conditions, Captain Finley couldn't afford the contents of the box.

That was over four grand worth of goods. Paid for with Gage's savings.

Captain Finley closed the flaps of the box and pushed it aside. "When I set a meeting, I expect you to rearrange your schedule to make it." She propped her elbows on the desk and stared at him over the steeple of her fingers. "Never change the time again."

Her expectations had been crystal clear from the beginning, but these were extenuating circumstances. "If I had come earlier, I would've been empty-handed, and I didn't want to disappoint you," he said, his tone casual.

Holding his gaze, Finley hit a button on her keyboard, and the printer spit out a piece of paper. "You disappointed me the moment you brought an uncleared person through my gate."

It wasn't *her* gate, despite the power trip she was on telling herself otherwise, but he wasn't there to quibble. "I'm sorry to disappoint you. Certainly, you were informed that it was a medical emergency."

She gave him a withering glance. "It was wrong for you to manipulate the gate guards, promising they'd be hailed as heroes. They're young and impressionable. The rules keep everyone safe. We're under no legal obligation to assist anyone beyond the boundary of Benediction for good reason."

"What about an ethical responsibility?"

Finley swiveled in her chair, took the paper from the printer and placed it in on her desk in front of her, ignoring his question. "Your actions tonight threaten our agreement," she said, her voice edged with acid.

They had forged a tenuous arrangement when he arrived last spring. One mutually beneficial to all parties.

Gage needed a place to lie low after his CIA team had been disavowed and put on a kill list. The irony of the tables turning—now he was the one being hunted—wasn't lost on him.

Getting into the town had been simple for him. He first became a resident of Benediction briefly as a child. His mother had married Claire's father, a townie who had been born and raised there. But an insulated life in the mountains of Virginia hadn't been for his mom, and the marriage only lasted a few years. Long enough for him to be documented as a former inhabitant and loosely considered a relative of a current native.

All of which had been sufficient to get him through the gates with Claire's dire medical situation and Dr. Steve Howland's support. Doc had been in Benediction forever and had known Gage as a child. Howland had vouched for Gage's character. Something he'd claimed didn't change. He had insisted Claire needed help to recover and the town required someone to manage her family business, which provided a critical service that Gage happened to have the rare qualifications to take over.

The right time, the right place, the right circumstances.

The problem was the background check Captain Finley wanted to send up through her chain of command as part of their security protocol.

There were no digital records connecting Gage to Benediction. He never included the town on his list of prior residences in his disclosure paperwork, and he had never shared the detail with a soul. If his name had been logged into the system, it would've drawn a bull's-eye around his head while giving the CIA his exact coordinates.

Gage had confided in Claire that a background check would be bad. As in disastrous. She told him about Finley's marital problems. Secrets were hard to keep in a small town. Finley was having a difficult time hanging on to her husband. A man of particular tastes, he loathed this remote assignment and the constraints it put on his own career and missed the creature comforts of a big city.

With Gage's connections and his rainy-day fund, he struck a deal for the duration of her assignment. Once Finley moved on from Benediction, she had promised the paperwork would appear as though he'd been properly vetted, so her replacement wouldn't ask questions. Not that Gage trusted her to follow through on her end.

She had two more years on her orders. Two years Gage could count on having sanctuary. For a disavowed CIA operative on the run for his life, two years could feel like twenty.

A feasible trade considering he had virtually no living expenses, even though the arrangement proved an irritating inconvenience.

Escape was not peace, he had discovered.

"These bimonthly deliveries of yours keep my husband happy. Living here is now tolerable for him. You've also found a way to make yourself indispensable to the town while somehow remaining invisible. Takes quite the talent to pull that off."

Well, he worked very hard at it. He'd stepped in for Claire while she was sick and still handled the less desirable aspects of the job for her. When the school's physical education teacher relocated, Gage offered to substitute, the same way he joined the fire department the moment they fell short on a required number of volunteers.

The trick was noticing a need and filling it while keeping everyone at arm's length. The more distance the better.

"I'd hate to dissolve our partnership and file this." Captain Finley slid the paper across the desk to him. "But I will."

Gage took the document and scanned it. A formal request for a background check on him.

He crumpled the paper in his fist but remained silent. Seething, he swallowed the bitterness rising in his throat. The threads of his long-suffering patience were beginning to fray.

"I can always print another and fax it," she said.

"Then how long until your husband leaves?" His tone was matter-of-fact as Gage steered the conversation back to her. "Every time he opens one of those boxes, I bet he feels like a king, relishing the extravagant commodities that didn't cost him a dime. Does he enjoy the surprises I include?"

Sometimes it was a tin of caviar, now and then a bottle of champagne that couldn't be found in a liquor store within a three-hour drive. Whatever Gage chose, it was sure to titillate the taste buds of Mr. Finley.

Apparently, the way to a man's heart was through his stomach. Or rather, his sophisticated palate.

Captain Finley's mouth twisted into an ugly expression that suggested her husband absolutely loved those little surprises.

Gage bit back a smile. It would've been mean to revel. There was no excuse to stoop to such a level, even though he'd been provoked.

"If those boxes stop, I give your marriage six months tops." Gage was treading a fine line. He'd made his point, and now he needed to ease off before he taunted her into lashing out. "Tell me what you want to maintain our accord."

"I want you to remember your place." She stared at him with barely concealed loathing. "I. Own. You."

No one owned him. Not even the CIA while he'd worked for the Agency. But if letting her believe that he was a harmless peon stuck under her thumb got him what we wanted, which was to stay, then so be it.

"When I say jump, you ask how high." She leaned back in her chair and put her feet up on the corner of the desk. "You stay invisible. You don't cause problems for me, like driving *trouble* through the front gate, making my life harder."

Hope was definitely trouble. On that, he and Captain Finley were in complete agreement.

"Mea culpa." He raised his palms in mock surrender. "But you'll be pleased to know that I have resolved the entire situation."

Finley arched a manicured eyebrow. "Resolved how?"

"I sneaked back into the clinic, got Ms. Fischer out of

Staff Sergeant Burton's handcuffs and drove her to Goode," he said, assured that Hope was actually safe at his apartment, where he'd help her get to the bottom of her sister's death.

Finley's eyes narrowed as she studied him closely. "But I gave explicit orders for you to vacate the premises of the clinic."

He nodded with a practiced look of contrition. "Your orders are the law around here, but I realized how upset you were going to be once I learned Ms. Fischer was on your blacklist. It's already snowing. No taxi will show up in the morning to take her to Goode. The roads will be too dangerous by then to travel. Danielle examined her. Ms. Fischer was no longer in immediate danger, and I thought it would be easier for everyone, you most of all, to simply get her out of town quickly and quietly."

"Is that so?"

Not the response he'd expected. An attaboy or pat on the back would've been more appropriate. "Yes, it is. Problem solved. You're welcome."

Captain Finley swung her legs down and put her feet on the floor with a harsh thud. "You won't mind if I verify that, will you?"

Corporal Livingston would confirm the time Gage left Benediction and when he returned. On the way out of town, vehicles were never searched, much less stopped. His truck had tinted windows, so Livingston wouldn't be able to say one way or the other whether Hope had been inside.

All the corporal could do was corroborate Gage's comings and goings.

"By all means, go right ahead," he said. *Knock yourself out.*

"Then I have your consent?" Her question sounded like a trap being set.

He nodded. "Of course you do."

Finley's face took on the look of a cat poised to catch a

succulent canary as she picked up the receiver of the landline phone. "If Corporal Livingston supports your story that you left town after the accident, as I'm sure he will, I'll have Staff Sergeant Burton check the clinic," she said, the words sounding magnanimous, but Gage was no fool. "And since you've given your consent, he'll then search your residence to be a hundred percent certain Ms. Fischer is gone."

The trap snapped shut.

Gage's temper flared at unknowingly giving Finley the upper hand and putting Hope in a vulnerable position. Hope was clever and audacious, but she'd proven that she reacted without thinking things through, examining all the angles.

He filtered his anger, keeping his face relaxed, his posture easy and his eyes soft. "Anything to put your mind at ease, Captain." What else was he supposed to say as a man with nothing to hide?

"If you're lying and she's found, you'll regret playing this game with me. I'll call my commanding officer first thing in the morning and relay my request for a background check on you verbally to expedite the process. Then I'll discover whatever it is you've been hiding out from here in Benediction."

Her smug expression was difficult to tolerate, but he crossed his legs and folded his hands in his lap. "Rest assured, it won't come to that," he said with a soft smile, hoping that was true, for everyone's sake. "Can the specialist make some coffee while we wait? It's been an exhausting evening. I could use something hot and strong to drink."

"Certainly."

This might all backfire on him in a million different ways.

No matter what, he wasn't going to let Finley call her commander to initiate a background check. If she did, all hell would break loose, turning Benediction into a bloodbath.

Under no circumstances would he allow the folks of this town to end up as collateral damage.

Chapter Seven

A combination of the heat from the fire and the brandy worked its magic, making Hope drowsy. By the time her glass was empty, it was hard for her to keep her eyes open. Fatigue had threaded through her, and her limbs had grown heavy.

Gage had encouraged her to sleep in the bed, but she didn't want to impose any further. Taking the sofa was the least she could do after the taxing evening she'd put him through and everything he'd done for her. She could only imagine how exhausted he must be.

As for her, curling up and drifting off was not an option while he was out there still helping her. How were things going with Captain Finley?

A car door slammed closed outside. Hope turned toward the window in the kitchen that faced the street. Blue and red lights were flashing.

The military police were there.

Hope scrambled to her feet. The room spun at the sudden movement. All the blood drained from her head, leaving her dizzy, but there was no time for weakness.

She hurried to the window, taking great care to stay low so her shadow wouldn't be seen. Not wanting to draw attention, she slowly slid the curtain to the side only enough to peek out and chanced a quick look below.

Her nerve endings prickled at the sight of Staff Sergeant Burton crossing behind his patrol car and striding up the walkway toward the front door.

Pulse skyrocketing, she ducked down.

Why was the staff sergeant there? Had Gage given her up?

Almost immediately, she dismissed the idea. Yes, Gage was a stranger, but he was a good person intent on helping her. That much she believed, even if he might have ulterior motives.

Something must have gone wrong during his talk with Captain Finley. It was the only reasonable explanation.

If the soldier was there to look for her, it wouldn't take him long to make his way up to the garage apartment.

Staying crouched, she scurried into the living room. After shoving on the canvas sneakers, she hid the blankets from the clinic and her wet shoes under the sofa.

It was better to leave the gas fireplace alone, so it looked as though Gage had forgotten and left it on. If she turned it off, Burton would be able to tell that it had been done recently.

She glanced around for any other evidence that she'd been there.

Two bowls and three glasses were on the rug. She scooped up the dishes, mindful not to let them clatter, and tucked them in the dishwasher.

The rumble of an electric motor came from below, followed by a soft rattle. The garage door was lifting.

Burton was searching the garage.

She had to get out of there, but she couldn't use the exterior staircase, and where was she supposed to go, anyway? Gage had proven the only friendly in Benediction, and she wasn't familiar with the layout of the town well enough to know a good spot to hide.

Pressure built in her chest as her mind buzzed. She breathed through it. *One step at a time.*

Knowing where to run was the least of worries. First, she had to leave, and then she could figure out the rest.

From the living room it was plain to see there were no windows in the bathroom. The only possibility was the bedroom.

Hope grabbed her purse, throwing the strap across her body, and hurried into the adjacent room. One small window was on the wall to the side of the wrought-iron bed.

Voices came from the exterior staircase. One female, the other male—Burton's.

She shoved the curtain aside and looked to see if there was

a way to escape. The window faced the rear of the property. A portion of the sloped lower-level roof ran beneath it. She might be able to use it to reach the ground.

The voices drew closer, coming to the landing. A knock at the apartment door sent her heart pounding. She was out of time.

"Gage, are you home?" asked a woman in a loud voice. It must've been Claire.

"You said no one was here. Why are you knocking?" Burton demanded.

Shutting the bedroom door halfway, Hope blocked the view of most of the bedroom from anyone entering the apartment.

"He's not here," Claire said. "You saw as well as I did that his truck is gone. Force of habit, I suppose. What are you going to do? Arrest me for having manners?"

Hope ran to the window and unlocked it but couldn't lift it open. It was stuck. Someone had painted over the bottom seam.

A fresh wave of anxiety flooded her system with adrenaline.

Footsteps pounded up the staircase. "Hey, Mom." A teenage voice outside the apartment door. Gage's nephew, Jason. "What's going on?"

Hope unzipped her handbag, fished out her utility knife and started working the blade from one tool across the sealed seam.

"The military police are looking for someone."

"An unauthorized outsider," Burton said. "Where have you been, Jason?"

"Next door, hanging out with Tyler. What do you care?"

"I think you should go wait in the house for your mother while we finish up here."

"The last time I checked, I hadn't enlisted," Jacob said. "So I don't care what you think."

Hope stripped the last of the seal, brushed the bits of scraped paint away from the windowsill and pried it open. She threw her leg over the edge outside and squeezed through the opening. A strange calm kicked in, the way it always did out on assignment whenever she took a risk for the sake of getting the perfect photo to capture a story.

"Open the door. Now!" Burton snapped.

Keys jangled, and the doorknob rattled.

As Hope lowered the window, she prayed it wouldn't squeak and give her away.

Shutting it quietly was easy, but she turned to move from the window and her foot slipped on the slick rooftop.

She grabbed on to the thin ledge of the sill, biting her bottom lip to swallow her scream.

Using her feet, she searched for a safe spot along the shingles, trying to gain purchase so she could crawl to the side. If Burton ventured a glance outside the window, he'd see her instantly.

Snow flurries whirled around her as the wind whipped the air. Hope heard them, inside the apartment now, their voices getting louder, drawing closer.

She had to move, but she was worried about making noise. There was only one choice.

Sucking in a breath, she abandoned her fear of falling and let go of the ledge. She tried to scoot from under the window, scrabbling with elbows and hands and knees. Another slick patch sent her sliding down the slanted roof as her stomach bottomed out.

Desperate, she clawed at the shingles. She caught hold of a vent stack pipe with one hand at the same time that her feet jammed into the rain gutter, breaking her fall.

Her heart was pounding in her throat, and the tangy taste of blood was in her mouth. During the fall, she'd bitten her lip deep, though slipping might have been a blessing.

The only way Burton would see her was if he opened the window and leaned out, which was still a possibility.

Jason yelled something inside the bedroom, but Hope was too far away to hear what he'd said. Burton shouted back. Claire's voice was caught between them, softer yet firm.

A moment later, there was silence.

Hope looked up at the window. She hadn't dropped far, less than four feet, but how was she supposed to get back inside? The roof was too slippery to climb. Was it even safe for her to try yet?

Had Burton been satisfied with his search and left?

"I need you to take me over there so I can search the place," Burton said, somewhere outside on the side of the house.

Guess that bloodhound wasn't satisfied.

"You don't have to do it, Mom! This might be Benediction, but it's still America and we have rights. Don't you need a search warrant?"

Their voices were traveling toward the rear of the house, where Hope was. She pressed against the roof and froze.

"Is this really necessary?" Claire asked.

"It is if you want to get me out of your hair," Burton said, sounding as if he were just below Hope.

"Instead of dragging this out," Claire said, "let's get it over with."

Something moved near Hope's head. Before she could stop herself, she shifted away in reaction. Her foot knocked leaves from the gutter to the ground as an owl flew away.

Hope looked to see if anyone had noticed.

Claire was walking across the yard, away from the house beside Burton, rubbing her arms to fend off the cold since she didn't have on a coat. They were on the path headed to the commercial building.

Where was Jason?

Hope glanced straight down over the side, and her breath snagged in her throat. Jason was staring right up at her.

Oh, no. Putting her finger up to her lips, Hope silently pleaded with him to say nothing.

Their gazes locked, and Jason looked at her for what felt like an endless moment before he turned toward the yard. "Mom!" Jason said, making Hope's heart clench. "Have fun with the Gestapo. I'm going inside."

"All right, sweetie," Claire said, raising her hand in a wave without looking back.

Staff Sergeant Burton was focused straight ahead and didn't bother to glance over his shoulder.

Hope let out a shaky breath. Her teeth chattered, but she wasn't sure if it was from the cold or fear.

Jason took off, disappearing around the side of the house, closest to the staircase, while Claire led Burton to the building several hundred feet away.

Two minutes later, Jason opened the bedroom window and stuck his head out, taking in her situation. "I'll help you up," he whispered.

Jason reached his hand down to her, and she did likewise, reaching up.

Their fingertips touched, but even if he'd managed to grasp her hand, he was no more than fifteen years old and didn't have the strength to lift her up.

"Hang on a second." He ducked back inside. It didn't take long for him to return. Jason draped the blanket from Gage's sofa out the window and held on to the other end. "Climb up. I won't let go."

Hope nodded. She took hold of the blanket and scaled the side of the roof, using the material for traction.

At the window, she grabbed onto the sill. Inside the room, Jason had his feet on the blanket, propped up against the wall, his back to the floor for leverage, and was holding the edge with his hands.

Smart kid.

Hope climbed inside, landing on the floor beside Jason on her hands and knees. "Thank you for helping me."

"You're welcome," Jason said, getting up. He pulled the blanket in, closed the window and, after drawing the curtain, turned to her. Standing taller than her, he was five-ten, maybe five-eleven. His hair was sandy brown and he had intelligent blue eyes behind rimless glasses. "Who are you?"

"My name is Hope." Grabbing on to the bed, she pulled herself up. Her arms shook from the climb, and she regretted not getting into the gym on a consistent basis.

"I know your name. Staff Sergeant Burton mentioned it. But that doesn't tell me who you are." His entire demeanor shifted. His eyes hardened, and his expression became inscrutable.

"Mind if we talk in front of the fire? I'm freezing." *Again.*

She stalked to the living room without waiting for a response and plopped down in front of the fireplace.

Jason turned off the bedroom light and followed, taking a seat near her rather than beside her.

"Thanks again for not saying anything to Staff Sergeant Burton," Hope said. "I really appreciate it."

"Why are they looking for you?"

If he already knew Hope's name, then his mother would later explain why she might be in town. Hope would rather tell her own story on her own terms. "My sister was a scientist here. She died. I'm trying to find out what really happened to her, and the military is making it very hard."

"Faith Fischer was your sister?"

She looked at him in shock, although she shouldn't have been surprised. It was a small town. Probably reasonable to assume that everyone had heard some version about how Faith had died. "Yes. Did you know her?"

He nodded. "She gave a couple of lectures at the school. Dr. Fischer was so excited about science and sharing what she knew, it made all of us want to learn more." Jason's eyes softened, and a smile tugged at his mouth. He'd obviously been taken with Faith, captivated by her, as everyone who knew her had been. "But how do you know Gage?"

"I'm an acquaintance of your uncle."

"He's my mom's *former* stepbrother. That doesn't make him my uncle."

"I heard Gage put his life on hold and helped your mom when she got sick. Doesn't that make him a family relation of some sort? Even if a distant one."

Jason rolled his eyes. "Did you know that the larvae of monarch butterflies are more likely to survive infection from certain flies if they're also infected by a protozoan?"

Was he calling Gage a parasite? "I bet you learned that in your biology class."

"I learned that from your sister. Regardless, where or how, it doesn't make it any less true."

Hope got the sneaking suspicion that she was treading in a family quagmire better left alone. "I don't know Gage that well or his relationship to your mom. But he saved my life when he didn't have to. At great risk to himself. I'd be dead if it weren't for him. *I owe him*, but he's the one still helping me."

"First my mom, then the fire department and the kids at my school, now you." Jason shook his head, disdain stamped on his young face. "That's his thing. Saving people, making them feel like they owe him, so they end up protecting him instead of the other way around."

Maybe this was worse than she first thought, but she was in no position to dismiss the kid's feelings. Not that Jason sounded like an ordinary teenager. "You saved me a minute ago when you could've turned me in to Staff Sergeant Burton, which would've been easier. Did you help me so that I would owe you?"

Jason shook his head. "No. Never."

"Then why did you help me?" Hope asked gently.

"I don't like the military. Or at least not the military in this town. They're bullies."

Hope was no fan of the MPs in Benediction and was itching to do an exposé on them, but she had seen the United States military do tremendous things, supporting liberty and preserving democracy abroad, too. No entity was entirely one thing, good or bad.

"Yeah, I don't like bullies, either." She'd always been drawn to photography, loved capturing the world through her lens, but when she realized that with her camera she could speak for those who had no voice—the downtrodden and disenfranchised—she'd found her calling. "Gage stood up to the MPs for me when he didn't have to."

Jason shook his head. "Don't believe anything he says. He wants people to feel like they can trust him, to like him, but he's worried that they might see who he really is, because he's hiding something."

Everyone had secrets and scars of one kind or another. Of course there was more to Gage beneath the surface. She would be a fool to think otherwise, but he was the one person she hoped she could trust. This conversation was making her reconsider, and she didn't like the unease stirring in her belly.

"Gage is not what he seems," Jason continued.

"In what way?"

"It's hard to explain." Jason lowered his head as if thinking and then looked at her. "A couple of years ago, my mom took me to a conference in New York City she had to go to for work. She gave me permission to explore around the hotel within a four-block radius. I saw these guys set up with a table doing a card trick. Three-card monte. For hours, people would bet, thinking they knew where the queen was. After a while, even I swore I knew which card it was, but I was wrong, and they kept losing, too. A few times, someone figured out the trick and won once or twice, got confident and bet bigger, only to lose even bigger. That's Gage." Jason looked at her expectantly.

Hope wasn't sure what to make of that, but she was ready for another brandy. "People aren't like card tricks." It was never that simple.

"Gage is." Jason stretched his long legs out and leaned back on his hands. "After my mom insisted that I call him uncle to show appreciation for how he helped us, I do. To his face, he's Uncle Monte. I told him why I call him that, but he's never chastised me or asked me to stop. Because he knows that I know the truth about him. It's the one honest thing between us."

Gage's words replayed in her head. *Please don't think I'm noble or anything close to it. Because I'm not.*

Maybe Gage had been trying to tell her something important about himself. But why would he bother unless he was a decent person?

It wasn't adding up, didn't make any sense.

"I'm sorry you have a difficult relationship with him," she said, being sincere.

Jason exhaled heavily. "You don't believe me. But just you wait, you'll see. Even my mom told me not to get too close to him."

Hope recoiled in surprise. "Really?" If Claire cautioned her son to be wary of Gage, then this was more than a teenage grievance and legitimate cause for Hope to be concerned. "Did your mom say why?"

"She said that she didn't want me to end up getting hurt."

The silence between them was absolute.

Hope couldn't write off the significance of a mother's warning to her child, but if Claire believed that Gage was a danger to her son, why would she allow him to stay?

The low rumble of the garage door opening cut through the quiet, and a vehicle pulled inside.

They exchanged a look. Gage was back.

Instead of feeling relieved, every muscle in her body was tight.

Gage crept up the staircase with the stealth of a thief, not making a sound. She didn't realize he'd reached the landing until the doorknob turned and he walked in.

Hope glanced over her shoulder at him. He hesitated near the door. Either it was her serious expression, Jason seated on the floor staring at the fire or the tension in the room that gave him pause. None of it was good.

"What are you doing up here?" Gage asked, his tone as neutral as his face.

"Saving your girlfriend from discovery," Jason said.

Hope gaped at the young man. Nothing was further from the truth, but she couldn't deny how the suggestion made her chest tingle. "I'm not his girlfriend."

"Whatever. It's none of my business." Jason got up, stuffing his hands in his jacket pockets, and faced Gage. "Aren't you going to thank me?"

Gage stepped deeper into the apartment. "Thank you." The tension in the room swelled. "There are some supplies in the back of the truck. Would you take them into the house? Your mom is expecting that stuff, and I got those comics you wanted."

"Sure, I'll take it in."

"Aren't you going to thank me? For the comics."

The room grew deathly still. Hope held her breath, sensing the delicate peace between them stretching like a rubber band that might snap.

"Thanks, *Uncle Monte*," Jason said with a sarcastic grin.

Gage didn't so much as blink. "Good night."

Jason shot her a look that screamed, *I told you so!* "Night." He strutted past Gage and left. His footsteps pounded against the stairs, fading until they were gone.

Hope let out a shaky breath.

"What happened when Burton searched the place?" Gage knelt beside her and closed a hand on her shoulder.

"Claire made a lot of noise on the way up the stairs and gave me time to sneak out through the bedroom window. Did she know I was here?"

"No, but she does now, or will once Jason tells her. I guess she was playing it safe. I'll talk to her tomorrow about the situation."

"I'm sure Jason will do that, too. I told him about Faith and why I'm here." In hindsight, it was probably risky to tell a temperamental teen the truth, but she didn't have much choice. "Will it cause more problems?"

He shook his head. "They'll both be discreet. For different reasons. How did Jason get involved?"

"I nearly fell off the roof and got stuck outside. He helped me get back in."

"I'm so sorry. The search was my fault." Gage cupped her chin, tilting her face up to his, and when their eyes met, a warm jolt shot through her like static electricity. "Are you all right?"

She swallowed hard, only managing to nod. What was it about Gage that had her nerves dancing in all the right places?

"The good news is Captain Finley believes that you're no longer in Benediction and that I took you back to Goode. Which means you'll have to keep a low profile." He stroked her jawbone with his thumb.

Driven by an impulse she didn't want to analyze, she leaned into his touch.

His fingers inched higher, caressing her cheek. "I'm glad you're okay and that Jason looked out for you," he said. "Grateful, actually."

Jason. The mention of him was enough to start her gut churning again with doubts. "Do you know why he calls you Monte?"

"Yes." Gage dropped his hand, but he didn't look away. "Do you?"

"I do." She waited for him to say something, to move, to do anything, but when he only stared at her like they were playing a game of chicken, she said, "Why haven't you defended yourself, tried to explain who you are to him?"

"Have you met Jason?"

Hope smiled. Teenagers were tough, but she got the impression that Jason was a special breed of difficult.

"Once he makes up his mind about something, there's no changing it," Gage said. "Besides, anything I could say about myself to him would only reinforce what he already thinks of me."

For a second, she was tempted to ask why Claire would warn Jason about Gage, but it had been a long night and they were both exhausted. The conversation could wait.

"You should get some rest," he said.

"I'll sleep out here. I don't want to deprive you—"

"Nonsense. I insist you take the bed. In the morning, you'll be thankful that you did, because I'm an early riser." The gleam in his eyes told her that she wouldn't be able to change his mind, so there was little use in fighting him.

"Fine. If you insist."

"When you wake up, we'll sit down and talk about Faith and the next step."

"Okay."

He gave her a hand up from the floor and walked her to the bedroom.

"Thank you, for everything." She rose on the balls of her feet and kissed him quickly on the cheek. His skin was cold and covered in day-old stubble, and she wanted to know what his lips would feel like against hers. Coming down onto her heels, she avoided eye contact. "Good night."

She hurried into the bedroom and shut the door behind her. *Why did you kiss him?*

"Talk about reckless," she whispered to herself. Even if it had only been on the cheek.

Hope sat on the bed near the nightstand that had a lamp on top of it. Bending over, she took off the sneakers. She rolled her shoulders and stretched her neck. Her gaze settled on the drawer in bedside table.

She grasped the knob and pulled, but the drawer didn't budge. Leaning closer, she spotted a keyhole. It was locked.

Her curiosity was too overwhelming to resist. She pulled out her utility tool—which she loved more and more each minute she spent in Benediction—and tried picking the lock.

If she got it open, Gage would eventually know that she'd broken into it, but she kept fiddling with the locking mechanism, anyway. Everything Jason had told her had sparked doubts. Niggling suspicions crawled in the back of her mind.

Finally, the lock gave way, and the drawer popped open.

Hope pulled it out farther. There was one thing inside. A black badge attached to a lanyard. She picked it up and turned it over.

Written across the top was *Nexcellogen*. There was a bar code in the middle. At the bottom, typed in all caps, was *Fischer, F.*

She stared at her sister's name, shock icing her blood.

This couldn't be, but it was.

Why did Gage have Hope's Nexcellogen ID badge? Did he have something to do with her death?

Clenching the badge, she struggled to understand what it could mean.

There was a light knock at the door, and she jumped.

"Do you need anything?" Gage asked.

Hope opened her mouth and then closed it. This was one of those times when she had to think carefully before she spoke, much less launched a verbal attack.

"No. I'm just really tired."

"I can imagine. Sleep tight."

She stared at the ID badge and shuddered.

Gage had saved her life without knowing who she was, and when he found out, he didn't abandon her to the military police like a killer eager to hide his crime.

But Jason had insisted in no uncertain terms that Gage *was* hiding something, Claire didn't want her son getting close to him, and there was the fact that he had Faith's work badge.

Hope locked the bedroom door and sat back on the bed.

If she was going to get to the bottom of things, she had to strategize. Come up with a plan rather than questioning him impromptu.

She needed to gather her thoughts and emotions and process everything first.

Then she'd find out if Gage had anything to do with her sister's murder, and if he did…so help him God, she'd kill him.

Chapter Eight

"Thanks for being so understanding about everything," Gage said, seated at Claire's kitchen table the next day.

"I knew something was up the second the staff sergeant knocked on the door." Claire poured herself another cup of coffee and sat across from him. "Honestly, I was relieved that it wasn't about Jason getting into trouble. I don't know what I'm going to do with him." She scrubbed a hand across her furrowed brow and ran her fingers through her light brown hair.

Jason was the spitting image of his mother, same hair, same sharp eyes, but the boy got his lean frame and height from his father. Gage had known Calvin from his earlier time in Benediction. They'd all been kids around the same age.

Claire had been in love with Calvin since she was ten, but it took him a few years to feel the same. When Gage heard about the car accident that had claimed Cal's life, Gage regretted missing the funeral, but he'd been away on a CIA mission.

"Just keep doing what you have been," Gage said. "Love him, be patient and tough when you need to."

They kept their voices low since Jason was in his bedroom. The town was so small there was only one snowplow, and it took time to clear the roads. The school had called a snow day.

She held her mug with both hands "It seems like all I show him is tough love these days. I'm terrified I'll push him away and even more scared of what will become of him if I'm not strict enough."

They'd been through so much. First, Claire's dad and Gage's onetime stepfather had died of a heart attack. Then two years later Cal passed away, and most recently, Claire had had a horrible lupus flare.

"The kid has lost a lot in a short amount of time." Gage took the last swallow of his coffee. "He almost lost you, too. He's grieving, angry and more scared than you are, but he's a fighter."

She sighed. "Don't I know it."

"In this case, that's a good thing. He's strong. As long as you listen to him and love him, he'll be okay. I wish there were more that I could do."

Claire clasped his forearm and patted it. "I'd let you, really, I'd welcome it if…" She lowered her head.

He nodded in understanding and agreement, even though she didn't see it. "It's what's best. If I got involved, I might do more harm than good in the end."

Her gaze lifted, meeting his. Tears filled her eyes. "I know. I just wish things were different."

"Me, too." And he did, more than anything in the world.

Gage was already separated from his team, his surrogate family, wondering if they'd evaded detection, if any one of them was alive or dead.

He couldn't risk forming any attachments in Benediction.

"This woman, Hope Fischer. Is the situation with her going to change things around here for you? For us?"

"It might. I'm going to do everything in my power to prevent that, but I have to help her."

"Of course you do." She gave him a sad smile. "Even as a scrawny kid, you were taking on bullies and fighting for justice. I'd never ask you to change, not that you would. I've always loved that about you."

Gage wanted to hug Claire, tell her that everything would be all right and how much he loved her, but his rules applied to her, as well. He wanted the best for them, to make life easier for her and Jason in the ways he could.

The last thing he desired was to become a source of pain for either of them.

"There's something I want you to remember," Gage said.

"What?"

"It's okay to go easy on Jason. If you ever feel guilty about it or worry that you're doing the wrong thing, remember that Benediction and all the rules are harsh enough. Try giving him mandatory cuddle time and movie night with his mom as punishment."

Claire laughed and wiped the tears from her eyes. "If only he saw how special you are instead of hating you."

Jason's contempt for him was Gage's own doing. Not deliberately, but if Gage could go back in time and handle certain situations differently, he would.

"I'll take his hate over hurting him any day," Gage said.

He got up and washed their coffee mugs while Claire wrapped a plate of food for Hope.

"Tell her I'm sorry about her sister." Claire handed him the warm meal. "If there was foul play, you find who did it and make them pay."

Gage nodded that he would, not only for Hope, but also to rid Benediction of a murderer.

Outside, the snow had stopped falling, leaving a little less than a foot on the ground. Not that it had prevented him from going through his morning routine of running six miles and doing a hundred push-ups and boxer sit-ups.

He climbed the exterior stairs and went into his apartment. The bathroom door was closed, and the shower was running.

Hope was finally awake.

Not a peep had come from the bedroom all night. Gage was normally a light sleeper, professional habit, but he wanted to be aware if Hope had nightmares, any trouble at all resting.

To avoid disturbing her after his workout, he'd cleaned up down at Claire's. Then he'd shoveled the walkway from the staircase and the sidewalk in front of the house and for the closest neighbors.

He set the covered plate down. The note he'd left explaining he'd be back and the extra clothes that had been on the counter were gone. Last night, he'd haphazardly grabbed what he could from the slim pickings in the dryer, not wanting to alert Claire that he had a woman stashed away upstairs. He should've asked her for a better assortment of things this morning. Sweaters, jeans, anything Hope might be comfortable in.

Once the shower stopped running, he sat down at the counter and waited.

The bathroom door opened, and he swiveled around on the stool and stopped. Stopped thinking. Stopped breathing. Of course he'd seen Hope before, but in the light of day... *Wow.*

Hope stood in the doorway with a towel in her hand drying her hair, which in the sunlight was a rich reddish brown, more brown than red. Her fresh face needed no makeup to accentuate her clear, tanned skin. She was so wholesome, so pretty in a girl-next-door way. Her lips were a rosy pink and kissing her was all he could think of. Until he realized what she was wearing—yoga pants and a white tank top. No bra.

His breath caught in his throat. The clothing molded to devastating curves, cupping breasts that were the perfect size for his palms, and it was hard for him to ignore the slight pucker of her nipples through the fabric. Then he wanted not only to taste her but to touch her, too.

"I didn't realize you were back." She followed his gaze down to her chest. Her cheeks flushed pink, and he lowered his eyes to the floor. "Excuse me a minute," she said, stepping into the bedroom and closing the door.

Way to make her feel comfortable.

He should've thought to call out to her, give her a heads-up that she wasn't alone in the apartment so she wouldn't wander out half-dressed.

The image of the tank top hugging her breasts and flat stomach was stuck in his head, and he couldn't shake the desire to kiss her. Which would be stupid and foolhardy. He was neither.

The bedroom door opened. She came into the kitchen wearing his hooded sweater zipped up over her top and had put on sneakers.

"Sorry for not warning you I was back." He grabbed a fork and set it next to the plate. "You slept through breakfast, but I've got lunch for you."

She sat on one of the stools. "What time is it?"

"A little after two." He studied her face. Up close, her eyes were a light green, soft and subtle as jade. "You must've really been wiped out."

"Took me a while to fall asleep. I had a lot on my mind." Pulling off the aluminum foil, she smelled the food. Meat loaf, mashed potatoes with gravy and green beans.

"It's simple but tasty. Claire made it."

Hope dug into the food. "Is she upset about me being here?"

"No." Gage poured a glass of water and handed it to her as he sat beside her. "She understands. Wishes you, *us*, the best in finding out the truth."

Hope coughed, choking on her food, and dropped the fork.

Watching her closely, Gage patted her back. She flinched and recoiled from his touch. Standing, she put the stool between them.

"Are you okay?" he asked. "What's wrong?"

"I was up half the night, thinking about Faith. After the military police came here looking for me, I couldn't shake the sense that I'm surrounded by danger." She pushed damp hair back behind her ear, avoiding his gaze. "I have no idea who's a threat and might want to hurt me."

Gage came around the stool, standing in front of her. He couldn't help but notice how she leaned back against the counter, away from him. "I'll do my best not to let anything happen to you."

"As much as I want to believe that," she said, finally meeting his eyes, "the truth is that you can't be with me every minute. I'd feel better if I could protect myself. Do you have a gun?"

"Do you know how to use one?" If she didn't, having one wouldn't make her any safer. In fact, it was liable to put her in more danger.

"Yeah, of course."

The pitch of her voice going a little too high and her eyes shifting to the left told him that she didn't. But why lie?

Gage lifted his wool pullover and withdrew the Sig from the holster at the small of his back. He handed her the weapon, handle first.

Hope grabbed the gun, not wasting a second to point it at him and put her finger on the trigger.

"What are you doing?" He slowly raised his palms to his chest.

"Explain this." She reached into the pocket of the sweater and held up the Nexcellogen badge. "Why do you have Faith's ID?"

She'd rummaged through his nightstand. He'd forgotten the badge was in there, but he wouldn't have expected her to pick the lock.

"It's difficult to explain. I think it might be easier if I take you somewhere and show you."

"Show me what? I'm not going anywhere with you until you start talking. And if I suspect that you're lying, for even a second, I'll—"

"What will you do? Shoot me?"

"Yes!" Hot emotions blazed in her eyes—grief, suspicion, anger, fear.

Gage set his feet and leaned into the Sig until the muzzle pressed against his sternum. "The report of the gun will be loud. Have you considered the attention it will draw? Not just from Claire and Jason, but the neighbors. Some of those neighbors are the military police. They only have to walk over to investigate." He stood still, his tone even, and held her wild gaze. "Hope, you're not a murderer. You're scared, and obviously finding Faith's badge has made you think you can't trust me."

"You're right about that. But even Jason told me not to trust you. Claire, the woman you supposedly took care of like some white knight, warned her son not to get too close to you."

White knight? Had she been listening when he'd confessed that he wasn't noble?

"Whose side are you on?" she demanded.

"My own." The truth was plain, and he didn't try to sugarcoat it. "And yours. The two don't have to be mutually exclusive. You can trust me, Hope. On my life, I swear it."

"Prove it, beyond a shadow of a doubt. Right here. Right now. Because I'm not going anywhere with you."

Anything he told her she'd question and doubt without first seeing what he wanted to show her. That left him one option.

Gage snatched the barrel of the gun and twisted it from her hand in a lightning-fast move.

Hope gasped, her eyes going wide.

Gage shuffled back two steps and held the gun up, barrel pointed at the floor. "Only put your finger on the trigger when you're prepared to pull it. And if you are, you had better make damn certain the safety is off and the gun is loaded." It'd also be a good idea to stand far enough away from her target so they couldn't take it from her, but he was confident he'd just taught her that last lesson.

He bent down and took out the sound suppressor he'd shoved into his boot earlier. Best to be prepared for any eventuality, especially with Hope being in Benediction with a killer on the loose. Gage attached the suppressor, screwing it quickly onto the muzzle.

"This is the safety." He pointed to it on the side of the weapon. "Flick it down when you're ready to shoot. The gun has a twelve-round capacity, and a bullet is already chambered. Extra ammo is in a shoebox in my closet and in the truck's glove compartment." He handed her the gun, once again handle first.

If that didn't inspire trust, nothing would.

Hope took the weapon and lowered it to her side. Pressing a hand to her stomach, she dropped down on the stool. "I wasn't going to shoot you."

"I know."

"You don't." She glanced up at him, looking like she might be sick. "Last night, when I thought you might have something to do with Faith's murder, I was going to kill you if I learned that you had. But as I was standing here, staring at you, all I wanted was to believe whatever you said, and I doubted myself."

He put a hand on her back, longing to comfort her, and this time she didn't pull away. When it came to Hope, his rules disappeared—maybe they didn't apply. They were two ships passing in the dark swamp of Benediction. She needed his help, a temporary situation, and beyond that she didn't have any expectations of him.

There was little chance of him letting her down, and if he died or had to take off again, he wouldn't leave a hole in her life. That knowledge was liberating. Freed him to care deeply for another and show it.

Hope took a deep breath, her gaze falling to the gun. "Ordinary citizens don't carry around silencers. Why do you have one?"

"I'm not ordinary."

"Then what are you?"

"Concerned, about you." Gage didn't trust lightly or easily, and neither did Hope. Her confidence in him had been shaken. Rocked to the core. They couldn't move forward until it had been restored. "Let's make a deal. You share your secrets, starting with why you were on that road last night, and I'll share mine."

She considered him a moment, her hands trembling. "What did you want to show me?"

"There's something you need to see to understand why I have Faith's ID badge," he said. "It's not far. Can I take you?"

"Okay."

Chapter Nine

The temperature had risen at least ten degrees from the previous day. Snow was already melting and wouldn't stick around long. Strange Virginia weather.

Wearing a coat and boots Gage had borrowed from Claire, Hope stared up at the sign hanging in front of the commercial building just yards behind the house.

Ferguson Funeral Home.

"Claire's dad owned and ran this place. Bequeathed it to her." He unlocked the doors that had beautiful stained-glass panels and ushered her inside.

She stomped off the snow from her boots on a mat and pushed back the hood that she'd pulled on so neighbors wouldn't be able to tell she wasn't Claire.

"My mom met her father at an NFDA convention in Washington, DC."

"What's NFDA?" Hope asked.

"National Funeral Directors Association." He led her through the foyer, past a desk and down a side corridor away from the viewing rooms. "They have conventions every year in different cities. Anyway, they clicked immediately, discovered that they'd both been widowed and lived in Virginia. He visited us for six months up in McLean, bringing Claire with him. Next thing I knew, they were married, and we moved to Benediction."

"You work here?"

"I ran the place while Claire was too ill. Now I handle the grunt work for her."

"You're a mortician?"

"I have a degree in mortuary science, but I haven't had an active license for years. No one asked when I took over—they were simply glad that someone could fill in for her."

They went down a flight of stairs to the basement, where he brought her into a large supply room. There were coffins and urns, but it wasn't set up like a showing room.

"After the doctor examined Faith's body, she was brought here. I was the one who cremated her. Nexcellogen handled shipment of her cremains to her next of kin."

Tears welled in Hope's eyes. She'd been Faith's primary emergency contact and listed as her next of kin. Faith had been the same for Hope. They figured if something ever happened to one of them, they wanted to break the news gently to their elderly parents and not shock them into cardiac arrest.

The same day a Nexcellogen representative had called to notify Hope of Faith's death, stating it had been suicide, she'd also received the urn in the mail.

The mail, for God's sake! No letter of condolence. Only Faith's supposed suicide note that had been typed and unsigned and the death certificate, along with a packing slip. Like her sister was an expired product being returned.

Her stomach roiled thinking about it.

Hope followed Gage to a desk at the back of the room.

"Claire turned over Faith's cremains, but she didn't know I had some of her belongings. I took the ID badge and kept it at the apartment."

"Why?"

"No one can get inside the Nexcellogen facility without it. I thought it might come in handy if they neglected to disable it. Small details fall through the cracks around here under ordinary circumstances. When your sister died, there was a lot of chaos." Gage opened the top desk drawer. "This is what I wanted to show you, besides the funeral home itself." He took out a small zip bag and gave it to her. "I wanted to mail it to her next of kin with a letter, but every time I tried to write it, I didn't know what to say."

Inside the bag was a necklace that Hope had given Faith. "As children we'd been joined at the hip, but as adults, both of our careers took us down different paths away from one another. No matter how many miles separated us, nothing weakened our bond. She gave me my favorite camera, the one I take with me everywhere." Hope hated being apart from it now, but she'd left the camera in her room at the B&B in Goode. "I gave her this necklace. She was wearing it when she died?"

Gage nodded. "She had it on when she was brought in."

Tears fell from her eyes. He brought her into his arms, wrapping her in a hug, and she wept.

The thought of Faith terrified with no one to help her as someone took her life tore Hope to pieces. Devastated her in a way she couldn't explain.

"I've got you," he whispered, his mouth against her ear. "It's okay to let it out." Gage tightened his embrace, his body steady and solid as a rock around her.

The kind gesture, the empathy and simple permission, broke her.

Her sobs deepened. Tears ran down her cheeks and dripped onto his shoulder. This was the first time she'd cried since finding out that Faith had died. It was as though her heart had been too congested with shock and denial to feel the agony of the loss.

How could her sister be gone? She was only two years older than Hope.

Faith had planned to take time off from work and fly out to LA for Christmas. Even their parents were going to come from Carmel. But now Faith was gone.

"It's so unfair. Faith was the brilliant one. Our parents swore she'd win the Nobel Peace Prize someday. She had this effortless beauty, glowed, radiated from the inside out. She was patient and caring and would never hurt a soul."

Hope was the reckless one, throwing herself into harm's way, crawling out onto battlefields, standing up to warlords with no fear of consequences, just for a picture. To tell a story.

"Faith was the one trying to make the world a better place. I'm only a stupid photographer. If one of us had to be taken before our time, it should've been me." Even her mother had expressed the same thing over the phone during the height of her own grief.

"YOUR SISTER IS GONE. Leave it alone! Let her rest in peace."

"She can't be at peace, Mom. Not until we figure out who did this to her. That's why I'm going to Virginia to look into it."

"Oh, please. Your conspiracy theories aren't really about Faith. You're going to Virginia because you need to make this about yourself, like you always do. Your sister is not some story for you to exploit."

"I'd never take advantage of Faith's death."

"Then stop this! Do you hear me? Let her rest and let us mourn. Why do you always have this constant need to be at the center of attention?"

"Don't you care about the truth? Don't you want to know what happened to her?"

"How dare you! It should've been you who died instead of my sweet Faith."

HOPE'S WHOLE BODY SHUDDERED.

"It shouldn't have been you, and it shouldn't have been her, either." Gage pulled her even closer, if that were possible, and swayed back and forth. He consoled her without trying to calm her down or stop her from crying. He let her feel, reassuring her that sorrow was all right. "Grief is like a tunnel," he said. "You have to walk through it to reach the light."

But there would never be any light until she found Faith's murderer.

They stood like that for a long time, with her cocooned in his protective warmth, her chest aching as though her heart might rupture.

Once she stopped sobbing and had gotten the worst of it out, Gage guided her down into the chair behind the desk. He crouched in front of her and peered up at her face. Taking her hands in his, he simply held them. Breathed with her, deep and steady, in and out. Neither of them spoke, their eyes locked. The moment stretched out—her jumping nerves stilled, the chaos inside quieted—thinning until it snapped and passed.

He must've seen or sensed the shift in her. A soft, sympathetic smile tugged at the corner of his mouth, and he handed her a box of tissues.

"Thanks." She took it from him. "Sorry that I lost it for a moment." As she wiped her eyes and nose, she realized what a wretched mess she must have looked. "Everything just poured out of me." It was good she hadn't been alone, because she might not have been able to stop. She needed his comfort, his kindness. "I wasn't able to cry before, for some reason."

Still squatting in front of her, he rested his hands on her knees. "This may have been the first time you cried, but it won't be the last, and that's okay. I lost my dad when I was seven. I know how hard it can be."

"My parents think I'm a nutcase for coming out here. They don't want to think about it or deal with it. They just want to accept this and move on." Which was bewildering. Her parents should've known better. Unlike Hope, Faith had been a devout Catholic. She was determined to be there for those she cared about. Committing suicide wasn't something she would do.

"They're grieving in their own way, like you."

She nodded. "But it'd be nice if they supported me in this."

He blew out a heavy breath. "The rumor in town is someone broke Faith's heart. Is it possible that she got depressed and—"

"No," Hope spit out, shaking her head, refusing to even

consider the preposterous idea. "Faith would never commit suicide." She didn't care what BS story Nexcellogen was pushing.

"I don't mean to come across as insensitive, but why are you so sure your sister was murdered?"

"Faith was happy. She had her dream job and had fallen in love with a guy in Goode. There was no breakup. Faith wasn't depressed." She was so excited about visiting Hope at Christmas and was planning to bring her boyfriend, too, introduce him to the family. "My sister was the type of person to see something through until the end. She wasn't a quitter, especially not on life. If you believe the rumors about suicide, why are you helping me?"

His fingers slipped through her hair in a soft caress. "I think there's a strong chance that you might be right."

Hope straightened and threw her tissues in a wastebasket. "Why?"

"A couple of reasons." He held her hands again like he was bracing her for what he was going to say next. "They claim Faith sat in her car in the garage and started the engine."

Hope's stomach twisted. The Nexcellogen representative who'd called her didn't have details and advised her to submit an official request for further information.

"Men tend to choose violent, more lethal methods," he said, "such as firearms, hanging and asphyxiation. Whereas women are more likely to overdose."

Hope squeezed her eyes shut, trying to stop her mind from spinning to all kinds of dark places, and breathed through a wave of nausea.

"Do you want to take a break?" he asked.

Opening her eyes, she shook her head. "Continue, please."

"In the case of suicide or suspected foul play—not that there has ever been a proven murder inside Benediction—an autopsy is supposed to be performed. But Dr. Steve Howland signed the death certificate without conducting one.

When I cremated her, I only knew the cause of death was asphyxia, but I didn't know how. Later I learned about the carbon monoxide because a neighbor had seen smoke coming from her garage. There should've been a cherry-red or bright pink tint to Faith's skin and red coloration of her fingernail beds because carbon monoxide binds to the hemoglobin, but there wasn't any."

"Do you think that means Dr. Howland was involved in covering it up?"

"It's possible, but not necessarily. I'm the one who cremated her, but I'm not a part of a conspiracy. Nexcellogen might have pressured Doc to wrap things up after a thorough examination. The same way they pushed to have the body cremated immediately, per Faith's instructions."

Wait. What? "Faith never wanted to be cremated. I assumed it was some mix-up in Benediction. She wanted to be buried in our family plot. I spread most of her ashes there."

Gage made his way to a file cabinet and took out a folder. He leafed through it and gave her a document with the Nexcellogen logo.

At the top of the form, the words *In Case of Death Instructions* were printed. It was an employee's declaration of how to handle their remains along with funeral wishes. Under internment request, the option for cremation as soon as possible had been checked, but that wasn't the only problem with the form.

"I'm not sure that's Faith's signature at the bottom," Hope said.

"What's wrong with it?"

Hope stared at the writing. "It's similar, very close, but something about it is off." She shrugged, unable to pinpoint what it was.

"This is an internal Nexcellogen form. Someone there must've forged it. Did Faith ever say anything about having problems at work with anyone in town?"

"No." Hope lowered her head. "Faith suspected the landlines here in Benediction were tapped and her calls monitored."

"Her suspicions were correct. Either Nexcellogen or the military police or both listen in on the lines."

"She never discussed her job on the phone. All I knew was that she worked in a lab with her team. Eventually, she started sending me letters, but there was never any mention of her project or conflicts with anyone." Her gaze fell to her lap. She opened the plastic bag and dumped the necklace into her palm. "Maybe this might be able to tell us something."

Gage picked up necklace by the chain and looked at the tube-shaped dangling pendant. "A mini cryptex."

"Yes. It's designed after the original sketches of Leonardo da Vinci. Faith and I were obsessed with puzzles and codes growing up. This was the best gift I could think of for her. Art, a puzzle and practicality all rolled into one." She spun the five cryptex rings one at a time, aligning them to the five-digit code she'd preset, praying that her sister hadn't changed it.

The mechanical combination lock clicked in place. The container opened, but instead of a secret piece of paper hidden inside, it was a USB flash drive.

"This holds 256 gigabytes of data," Hope said.

"Let's take a look and see what's on it."

Chapter Ten

For hours, Gage sat beside Hope, poring over the contents of the thumb drive. Her fingers flew across the keyboard of the funeral home's laptop, accessing every file.

They took their time reading document after document. There was a mountain of data.

"This is more of the same," Hope said as she stared at the screen. "Results of a compound tested on mice. This is sample 180. Again, a different chemical ratio from the last. Always the same intervals of time. A dose administered to the mice either one month, one week or one hour before *the event*." Hope sighed. "What event?" Most of the markers were color-coded in red, others in yellow, but a few had green bars on the graph. "With so much red, I'm guessing this one didn't work, either." She skipped to the last test marked sample 221. "Looks like progress compared to the others. It's mostly green. But what do you think this long bar of red represents?"

"You've got me. Try this folder." He pointed out one they hadn't opened. "We need to find something that explains what she was testing."

Hope clicked on it. More documents. She opened the most recent one. This time, they weren't test results. "Finally, her notes on the tests and findings. Everything she'd use to write a scientific paper. Here. The drug is a neuro pathway beta-blocker, and the event they subjected the mice to was…a series of small shocks."

Gage skimmed the page Hope indicated. "She was working on a drug to prevent post-traumatic stress disorder in soldiers. Regardless of which war or conflict you look at, there are high rates of PTSD in veterans. Soldiers' lives are completely ravaged by the things they had to do in combat."

It happened to CIA operatives, too. "Only a few treatments are effective, and as far as I know there are none that can prevent it. A drug that could block the effects before it took hold, to be used to inoculate soldiers from the devastation of PTSD before they go into combat, would be revolutionary."

"Worth a lot of money. The government would pay any amount for something like that. Probably the closest they could get to creating a super soldier."

"That's why they're working on it here in Benediction instead of the labs at Nexcellogen headquarters."

A confused look crossed Hope's face. "Faith didn't think there was anything strange about the transfer from Herndon out here. She said it was for security reasons."

"This town has a weird history. When I lived here as a boy, I heard stories about government testing on humans, soldiers, not just mice. An endeavor to make the ultimate warrior."

"Oh, come on," Hope said incredulously. "I was kidding a minute ago."

"The townspeople believe the stories. Claire's father did."

"They also believe the story about Faith."

"What I know for a fact is that the military has a stake in whatever that company produces. Years ago, a lot went wrong with their testing on soldiers and Benediction was almost shut down, but then Nexcellogen won the bid for a new contract and replaced whatever pharmaceutical company was here before. A drug like this—" he gestured to the document up on the screen "—would benefit soldiers greatly and falls in line with the mission objective of this town."

"But the drug isn't effective." Blowing out a breath, Hope sank back into the chair and scrolled through the document. "The only one that showed promising signs had been administered one hour before the stressor. Those mice exhibited no freezing when they returned to the test environment, a higher threshold for pain, but some demonstrated violent tendencies. They would need a dose given one week to one month in ad-

vance that didn't potentially turn someone homicidal for it
to have practical applications for the military."

"Do you think Faith might have been working with another company on this?"

"You mean corporate espionage?"

Gage nodded. They needed to explore every possibility.
"If she were, it would be a motive. Maybe someone at Nexcellogen found out and wanted to stop her. Or the rival company received the data and needed to silence her."

"Faith would never spy. She was loyal to a fault."

"She risked sneaking this data out of the facility for a reason. It must be important somehow."

"But I have no idea what to do with it or how it explains
why she was murdered. I was hoping for something concrete."

A smoking gun would've been nice, but far from realistic.
Few people planned for their own death, lining up dominoes
to fall and point to their killer.

Gage did, but no one would miss him other than his disgraced teammates, and no one would seek justice on his
behalf.

But maybe he could help Hope find answers. "At least this
gives us somewhere to start."

"How? This feels like a dead end."

"Faith was obviously worried about whatever was going
on in her lab. We need to find something to help us make
sense of why she had this data on her thumb drive."

"Where do we look?" Her gaze drifted, then she straightened and met his eyes like she had an idea. "Nexcellogen.
We break in using Faith's ID badge."

"Absolutely not. Getting in would be one thing. Finding
evidence of a crime and getting back out undetected is another thing entirely. That should be a last-resort measure. We
have to tread with care."

"Do you have a better suggestion?"

"Maybe she smuggled out more than what's on this thumb

drive. It's possible she may have kept notes on her personal laptop for her own reference since there was no chance of anyone hacking into it from the outside."

"You think we should search her place." A statement, not a question.

Hope was close.

"They boxed up her all her belongings and removed them from her townhome. Everything is sitting in the evidence room at the MP station," he said, and she grimaced. "I have an idea on how we can get to it. Discreetly."

"I bet you do." Hope eyed him. "Don't take this the wrong way, but I need to know why Jason doesn't trust you. Why Claire is worried about her son around you."

Exhaling, he lowered to a knee and cradled one of her hands in both of his. "I am hiding things. Hiding *from* things. It's the reason I keep him and Claire at a distance. Because I don't want to hurt them when I leave." Or when his past caught up with him and put him six feet under. "Jason has been through a lot. He needs stability, people he can rely on no matter what, like an anchor. That's not me. I can't be that for him and Claire. She understands, though she doesn't know why, and we both agree on this. But I've made mistakes with Jason. I handle sports for the kids at the school. I'm friendly with them in a way I'm not with him. They see me for forty-five minutes once a week. Whereas I live with Jason. I need to be careful not to let him form any attachment to me. For his sake."

"That's why he thinks you're not what you seem."

"I'm one way with others and another with him. To protect him. He believes my compassion toward others is fake because he doesn't think I have any for him. But I love that kid and Claire."

She tangled her fingers with his. Her light green gaze had a gravitational pull all its own, tugging the tide of his focus toward her.

"What about how you are with me?" she asked. "Can I trust it to be genuine?"

More than he cared to admit. "Yes." There was a kinship between them. Not just the fight for justice, the empathy of needing to know what happened to a loved one, but there was mutual recognition of a fire burning in the soul of another.

"Then we should go through my sister's personal belongings."

"We'll eat dinner and wait until things in the town wind down." Gage unplugged the flash drive. Handed it to Hope for safekeeping. Packed up the laptop to take with them just in case they needed it later.

As they walked up the stairs, their arms brushed. He took her hand, and she interlaced their fingers.

Bringing her to the funeral home had been the right call. She was no longer wary of him.

Being close to her physically came naturally to him, had him craving more. Not fighting it had her opening up on an unexpected level. One he hadn't planned.

One he liked.

Living in Benediction, detached from everyone, his emotions caged, was hollowing him out. Leaving a shell of a man.

Hearing Hope's pain, seeing the rawness of it, comforting her, touching her, soaking in her presence, made him want to stop hiding who he was. One day a kill squad might come for him, and if they did, then he wanted to connect with someone before that happened. To be known. To be seen. To be accepted.

Sounded simple, a small desire, but it was the greatest thing he could imagine.

They walked down the corridor that led to the lobby.

Right before they came to the corner, she stopped him. "Hey, thank you." She cupped his jaw, her thumb caressing his cheek. "I mean it. No one has ever done this, put themselves out there, on the line for me. I couldn't do any of this without you."

The sincerity in her eyes filled him with a bubbling warmth, but her gaze heated in a way that told him this was more than gratitude. Convinced him there was something between them beyond what he imagined in his head—call it chemistry…inevitability.

Her hand slid up into his hair, and she tugged his head down slowly as she rose on her toes. She kissed his jawline, his cheek. Warm, soft lips gently brushed over his, barely touching, almost teasing him with the invitation to do what he'd longed to do since pulling her out of Goode Lake. Needed to do now more than he'd needed anything in a long time.

Wrapping his arms around her, he kissed her, gentle at first, eased into it like sliding into a warm bath. He guided her back to the wall, their bodies pressed together. He breathed her in. Kissed her with growing urgency, more intensity, and Hope made a provocative, needy sound that rocked straight through him.

For one delicious instant, he forgot everything else. His mind went blank; his brain shut right off. His equilibrium was lost, but his center of gravity was found. There was only the sensation of her body moving against him. The feel of her hot tongue. The sweet taste of her mouth. Her scent. His heart thundering in his chest.

Just a heady euphoria that had him leaning into her, yearning for something deeper, more satisfying—until he heard it.

A slight squeak of a hinge that had his eyes flying open.

Hope was oblivious, kissing him, her fingers clenched in his hair.

He stilled. Pulling his head back, he covered her mouth with his palm.

The front door closed. Someone entered the lobby, shuffled to a stop and trod lightly.

Her brow creased with worry, but he pressed his mouth to her ear. "Stay here. Don't make a sound. I'll get rid of whoever it is," he whispered.

After she nodded, he handed her the laptop and rounded the corner into the lobby.

Dr. Howland walked toward him. A sociable man in his seventies with curly gray hair, he waved and smiled, deepening the wrinkles at the corners of his eyes and mouth. "Hey, Gage. I've been trying to track you down."

"Oh, yeah?" Gage walked up to him, keeping the doctor near the door. "Eager to get back the sweats I borrowed? I'll have them washed and delivered tomorrow."

Chuckling, Doc adjusted the tweed flat cap on his head. "No, no rush on that. Take your time."

"So what brings you out in the snow?" On a day like this, Danielle would be running the clinic whether she was scheduled for duty or not, and Doc would be curled up in front of the fire reading a book and sipping whiskey.

"I wanted to get some information regarding the woman you saved. Hope Fischer. I wanted to talk to her."

Gage shoved his hands in his pockets. "Really? About what?"

"Danielle called me last night and told me about her. I think she mentioned it to you," he said in a dismissive way, as though it were no big deal, with a little bob of his head, his eyes cast down.

When someone in Benediction downplayed something, you needed to pay close attention, because the details they didn't want under a spotlight were the ones that mattered.

"I recommended she stay overnight, to be certain she was well. I wanted to follow up with her. See how she's doing. Captain Finley mentioned you took her to Goode. Is that right? Where exactly did you drop her off?"

The question struck Gage as wrong. Howland was a good doctor and was known for checking up on patients, but Hope hadn't been his patient and tracking Gage down in the snow seemed a tad much.

Gage wanted to give Doc the benefit of the doubt, but this was how people tied up loose ends. Track the person down and finish the job. "Did you also hear she thinks her sister didn't commit suicide?" Gage stepped closer, studying him. "That she was murdered?"

"I did." Doc met his gaze. His gray eyes narrowed a bit, only for a second. "That's also part of the reason I wanted to talk to her. To apologize."

Well, wasn't that interesting? Not the response Gage had been expecting at all. "Apologize for what?"

"Not doing an autopsy on her sister." Howland, the primary physician and medical examiner, was aware a mortician would know whether one had been conducted. "If I had, it would've closed the door on any doubt for her. It's upsetting to think about a young woman wasting time chasing ghosts."

"Why didn't you perform one?"

"For starters, they said she'd been depressed for months. A suicide note was found on the dashboard in her car."

"Signed?" Probably forged the same way the form authorizing cremation had been, Gage was willing to bet.

"No. Typed but not signed." Doc removed his cap and ran a hand over his thinning mop of silver curls. "My preliminary examination of the body confirmed asphyxiation. When they asked me to expedite the process, for the sake of the family, I did. In hindsight, I shouldn't have if her sister has lingering doubts."

The story was good. Even to Gage it sounded plausible. Doc looked believable. But this was Benediction.

Gage needed to push, hard, to get to the truth. "I looked at the body, too. There was no cherry-red lividity to her skin or discoloration to her fingernail beds. I consulted with the coroner in Goode, and Faith Fischer may have died from asphyxia, but not CO. Not in her car." The lie was a bluff, and he had an excellent poker face.

"Oh, please, Gage. I've been a doctor fifty-plus years and you're a mortician still wet behind the ears. The slight flush of the skin was there, but subtle. You must've missed it. Not as if you have an expert eye." He made a waving motion with his hand.

Trying to downplay it. Again.

"I know she didn't die of carbon monoxide poisoning," Gage said. "So why did you lie?"

"That's ridiculous. You don't know what you're talking about."

Gage snatched Doc by the coat collar and spun him, shoving him up against the wall.

Doc's eyes glazed over with panic. "What are you—"

"Who paid you to sign the death certificate as a suicide?"

"Are you crazy?" Howland jutted his sharp chin up in the air. "I'd never do such a thing, accept a bribe!"

"But you did. And I want to know why."

"Benediction is starting to get to you, son. The isolation, the rules, they're messing with your head."

It was time for Gage to mess with Doc's head. "I never cremated Faith," he said. "Her body is downstairs in the mortuary fridge."

Doc's florid face went pale. "I don't understand. You told everyone that you cremated her. Nexcellogen shipped the remains to her family."

"I drove two towns over, had a deer cremated and those were the remains I handed over." When a body was incinerated, it was reduced to the skeleton. Not ashes. Then the bone matter was pulverized, ground down into a fine, grainy powder. To the naked eye, human and animal cremains looked the same, but the weight had to be right. "Five point seven pounds. How about I take Faith's body to Goode and see what the coroner there has to say about the cause of death?"

"No! Don't."

There was only one reason why he wouldn't want that to happen. Faith had been murdered.

"How could you?" Gage asked, disgusted with Doc. "Sacrifice your principles and integrity?"

"It's not what you think. If you had questions, why didn't you come and talk to me?"

"I knew something about this was wrong." That much was true. He wished like hell he had pushed for the details of how she'd died and questioned the fact that there hadn't been an autopsy. Though it didn't make him complicit like Doc, Gage was ashamed he'd toed the line. His gut burned thinking of it. He had a responsibility to help Hope that he wouldn't ignore, and if he were being completely honest with himself, guilt spurred him on, too. "How much did they pay you?"

Lowering his head, Doc sighed. "Nothing. I wasn't paid one red cent."

"Then why? Tell me the truth."

"The night I examined Faith Fischer's body, I was drunk. I had been in the pub earlier, drinking with some of the guys. Faith had come in, picked up an order for dinner like she often did. One of the boys mentioned how sad she looked, depressed. That it must've been over her breakup. I wasn't too far gone at the point, and it was plain to see that she wasn't herself, had a weight on her shoulders. Something was troubling her. Later, when I examined Faith, it seemed obvious that it was suicide."

"Obvious that a woman who was so depressed she wanted to kill herself that she would bother picking up dinner?"

"Everybody thought it was suicide and said so. We've never had a murder in Benediction."

"Who is everyone?"

"I don't know." Dr. Howland shrugged. "The MPs were there. Captain Finley. Ms. Lansing."

"Who asked you to expedite things?"

"No one. I said that to you now to cover my negligence. I'm so ashamed."

Gage was aware of Howland's fondness for 101-proof Wild Turkey. It packed a mean punch on a modest budget. "Why are you looking for Hope Fischer?"

"I told you. I only wanted to make sure she was okay and convince her to go home. I feel bad that poor woman is out here because of me, because I neglected to be thorough. It's the God's honest truth."

Dropping his hands, Gage stepped back. "If you mean Hope no harm, stop looking for her and leave her alone."

"All right. I will." Doc nodded. "Gage, you're right that the lack of discoloration to Faith Fischer's skin would indicate that she didn't die in the car from carbon monoxide. Though it did look like asphyxiation to me. But that would mean someone wanted it to look like suicide." Doc wrung his hands. "If you take her body to Goode, I'll lose my license. I'll be disgraced." His face was quivering, his eyes moist, near tears. "My job is all I have. I'm a good doctor when I'm sober. You know that. I saved Claire's life. I never drink if I'm going to be at the clinic. Never. Danielle makes sure of it. Please, Gage."

It was despicable that even now, sober and lucid, Howland was more concerned with covering his own tail than helping Faith's family get justice. "Her body isn't here. Her cremains *were* given to her family."

Doc's face twisted in disbelief. "You lied?"

"I bluffed." The gamble had paid off, too. "It was the only way to get you to tell me the truth. I needed to know. For my own sake." And most of all for Hope's.

Doc wiped his brow with the back of his hand. "If you're smart, you'll drop this. It's dangerous. If someone was willing to kill once, they'd do it again." He turned and scurried out the door.

Gage hesitated a minute. Once he was sure the doctor was

gone, he went back around the corner and found Hope leaning against the wall. She had the laptop pressed to her chest and her arms curled around it.

"Did you hear everything?" he asked, cupping her cheek.

"Faith was murdered, and the doctor helped cover it up with his negligence."

"Are you okay?"

"I won't be okay until we find out who killed her and why. But there was something the doctor said about Faith's suicide note that got me thinking. It was mailed to me along with her remains, but it wasn't signed." She took out the Nexcellogen document. "If whoever forged her signature on this killed her, then why not sign the note, too?"

Gage considered that, ran through possibilities. "That document," he said, pointing to the one in her hand, "is an internal corporate form that they only share a copy of with the funeral home. We usually shred it when we're done. I only kept it after learning about the carbon monoxide discrepancy. I don't think her killer ever expected you to see it."

"How high do you think the cover-up goes?"

It was hard to tell. "Michelle Lansing has been the director of Nexcellogen operations in Benediction for six years. She's as high as it could possibly go here."

"Tell me more about her as a person."

"Michelle is agreeable, diplomatic, but she's also the corporate type. A bigwig. She has a considerable amount of power and influence and likes it. Works seven days a week. She has white hair but makes fifty look like the new forty. Her hair is the only thing that gives away her age. She's always the center of attention at functions. She even gave the eulogy at the memorial service for Faith."

People were happy with her in charge, and unlike most outsiders, who found it hard to adjust and hated it here, Michelle loved Benediction.

"I think we need to look at everyone who was close to Faith," Gage said. "Who worked with her on her research?"

"Faith was the lead on the project, and she brought in Paul Kudlow. He's been here working in the lab with her from the start. I met him a few years back when they were in Herndon. We all had dinner together a couple of times. They were friends. Last year, she requested that an extra scientist join her team. Neal Underhill. She called him a rising star with lots of potential."

Gage was familiar with both men from a distance. Kudlow was happy-go-lucky, the kind to crack jokes not everyone found funny. Underhill was astute and serious, a bit of a cliché in a geeky way, wearing glasses and MIT Nerd Pride T-shirts.

"Why did she wait until last year to bring on Underhill?"

"She only said that he was going to be a good addition to the team."

He rubbed both her arms. "We have to see if there's anything in your sister's stuff that can shed some light on this."

She agreed. "Do you think Dr. Howland will tell anyone about your conversation?"

Gage shook his head. "I don't have any proof that could hurt him, and I don't see him wanting to unburden his soul to anyone else. But Doc was right."

"About what?"

If they asked more questions, eventually someone was going to take notice.

With this, he couldn't be on his own side and Hope's. The two were mutually exclusive. He was wrong to think otherwise.

Digging around would rile a hornet's nest and make staying in Benediction impossible.

So, now there was only Hope's side.

"This *is* dangerous," he said.

"If you're reconsidering, I understand."

"I swore to see this through with you. To take it as far as you dare go. I stand by that." And by her, because she wasn't going to let anything stop her.

Holding his gaze, Hope straightened. The fierceness he so admired blazed in her eyes. "Then I want to take it all the way."

Chapter Eleven

Benediction was so quiet and serene with an almost idyllic quality at night. But if you peeled back the holiday-themed veneer, beneath the surface this place was rotten, festering with corruption like a disease.

Hope was bent low inside the truck as Gage parked close to the MP building.

Replaying the plan in her mind, she pulled the hood of the zip-front sweatshirt over her head, tucking the strands of her ponytail inside, and tied the draw cord under her chin.

"You mentioned there are cameras inside and that you had a way for me to avoid detection. This feels like a good time to share."

Gage flashed a grin that demanded her full attention. "Take this." He handed her a black device resembling a remote that fit in her palm. There was a small antenna at the top and a single switch in the middle. "It's a hybrid analog/digital video scrambler, a little something I picked up when I knew I was heading back to Benediction."

"Did you get this at the same store where you *picked up* a silencer for your gun?"

"No. I already had the silencer."

His attempt at humor was awful, but he had her smiling nonetheless. "Ha-ha."

"I'm not joking, Hope."

Under different circumstances, with a different man, the statement should've unnerved her. She didn't know Gage's past or the secrets he was hiding from. What she did know was that she could trust him. That was enough.

"What exactly am I supposed to do with it?" She held up the scrambler.

"You have to be within five feet of any video camera for it

to blur the feed. You'll be within partial view of the camera on the exterior before that, so you'll have to approach from the side. If you stay as close to the wall as possible, you'll be in the camera's blind spot once the scrambler becomes effective. But to be on the safe side, never look up at the camera and keep your head down."

"Got it. I guess I just flick the switch."

"Yep. You'll need this, too." He unzipped a case the size of a mini manicure kit, revealing instruments she recognized.

"You failed to mention I'd have to pick a lock."

"It's a skill set you already possess. I didn't think it'd be an issue."

She narrowed her eyes at him. "What kind of lock are we talking about?"

"Padlock." Quickly, he pointed out the tools she'd need and explained how to use them. "Got it?"

"Yeah, I think so."

"I'll keep whoever is on duty distracted for as long as I can. Ready?"

"As ready as I'll ever be."

He covered her hand with his and gave her a reassuring look. The anxiety dancing in her stomach eased, and she nodded that she was okay.

"On my count," he said. "One." They opened both doors at the same time. "Two." Out of the truck. "Three." They closed the doors in unison.

It needed to sound like one person got out of the truck rather than two in case the guard inside was paying attention.

She scooted around to the rear of the truck while Gage sliced his tire.

They gave it a minute, with her crouched low and him pretending to inspect the flat, before he went inside to ask for assistance.

Hope wanted nothing more than to bounce, pace, work off her nervous energy with movement. Instead she drew in deep, steady breaths, focused on the steps she needed to execute and stayed still.

"Thanks, Specialist Porter," Gage said moments later.

"No problem. I've a got a jack in my vehicle."

"Getting a flat is bad enough, but getting stuck without a jack is the absolute worst. I didn't want to risk driving home and damaging the rim."

Their voices drew closer, and she braced to spring into action.

"We're here to help." The trunk of Porter's car popped open.

That was the cue.

She dashed to the side of the building on the balls of her feet and switched on the scrambler in her pocket.

Gage was chatting up Porter behind the trunk door, where the young man's view was obscured.

A quick look around, then, following Gage's instructions, she made a beeline for the entrance with her back close to the brick wall. She slipped inside the building and pulled the door closed behind her before Gage and Porter headed for the truck.

It'd been a short run, but her heart was slamming against her chest. Air punched in and out of her lungs. She was fit, did more yoga than cardio—still, her shortness of breath was startling.

Adrenaline. It intensified her body's response. Nature's way of fueling her through this.

She looked around the MP station. Gage had drawn a simple diagram of the one-story building. There weren't many rooms, and only one was her concern.

She ran around behind the receptionist desk and checked the camera screens on the monitor. Complete picture degradation, as promised by Gage. She hustled down the main hall. After passing what looked like a supply closet, she came to the evidence room.

Lowering down on one knee, she took out the tool kit. She inserted the bent end of the tension wrench in the lock opening. Applying pressure to hold the opening over the lock hole, she turned the wrench in the direction the key would go in as far as it'd budge. She pushed the rake-shaped tool in with the teeth and ridges against the locking mechanism. Jiggling it, she moved the instrument in and out. A click, and the lock popped open.

Voilà. Not as easy as the nightstand drawer, but she'd managed. Maybe she did have an innate talent for lock picking.

She opened the door and hooked the padlock on the loop of the fastening.

Inside, she disregarded the locked cage of evidence bags and headed to the stacked boxes in the corner. Each one was labeled *F. Fischer* and had been sealed with bright yellow tape.

Anyone checking the boxes later would know someone had been in them. It could draw the MPs to review the videotape. The obscured footage would raise more questions than answers.

Until Porter rehashed the events of the night.

Damn.

But Gage must've considered that. Little to nothing escaped him. He was a man who paid attention to details. If anything went wrong, he had to know everything would lead to him.

With sudden clarity, the magnitude of how much he was risking hit her. Pressure built in her chest. Her thoughts raced. There had to be a way to cover her tracks and protect Gage.

Stop. Focus.

There was no turning back, and time was running out.

She sliced the tape on the first box, removed the lid and riffled through it. Item after item dredged up memories, forced her to think about Faith's life here, her death, brought a wave of grief that she had to push aside.

All the clothing, toiletries and thick science manuals she left. A small flipbook of pictures of her and Faith as children and highlights of her sister's accomplishments Hope set to the side to take. It was sentimental and contrary to why she was there, but she couldn't bear to leave it behind.

Noticeably missing from the boxes was a personal laptop. Gage had thought she'd have one, and so had Hope. Faith liked to work late in bed when she couldn't sleep. But there was no computer and no printouts of additional data.

She opened the last box. Inside she found a copy of *To Kill a Mockingbird*. It was Hope's favorite book, not Faith's. She rummaged through the box, looking for *Wuthering Heights*, which her sister reread at least once every year, but there wasn't a single edition. It seemed odd for some reason.

Her gaze fell to a notebook. Faith wasn't the type to keep a diary. Hope leafed through the pages, expecting to glance over paragraphs about Faith's boyfriend, a clue as to how the data on the thumb drive might be related to her death, but what she stared at instead left her bewildered.

Pages of gibberish. Random words and numbers scribbled throughout. Most written in nonsensical patterns. None of it appeared connected. To anyone who didn't know Faith, they might see this and suspect she was losing her mind.

But Faith had been sane. Lucid and logical. Not depressed or losing her faculties.

Another dead end?

Cursing her luck, she was ready to scream in frustration and kick one of those boxes across the room, but then she saw it. Five words that made absolute perfect sense.

One does not love breathing.

Of course. Turning through the pages again, now she understood, saw the connection. "Thank you, Faith."

Hope grabbed the journal along with the Harper Lee book and put them on the pile of stuff she was taking.

Spinning around the room, she searched for the one thing

she needed next. Yellow tape with the word *Sealed* printed across it.

A roll was sitting on a shelf.

Moving like her life depended on it, she threw the lids back on the boxes and only added tape over the seams. She scooped up the items from the floor. Closed the door. Locked it.

Still not a sound in the station. She crept down the hall. At the front door, she peeked outside.

The guys had changed the tire and Gage was talking Porter's ear off while keeping the young man's back to the entrance.

Gage nodded, as though in response to something Porter had said, but she caught the subtle flicker of his gaze in her direction.

Gently, she opened the door and slipped out onto the sidewalk. There was no way for her to make it back to the truck without being seen by Porter. Staying close to the wall, she hurried along the walkway, moving swiftly and softly. She darted around the corner and pressed her back against the side of the building.

Her heart thundered in her ears, and her legs shook.

When Gage pulled up beside her, she couldn't wait to jump in.

As soon as Hope dropped into the passenger seat, Gage took off, headed back to the house.

"Get down," he reminded her. She had done well. But caught in the adrenaline high she must be feeling, it was easy to slip up and make the simplest mistake.

She slid down low in her seat, clutching the things she'd taken from the station. "There was no laptop."

"It was a long shot. Nexcellogen must've confiscated it before packing up her belongings." He slapped the steering wheel as he pulled into the garage. "I thought her personal effects might have been one of those small details they could've overlooked. Guess not." The garage door lowered closed. "They probably took everything of any value to us."

"Not everything."

He stared at her. "I'm on pins and needles. Spill it."

"Upstairs, where it's warm and we can talk."

That was best, and it went without saying that they needed privacy. Not for Claire or Jason to wander into the garage. "All right."

After he made sure the coast was clear by the exterior staircase—no neighbors taking a late-night stroll, no one peeking out their curtains—he ushered her up the stairs and into the apartment.

He turned on the kitchen light and the fireplace.

Hope sat at the counter, laying out the items. Gage came up beside her. Standing with an arm around the back of her stool, his chest brushed against her shoulder, and a ripple of warmth slid through him at the simple contact. He ignored it and tried to focus on what she discovered.

"I think this is important." She opened the journal and flipped through it for him.

Gage stared at the pages. "It looks like a bunch of scribbles, random thoughts. Am I supposed to know what this means?"

"No." Hope smiled like that was a good thing. "I don't think she wanted anyone who stumbled across it to understand. Faith was clever not to use a consistent pattern to hide what she was really doing."

"Why are you happy about that?"

"Because I understand it. When we were little, we use to talk in code around our parents, loved to put together puzzles. We even created our own ciphers."

"Are you saying this is some kind of code?"

"This is evidence that she wrote something *in code*." She

handed him a book, *To Kill a Mockingbird*. "That's the cipher she used."

He shook his head, still lost. "Okay. We know how to break the code, but we don't have anything to decipher."

"Not yet." She peered up at him, bring their faces close. A sssssssssss apart. "We, um—" She licked her lips, and her gaze dropped to his mouth for a second and bounced back up, meeting his eyes. "We just have to get—"

"Please don't tell me we have to break into Nexcellogen."

"Nothing like that."

"Glad to hear it." When she didn't look relieved, he searched her face. "But I don't like to be kept in the dark. So, tell me what I'm missing."

"You might want to sit down first."

Straightening, he stiffened. "I'm not a take-bad-news-sitting-down type. I prefer standing while drinking. Just spit it out."

"Faith had been here four years, but she didn't start writing to me until a few months ago. I think the code is in the letters she wrote me. They're in my suitcase back in Goode. I brought them on the off chance they might come in handy."

Exhaling, he sat next to her, delighted he didn't need that drink after all. "That's not so bad. I'll go there tomorrow and get them."

Hope grabbed the bottle of brandy on the counter. "While you're there, I need you to speak to the sheriff for me. Ryan Keller."

Gage got a bad vibe. Dealing with Captain Finley had proven tricky enough. Having a conversation with any more law enforcement was not on his to-do list. "Why?"

Pursing her lips as though she tasted something sour, she poured two fingers of brandy in two glasses. "If you don't tell him that I'm all right, he's going to come here to Benediction looking for me. He'll make a lot of noise, blow this whole thing, and then the MPs will know that you never took me back to Goode."

That bad vide turned into a terrible one. "Why is he going to come looking for you?"

Hope took several deep breaths, like someone standing on the edge of a high board looking down at a ten-meter drop. "There's something I need to tell you, and you're not going to like it." She handed him a glass of brandy and took the plunge. "The reason I was on that road the other night was because it was part of my plan to get inside Benediction. The sheriff helped me…by running me off the road."

Gage's heart throbbed, beating slow but hard, booming in his ears. He gulped the liquor. Let it burn away the sudden cold racing in his veins as he gathered his thoughts. "The accident was deliberately orchestrated?" Saying the words out loud magnified the absurdity of it. The sheer horror of it.

She sipped the brandy. "Yes and no."

"You almost died!"

"That part was a mistake."

"I should hope so."

She gave him a look devoid of humor. "Ryan is a good guy. He fine-tuned my plan. If at any point I changed my mind and wanted to back out, all I had to do was put on my hazard lights as the signal to call it off. But I didn't. Because I was determined to see it through."

"You being a reckless daredevil, I get. A sheriff? Not so much."

"I was supposed to crash into a tree. He had it marked out for me. He even talked me through what I should do if I hit black ice. But I panicked, slammed on the brakes. The car went into a skid and spun out of control. I completely missed the tree and ended up in the lake."

Gage poured himself another drink. "He just left you there. What if I hadn't stopped?"

"The plan was for him to watch in his rearview mirror

and make sure someone stopped to help. We timed it. He was watching the gate with binoculars. When he saw someone leave, you, we—"

"How crazy are you? And this sheriff must be even crazier for going along with such an insane, dangerous, reckless plan."

"It wasn't insane. It was clever, and it worked. I'm here." She finished her drink. "And I'm not crazy. I was at my wit's end getting stonewalled by the people here. The desperation inside to find the truth about Faith had taken on a life of its own. Grown into this wild thing, gnawing at me day and night."

Grief wasn't a dark cloud hanging over your head. Grief was animate. A beast with sharp teeth and claws, a predator that devoured. If you didn't conquer it first.

Hope took the bottle. Poured another. "I know it was risky."

He grunted. "That's an understatement."

"I've risked my life for stories. To get the picture that was worth a thousand words. How could I be willing to do that for a job and not for my sister?"

"You were gone." He caressed her cheek. "Unconscious. Water in your lungs. If I had been anyone else, someone who hesitated, someone unable to break your window, someone who didn't know CPR, someone not willing to fight for medical treatment, you would be dead."

She cupped both his cheeks and looked him straight in the eye. "But it wasn't someone else. It was you. A good man, the right man, who at great personal risk is still helping me."

The way she touched him, called him the *right* man, almost took the sting away from everything else. Almost.

"I guess us good men are a dime a dozen. You've got the sheriff. Me. Anybody else I should know about waiting in the wings to assist?"

She recoiled, dropping her hands from his cheeks. "No, and you are not a dime a dozen."

He swiveled in his seat, facing her. "Maybe you're just extremely persuasive. A witch who casts spells on good men." That would explain why he had an uncharacteristic need to get close to her, connect with her.

God, she'd probably done the same with the sheriff. Bewitched them both.

"Maybe I am." She sighed. "Are you trying to imply something else? If you want to ask me something, just ask."

The words danced on his tongue. He hated the pent-up energy whipping around in the pit of his stomach. It was unfamiliar and grating, and if he didn't know any better, he'd call it jealousy. "How close did you get with the sheriff before he agreed to risk his job and reputation to run you off the road, as a favor?"

She threw back her drink, stood up in between his spread legs and brought her face so close they were practically nose to nose. "Ryan is the man Faith was seeing. They were in love. She was going to bring him out to LA to meet the family, because they were serious. Ryan told me he was planning to propose at Christmas, in front of all of us. I even saw the ring. So it didn't take much persuading on my part. I just had to promise to find Faith's killer."

Hope stepped around him and stormed off into the bedroom, slamming the door.

Gage clenched his hands into fists, wanting to throttle himself.

Asking her that had been rude and insulting. He wasn't proud.

He was afraid. Terrified that he cared too much, had feelings unlike anything he'd ever experienced for a woman he'd known less than forty-eight hours.

This was madness.

But it was as though he'd known her far longer. Regardless of time, he could easily end up in love with her. Maybe he already was. He'd made her fight his fight, and there was no noble reason behind it. Hope was the reason.

She was special. He had to hand it to her that although her plan to get inside Benediction had been reckless to the nth degree, it had been smart. And it had worked.

Was he upset because he felt like a sucker?

He growled his frustration.

If his team could see him now, Hunter, Zee and Dean, they would think that he had a screw loose in his head for falling so hard, so fast for any woman. Then they'd have a good laugh at his expense. Then Zee would tell him to apologize.

For calling Hope crazy and her plan insane. For implying things about her and Ryan, the good sheriff who had no problem running Hope off the road. The bit about a witch with a spell was bad, too. It had crossed the line and been over-the-top.

"Yes, Zee, you're always right." He missed them all so much. The only people in the world he'd ever let in and would do anything for.

Gage looked at the bedroom door.

He did owe Hope an apology and reassurance that he'd get the letters *and* alleviate Ryan's worries. If she wanted to slap him and kick him out after that, he deserved it.

Chapter Twelve

Gage's words had sliced deeper than a knife. In all her life, Hope had never met any man so infuriating. Insulting.

But damn hot. Bold. Generous and perceptive.

She unzipped her sweater—his sweater—and took it off. Tossed it across the room. Paced back and forth, needing to get the blood moving in her legs.

The worst part was the attraction to him tugging at her to go back into the living room and hash this out.

She shouldn't have lied to him about Ryan. The sheriff did love Faith, planned to marry her, that was true, but he'd wanted nothing to do with Hope's plan. He'd called her all the things Gage had.

Ryan didn't want her to end up like Faith. Hope had had to guilt-trip him into helping her.

Not her finest moment, but she was so close to avenging her sister now. She just needed those letters.

She'd anticipated Gage would be upset, but after he implied something offensive, she couldn't admit she had roped Ryan into her scheme.

Gage was different. He'd offered her his help, no strings attached, with such conviction and dedication it left her breathless in amazement.

Calling him a good man wasn't meant as a platitude or to butter him up to speak to Ryan. Nor had there ever been the right man under any circumstances. In less than two days, she had come to trust him as she had trusted no one since Faith. She'd never felt so close to a guy. Tethered to something that wouldn't crumble to dust. She knew little about him, but on the other hand, she knew him better than her longest boyfriend or anyone in her life. Understood what was at his core, his character, the nature of his spirit, the essence of his heart that dictated his actions.

To do what he was doing for her, surely, made him exceptional. Singular. The right man for her, and she wanted him so much.

The bedroom door flew open, and Gage stalked in.

"I'm sorry," he said. "For, well, everything. I shouldn't have been such a jerk. You could've lied about the accident and simply said Faith's fiancé would worry, but you were honest. It's just the idea of something happening to you, deliberately, makes me physically sick and—"

Hope threw her arms around his neck and kissed him. No hesitation. No flirting.

Curling his arms around her, he spun her and pressed her against the wall. He kissed her deeper, harder. So completely that heat overwhelmed her.

She lifted her head to get air and smiled. "You had me at sorry."

"Really?"

She nodded, melting against him. "Really."

"Z always said a sincere apology could solve most problems and that men were idiots. Who knew she was right?"

"Who is Z?" An old girlfriend? An ex-wife? Someone who still meant something to him?

Gage flashed her one of those grins that made her belly quiver. "Unimportant. I'll tell you later."

He lowered his mouth to hers, and she welcomed the touch of his lips. What started out as sweet turned rough, hard and blistering as he pulled her closer.

Every nerve ending sparked to life. She circled her arms around his neck. Opened to him as their tongues came together.

Her insides churned with need. "I want you, Gage."

He looked down at her, and raw yearning gleamed in his eyes. "The feeling is mutual." Pressing his lips to the hollow of her throat, he explored the rest of her body, his hands skimming and groping until she craved more.

All the uncertainty and grief of the past few days evaporated. She might've only known Gage for a short time, but she trusted him, knew she was safe with him. Intimacy was about sharing your heart and soul as well as your body, and if there was anyone on the planet that she was willing to take that risk with, make herself vulnerable to, it was Gage.

There was only him and this moment. She wanted to touch him, strip his clothes off, have skin on skin. Friction.

The room spun as he lifted her into his arms and carried her to the bed. He didn't toss her to the mattress, treat her as if she were a piece of meat. No, it was the opposite of what she'd received in the past.

He lowered her slowly, his eyes never leaving hers, like she was the most precious thing in the world.

He pulled off her tank top and unhooked her bra. Filling his hands with her breasts, he took a hard tip into his mouth.

Her mind went blank, but her body burned. A soft sound escaped her throat. He kissed his way down her stomach while his hand drifted lower, between her legs, palmed her through the soft sweatpants until she was writhing beneath him.

Every inch of her throbbed and ached from the sensual torture. He peeled the sweatpants off her legs and touched her with no barrier between them.

His skillful fingers teased and played before sliding inside her. Deep but tender, coaxing her to soften to jelly around him. His fingers stroked with the same rhythm as his tongue in her mouth. The pleasure grew so intense she was shaking.

"Hope," he whispered. No man had ever said her name like that. With the reverence of a prayer or a vow. His eyes ran over her, growing darker. Hungrier. "You're so beautiful." His voice was so husky she almost didn't recognize it.

She opened the button at the top of his jeans and lowered his zipper.

"Wait," he said as though he'd remembered something. "I don't have protection."

"I've never been with someone without it. Usually I bring my own." Then she remembered she had her purse and there was probably a prophylactic package in the inner pocket.

He sat back. "I'm not ready to be a father."

No complaints. No cajoling. No trying to convince her that they could do *other things.* Things which were in some ways more intimate because people usually didn't use protection when they did them, and that was the reason she abstained from such acts with strangers. It required a great deal of trust.

She might not know his past or what brought him to Benediction, but she knew his heart.

In that moment, with hunger gleaming in his eyes and his willingness to back off without protest, she was certain—she was falling in love with him.

"I'm not ready to be a mother, either. With all the travel I do, I get a birth control shot every three months. I'm not due for my next one for a few weeks. But I might have a couple of condoms in my purse."

If she was mistaken and didn't have any, then she'd find out whether there was a medical reason they couldn't have unprotected sex since she was on birth control. Gage had saved her life more than once and he was the most trustworthy guy she knew. Making love to him, with nothing between them, being intimate in ways she hadn't with anyone else, felt right.

He grabbed her bag from the nightstand and fished out one.

Part of her wished she didn't have any, but that was another conversation for a different time.

"I want you." She reached for his shirt, and he wrapped his hands around her wrists, stopping her.

"I have scars from my previous line of work. Not as bad

as some, but enough to surprise you. To put you off, even."
He stared at her, and it was the first time she'd seen him look
uncertain. Vulnerable.

This was what she wanted, for them to be unguarded and
exposed.

"Let me see you, Gage." She pulled his sweater off over
his head. There was another layer, a thin thermal shirt that
clung to his body. She removed that, too, along with his jeans,
and took in the sight of him.

Sitting up, she traced the marks on his body with her
fingers.

Cuts and scars—some she recognized as healed bullet
wounds, dozens, were all over his body. She kissed them as
she swept her hands across his sleek muscles. He made little sounds of pleasure, and slowly, the tension in him eased.

"Will you tell me about them, later?" she asked, taking
him in her hand and stroking his erect shaft. Right now, she
didn't want explanations—she only wanted him.

He groaned, his eyes rolling back into his head. "I promise."

Gage drew her back down and kissed her. The weight of
his body settled on her, and she loved the heaviness of him,
the hard angles, the strength and heat of him. He nipped at
her neck, tiny bites that heightened other sensations before
licking up her throat.

As he lifted on one forearm, she saw the condom in his
hand. Unwilling to wait, she took it and ripped the wrapper
with her teeth. Smiling at her, he took it from her hand and
rolled it on while she watched. The moment was sensual, intimate, instead of awkward.

Wrapping her legs around his hips, she dragged his mouth
back to hers. He pressed inside her wet, aching body and
swallowed her moan. He kissed her so long she was lost in
her own answering need.

They fit together, snug and perfect, as though they weren't simply joined, but attached. A part of one another.

Sensation bloomed, and that's all there was. His hands caressing her body. His mouth kissing her, tasting her. The feel of him moving inside her. Thick and hard. The tension building, tightening. Their breaths mingled in a haze of heat and pleasure. Pressure so excruciating and sweet she thought she'd shatter.

HE'D GIVEN HIMSELF permission to love her, thought only of Hope as he had touched her with exquisite care and did his best to make her only think of him. The pleasure of her tight as a glove around him as she'd cried out his name came back to him in a rush. His throat tightened recalling it.

The toilet flushed and the water ran. Seconds later, Hope was back under the covers.

He drew her close against him, and she slid her leg between his thighs. Emotion welled in his chest, threatening to swamp him.

"The scars," she whispered, running her nose up his neck. "Are they related to why you're hiding in Benediction?"

"Yes." He'd never told a soul what he'd done for a living, why he was running. Not even Claire knew, and his work family, his team, didn't count. Though he formed the words in his head, they wouldn't leave his mouth.

"Do you not want to tell me?" she asked in the wake of his silence.

"You can want a thing and fear it at the same time."

She leaned up on an elbow and looked down at him. "I've trusted you with everything, and you've shared the burden of helping me find my sister's killer. To be in something with a person, for them to care enough to share the burden, is beautiful. A small miracle. You've done that for me. Let me do the same for you."

He gave a long exhale and shuttered his eyes. There was

no easy way to tell her. "I used to work for the CIA." That was already saying too much. Things never ended well when you confided in people about CIA business.

"Look at me." She pressed a palm to his cheek. "Please."

He opened his eyes and met hers. She stared at him without frustration or disappointment, but with the studious expression of someone trying to sort out a puzzle, put the pieces together.

"You can trust me," she said.

"It's not that." He did trust her. Odd as it might seem, considering she was a photojournalist. "If I tell you anything else, it'll endanger you." To involve her would be unfair. "I want you to have the luxury to walk away, the freedom to go back to your life. Getting too close to me could put a target on your back. I don't want that for you."

"This is a two-way street, Gage. Let me be in it with you, share the burden. Tell me what you're up against and I'll decide for myself. Okay?" After he nodded, she asked, "Is Gage your real name?"

"I was born Gage Graham." Hope was the only person he'd slept with who knew that. "The people I worked with knew, but I had an alias on the job when interacting with others." Using an alias in Benediction would've been impossible. There was Claire and hard-copy records from his childhood as proof of the truth.

"What did you do for the CIA? From all the scars, I take it you weren't an analyst sitting at a desk."

There was no telling what she'd think of him, how she'd react, after he told her, but he'd opened this door based on a gut feeling and instincts about her. "I was a member of a kill team. Our job was to take out the bad guys. Make the world a safer place. We eliminated dictators and terrorists." He swallowed hard and searched her face.

Shock and concern were evident in her eyes. He was waiting for the judgment, but it never came.

"Go on," she said, softly.

"My team's code name was Topaz. We were a close group, solid, tight like family." They'd only had each other to talk to openly, as he was doing now. "Hunter was our team leader. Zee, Zenobia, was our tech guru. A wicked hacker. Dean was the point person." Nice way of saying he was the team assassin.

They each had a specialty but were also skilled operatives, proficient with a variety of weapons and hand-to-hand combat.

"What was your role on the team?"

"I was the cleaner. When a body needed to disappear without a trace, or if we needed to doctor a scene to mislead anyone snooping, I took care of it. Did whatever was necessary to make sure it wasn't tracked back to the CIA."

"So what happened?" she asked, stroking his forehead and running her fingers through his hair.

It was a mystery to him how she could even look at him, much less touch him.

"I wish like hell that I knew. On our last mission something went wrong. We were supposed to take out an extremist, Khayr Faraj, in the mountains of Afghanistan, along with his financial backer, and thought we had."

"Faraj? I've heard of him. He's still alive. They say in a couple of years he'll be more powerful and dangerous than Osama bin Laden ever was."

"That's why we were so eager to get him. There are no pictures of Faraj, but the file we were given had a description. He purportedly had a birthmark on his cheek. The information we had indicated he'd be with a group of other terrorists and meeting with a corrupt Afghan official who was secretly funding him. We were instructed to use explosives. Take everyone out. It was odd, because normally we decide which method of elimination is best."

"If Faraj wasn't there, who did you kill?"

"Turned out to be a tribal leader meeting with the Afghan official."

"How did the mistake happen?"

"I don't know. We never got a chance to ask. Our planned extraction was compromised. A kill team had been waiting for us. We weren't sure at the time if it had been a CIA hit squad. Fortunately, Hunter always has a contingency ready. We camped out for weeks in shipping containers on a freighter until we were back Stateside." Not his fondest or prettiest memory. "Hunter tried to meet with our CIA handler, but everything went sideways. Instead of Kelly Russell showing up, another kill team did. Mercenaries. Ruthless, with no regard for collateral damage. And no interest in asking us questions or taking us in alive. Then we knew for certain that it was the CIA trying to eliminate us. We had to split up. We've been lying low ever since."

She put her hand on his chest. "My goodness. I can't imagine. Losing your career. Your team. Forced to run and hide. With no idea why."

"It's been a living nightmare."

"At least you have Benediction. The CIA isn't looking for you here."

"This is temporary. I trust Captain Finley about as far as I can throw her to keep her end of our bargain."

"What bargain?"

"I procure items for her husband, to keep Mr. Finley happy. This town can be hard on spouses. In return, she conveniently forgets to run a background check on me. When her assignment is close to ending, it'll be time for me to move on. Somewhere."

Finding a safe place to hide out was tough and next to impossible to do on short notice, but he had two years to pinpoint where to go.

"Well, you have me." She brushed her lips over his and caressed his face. "This—us—it doesn't have to be temporary."

This woman was amazing. After everything he'd told her, she wasn't running for the hills or horrified. In fact, he didn't see one drop of fear in her eyes.

As much as he would love to explore a relationship with Hope, the logistics didn't seem feasible. "I'm holed up in a town that you're not allowed to be in. Your life is in LA, a city with a ton of closed-circuit cameras, which isn't conducive to a wanted man staying under the radar."

"I'm a freelance photojournalist. My life, my home base can be anywhere. Except Benediction."

They both laughed.

Hope. That's what she was, his hope, opening him to new possibilities. In a million years, he never would've dreamed this could happen. That he'd meet a woman he wanted to bare his soul to, who made his pulse race every time he touched her.

"I've been on my own," she said, "for a long while. So long I'd convinced myself that I wasn't lonely and that solitude was better. That there's freedom in not getting attached to anyone. Not relying on anyone. I can take care of myself, but in the short time I've known you, I've realized how nice it is not to have to. Nice to be able to depend on someone. To have him hold my hand, let me cry on his shoulder, to help me without asking for anything in return. I've never had that before, and I don't want to lose it." She pressed a kiss to his lips, and he tightened an arm around her.

His heart swelled until his chest tightened, as though his lungs were crowded and fighting for space.

He had to move on from Benediction eventually. Maybe she could stay in a nearby town—preferably not Goode, where she was friendly with local law enforcement—but somewhere within an easy drive, and they could explore this.

Take things slowly, giving them both an opportunity to come to their senses. Who was he kidding? Give her an opportunity. He didn't need one.

"Spending time with me could be risky," he said. "Life would be easier, simpler for you if you didn't even consider it."

"Haven't you learned who I am by now? Hello." She took his hand and shook it. "I'm Hope Reckless Fischer."

He was well aware of whom he was dealing with. "Nice to meet you, Ms. Fischer. I hear they call you Trouble for short." He cupped the back of her head and brought her mouth to his.

She had no idea what she was suggesting. How dangerous it could be for her. He needed to make her understand. Which wasn't going to happen while their emotions were clouded with all the endorphins running high in their systems.

"I'll make you a deal," he said. "Let's find your sister's killer first, starting with me getting those letters and having a chat with the sheriff. Then we'll talk about us. Outside of the bedroom with clothes on."

"You've got yourself a deal."

"Any idea where I can find the sheriff? Besides the station."

"He has breakfast in a diner on the same street as the B&B I stayed in. Pretty early, before the rush."

"I can work with that."

"Thank you." She gave him a quick kiss. "Since we have to be up early, are you ready to go sleep?"

"Sleep isn't really what I had in mind." He pulled her on top of him and ran his hands down her back and lower. Yes, he wanted her again, but his deeper desire was for what would come after, when she'd ask more questions and he'd give answers, letting her peel back more of his layers.

She smiled. Her direct gaze pierced right through him. "Good, because I'm not tired."

That terrible vibe he had still niggled at him with the irritation of a splinter under the skin. If destiny was whispering to him this time, he couldn't hear what it was saying.

Hope slid down his body, kissing and licking him along the way. Then she took him into her mouth and everything else slipped away.

Chapter Thirteen

At seven o'clock on the dot, Ryan logged off his computer, finished checking emails that might have come in overnight. Sunlight streamed through the wall of windows into the office. At least it wasn't a dismal day. Then he reminded himself that didn't mean it would be a good one.

He put on his jacket and campaign hat, tucking the brim down low.

"You want me to grab you breakfast?" he asked Dwight on his way to the front door.

Aimee wasn't in the office yet, but she would be there by the time Ryan returned.

"I had a big bowl of oatmeal. I'm good." Dwight typed away on his keyboard, completely focused for once. "Thanks for letting me take care of this paperwork this morning instead of last night."

"Yep, I'm just glad Finn is going to be all right."

"He'll be in later, at five o'clock. For the evening shift."

Shaking his head, Ryan took out his sunglasses from his jacket pocket and put them on. "I told him to take the day off." Ryan was prepared to work a double and had already coordinated with the home care helper to spend the night.

"He said he was fine and wanted to come in."

Ryan shrugged. "Suit himself. I'll never complain about having more deputies on hand. Be back in an hour."

Dwight waved and turned back to the computer.

This used to be Ryan's favorite time of day, that brought him a sense of peace. Everyone was just waking up. The streets were clear and quiet, and he could hear himself think as he walked. Once he'd enjoyed that. Before Faith.

They'd met four years ago when she was staying at the B&B until her housing in Benediction was finalized. Like a fool, he'd waited a year to ask her out. Thinking no one that pretty and sophisticated from a large city would have any interest in a simple man who was a bit rough around the edges and the sheriff of a tiny town.

Physically, Hope resembled Faith. Both attractive and slim without being rail thin, but Faith had had a glow about her. She wasn't afraid to eat pasta or pizza or split a piece of pie. Most of the time, she'd stolen his. Hope's brown hair had a hint of red that matched her fiery spirit. Whereas Faith's had natural blond highlights, giving it a golden sheen in the sunlight. She was the kindest, gentlest person and the only one who could get his father to smile. She would read Ryan's thoughts by the expression on his face and finish his sentences.

He'd felt blessed to be in her presence, to have her love, and tried every day to be worthy of it.

How could the universe be so cruel to give him his soul mate and then take her away?

They never had a chance to get married, have a family and grow old together the way they'd planned. He never should've waited a minute to ask her out.

Now he walked these quiet streets, decorated for the holidays, rubbing the engagement ring resting against his sternum that he had planned to give her at Christmas, his blood boiling and his heart bleeding. After Faith was gone.

He rounded the corner and stopped cold.

A man he'd never seen before came skulking out from the walkway that ran between the bookstore and the B&B, carrying a suitcase. A *blush* Tumi carry-on that sure as hell wasn't his. Not that a dude couldn't own luggage in any shade he desired, but Hope had clarified the color wasn't pink, as Ryan had called it, but blush. When he'd been notified that a woman bearing a striking resemblance to Faith had checked in, he'd gone over to investigate and met her sister.

The stranger hadn't left the B&B through the front door

as someone who belonged there would. He put the luggage inside a truck, locked the door and crossed the street, entering the diner. The man had the build of an athlete, nothing soft about him, and walked like he knew how to handle himself.

Not with the swagger of someone looking to advertise what they were to the world. That man was far more subtle. He had the prowess of a mongoose.

Looked so harmless most wouldn't bat a lash at him, but Ryan was certain he was deadly enough to kill.

Ryan hung back, collecting himself, letting the steam of wild ideas burn off in his mind.

Nexcellogen, the military police or some other group inside Benediction had Hope. They'd sent that man to dispose of her things. To tie up loose ends.

So they could make Hope disappear.

Ryan pushed off the wall and headed to the diner. Walking in, he looked around. Folks at two booths, one table. The stranger was at the counter at the far end away from everyone else, reading a newspaper.

"Morning, Sheriff. Bring your usual over?" Sally gestured to the booth where he always sat.

"The usual, yes, but I'll be sitting at the counter. Change things up a bit."

She appeared flustered a moment, but she nodded. "Okay. Change is good in Goode." She smiled.

"I like that. Sounds like a campaign slogan." Ryan headed to the back of the diner. Tipped his hat to patrons acknowledging him with a smile or a wave. Everyone he recognized, knew by name, but he didn't want to get bogged down in idle prattle, so he kept moving.

He sat next to the stranger, though every other seat at the counter was empty. The gesture would speak volumes.

Mongooses were territorial.

Ryan took off his Stetson, placed his sunglasses inside and

dropped it on the stool on the other side of him. Sally brought him an orange juice and hurried back into the kitchen.

The stranger picked up the glass of water in front of him, took a healthy gulp, set it down. "How's it going, Sheriff?"

He was a smart mongoose. Those were even deadlier.

"Good. The snow is melting, and the sun is shining." Ryan drummed his fingers against the orange juice. "No complaints."

"I heard differently," the stranger said dryly.

"Come again?" Ryan looked at the man, but the stranger didn't meet his eyes, still pretending to read the paper.

"Heard you were worried about a woman in Benediction."

A tingling sensation crept up Ryan's spine. He pushed his orange juice away and turned to him. "Did you? Who did you hear that from?"

"Hope Fischer." The stranger's voice was low, barely audible.

"Do you know her?" Ryan leaned toward him, his heart pelting in his chest. "Have you seen her? Is she all right?"

"Hope is in Benediction." The man turned the page and flicked the newspaper. "She's okay. Trying to track down the person you both want to find."

Sucking in a deep breath of relief, Ryan regained his composure. "Does she know who did it? Who killed Faith?"

The man looked around as if concerned others might notice them talking.

Ryan faced forward and drank his orange juice.

"No, she doesn't know yet," the stranger said. "But we know it was murder. The death certificate was falsified."

We. Ryan hung on to that word. "Is there anything I can do?"

The stranger finished his water. "No."

"When will I hear from her?" Ryan needed to talk to her firsthand to be sure she was all right and put his mind at ease. If something suspicious happened to Hope while she was in Benediction, no one would be the wiser.

Sally came out of the kitchen, carrying a white paper bag of food. She set it down in front of the stranger. "There you go. Two Goode special breakfast sandwiches."

Faith's favorite. Hope's, too. Was the order coincidence or did it mean Hope was okay?

"Enjoy." Smiling, Sally left to greet new customers— the boy with the paper route and his mom.

"I don't know when you'll hear from her." The stranger glanced at Ryan, his gaze steady. Cool? Detached? "Once she's ready to leave Benediction. She can't contact you until then."

Convenient. That could be days, weeks, plenty of time to dispose of Hope and erase any trace that she'd been there. The sort of tactic he'd expect from Benediction.

Everyone in that town was shady, and none of them could be trusted.

Ryan clenched his hands. "Who are you? How do I know you haven't hurt her?"

"Me?" The man folded the newspaper, laid it on the counter and swiveled in his seat, facing him. "You're the one who almost got her killed," he said, his voice low and tight. Razor-sharp. But his face remained impassive, like they were having a conversation about something as interesting as the weather. "Rammed her car and sent it into the lake, where she almost drowned."

Drowned?

Nausea washed over Ryan. He'd sworn to look out for Hope as a brother would, and he'd let her down. From the moment he agreed to help her carry out her plan, he'd regretted it, but it was the only way to find out what really happened to Faith.

"I never meant for that to happen," Ryan said.

The stranger cleared his throat. "The road to hell is paved with good intentions, Sheriff."

"Don't talk to me that way." Ryan spun toward him but kept his tone hushed. "You don't have the right to lecture me."

"Why not? Because Hope didn't die?"

Ryan pulled out the engagement ring from his sweater and pointed to it. "Because I've been in hell ever since I lost the woman I love. Because I've been hanging on to find Faith's killer. Who the hell are you?"

The stranger's eyes narrowed, burning with anger. "I'm the one who stopped on the side of the road to help. I'm the one who gave Hope mouth-to-mouth, saved her and took her to the Benediction clinic." Lowering his head, he turned toward the counter and tossed two twenty-dollar bills next to his glass. "The way I see it, you're the one who needs to be lectured, because you've got lousy judgment. You couldn't protect Faith, and you almost killed Hope yourself."

"Bastard!" Ryan jumped up, his fists clenched, hanging on to his self-control by a fraying thread. "How dare you!"

A hush fell over the diner, and he knew everyone was staring even though his back was to them.

Grabbing the bag, the man stood. "If you want to keep her safe, stay away from Benediction. Don't ask questions about her." Then the stranger was gone.

Ryan did want to keep Hope safe. He owed Faith that much. But he didn't take kindly to condescension, arrogance or disrespect.

If that man had been telling the truth, Ryan would stay away from Benediction, but he didn't know that guy from Adam and had no proof of what he'd claimed.

Not asking questions about Hope didn't mean he couldn't ask questions about other things.

Sally wiped down the counter and went to take the stranger's glass.

"Wait." Ryan held out his palm, stopping her. "Grab a plastic bag from the kitchen. I want to take that glass with me."

"Why, Sheriff?"

"Get the bag."

Sally spun around, shuffled to the kitchen and returned with a resealable plastic bag.

Picking up the edge of the glass with a napkin, he dropped it into the bag she held open for him. "Thanks, Sally," he said, standing.

"What about breakfast?"

"Wrap it to go. Have that kid, the one with the paper route, deliver it." It was another snow day for school. "I'll pay him ten bucks."

"I'm sure he'll get a kick out of it," she said, grinning from ear to ear, her plump cheeks rosy. "That's more than he makes in a week."

Ryan left the diner, holding the bag with the glass, and headed back to the station.

There was something about the stranger he didn't trust. And a whole lot about him that he didn't like. The shifty eyes. The smart mouth. The contemptuous tone. The cocky, I-can-kick-your-butt demeanor. Giving the sheriff orders and telling him what to do in Ryan's town. Pretty slick for Benediction. The stranger might be security for Nexcellogen trying to throw him off Hope's trail. Ryan wouldn't believe everything was all right until he heard from Hope firsthand.

He walked into the station and handed Dwight the bag. "Run the prints on that glass. As soon as you have something, I want to know."

"Will do. I'll get to it as soon as I'm done with my paperwork. How deep do you want me to dig?"

"Every database. Even if there's no criminal record, I want to know about any arrests. Leave no stone unturned."

A NEW FRISSON of amazement ran through her when the door to the apartment opened and Gage walked in. He'd been gone for so long she'd started to worry.

As he set her suitcase on the rug, she uncrossed her legs and got up.

Hope ran her hands over his chest. "I thought it might have been too conspicuous for you to bring my whole bag."

"You're right, but I figured you'd want your own clothes and other stuff. I mean, what's a photojournalist without a camera?"

Even without asking, he'd brought all her things, knew she'd miss her camera.

Cupping his face, she pressed her mouth to his and kissed him. Hard.

It occurred to her she'd never tire of this, even if she kissed him every moment of every day.

Smiling, she had thought the romantic in her had been lost, missing in action, years ago. So nice that it wasn't. "You taste like bacon and avocado."

He lifted the white paper bag in his other hand. "Ate mine on the way back. Yours is cold. Sorry it took me a while, but the pharmacy in Goode didn't open until nine, and I needed to pick up a refill for Claire's prescription. Do you want me to pop the sandwich in the microwave for you?"

"Thanks, but I'm too anxious to eat." Hope dropped to her knees and unzipped her bag. She grabbed her small jewelry case beside her camera and took out the cremation urn necklace. A heart surrounded by silver angel wings. "Inside are the last of Faith's ashes," she said, holding it up. "I got it so that I'd always have a piece of her with me. I left it in my bag for safekeeping."

"Do you want me to help you put it on?"

"Thanks."

Hope pulled her hair out of the way while Gage draped the chain around her neck and clasped it for her. She put it inside her top. The silver was cool against her skin but quickly warmed.

The heart and wings rested beside Faith's cryptex pendant, which Hope also wore.

She turned back to the carryon. The four letters, bundled and tied together with a white silk ribbon, were in the top left corner.

"We should begin in chronological order," he said, sitting next to her. "See what made her start writing to you."

Hope opened the first letter, dated August 23. "Take a look." She handed it to him. "Faith deliberately mentioned she was reading *To Kill a Mockingbird*. At the time, I didn't think anything of it that she'd specified mass market paperback and the fiftieth anniversary edition."

"She wanted to make sure that you two would be on the same page. Literally."

"Exactly." Hope leaned over and pointed to the bottom of the letter. "After she signed it, she put a quote from the book."

"Hey, I think I see the difference in Faith's signature. Can you grab the Nexcellogen form?"

Hope reached for the jacket on the sofa and pulled it out, handing it to him.

"Now that I'm looking at the real deal in comparison, it's obvious. Faith was left-handed?"

"Yeah. Why?"

"Whoever forged her signature was right-handed. A leftie makes strokes in a right-to-left direction, and the slope of letters has an inclination in a backward direction. But when you compare it, on the forgery, the person did come close, but the letters want to slope in a forward direction, which is the natural inclination for a right-handed writer."

"It was hard for me to pinpoint what it was about the other signature. But now that you say it, I can see what you mean. It's so subtle."

Fortunately, he knew what to look for. Did he ever have to make someone's death look like a suicide, forge letters?

One day she'd ask, but at the moment, there was too much for her to think about.

"With the quote at the bottom of the letter, do you think it corresponds to a page number?" Gage asked.

"I doubt it." Hope opened the book and found the first quote on page 112. "It's the fourth line down on the page. Let's circle every fourth word in the letter. If that doesn't get us anywhere, we'll go by paragraph."

As Gage got her a pencil, her pulse kicked up a notch. With any luck, this would get them one step closer. She began the process, counting and circling. An eerie tingle raced down her spine as the words came together. The message was simple and clear.

"'No success at work. Only failure. Pressure. Don't know what to do. May have a bigger problem. Sidekick is up to something,'" she said, reading the coded message aloud.

"Who is sidekick supposed to be?" Gage asked.

"A sidekick is a buddy, a friend. It must be Paul. She liked Neal and I'm sure they became sociable in this small town, but she never talked about him as if they were buddies."

He stared at her with an analytical frown, as though he was working out an equation in his head. "Look up the next quote."

The letter was dated October 1.

Thank goodness Faith had chosen this particular book and quotes that stood out. Hope had read it so many times, she knew where to pinpoint them without much effort. "Six."

Gage highlighted each word this time. "'Higher-ups in big city expect results that I can't give. Worried I'll be transferred. Forced to move. Can't leave my love now.'"

"We didn't speak on the phone every day," Hope said, "but a few times a month at least, unless I was overseas. She never mentioned anything about the possibility of having to move back to Herndon. Why wouldn't she come right out and say that to me?"

"Remember, she suspected the phone line was tapped, and obviously, she was worried that someone might even check her mail. Maybe she wasn't allowed to talk about the project at all. To admit that she might be kicked off the project meant something was wrong with the drug testing. But I'd like to know why she wouldn't say anything to Ryan if they were in love and on the verge of getting engaged. I didn't think highly of him before, and after meeting him my opinion hasn't changed."

She understood he was upset with Ryan for going along with her plan, but she needed Gage to look at the facts without bias.

"Faith would never want a boyfriend to feel forced or manipulated into proposing. If Ryan thought there was a chance she might have to leave, then he might've felt compelled to pop the question or lose her. She believed in fairy tales and wanted things to progress in their own time. I could see her not telling him outright."

"I'm sure Faith had her reasons, but I don't trust Sheriff Ryan Keller. He has poor judgment. I don't understand how he could endanger you like that."

Setting the letter down, she scooted closer to Gage. "I wasn't totally honest last night. Ryan didn't want to help me with my, and I quote, harebrained plan. He called me foolhardy, truth be told, but I guilted him into doing it. I shouldn't have misled you, and I don't want it to skew the way you see him."

Gage put his fists on his thighs and shook his head. "You didn't force him. He had a choice and made the wrong one."

They weren't going to see eye to eye on this.

Hope put her left hand on his right fist.

A ghost of a smile touched his lips. He opened his hand, turning it palm up, and enfolded hers. "Moving on."

A small laugh escaped her, and she nodded in agreement.

Hope found the third quote in a letter dated October 27. "Ninth line down."

Gage made quick work of piecing together the message. "'Unbelievable. Brutus wants my job. Promises better results. Lies. Merlin without magic.'"

"This doesn't sound like the Paul I met in Herndon. Perhaps this is about Neal."

"We should read the last message."

"The letter was dated four days after Thanksgiving."

Gage looked over at it. "She was killed the next day."

Hope shivered from a sudden chill, and Gage wrapped his arm around her shoulder.

"I was in Syria when she wrote this. She'd called, left a message, sounded upbeat, ecstatic. Said Ryan was coming for Christmas and everything was falling into place."

"Something must've happened. What's the number for the last quote?"

Pushing aside the grief welling in her chest, she looked it up. It took her a minute, but she found the line. "Five."

She tried to picture Faith happy and smiling, excited to introduce Ryan to the family. That was the one thing Hope could take comfort in.

"'Had it wrong,'" Gage said, reading the message. "'No one can be trusted. Think crony is misusing drug. Selling. Recreational. Horrible. Need proof.'"

"That's definitely about Paul. I can't believe he was using their research to make recreational drugs. But why?"

"Money?" He rubbed her back. "Money, power, passion, revenge—those are always the biggest motives for murder when the victim and perpetrator know each other."

"Paul is nice, the life of the party. Not a scumbag drug dealer."

"How many of those have you met?"

"I see your point. Do you think Paul could also be Brutus?

Taking her job and overseeing the lab would have given him more control and leeway to do what he wanted."

"It's possible," Gage said. "Hang on a minute." He read the letter in its entirety. "She talked about a new illegal drug flooding the area called Zion. How Ryan was trying to find the person distributing it in the area and she wished she could help him."

"I had no idea she thought the source might be coming from her lab." She pushed her hair back behind her ears and grunted her frustration. "I feel like such an idiot. Faith handed me all these breadcrumbs with quotes from my favorite book, and I never put it together."

"You are now."

"But what if I had done it sooner, while she was still alive? Maybe I could've come out here and helped her. Saved her." Regrets spiraled in her mind as her chest tightened, making it hard to breathe.

Gage stroked her cheek with the back of his fingers. "You can't beat yourself up with what-ifs. They'll get you nowhere useful and only make you miserable."

When he flattened his palm against her cheek, she nuzzled into it, allowing herself a moment to absorb the comfort he gave her. She knew he was right, but it was hard to forgive herself for the oversight.

He lowered his hand and pressed a soft kiss to her temple.

"We have to question Paul," she said. "Do you know where he lives?"

"Next door to Faith's old townhome. Near the entrance of the residential area. His place backs up to the woods."

"It's a Saturday. The odds are good he won't be at work. He might be at home." Hope got to her feet. "What are we waiting for?"

Gage stood, meeting her gaze head-on, and closed his hands on her arms. "We should wait until it's dark."

"We finally have a motive and a suspect. I don't want to wait."

"Listen, you haven't eaten today. It's already lunchtime, and I'm hungry. Let's have a bite and talk this through with clear heads."

"Fine. I'll eat, but if you think I'm going to sit here and stew for several hours, you're the one who's crazy."

Chapter Fourteen

"This is a bad idea," Gage said to Hope an hour later, dressed in all black with a wool hat and gloves, even though it was warmer today than it had been yesterday. He crept through the woods adjacent to one of the running trails that butted up against the rear of Kudlow's property.

He'd gone insane. That thought spun in his head over and over again.

The snow was practically gone, making their trek relatively quiet, and there were plenty of evergreens for great conceal-ment. But it was still broad daylight. This kind of operation was supposed to be conducted under the cover of darkness.

"This is happening." Jogging beside him, she wore blue jeans, winter booties, a dark turtleneck and his black zip-up with the hood covering her hair. She nearly fell when her boot got caught on a gnarled tree branch, but she pressed on through the underbrush. "We do this now," she said, de-termination sharpening her tone, "and we get answers, no matter what it takes."

Gage hadn't spent his life looking for a partner, trying to find someone like Hope, but now that he was with her, he didn't want to imagine being without her.

Years of retreat and evasion had ended last night when he opened up and revealed himself to her. Told her things only his team—the family of his choosing—knew about him. Told her things they didn't know. There was no one reason that could explain why he'd broken down his carefully erected walls, or why with her. Though he'd given it considerable thought on the drive to and from Goode.

This wasn't love at first sight. He didn't believe in such nonsense.

Maybe it was a series of events that made real the cost of

his choices. How her survival and safety hinged on his actions that bound them together.

In her face, he saw his own vulnerability. And his strength, too.

He never wanted to stop looking at her.

"It's this one," he whispered, stopping and crouching low in the thick trees. He scanned the area.

There was twenty feet of lawn and some trimmed hedgerows between the woods and the back door of the townhome. The unit to the right had been Faith's and was vacant. They only needed to worry about the neighbors on the other side possibly hearing anything.

All was quiet in this pristine section of the residential area, apart from the voices of children, probably unsupervised, enjoying their Saturday afternoon on the playground. No movement in Kudlow's kitchen or the bedroom that faced the rear. It was the same next door. A dog barked somewhere down the block, too far to be of any concern, but then it quickly stopped. Silence settled once more.

Considerate neighbors didn't allow their pets or their kids to be a nuisance. Didn't play their music too loud, didn't throw noisy parties and most certainly didn't break in. Everyone in Benediction was a considerate neighbor.

But once again, Gage was about to become the exception to the rule.

He scanned the area one more time, since it was the middle of the day. "All clear," he said. "Ready?"

Hope pulled out the Kylo Ren mask he'd given her and slipped it on. He did likewise, wearing Darth Vader's. They were from costumes he'd bought for him and Jason, so they could dress up as characters from Jason's favorite movie franchise. The kid had had an incident with the military police the week before Halloween. Gage had thought while handing out candy together to a handful of trick-or-treaters, he'd talk some sense into him. But Jason had flat out refused the gesture.

Too little, too late on Gage's part.

The masks had gone unused until now.

"Remember, let me do the talking," he said, not sounding like himself thanks to the voice changer inside the mask. A fortuitous purchase since he was about to break into the house of someone who knew him.

"Got it." Hope's voice was distorted, as well, but he wanted her to take a back seat on the interrogation, worried she might get emotional and deviate from the plan.

He darted through the trees. Took a knee by the back door.

No home security system to worry about, and if he was in luck, he wouldn't even need the lock-picking tools in his hand. Given that the town was so insulated with high-level security, most homes had either unlocked windows or doors or both. It was usually the MPs or some of the Nexcellogen outsiders who bothered to lock up, more so out of habit.

Gage tried the knob—it turned, and the door opened. He gestured for Hope to hurry over.

She looked around before dashing from the tree line. She entered the house and he followed, closing the door softly and swiftly behind him.

Gage handed her the kit to hang on to and crept through the kitchen toward the living room, where a television was on

From the sound of it, Kudlow was playing a video game. Alone. A shoot-'em-up game with aliens.

Gage drew his gun and swept into the living room.

Kudlow was sitting in a recliner chair, wearing a robe, boxers and a plain tee underneath, and slippers. It took a second for him to catch the movement and notice Gage because he was so involved in the game.

His eyes flared wide, and his lips parted with soundless shock.

"Get up," Gage said over the television.

Finally, Kudlow blinked and raised his hands, dropping

the game controller. "What's going on? Is this some kind of prank?"

"Up! Now!"

Shaking, Kudlow rose from the chair and then froze. "Neal? Is that you? This isn't funny."

Gage stalked up to him and pushed Kudlow into the hall, away from the front of the house, where there was street traffic and a passerby might overhear something. Even though there was little chance of that with the volume of the video game.

Kudlow scurried down the hall with his hands up by his ears. "What's happening?"

"Shut up," Gage said in a tight voice.

"Who are you?"

"A concerned citizen." Gage shoved him into the kitchen. "Sit."

Kudlow dropped into a chair at the dining table. "What do you want?"

"Answers." Gage nodded for Hope to restrain his hands with zip ties the way he'd shown her earlier—behind him and attached to the lattice-back chair that came standard in the furnished places. She did so without hesitation.

"Ouch." Kudlow grimaced as she secured the restraint. "That hurts."

Good. Better for it to be too tight than too loose.

Gage lowered the weapon. "Tell me about the illegal drug you're selling."

"Wh-what?" Kudlow's terrified gaze bounced between them. "I don't know what you're talking about."

"I'm talking about Zion," Gage said.

"I've got nothing to do with that." Kudlow paused. His Adam's apple moved and up and down as he swallowed hard. "You've got the wrong guy."

"Either you cooperate and talk, or we do this the hard way." Gage aimed the Sig at the man's knee. "I induce cooperation, which will be very painful, and in the end, you'll still talk."

"What do you want to know?"

That was more like it. Gage lowered the gun. "Where does Zion come from?"

"I—I—I make it."

"Why?" Gage asked.

Kudlow looked perplexed by the question.

"You're a scientist," Gage said. "You're supposed to be making the world better. Why are you selling drugs?"

"Because I can. For the money." An edge of panic shook his voice, rushed his words. "You think I want to rake in five figures a year while corporations like Nexcellogen make billions off my work?"

"Off Faith Fischer's work," Hope said.

Gage had warned her not to speak. Leave the interrogation to him. It would be quicker and more efficient that way.

"Yeah." Kudlow looked between them. "So what?"

"So you killed her over it," Gage said.

"Me? No, no, no," Kudlow sputtered. "I would never hurt Faith."

"Liar," Hope said, coming up next to Kudlow. "You killed her because she found out the truth about what you were doing and was going to expose you."

"How do you know that?" Kudlow asked, his face contorted with fear.

The man was too unnerved to deny it. "Doesn't matter how we know." Gage stepped forward and eased Hope to the side. "Tell us exactly how you did it."

"She committed suicide. I didn't kill her! I wouldn't, couldn't. Never. She was my friend."

"You would for money." Gage bent over and got in Kudlow's face. "To save your reputation and your career. To keep your drug enterprise running."

"No, that's not what happened!"

The guy was scared and flustered, but he needed a push. "Then tell us," Gage demanded, slamming a fist down on the dining table.

"Yes, I wanted her out of the way in the lab, okay, but for her to go back to Herndon!" Kudlow was sweating and shaking. "Neal stumbled upon what I was doing long before Faith. He promised to keep it quiet if I helped him take her job. It would be a win-win for both of us." His wide eyes were starting to tear, his gaze everywhere, not settling on one spot for more than a second. "I'd get to continue manufacturing my drug and he'd get the glory once we had a breakthrough. Neal would be able to write his own ticket then. But something happened over the Thanksgiving weekend she spent in Goode to make her connect Zion with the drug we were working on in the lab."

"Do you have any idea what it was?" Gage asked.

"No. She didn't say."

Gage studied him, assessing more than his words for the truth. "What was she doing Thanksgiving weekend?"

Kudlow shrugged. "Spending it with her boyfriend, I think. Faith was private. She didn't really talk about that stuff. I just assumed she was seeing someone since she went to Goode so often. After her suicide, there was talk she'd gone through a bad breakup."

"She didn't commit suicide," Hope snapped.

Gage raised a palm to her, needing to keep things on track.

She huffed, folded her arms and crossed to the other side of the kitchen.

"So, Faith came back to work after Thanksgiving and suspected that Zion was being produced in her lab," Gage said. "She learned it was you, and you killed her to keep her quiet."

Kudlow shook his head. "I didn't lay a finger on Faith."

"But she did know you were producing Zion," Gage said.

"Faith started snooping around and suspected me, but she couldn't prove it. She needed a sample of Zion to test and compare to the ones in the lab. But she figured out that Neal must've known what I was doing and that was the reason I was supporting him to take over the project."

"Faith trusted you!" Hope said. "She thought you were loyal, that you were her friend."

"I remember the look on her face." Paul was crying now, tears streaming down his cheeks, white spittle gathering at the corner of his mouth. "Faith said I was a contemptible weasel and called Neal Brutus. She was so mad. So hurt. She was going to disclose the truth about the failing drug trials in the annual report. That meant corporate would shut us down. Everything would end."

The words shocked Gage. He was a man who kept his ear to the ground and hadn't heard anything close to that. "What do you mean, shut you down? Aren't there several ongoing projects?"

Kudlow nodded, with tears spilling from his eyes. "But ours was the shining star, the great hope for Nexcellogen. We had to meet a certain benchmark in the annual report. Show we were ready for human clinical trials. But if we couldn't pull off what we promised, this miracle PTSD vaccine, they were going to pull the plug on funding. That meant us, the company, leaving Benediction by springtime."

Interesting. That was a big statement with even bigger repercussions for the whole town. It meant the death of Benediction if what he said was true.

Then again, the town had been close to dying before and always pulled through.

Gage must've been silent for a moment too long, thinking, because Hope prowled up to Kudlow

"When you couldn't get Faith replaced and she discovered what you were doing, you decided to kill her," she said. "Admit it and we might let you live."

"Stop," Gage warned her. It'd only muddy the waters if Kudlow admitted to a crime he hadn't committed out of fear, thinking it was the only way to survive. The guilty always wanted to convince you of their innocence. Better to let them talk, dig their own grave.

Invariably they'd say something that could be proven or disproven or get caught in a lie.

"Why should I stop?" Hope asked. "He had every reason to kill her. He had a motive, probably opportunity, too, and no alibi."

"That's not true!" Kudlow said frantic. "I do have an alibi. The night Faith died, I wasn't in town. I was with my distributor. We negotiated new terms. Talked about expansion. Ways to increase production outside the lab, so Faith would never get proof. We ended up partying and I got drunk, wasted. I couldn't drive, crashed at his place."

"Who is your distributor?" Gage asked.

Kudlow squeezed his eyes shut and lowered his head, like he regretted mentioning the alibi and wanted to suck the words back into his mouth.

"Who?" Gage pressed.

"He, uh…" Kudlow hesitated, his bottom lip quivering as though he were more terrified of his accomplice than them. "He'll kill me if I tell you. Please."

This was the part of the interrogation where threatening death worked. "*We'll* kill you if you don't."

Kudlow raised his head. Tears and snot glistened on his face. "He's in the sheriff's department."

Hope's gaze flickered to Gage. The same question he had was evident in her shocked eyes.

If the distributor was Ryan Keller, Gage was driving back to Goode to shoot the man himself. "Give us a name. Now." He put the tip of the silencer to Kudlow's leg. "A bullet in the knee is excruciating."

"Dwight!" Kudlow snapped up. "Dwight Travers. One of the deputies. The MPs, they can verify that I left Benediction after work at five and didn't come back through the gates until the next morning, around, um, nine or so. Faith had already been found by then. The whole town was abuzz about it."

Kudlow was right. Faith had been brought to the funeral home shortly before midnight. According to Dr. Howland's report, the time of death was between seven and eight, and a neighbor whose account of being out for a jog and seeing smoke coming from Faith's garage substantiated at least that part of the doctor's findings.

"Then are you saying Neal killed her?" Gage asked.

Kudlow shrugged. "I don't know who did it," he said, looking as though he truly had no clue who had murdered Faith. "Neal wanted her job and, eventually, he got it, but that doesn't make him a killer."

"But it does make it convenient for both of you now that she's gone." Gage crouched down in front of him. "Maybe Neal killed her and you knew about it. Helped him cover it up. Spread the rumors about a breakup."

"No. That's nuts!"

Hope paced in the kitchen. Gage could feel the rage and tension emanating from her. She was barely holding it together, but he admired the fact that she was.

"Sounds plausible to me," Gage said. "Maybe I should shoot you and Neal, too."

"Please," Kudlow pleaded, sobbing. "Don't."

"Give me one good reason to believe you and Neal didn't do this together."

Kudlow looked up and around as if searching the room for a way to escape. "Wait. Uh, Neal told me that he was working late in the lab the night Faith died. We have to badge in and out of the building. There's an access log in security. I wasn't in Benediction that night. I have an alibi. If you can get the records in Nexcellogen, you'll know if Neal was in the building or not."

"If it turns out that Neal was in the building that night, who else would have benefited from Faith's death?" Gage asked.

"The whole town. Right? I mean, if Nexcellogen pulled out, Benediction would shut down. These townies are crazy about this place. They'd do anything to keep it thriving."

They would. They were fiercely protective of this place, as if it were a family member.

"But the possibility of the company leaving wasn't common knowledge," Gage said, thinking it through aloud. The townies were gossipy. Something of this magnitude would've spread like wildfire if even one permanent resident had known. "None of the townsfolks knew. I'm guessing they wouldn't have heard about it until after the annual report came out and the company made their decision public." Which brought everything full circle back to the perpetrator being someone inside Nexcellogen. Only an employee would've been able to change and forge Faith's In Case of Death form.

"That's not going to happen now," Kudlow said.

"Why not?" Hope asked, breaking her silence.

"Neal altered the annual report. Made the results look far more promising than they really were to buy us time. We're close to a breakthrough on that drug. I just know it and so does he. We can make it work."

"Did Michelle Lansing know the report was falsified?" Gage asked.

"Are you kidding me? She would've fired both of us on the spot for even suggesting anything so unethical."

Gage believed him about Michelle, who'd always struck him as ethical and reasonable, and it was possible that Kudlow was also right about Neal Underhill. But they needed more than gut instinct. They needed proof.

"Pen and paper," Gage said. "Where can I find it?"

"Top left drawer." Kudlow gestured with his chin.

Gage grabbed it and sat. "You're going to give us the

names of all the project team leaders." All of them had something lose if Nexcellogen pulled out of Benediction. "And I want to know the layout of the building and exactly what to expect inside. Any security protocols, how many people typically work on a Saturday. No detail is too small. Do you understand?"

Time spent in reconnaissance was seldom wasted.

"Okay." Kudlow nodded. "Yeah."

Kudlow spilled his guts, describing every inch of the building that he'd seen.

It took over an hour, but Gage wanted to be thorough, going over every aspect several times. Gage listened for any changes or slipups, to be sure the information was credible. While he did that, Hope searched Kudlow's things for any clues they might have overlooked.

She came back into the kitchen, holding two white lab coats and other items with the Nexcellogen logo on it. Catching Gage's eye, she shook her head. There was nothing else useful.

Once Gage was satisfied with the details of the building, he folded the paper and slipped it into his pocket. "How many guards on duty?"

"Four, Monday through Friday. Two on the weekend. One in the lobby and the other in the security room."

"What time is shift change?"

"Seven. Always at seven."

According to the security procedure, every individual had to scan their ID badge to get through the gate turnstile in the lobby that was designed to make piggybacking impossible. Which was a good thing. The access records would be accurate, reliable, and anyone who had been inside the building at the time of death could be eliminated as a suspect.

It also meant they'd need two badges, and both had to work. "Where's your badge?" Gage asked.

"On the counter, next to my wallet."

Gage grabbed it and then nodded again to Hope. This time she took out duct tape and placed it over the scientist's mouth.

Kudlow's eyes widened with renewed alarm as he shook his head.

"Sorry, but we can't have you screaming for help," Gage said. "You'll be set free later. But if you've lied about anything, conveniently forgot to tell us something about security protocols, no one will look for you until Monday." He'd figure out a discreet way to have someone stumble upon Kudlow and release him without it leading back to Gage.

Getting their hands on the Nexcellogen entry and exit log was imperative, and they couldn't risk Kudlow notifying someone beforehand.

It looked like his last-resort measure was their next step.

Chapter Fifteen

Dwight knocked on Ryan's office door and poked his head inside. "Nothing came back on those fingerprints, Sheriff."

"Really? Nothing?" Ryan leaned back in his chair, more than a little disappointed to hear the news. But just because the stranger from Benediction didn't have a record that didn't mean Ryan was wrong about him. Simply meant he hadn't been caught. Yet.

"Yeah," Dwight said. "There were two sets, but I only got a hit on Sally's prints."

Ryan shot him an incredulous look. "Sweet Sally who wants to put a smile on everyone's face?"

"She recently got her real estate license. Remember?"

"Oh, okay," Ryan said, recalling the party for her at the diner. Part of the process of obtaining your real estate license was submitting your prints to the Virginia Central Criminal Records Exchange for a state and national fingerprint-based criminal history check. "You checked all the databases?"

"Yep. FBI, Department of Defense, Department of Homeland Security and even the Foreign Biometric Exchange," Dwight said, referring to the database that was a collection of high-value biometrics on persons of interest from foreign law enforcement in partner countries. *"Nada."*

"All right. Thanks." Ryan turned to his computer.

"One more thing." Dwight leaned on the door frame and crossed his arms. "We got a call from Gary Metsos about ten minutes ago."

Ryan looked back at him. "What about this time? Old man Metsos see another UFO?"

Dwight chuckled. "No, he only sees those late at night. But it was the strangest thing. He said a helicopter landed on his farm."

"Emergency landing? Do some people need help?"

"I don't think so. He said that he was going to talk to them, find out what was going on, but a big black SUV pulled up alongside the state road, in front of his property. Those men loaded in, drove off, going east, and the chopper left."

"That is odd. Did Gary say what they looked like?"

"Yep. Tactical."

"As in armed?"

Dwight nodded.

Terrific.

"Assault weapons," Dwight said. "You want me to check it out?"

Swearing under his breath, Ryan drummed his fingers on his desk. It was going to be another wretched day in Goode.

Firearms with magazines capable of holding more than twenty rounds were classified as assault weapons, but they were legal here. Unless those men had fully automatic machine guns or sound suppressors—silencers—there wasn't much the sheriff's department could do in this county. "If those men are on the state road going east, then they're headed our way and we'll…" Ryan glanced out the window as a black Chevrolet Suburban SUV with dark-tinted windows parked right outside the station. "Well, well. What do we have here?"

"I guess that answers my question," Dwight said.

Only the front passenger door of the vehicle opened. A man with slicked-back hair, dressed in a black suit and wearing sunglasses—despite the fact that the sun was already low on the horizon and it'd be dark soon—got out and closed the door.

"You think they're govvie?" Dwight asked, frowning, and sucked his teeth.

Government preferred this type of vehicle. The suit screamed three-letter alphabet agency—take your pick, FBI,

DOJ, DOD, DHS. Not that it mattered, because no local sheriff was going to trust them until they proved their worth.

Fastening the top button on his suit jacket, the man proceeded inside the station. He stopped at the receptionist desk and spoke to Aimee. She picked up the phone, presumably to notify Ryan that someone wanted to speak with him. But the man stopped her, offering a tight smile that played closer to a grimace, and waltzed across the open floor space, past Dwight into Ryan's office.

Still wearing his sunglasses.

What nerve.

"Boss, you want me to stick around?" Dwight asked, scrutinizing their visitor from head to toe.

Ryan waved him off. "I've got this."

"Okay," Dwight said. "Holler if you need me."

As Dwight's determined footsteps drifted away toward his desk, the man took it upon himself to take a seat across from Ryan.

"Hello, Sheriff. I'm Agent Joe Smith." He reached into the inner pocket of his jacket, but instead of taking out a business card as Ryan had expected, he pulled out his cell phone. "It's come to our attention that this man might be in the area." He turned the screen toward Ryan, and on it was a picture of the stranger from Benediction. Shorter hair. Same shifty eyes and severe expression. But without a doubt, it was the same man.

A fine sweat chilled the back of Ryan's neck.

"Have you or anyone in this office seen him?" Smith asked.

"Who is that man?"

"A fugitive. Real menace to society wherever he goes. He's wanted for several crimes. Do you or your deputies know his current whereabouts?"

"What did you say his name was?"

"I didn't." Smith lowered the phone. "Sheriff, I'm all for quid pro quo, but it's rude to answer a question with a question."

"And it's rude to wear sunglasses indoors and just plain stupid to do so at night. I guess we could both use etiquette lessons."

Smith flashed another tight smile and removed his glasses. "The man we're looking for has used many aliases. The last one known was Taggert Jenner. He should be considered armed and dangerous."

"Sort of like your posse in that vehicle?" Ryan pointed to the SUV. "Do you have a permit for open carry?"

"In a vehicle, a firearm isn't considered openly carried unless it's openly visible. Ours are not."

"Mr. Gary Metsos saw you boys on his property with weapons. That would be open."

Smith sat back and crossed his legs. "Unless I'm mistaken, in this county open carry is allowed without a permit for people eighteen years of age and older. And I'm never mistaken."

"I see you've done your research." Which was rather disquieting. "What exactly are y'all armed with?"

"Assault weapons. Semiautomatic. Would you care to see?"

Okay, he'd bite. "Sure." Ryan stood, grabbing his hat.

But Smith stayed seated, punched in a number on his phone, speed dial, and put it to his ear. "The sheriff wants to see what the boys are carrying. Come on in." He disconnected.

Three doors opened, and three men stepped out of the SUV. The lot of them were dressed in tactical gear with bulletproof vests. They all looked grim. Had holstered sidearms on their hips. Assault weapons in their hands.

"Hey, boss, what's up?" Dwight asked in a loud voice, crossing the open space of the station while staring outside.

"They've agreed to show me what they're armed with," Ryan said. "Go back to your desk."

The men entered the station, poured into his office single

file and stood around the periphery while Aimee watched like it was any other day.

People carrying assault weapons wasn't anything new. This was Virginia—most folks in the area supported the Second Amendment and proudly showed it.

Smith pointed to one of his men.

The guy stepped forward, holding up the assault weapon to the side, muzzle pointed toward the wall. "This is an MP5K in nine-millimeter semiauto. Magazine capacity is fifteen rounds. Would you like to inspect further, sir?" He offered the firearm, handle first.

"No, that won't be necessary," Ryan said, noting the muzzles were all threaded so you could screw on a suppressor. He'd bet dollars to doughnuts those men were carrying silencers in their cargo pockets or had left them in the vehicle.

This was a good show. Appeared cooperative.

Ryan might be guilty of answering a question with a question, but Joe Smith—and no, Ryan did not think his name was really Joe Smith—responded to questions with a whole lot of baloney without ever giving a legitimate answer.

In the past fifteen minutes, Ryan still hadn't learned the name of the stranger from the diner. Joe had only shared the last known alias used.

Ryan looked around at the tactical contingent in his office. Their bulletproof vests were plain, devoid of any words like Police, SWAT, FBI. "What agency did you say you were with, *Joe Smith*?"

The rubbery smile loosened. "Sheriff, this is a matter of homeland security." Joe held up the phone, showing Ryan the picture again. "Where's the man we're looking for?"

"Homeland security, huh? I'd love to see some DHS credentials. Preferably a badge with your real name on it."

Smith leaned forward. His pupils were dilated such that the black pool at the center of each iris appeared to equal the area of surrounding color. Two black holes in space. "You could save us all a lot of time and energy by cooperating. Because before I leave your station, you're going to answer all my questions to my satisfaction, and once I am gone, you still won't know my real name."

Ryan chuckled, interlacing his fingers and pressing his palms to his stomach. Two Yankees in one day who wanted to be cowboys. "You're a funny man, Joe."

The other men remained stony-faced and silent.

Smith dialed another number. A pause. "It's me. I'm sitting in Sheriff Ryan Keller's office in the Podunk town of Goode. He's refusing to cooperate." He listened a moment, his gaze never wavering from Ryan's. "Thank you." Smith hit the end button and put the phone back in his pocket. "My men and I are going to grab a cup of coffee. You are going to receive a phone call shortly. After you do, I'll sit back down in this chair, and then we'll see who's laughing."

Smith stood and strolled out. His men followed, leaving the door open. They asked Aimee a question. She jumped up and hurried to the break area, since it wasn't a large enough station for a break room, and started pouring cups of coffee.

Ryan had assumed they'd leave, make their way to the café or to the diner while he received this mystery call.

Anxiety rippled through him. He signaled to Dwight, discreetly, urging him to get his tail in there.

Dwight hurried over without looking like he was rushing. "Yes, boss?"

"You said that nothing came back on those prints, right?" Ryan whispered.

"Yeah, boss. No results found in any of the databases."

How in the hell did these guys know to show up here? "Okay, thanks."

Their visitors gathered in the entrance, sipping coffee.

Aimee sat back down as the phone rang. A second later, she buzzed Ryan. "It's the governor on the line for you."

Holy. Hell. Ryan hadn't known who to expect a call from, but it sure as heck wasn't the governor.

Standing near Aimee's desk, Joe Smith looked right at Ryan. Satisfaction gleamed in his eyes as he gave Ryan a two-finger salute, then lowered his index finger, leaving his middle one up.

Ryan looked away and cleared his throat before picking up the phone. "Hello, Governor. This is Sheriff Keller."

"Before today, I never knew the town of Goode or you, for that matter, Ryan Keller, existed. The only reason I care is because I don't like it when I receive phone calls from people who have the power to make my life difficult. The reason you should care I'm on the phone now is because I can make your life very difficult. Do you understand?"

"Yes, sir, I do." Ryan straightened in his seat.

"There is a gentleman in your office who wants to ask you questions. I want you to answer him. Fully. Truthfully. The more information the better."

Joe Smith would ask questions to connect the dots. Why had the stranger been in Goode? Had he committed a crime? Why had his fingerprints been run since no crime had been committed? What had the stranger discussed with Ryan in the diner?

Those dots would lead to Hope.

Ryan had almost gotten her killed. Throwing Faith's sister to the wolves—who were armed with assault weapons and most likely had sound suppressors— wasn't going to happen without a legitimate reason.

Who were these men? Why were they looking for the stranger? Could Hope be implicated in some crime due to her association with him?

Ryan had no idea what Hope knew about that man or her connection to him. But when Smith and his men found the stranger, Hope would be with him, and she might get caught in the crossfire.

"With all due respect, Governor, I don't answer to you. I was elected by the people of Goode and answer to them. You have no authority over me." The governor could not fire him, nor officially reprimand him, and had no direct control over any funds for his department. It would take effort on the part of the governor to make his life difficult, but Ryan had been polite earlier, allowing him to flex his muscles. "Unless I know where these men came from, I don't have any answers for them."

"I'll spell it out for you in language you'll understand. Their business concerns national security and is above both of our positions and pay grades." There was a long, uncomfortable pause. "Now, you're going to be a patriot and answer Mr. Joe Smith's questions, so I don't have to field any more calls from government spooks or, heaven forbid, the White House. Are we on the same page?"

Smith and his men must have been CIA, which would explain a lot. For starters, how Ryan's office could run prints that turned up zero results but triggered the arrival of a tactical unit. The CIA had absolutely no authority to act on American soil, making this a sticky situation. But if Smith had reached out and touched someone who in turn had touched the governor in five minutes, then this was official. It was serious.

It was big.

Bigger maybe than him, Hope or Faith. What he wouldn't give to know.

"Yes, sir," Ryan said. "We're on the same page."

The line went dead. Ryan hung up and drew in a breath.

After Smith sent his men back to the SUV, he tossed his coffee cup in the trash and stalked into the office. Taking a seat, he said, without sarcasm or gloating and getting straight to business, "Let's try this again." He held up the phone with the picture of the stranger on the screen once more. "Someone in this office ran this man's prints today. Who and why?"

"I ran them after talking to him earlier this morning in a diner. Something about him bothered me." Much in the same way Smith bothered Ryan. But Smith was worse. If the stranger was a mongoose, Smith was a shark. "That's why."

"This man doesn't draw attention," Smith said. "He's adept at blending in. If he caught your interest during a conversation, there's an extraordinary reason. What did you two discuss?"

Ryan shifted in his chair. Crossed his legs and uncrossed them. Leaned back and sat forward. Nothing he did changed the boxed-in feeling he had. "Not what, who. We talked about a woman."

"I want to know exactly what was said, word for word, and please, Sheriff, don't insult my intelligence or waste any more of my precious time by trying to lie."

Ryan's palms itched. "This woman is innocent of any wrongdoing. I need your word, your assurance, that she won't be hurt as you go after your target."

"We're both professionals and know there are no such guarantees. If I gave one, you wouldn't trust it," Smith said, and Ryan had to agree. "What I can say is that she is in imminent danger right now if she's with that man. You want to protect her, save her from herself? Then tell me about the discussion you had, starting with the name of the woman."

The itching worsened. Ryan scrubbed his palms on his pants. He was caught between a rock and a proverbial hard place. Between national security and loyalty to the woman who should've been his sister-in-law. Loyalty to Faith.

His stomach twisted, but there was no way around it. "We talked about… Hope Fischer."

Chapter Sixteen

Hope watched the sun set against the backdrop of the lake and the mountains. Faith had loved this town. The picturesque setting that had made her feel like she was on vacation every day. The quiet, low-key lifestyle. No time wasted stuck in traffic. No hustle and bustle. Making caramel apples for the kids at Halloween, confident parents would let their children eat them without fretting that they might be poisoned. Getting to know her neighbors. The sense of community that her sister had called a blessing.

Turned out that it was also a curse. One of those neighbors had killed Faith.

The alarm on Gage's watch buzzed. It was five o'clock.

Although the scientists at Nexcellogen tended to be workaholics given their dedication and isolation in Benediction, Kudlow had assured them the foot traffic in the facility would be at a bare minimum and practically empty by four on a Saturday. Gage had wanted to give it an extra hour to be on the safe side.

"It's time," Hope said, more out of anxiousness than the need to inform Gage.

She could tell he was cognizant of everything. The time. Which way the wind was blowing. Her eagerness to break inside Nexcellogen that wrestled with her desire to hang on to this moment of calm. The temporary sense of peace dancing in her heart.

Seated on the sofa beside her, Gage hadn't dragged his gaze from her for the past few minutes. The air between them vibrated with an almost palpable awareness. They were in this together. Of that she was certain. But there was something he wasn't saying.

She rested her hand on his leg. "What is it?"

"After they question Kudlow, they'll suspect me. Suspicion I can handle, divert. But once we're inside that facility, the security guard in the lobby will be able to identify me. So might the one in the security room if I can't subdue him without him seeing my face. Then they'll know for certain it was me."

"Gage, I don't want to ruin your life in my pursuit of justice for Faith."

"The CIA destroyed my life long before you came along." He placed his hand over hers. "It's just being on the run is hard. The hardest thing I've ever done. If they know it's me, my back will be up against the wall and I'll be forced to leave. Running unprepared with no safe place to go is..." His gaze fell.

"Dangerous."

Gage looked up at her. "It's suicide." He released a long, heavy breath. "Being on the run, staying at a random place, even for a night, is like flying aboard a tin can that could fall apart at any minute. Crash and burn like that." He snapped his fingers. "So I need to make damn sure that my next hiding place is certified safe. That takes time and preparation, and while I'm looking, I risk exposure."

She got the gist of the metaphor. Gage was a formidable man, but his situation was as fragile as glass. "Who says they have to see your face?"

"I can't go inside Nexcellogen wearing a Halloween mask. Neither can you."

"Why not?" When he made an incredulous face, she said, "Hear me out. Waltzing in together after five on a Saturday would draw too much attention from the guard in the lobby, anyway. We go in separately. We'll both wear Nexcellogen ball caps. Once I'm in range of the cameras outside the building, I'll tip my head low, keep my face down." Just like he'd taught her to do at the military police station. "Kudlow said the guard on duty in the lobby is a formality for visitors. The guard doesn't even check employee ID since the gate turn-stiles ensure secure entry and exit. I'll go in first, but as I do, you create a distraction to lure him out. That way he's focused on the diversion instead of what I look like. While the guard is busy outside, you slip in without him seeing you. You keep the video scrambler with you the entire time. As for the guard in the security room, that's when you use the mask. No one will have a good description of either of us."

"That all sounds good in theory, but there is a guard in the security room monitoring the feeds of the surveillance cameras throughout the facility. All it takes is for him to see one fuzzy camera screen followed by another and he'll sound the alarm before I have a chance to restrain him."

In her short time in this town, she'd come to learn something important. This was Benediction, where no one expected murders, robberies or coups d'état in science labs. It was slow, quiet, predictable. "The odds are extremely high the guard will be reading a book, doing Sudoku or a cross-word puzzle. Not watching the hallways. On the slim chance that he is, his first assumption will be technical difficulties. Not that someone is breaking in."

"That's a huge gamble. Someone in Nexcellogen killed Faith. The logs will help us narrow down who, but we've got one shot at this."

"It's worth the risk." He was worth the risk.

She wanted to take a chance on him, though the stakes were incredibly high. When she thought about what she wanted tomorrow to look like for herself, she pictured Gage in it. She was holding tight to that vision now.

"All right. We can try it," he said. "But this time, I'll bring my ski mask if I need it."

"What do we use as a distraction?"

Gage thought for a moment. "I've got some leftover fire-works from the Fourth of July in the garage. I think I can make it work. But you can't hang around in the lobby waiting for me. It'll look suspicious." He took out the map of the building and looked at it. "Think you can meet me near the security office by the east stairwell? There's a restroom." He pointed it out. "You can wait inside for me."

"It's not far from the lobby. I don't see why not."

He stood, pulling her up with him, and hauled her into his arms. "We'll be separated for a short time inside. While we are, be safe. Be smart." He withdrew his gun with the sound suppressor attached and handed it to her. "I doubt you'll need it. The Nexcellogen security guards are only armed with Tasers."

She nodded and glanced down at the weapon. It felt heavy in her hand, but she wouldn't need to use it. The gun would never leave her bag.

They grabbed the items they needed—lab coats, ball caps and messenger bags. Kudlow had had a ton of stuff with Nexcellogen logos in his closet, as though the company were constantly handing out things. Or, in addition to being a drug dealer, he was a kleptomaniac, too.

In the garage, she climbed into the truck while Gage loaded the box of old fireworks into the back.

He hopped in behind the wheel. "Provided the details about the security protocols are correct, you won't have any problems. If you do run into a major issue, shoot to injure, not kill. For anything minor, bide your time. I'll be there."

Three words she trusted and believed in, that meant more to her than *I love you.*

I'll be there.

Because he would. No matter what.

Her job had taken her to ugly places, and through the lens of her camera she'd captured terrible things, making her cynical. She had come to see the world as a place in which corruption and greed reigned supreme, promises were broken, trust was betrayed and integrity no longer mattered.

Then Faith had fallen in love with an honorable man and inspired Hope to dream. To imagine.

To hope.

But it was Gage who had proven to her that there was still goodness in the world. Promises that would be kept. Trust that would be treasured.

There were people who would stand with you and not let you down.

She cupped Gage's face and caressed his cheek. "I know you will."

WATCHING JOE SMITH walk out of his office and climb into his black Suburban, Ryan felt sick to his stomach. He'd answered all Smith's questions, and now Ryan wanted to take a shower and scrub off the experience.

Something wasn't right about this situation.

Not for a minute did he doubt that the stranger was a fugitive, but why wasn't he in the database?

Ryan had cooperated fully, as instructed by the governor, and he hadn't received one straight answer in return for his effort.

Hope was in imminent danger. From Joe Smith and his men. Ryan sensed it in his gut. Smith was the type to cut through a human shield to get to his target and call it collateral damage.

The thought of Hope being a casualty in the crossfire because Ryan had been forthcoming made something inside him crumble.

He sat behind his desk, second-guessing everything, itching to do something, anything. But what could he do to help Hope?

Damn. Too bad he didn't know the stranger's name. Otherwise he could call Benediction, give the man a heads-up about Smith. That way, the stranger could watch out for Hope and ensure she wasn't inadvertently in the line of fire that was about to come flying his way.

Then again, maybe Ryan didn't need to know his name.

He buzzed Aimee, and when she picked up, he said, "Get me the number to the clinic in Benediction."

"Benediction?" She spun in her seat and stared at him through the glass.

"You heard me."

The stranger had given essential details that Ryan could use to track him down. The man had been the one to bring Hope to the clinic. Someone there must know who he was. Ryan could probe until he got contact information without letting on that Hope was in Benediction. Those townies didn't have cell phones, but they sure as heck had landlines.

Dwight got up, passing Finn—who had trudged in late, after five, looking worse than warmed-over dog food—and made a beeline to the office. "Hey, boss, what did those ya-hoos want?"

"They're looking for someone. A man. You ran his prints today. We still don't know who he is, but Joe Smith and his merry band of men do."

"Anything for us to do on this matter?"

"Us? No." Ryan grabbed his Stetson. "Me, yes." He slipped on his jacket and left his office. "Aimee, you got it?"

She tore off a slip of paper with a phone number on it. "Here you go."

"I'm heading out to check on the boys that were just in here," Ryan said.

"You want me to ride along?" Dwight asked.

"Nope. Sit tight." Ryan made his way to his SUV and sped off after Joe Smith. Catching up to them was unlikely and not what Ryan desired, anyway. Getting them in his sights and keeping them there was. He'd have cell phone reception for the next fifteen miles, then he'd lose it on that blasted road to Benediction.

Time was a-wasting, so he'd better get to it. He dialed the number Aimee had given him.

"Benediction Clinic. PA Varma speaking."

"Evening. This Sheriff Ryan Keller from Goode. I'm trying to get in contact with someone in Benediction. A man, early thirties, dark hair, about six feet tall. I don't know his name, but he saved the life of Hope Fischer. I believe he brought her to the clinic for medical treatment. It's important I speak with him. I'd like to thank him for being a good Samaritan, but I also have some urgent news for him. Can you help me?"

Chapter Seventeen

Hope threw on a lab coat and ball cap identical to what Gage was wearing. Her hair hung loose, framing her face. Faith's badge was already around her neck, hanging from a lanyard.

Gage hit the remote button, opening the garage door, started the truck and backed out.

She ducked down and stayed low as he drove until he parked behind the church. It was the closest building to the Nexcellogen facility.

"Maintain a steady pace as you approach the building," he said. "Leisurely, not too brisk. That'll give me a chance to set up and time it for when you enter."

She put the gun in the messenger bag. "Will you be all right without a weapon?"

"Don't worry about me." He smiled, but his eyes remained deadly serious. His gaze dropped to her chest, and his expression changed. "Switch badges with me."

"Why?"

"In case they deactivated Faith's. Take Kudlow's instead."

They exchanged ID badges. "What are you going to do if Faith's doesn't work?"

"Improvise," Gage said. "I'll get in."

Three more words she trusted. "I'm sure you will."

"Focus. Keep your head in the game."

She slipped a hand around the back of his neck and kissed him. "Keep your head attached."

"I'm pretty good at that."

Hope slipped out of the vehicle, walked around the church and crossed the main road. There were only a few scattered light posts. Enough to make a person who was out for a stroll or jogging at night feel comfortable without lighting up the area like a football stadium.

There was no gate around the facility. Not that they needed one, when there was an electrified fence and wide buffer of trees between the entire town and the outside world.

She walked through the parking lot. There were plenty of spots, which would've been a dream in LA or NYC. Along the side of the facility she noticed bicycle storage racks and a dumpster.

Getting closer to the guard and cameras posted at the main entrance, she tilted her head slightly down, in a casual way but not so much that it would appear suspicious.

She passed one row of parking about three hundred feet from the door.

Still no distraction from Gage. She wondered how he was supposed to time his diversion without having a visual of her approaching the entrance, but she had confidence in his plan. As long as she followed his instructions and didn't walk too fast, his timing would work.

Crossing the last of the parking spots, she was two hundred feet from the building. The pavement between her, the cameras and the front door shrank with each step she took.

One hundred fifty feet.

She sauntered at an easy pace as her palms grew clammy and her stomach rolled.

One hundred feet.

The thick rubber soles of her ankle boots were quiet. The air was crisp, cool. There was barely a breeze.

Fifty feet.

Twenty.

A loud pop shattered the night. The sound had come from the east side of the building. If she hadn't known better, she would've thought it was gunfire.

She hurried through the front door. Once inside the atrium that featured a large skylight, she hesitated.

Most lobbies were designed with aesthetics and convenience in mind. This one was the opposite. Security had been the primary concern. A physical wall separated the vestibule from the secured portion of the building. Within the wall were two full-body turnstiles that controlled access to the facility.

Kudlow had described it in detail, but hearing about it and seeing it were two different things.

Hope kicked her brain into gear. She dared to wave at the guard posted at the desk. "There's something going on outside," she said, holding up Kudlow's badge to the card reader.

Another bang echoed. The guard shifted in his seat as if trying to pinpoint the direction of the noise and stood.

The light on the turnstile reader stayed red. Her heart lurched.

Why didn't it work?

If Kudlow had gotten loose or someone had found him early, he would've warned the folks at Nexcellogen. His badge wouldn't have simply been deactivated. Guards would be waiting to apprehend her and Gage.

Bang.

Bang.

Hope's throat grew dry as sandpaper. Staring at the bar code facing her, she flipped the badge to the other side. Tried again.

The security light winked green and beeped. Hope exhaled in relief, pushing through the turnstile. "Walking through the parking lot it sounded pretty loud and scary," she said to the guard.

"It's probably just some kids messing around. Bored teenagers." The guard came around the desk and made his way toward the turnstile. "I'll go check it out. Scare them off."

As they passed each other, Hope lowered her head, pretending to search for something inside her messenger bag.

The guard stepped up to the turnstile with his badge in hand. A second later, the card reader beeped, and he pushed through into the vestibule and went outside.

Cautious to keep her head angled away from the cameras, she bypassed the elevators and took the corridor that led to security. She used her hair and the bill of the cap to shield her face.

She spotted the door to the east stairwell first, then the restroom, which was next to the security office. It was unisex, single occupancy. *Perfect.* The one detail that Gage hadn't grilled Kudlow about had been the type of bathrooms.

Hope tried the knob.

The door was locked.

Her heart skipped.

"Be out in a second," the guy inside the bathroom said.

Hope shuffled backward, shifting a glance down either end of the hall. It wasn't as if she could stand there and wait. She turned and ducked into the stairwell, shoving the door closed behind her.

Pressing her back against the wall, she looked through the glass panel in the top of the door and waited.

The bathroom door opened. She ducked down a second to give the man time to pass.

Once she thought it was clear, she got up, inching her way along the wall, and peeked through the small window.

The guard entered the security office, but the door didn't close. Another man came out and stood on the threshold, holding a bottle of rum.

His dark hair was coiffed. Black pants. White shirt. Red sports coat with Nexcellogen Head of Security printed across the chest.

Hope had met him briefly in the clinic. Ian McCallister.

"Leave the camera in Ms. Lansing's office disabled," Ian said.

"I have no interest in spying on you two," the guy replied. "Why don't you go to her place or take her to yours?"

"She prefers discretion, and I'm a gentleman. The residential area is like living in a fishbowl. She doesn't want anyone to see me coming and going from her house or vice versa. Besides, she ordered an extremely comfortable sofa for her office."

"I understand. Gossip spreads fast around here. A lit match through dry brush."

"Tell me about it." Ian chuckled. "I'm going to head up."

Up?

Her heart drummed in her chest. What if he planned to take the stairs instead of the elevator?

Hope raced up the stairwell on the balls of her feet. The messenger bag, hanging from her shoulder, flapped against her hip. She held it to her stomach to keep the bag from making noise.

On the second floor, she pressed the badge to the card reader. The light didn't change, and the handle wouldn't turn.

Damn it.

She recalled Paul saying that the two upper floors contained the labs. But a person could only access a floor or lab if they worked there. The only badges that opened every door were Michelle Lansing's and the security guards'.

Hope bolted up the next flight of stairs.

The door creaked open on the bottom floor. "Yeah, okay," Ian said. "Don't leave any beer cans in there this time."

At the top landing, Hope put the badge to the card reader. The light flashed green. No beep. *Thank God.* She eased the door open, slipped into the hall and gently pulled it closed.

Lansing's office was also on the top floor. Ian would be up there in no time.

Hope looked around and spotted the elevator on the right. Michelle Lansing's office was down that end of the hall. According to Paul, the lab he'd worked in with Faith was on the other side closer to the break room, which was across from a conference room.

Six labs were on the third floor. The one she needed to hide in should be two doors down on the left.

Turning, Hope took off.

There were no lights on in any of the labs. This section of the hall appeared deserted. She found the room, the only one her badge would open.

A light tap to the scanner. The door slid open with the softest whisper that shrieked of money. She ducked inside and shuffled backward, deeper into the room.

The lab took up six to seven hundred square feet of space. Like the others she'd passed, it had an open plan and floor-to-ceiling windows treated with privacy screening to provide natural daylight and to prevent the scientists from going stir-crazy. Every wall was transparent. Most likely to enhance collaboration, sustainability and safety.

Perhaps the glass walls were the reason some scientists worked late. To have privacy. To plot. To produce illegal drugs.

But this lab had been Faith's, where she'd spent countless hours, working side by side with Paul Kudlow and Neal Underhill, surrounded by traitors and a murderer.

Hope wandered through the room—glancing at computers, microscopes, petri dishes, a centrifuge, test tubes, pipettes, forceps—wondering which workstation had been her sister's.

All Faith's bread crumbs had led Hope here.

Emotion clogged her throat as she spotted a gift that she'd given Faith for her thirtieth birthday.

Newton's cradle. Such a cliché thing to give a scientist, but Faith had claimed to adore it. Hope drifted closer to the desk and ran her fingers across the upper bar of the toy.

The contraption was simple. Five small silver balls hung in a perfectly straight line, just barely touching one another, suspended by thin wires that connected them to two parallel horizontal bars attached to a base. When a ball on one end of the cradle was pulled from the others and released, it struck the next ball with a click, but instead of the four remaining balls swinging, only the ball on the opposite end of the row was thrown into the air. Then the metal ball swung back to strike the others, causing a chain reaction again in reverse.

Despite its simple design, Faith thought the gift had been perfect. To her, it represented the most fundamental laws of physics and mechanics.

A conservation of energy, momentum and friction.

Hope sat down and pulled one ball on the end of the cradle and let it go.

Watching it in action after so much had happened, it was easy to see that same principle reenacted in life.

Faith had been the first ball to be pulled, colliding with the others. Hope had been the second. Gage the third. A serious of chain reactions. Energy, momentum and friction carried on.

But what or who would be the next ball to strike back?

GAGE RELEASED THE last firecracker on the east side of the building in a blind spot of the cameras.

Knowing the security guard would come from the south, where the entrance was located, he raced to the north side. Just as he rounded the corner and peeked back, he caught sight of the guard coming around the bend.

Gage sprinted along the north wall and down the west side, passing a dumpster and bike rack.

To be sure the guard hadn't simply doubled back without further investigation after discovering no one, Gage sneaked a glance.

The entrance was all clear. He dashed for the front door.

Inside, he glossed over the atrium while catching his breath and went to the turnstile. *Centurion* was printed on the top of the security pad. Just as he was about to put Faith's badge up to the scanner, he stopped.

Deactivation was a possibility he'd considered, and he

had a Band-Aid solution in that event. But what if using the badge triggered an alarm?

Or worse, a silent alarm that he wouldn't be aware of until it was too late.

Then it would be game over. With Hope trapped inside.

That was unacceptable. He spun on his heel and pushed through the front door outside.

The security guard was already headed back to the entrance.

Gage strategized his options like in a game of blitz chess. Less than ten seconds to make his next move. He lowered his head and beckoned to the guard with a hand. "I was looking for you. Some kids are spraying graffiti on the other side of the building," he said, deepening his voice with a slight Southern twang and looking toward the west side, away from the man. "Come on. If we hurry, you can catch them."

The guard swore and took off, running past Gage, determined to catch those troublemakers.

Gage was right behind.

After they turned the corner, the guard stumbled to halt beside the dumpster and stared. No doubt perplexed.

Gage swept up behind him and locked his right forearm around the guard's neck in a chokehold. They were roughly the same size, but the man's neck was thick, and he was putting up a struggle. Fortunately, the element of surprise helped, and the guy was panicking instead of thinking, which was always a mistake. Gage tightened the hold with all the strength he had, pinching the man's neck in the crook of his elbow until the guard's body went limp, rendered unconscious.

Not slowing for a beat, Gage checked his surroundings. Then he wrapped duct tape around the man's wrists, ankles and over his mouth. He removed the guard's ID badge, pocketed his Taser and opened the lid of the dumpster. Hauling the body up and tossing the man inside left Gage huffing and puffing, but he made speedy work of it.

He flipped the lid down and strolled to the entrance, winded. Another check of the area and he was confident no one had seen him.

Once he cleared the turnstile in the lobby, he activated the scrambler and hustled down to the restroom next to security. Three light raps of his knuckle on the door and he waited, listened.

Nothing.

Gage tried the knob and opened the door. The bathroom was empty.

Hope, where are you?

Gage reached into the messenger bag for his ski mask and pulled on one made of a breathable polyester fiber that covered his face, save for the band of his eyes.

Leaving the bathroom, he darted a couple of feet down the corridor. On the wall beside the door to the security office was a card reader—one presumably only a guard could access.

Kudlow hadn't mentioned that.

Not that it mattered, since Gage was wearing the badge that belonged to the front guard. He put the ID to the scanner, opened the security room door and swept inside with the Taser in his other hand, low by his side.

The security guard was glued to a paperback, holding a beer and oblivious to the monitors.

Gage recognized him.

Sylvester Faliveno. Laid-back and not the sort to make a fuss.

Probably no need to tase him.

Chuckling at something on the page, Sylvester glanced up from the book. "What's up—"

"Get down on your knees, facing the wall, hands behind your head and I won't hurt you," Gage said in the same fake voice he'd used outside.

With a placid expression, Sylvester closed the book, set his beer down and complied.

Gage trussed him up and sealed his mouth with duct tape. To make things easier on them both, he put Sylvester down on his side, still facing the wall.

Spinning one of the stools on its wheels, Gage sat in front of the large monitor with six rotating screenshots from every camera. Two minutes for them to cycle through all the surveillance feeds: exterior angles, lobby, offices, labs, conference rooms. One screen was dark, but before he investigated it, he found Hope. She was upstairs in Faith's lab, sitting at a desk.

He had no idea what had possessed her to deviate from the plan.

But she was safe.

Gage scooted the stool a foot to the side and turned ninety degrees to face the other computer that was already logged in. He glanced at the icons on the screen. Grabbing the mouse, he double-tapped on the app labeled Centurion.

Sure enough, it was the entry and exit records.

Time to check the log on the night Faith was murdered.

Chapter Eighteen

Hope stared at Faith's computer, listening to the click of the metal balls from Newton's cradle.

During her sister's last days, Faith had taken the risk of copying clinical tests and reports. Hours of documents saved to the concealed thumb drive. Gage had insisted the information must be important. There had been a reason Faith had copied them.

But none of the bread crumbs had spelled out why.

The single word repeated in her head slowly to the rhythm of the clicking. *Why...why...why?* Like a prayer begging for an answer.

Hope stilled the metal balls in the device, and in the silence, it came to her, loud and clear as a clap of thunder.

She realized how Faith had planned to use the data.

"Faith?" The smooth female voice was like an electric shock jolting through Hope.

She looked up, her heart throbbing in her throat.

An attractive woman with soft white hair that framed a face that looked fortysomething stood in the lab holding an ice bucket with a plastic liner. In the moonlight coming in through the windows, her narrowed eyes shone blue. She wore dark slacks, tailored with a meticulously pressed crease, and a light blue silk blouse. There was an unmistakable air of authority to her.

Hope recognized the woman from Gage's description.

She was Michelle Lansing.

The woman drew closer. "Who are you?"

"I'm Hope." She rose and edged back from the desk. "Faith's sister."

"For a moment, I didn't know what to think. Maybe I was seeing a ghost. I was going to get ice from the break room."

Michelle sat the bucket down on a table and stepped deeper into the space with bare feet. "And I saw you." She shook her head. "You look so much like her. *Faith*." Michelle's face changed as if she were waking from a dream. The surprise knitting her brow lifted, the lines of confusion across her forehead smoothed. Her bewildered gaze turned to a sword-sharp stare, but her voice softened. "I heard you were at the clinic the other day, dear."

Michelle eased toward the desk.

Hope backed away, skirting around the other side of the workstation in the opposite direction, keeping her eyes on the woman.

"How did you get into the building?" Michelle's gaze flickered down to the computer, as though she were checking to make sure it hadn't been accessed, and then bounced back up. "What are you doing here?"

"I'm here to find out who murdered my sister," Hope said, lifting the flap of the messenger bag and stepping back in the direction of the door. "So she can finally rest."

"Murder?" Michelle recoiled. "I'm sorry, dear, but Faith took her own life. It's horrible, terrible, I know, but I saw her body myself."

"I don't care what you saw. What I know is that Faith was happy and in love and not rebounding from a breakup or whatever story you all have been spreading."

"Why on earth would anyone want to harm her?" Michelle stepped forward. "She was a lovely person. Bright and warm. Everyone who knew her liked her."

Hope pulled the gun from the bag and aimed.

Michelle stopped walking, but she didn't flinch. Didn't even blink.

"Her project was the *shining star* for Nexcellogen," Hope said. "But if it continued to fail, the company was going to give up on the research and pull out of Benediction."

Michelle stiffened. "How do you know that?"

"It's true, isn't it?"

"It *was* true, but that's no longer relevant," Michelle said, her voice gentle yet firm, her composure unflappable. "We've had a breakthrough and we're staying. If only Faith could've held on long enough to see it, maybe things would've turned out differently."

"Nothing has changed," Hope said. "Your clinical trials are still failures, and I think you know that."

"Dear—"

"Think carefully before you speak. Because if you lie to me about this, then I won't believe you when you try to convince me you didn't murder my sister." Hope slid the safety off and put her finger on the trigger. "You know the report Neal Underhill gave you is fraudulent, don't you?"

"The trials aren't failures. They simply haven't been a complete success. And yes, I'm aware the data was made to look more promising than it is."

"How could you go along with falsifying data?"

"Our contract with the government is worth billions. Once we're able to inoculate soldiers against PTSD, the civilian applications will be endless. This project is too important and lucrative to have it scrapped when we're this close."

"That's why you killed her?" Hope asked. "Over money?"

"I admit, dear, there's no way I would've made it this far without being a cutthroat in business, but I am not a murderer. Your sister had a choice. She could either play the game or be transferred back to Herndon and Neal would replace her. I'm a civilized woman. The only weapon I use is negotiation."

"Faith would've rejected going along with your scheme outright. There's no way she'd let you pass off false data."

"Your sister was considering my offer, which would've come with a nice bonus and excellent terms that would've allowed her stay in Benediction the way she wanted."

Was that possible, that Faith had contemplated this deal with the devil?

It would've given her what she wanted. To stay in Benediction, close to Ryan. To continue on the project, committed to helping soldiers. To work. Even if she had quit and stayed in Goode, her career as a scientist would've been over. The best she could've gotten in this area was a job as a high school science teacher. Provided there was an opening.

"She was supposed to give me her answer sometime after the Thanksgiving break," Michelle said. "That's when she must've gotten her heart broken and went into a tailspin of depression."

No, that's when something happened to make her connect Zion to the drug in her lab. She must've confronted Paul and Neal, and Faith must've drawn a line in the sand.

Hope shook her head. "After the Thanksgiving break, Faith did make a decision, but it wasn't to play your game or to go to Herndon."

Michelle's gaze shifted over Hope's shoulder.

Hope pivoted as she redirected the gun.

Ian entered the lab, blocking the door. "Michelle, are you all right?"

"I'm fine, but this young woman is crazy," Michelle said.

"Move over there—" Hope gestured to Ian "—away from the door." Hope and Ian both turned in a half circle, so that Hope was closer to the door and facing them. "The annual report you submitted to headquarters is as bogus as my sister's death certificate. I have the evidence to prove your data is falsified." That's why Faith made a copy. To serve as proof. "I'm going to do what Faith would've wanted. What she would've done if she was still alive. I'm going to expose the fraud going on here, but before I do, one of you is going to tell me what really happened to my sister."

Ian clenched his hands.

That's when Hope heard it, the creak of leather. Then she saw it. He'd put on gloves before he came into the lab.

Ian grabbed the ice bucket from the table and lunged.

Faster than a blink. He swung. The hard plastic collided with Hope's hand, knocking the gun loose.

The weapon clattered to the floor.

Michelle's hand fluttered near her mouth, her eyes wide, as Ian kept swinging.

The next blow struck Hope on the shoulder and sent her spinning.

Ian dropped the bucket but kept hold of the plastic liner. In one fell swoop, he slipped the bag over her head. Ian was behind her now, tightening the plastic around her neck.

Hope gasped for air, sucking the plastic over her mouth. She scratched and clawed at his hands. Her nails scraped thick leather. Not skin.

That's why he'd worn the gloves.

"Ian!" Michelle said. "What are you doing?"

"Protecting you, as I always have." Ian jerked Hope from side to side, keeping her off balance as she struggled to breathe. "You want to know what happened to Faith. I'll tell you. I happened. I killed her just like this and then dumped her in her car."

Michelle reeled back. "Ian, let her go."

"I can't. For you, I have to kill her. That's what I do, sweetheart. I watch, I listen, I do whatever is necessary to protect you."

Hope fought against her instinct to scratch at her throat to get the bag off. His hold was too tight. Too absolute. She clawed at the plastic over her face instead. Punctured a hole in it near her mouth. Gasped for air.

She shredded the plastic covering and widened the hole with her fingers and breathed.

"Why?" Michelle asked, clutching her chest. "Why kill Faith?"

"Because she fought with Neal and Paul and wanted to send the true results to headquarters, your deal with her be damned. Faith didn't care about the repercussions to anyone else. She was selfish. Shortsighted. She needed to go. Just like her sister."

Hope reached out to grab something. Desperate for anything that might help her. She desperately sucked in gulps of oxygen through her mouth. Her nose was still covered by the bag.

"With Faith, I didn't have this problem, because I used a tear-proof trash bag." Ian tightened the remnants of the bag around Hope's throat to strangle her.

Her windpipe closed, sealing off her airway.

THE ENTRY AND exit logs didn't lie.

Gage looked over everyone who'd been working the night Faith died. Neal Underhill, Michelle Lansing and four of the other nine team leaders had been in the building during the time of her death.

But one thing stuck out.

Ian McCallister had exited the building at five but swiped back in at seven thirty. He was gone during the window when Faith had been killed, sometime between seven and eight. Thirty minutes was plenty of time to commit the murder and get back in the building.

Looking farther down the log, Gage noticed that Ian had left Nexcellogen again later at nine, right after Michelle Lansing. Mostly likely in response to the call notifying them about Faith.

But what was he doing for two hours between five and seven, and why did he kill Faith at all?

He needed to tell Hope.

Gage turned, glancing at the monitor with the surveillance feeds. He waited for the screens to cycle through, to be sure she wasn't on her way down. Still, one camera was out and the screen black.

Finally, the lab that Hope was in popped up on the monitor. Gage's heart plummeted, and he bolted out of the office.

HOPE CLUTCHED AT Ian's hand, struggling to pry his fingers loose. Spots danced in front of her eyes as he jerked her from side to side.

"My God." Michelle shuffled backward. "How could you, Ian?"

"I got Doc hammered at the bar. Bought lots of rounds, knowing that lush couldn't resist. Planted the seeds about Faith's depression and a breakup. In a bar, nobody cares about the truth, but they all love a good story. I whispered to the MPs, even you, Michelle, that it must've been suicide. Poor brokenhearted Faith took her life. You all agreed, regurgitated it back to Doc. That boozer believed it, signed the certificate. None the wiser I was playing him like a fiddle."

Hope reached out with her right hand. Groped the table for something heavy, sharp.

"Oh, Ian. Please, let her go!"

"I'm doing this for you. For us. In Benediction, we found everything we've both wanted. A second chance at love. Greatness," he said, panting. "We run this town, you and I. Together. You did say reigning in hell is better than serving in heaven."

Hope knocked over test tubes. Glass shattered.

Ian danced her body away from the desk.

She kicked backward. Her heel struck bone. Ian grunted in pain and stumbled, sending their weight skittering, and her hip slammed into another table.

"I never wanted you to kill anyone," Michelle said. "You have to stop, do you understand? Let her go!"

Pressure built in Hope's chest, too familiar, too painful. Breath backed up in her lungs. Her legs grew rubbery. She swept her hand over the table. Frantic. Out of air. Choking.

"No, sweetheart," Ian said. "We're too close now to stop. The annual report has been filed. This empire is ours. Just one more loose end and everything will go back to normal. Then you'll thank me."

It was so hard for Hope to hang on. To fight. Darkness clouded her vision. Her fingers closed around a piece of cold steel. Forceps. She jabbed the sharp, pointed end backward into Ian's leg.

Ian howled, but he held on to her.

She stabbed him again and again.

His hands opened, and he shoved her away as he cursed and screamed. Coughing and gasping, Hope tore off the plastic bag and moved, needing distance from Ian.

The door opened. Gage stormed into the lab like a madman, wearing a black mask over his face. At the same time, Ian dived for the floor. Toward something that glinted in the moonlight.

The gun.

Gage charged, tackling him.

The two men rolled on the floor, fighting over the gun for a long, terrifying moment that twisted Hope's stomach in a knot. Ian clutched the gun, the barrel pointed down between their bodies, as Gage tried to wrest it away from him.

A whisper of a bullet.

Hope froze as Michelle gasped.

Neither man moved.

Not Gage. Please, don't let it be Gage.

Chapter Nineteen

Gage waited for pain to pierce him. But it never came. For a split second, he prayed a stray bullet hadn't hit Hope.

He looked up.

Ian was on top of him. The man's eyes were open and still, his lips parted in a gasp.

Gage rolled the dead body off him to the floor, grabbed the gun and sat up.

A red spot on Ian's shirt grew as the blood from his wound spread. There was blood on Gage's lab coat and some on his sweater, but the wool was dark.

Hope rushed to his side and threw her arms around his neck, holding him. "Thank God, you're all right."

His heart squeezed. "Ditto." If they'd been alone, he would've allowed himself to feel the relief that was just out of reach, would've told her what he was thinking, feeling, but he had to keep it bottled up.

"I don't know what I would've done if I lost you," she whispered in his ear. "Like this. Because of me." She sat back on her heels and stared in his eyes. "Or if I lost you at all."

Gage wrapped an arm around her, the sentiment echoing deep inside him. The prospect of losing Hope had held him hostage from the nanosecond he'd seen the plastic bag over her head until the moment he realized that he hadn't been shot.

He wanted a day, a week, a month with her, as much time as fate would let him have to just be together without these other…distractions. To unwrap this rare gift he'd been given. To know her. Love her.

Be loved in return. If such a thing were possible for a man like him.

They climbed to their feet.

Michelle crept over to Ian, without making a sound, and looked down at him. "Why, you fool? We didn't need everything. Not when we had each other," she said low, under her breath.

"Were they in this together?" Gage asked Hope, referring to Michelle.

"I don't think she knew he killed Faith. Or maybe she didn't want to know. Easier to stick her head in the sand for plausible deniability. But Ian was responsible. He took her life." Hope looked at Michelle. "I'm going to release all the data that Faith downloaded, proving your annual report is bogus. Your headquarters and any news outlet that wants the story is going to know what you did, what your boyfriend did, and how my sister lost her life over a contract."

Michelle straightened, holding her head up high. "If you think I'm going to apologize, you're wrong."

Hope stepped closer to Michelle and slapped her in the face. The sound sliced through the room like a machete. "You're not going to reign in hell. You're going to burn in it."

A flare went off in the dark sky outside the window, soaring in a blazing arc. A second one. Then a third.

That signal meant doomsday.

Gage had given Claire the 26.5-millimeter flare gun. It resembled a snub-nosed revolver with a fat barrel. He'd told her that if there was danger, the-sky-was-falling kind of danger, to fire the flare from the woods across the street from the house three times. "We have to go. Now."

"Good luck," Michelle said, rubbing her cheek. "You won't make it to the lobby before I lock this building down."

They didn't have time for this. There was no telling what was happening beyond the walls of Nexcellogen to make Claire use the flare gun.

Gage took the Taser from his pocket, turned it on and jammed it into Michelle's side. Her eyes rolled up into the back of her head as her body shook violently. Pulling it away, he turned it off.

Michelle dropped like a sack of potatoes.

Gage grabbed Hope's hand, and they made a beeline for the stairs.

They were out of the building in less than a minute flat.

"What's going on?" Hope asked as they ran through the parking lot.

"I don't know. But those flares were for me."

"How can you be sure?"

Besides the fact that they'd been fired in the vicinity of the house and there were three in short succession, as he'd instructed in case of an emergency, he said, "I never leave Benediction without telling Claire or leaving her a note, since we don't have cell phones. She knows I'm here, somewhere. And she just used the signal I gave her."

They crossed the road and got in the truck. Both of them removed the white lab coats.

"Are we going to the house?" Hope asked.

Gage tugged the ski mask off and shoved it into his pocket. "No. In case of an emergency, the rally point is the funeral home."

RYAN SHUT OFF his headlights and pulled over on the side of the road a half a mile from Benediction's gates. He grabbed his binoculars and hopped out.

The Suburban with Joe Smith and his men had stopped at the gate. All four doors opened.

But five men climbed out the Suburban. *Five.*

One must've stayed back in the vehicle when the others had come into Ryan's office for some reason. Dwight hadn't asked Mr. Metsos how many guys got out of the helicopter and into the SUV, and Ryan had assumed it had been only the four.

The two military guards drew their weapons, but Smith

and his men attacked them. Bright flashes came from muzzles with attached sound suppressors. Both MPs dropped.

"Dear Lord," Ryan muttered.

Smith's men picked up the bodies and hauled them into the guardhouse.

They'd killed those innocent boys in cold blood when they could've wounded them or disarmed them instead.

There was no telling what they'd do if Hope came in between them and their target.

What have I done?

He crossed his fingers the call he'd made earlier would help.

PA Varma had given Ryan two phone numbers. One for Gage Graham and the other for his stepsister. Gage hadn't answered, but Claire had. Ryan had told her everything he could without mentioning Hope was in Benediction. The stepsister, Claire Ferguson Coughlin, had thanked him and promised to relay the message, right before his cell stopped working.

Ryan looked back through the binoculars.

Three flares shot up into the night sky, one right after the other, somewhere in Benediction. Near trees.

It could be a coincidence, the timing of those flares, but Ryan didn't think so. He didn't believe in coincidence.

He refocused on what was happening at the guardhouse.

The gate was now open.

Smith removed his suit jacket, threw on a bulletproof vest and got back in the vehicle along with the other men.

Not a bad idea. Ryan dumped his jacket in the trunk, trading it for a vest, and added his sheriff's star to the front.

Another peek through the binoculars.

Smith was inside Benediction.

GAGE THREW THE truck in Park beside the funeral home. Claire and Jason were standing outside by the entrance.

Worry was stamped on his stepsister's face. Jason had his hands shoved into his jacket pockets and yawned.

If Claire had set off the flares, then something awful—something awful in particular to Gage—had happened. But seeing Claire and Jason, standing, breathing, and having Hope healthy by his side were all that really mattered. The people he cared about were alive.

He'd work through the rest.

Gage and Hope made their way to them.

"Are you okay?" Claire asked, looking him over.

"Yeah, what's happened?"

"Sheriff Ryan Keller from Goode tracked you down."

Gage and Hope exchanged a glance.

"He had a message for you," Claire said. "He owed you two apologies. First, he never thanked you for saving Hope's life. For that he's sorry."

"Was that all?" Gage asked. If so, the flares were overkill. Then he remembered. Two apologies.

Claire shot him an exasperated look that told him she wasn't finished. "Four men were in his office today, led by a man called Joe Smith. They were looking for you."

"Did he say why?" Gage asked.

"Yes, and it's the reason for the second apology. He took your water glass from the diner this morning and ran your prints."

The sudden noise in Gage's head, filling his ears, the hiss and grinding whir, weren't his imagination. That was the sound of his sanctuary being flushed down the garbage disposal.

Jason snickered. "Are you a criminal, Uncle Monte? Running from the law?"

Claire shushed her son and turned back to Gage. "Ryan wanted you to know that Joe Smith knows you're here with a friend and is on his way. They might even be here already. Benediction isn't safe."

Time slowed, stood still for one perfect second. Where he could breathe and think.

Then he moved. "Come with me." He unlocked the door and led the way into the funeral home.

Jason went to turn on the light.

"No," Gage said, using a tone that discouraged questions. "I'll turn on the light in the basement." He locked the door behind them this time, not wanting anyone sneaking in and creeping up on them. Once was enough with Dr. Howland.

In the basement, Gage flicked on the lights. "Jason, go to the supply closet and grab the sledgehammer."

"But we don't have one."

"Yes. We do." Gage had purchased one in preparation just in case this day came.

Jason dashed down the hall as if he understood the urgency, even if he didn't respect the fact that Gage was at the epicenter of the situation.

Gage hustled to the desk and shoved it to the side.

Jason ran back and handed Gage the sledgehammer. "Wouldn't a gun be more useful?"

Gage withdrew the Sig from the holster at his back. "Like this? That's sort of the idea." He handed Hope the gun so it wouldn't restrict his movement. "Stand back."

Everyone shuffled a few feet away.

Gage swung the sledgehammer at the wall, punching a hole through it. Battered the spot until it was roughly twenty-five inches in diameter. Throwing the sledgehammer to the side, he reached into the hole and pulled out a duffel bag that he'd hidden there his first week in Benediction. He unzipped it, revealing the contents.

Everyone stepped forward and peered inside his go-bag.

"Oh, snap!" Jason said, staring at bundles of cash in different currencies, passports, weapons and other essentials.

Going through the gates of Benediction wasn't like crossing

the border of a foreign country, where customs searched your belongings. Besides, firearms and his other items were legal.

"I'm not a criminal," Gage said. "All I have ever done is serve my country. I can't explain why there are men coming here to find me. Or why I have to run. What I can say is that when I am put six feet under, it will be with a clear conscience. If those men survive and I don't and they question you, renounce me as family. Say you know nothing about me or where I came from."

"Oh, my God," Claire said, clutching her chest.

Gage clasped both of her arms. "Even though we didn't stay in constant touch over the years, you've been the best sister that I could ask for. You've helped me without question, and it means more to me than you'll ever know."

Claire dragged him into a hug. "I want you to be safe. I want you to be happy."

At this point, Gage was just looking to survive the night. "I love you. Since the day you called me your little brother and dared any kid in Benediction to treat me like an outsider."

Claire tightened her embrace, squeezed and let him go.

Gage dug in the bag and offered her a bundle of US dollars. Ten thousand.

"I can't accept this," she said.

Better for it to go to her than the Finley family. "My contribution to Jason's college fund." He shoved the money into her hands. She stuffed it in the inner pocket of her coat. Then he turned to his nephew. "You were right that I was hiding something I didn't want anyone to figure out. That's why I let you call me Uncle Monte. I knew this day would come, and I couldn't let you get close to me because of that. You've lost too many people you've loved. I didn't want to be one more person on that list. But you blow me away, kid, in the best way. Your brains. Your spunk. Your courage. But most of all, your big heart. Be nice to your mom and listen to her. She'd do anything for you."

For once, Jason was speechless, but he nodded.

Gage turned to Hope.

"If you try to say goodbye to me," Hope said, "I'll slap you, too."

What was it about this woman? He couldn't help but smile.

"You told me the risks," she said. "I'm willing to take them. After everything…let me help you. Let me go with you."

Gage drew a deep breath, debating, but in the end, he said, "Okay." He'd learned there was little use in fighting Hope on an issue once she'd made up her mind, and there was no time to waste arguing. Once he dealt with the immediate threat, he'd give her a chance to come to her senses. Gage looked at Claire. "Take Jason to the fire station. Stay there until this is finished." There were two full-time firefighters at the station, though one was probably out checking to see who'd fired flares. "Tell them to call the volunteers for backup and that there are violent men in Benediction. They won't let anything happen to you."

"Be careful." Tears glistened in Claire's eyes. "I love you, too, little brother."

"One last thing," Gage said. "Paul Kudlow is tied up in his house and needs to be cut loose. Along with a couple of guards at the Nexcellogen facility, in the dumpster and security room."

Claire's brow creased with concern again. "I'll have someone check on them. After." She kissed his cheek, then she wrapped an arm around Jason and hurried up the stairs.

"How can I help?" Hope asked.

"You need to understand what we'll be up against. The CIA sends operatives like me and my team after international targets. But they contract cold-blooded mercenaries for an op such as this. Going after their own people, especially on American soil. It provides a layer of distance and deniability. They're not here to capture me. They have one objective. To kill me."

"What do you want me to do?" she asked without hesitation.

Tenacity ran through this woman hot as a live wire.

"Your job will be a two for one." He passed her the one bulletproof vest that he had, and she put it on. "The first part is facilitating our exit out of Benediction."

"What's the second part?"

He hooked the sheath of his Venom knife on the back of his belt. "Well, the first will draw attention."

"Wait. Am I supposed to be bait as the second part of my job?"

"It's unavoidable. But I'm the top priority for Joe Smith or whatever his real name is, not the bait. Anyone who helps me, anyone near me out there, they'll try to use as leverage." But once they no longer had any use for her…

There was no way in hell he was going to let that happen.

He removed the sound suppressor from the Sig Sauer Hope had and screwed it onto his HK MP5K. A weapon of choice in his line of work. Extra magazines he stuffed in his pocket.

"If I use this," Hope said, glancing down at the gun in her hand, "they'll hear it."

"Not if. You *will* use it. With what I need you to do, they're going to hear it, anyway." Gage cupped her cheek, held her gaze. "I won't let anything happen to you. Follow my instructions. No deviations like earlier."

Going off script had almost gotten her killed.

"Understood," Hope said. "Tell me what to do. I'll do it."

"Remember where we entered the woods, on our way to Kudlow's?"

"Yes."

"That's the area where Claire set off the flares. The men that are mostly likely already here in Benediction will start there. Or close to that spot. We're going to go there together."

The flares were as much a signal to Gage as they were a lure for anyone hunting him. He knew those woods, every tree, every berm, every shrub, every inch. Ran through them in the day and in the dark. Walked them, too. He was outmanned and outgunned, but in war, like in business, it was the terrain that mattered.

"Why are we going toward them instead of away?" Hope asked. "We don't need to leap into a bonfire to know it's hot."

The analogy was fitting. "In that area of the woods, we took a left and ran parallel to the hiking trail to go to Kudlow's house," he said, and she nodded, listening. "I need you to go straight instead, all the way to the fence line. There's a standing unit that powers the electric fence. You're going to shoot the power source. Disable the fence and cut through it."

"With what?"

He pointed out the bolt cutters and a screwdriver in the bag. "The handle of the screwdriver is solid plastic. Use the metal part to test the fence and make sure it's down before you use the bolt cutters."

"What if I run into trouble?"

"Once again, not if. You will." He picked up the bag and slung the strap over his shoulder. "All you have to do is follow my instructions. Do you trust me?"

"I trust you with my life."

Gage stared into her eyes, fiery, determined, so beautiful. All he wanted to do was kiss her, wrap her up in his arms and hold her there forever, but there was no time. He had to act now.

He put on the ski mask to better help him blend in with the woods. Next, he grabbed his monocular night-vision headgear and unfolded the unit. It fit securely, hugging his scalp, and the high-resolution lens was positioned over one eye.

Unless the men who came for him were wearing a set of their own, they wouldn't be able to see more than ten feet away in the woods at night. No doubt they were well-trained specialists, but the probability was high that they were also a bit cocky. Four against one, thinking they had the drop on Gage and that he was completely unaware. Ego got the best of lots of men.

Guess Ryan was good for something after all.

Taking Hope's hand, he described her part in the plan as they left the funeral home. The explanation was short and simple, and when he was finished, she didn't have questions.

Outside, it was quiet, and all was still.

The calm before the storm.

They took off for the woods on foot, headed toward the section that was far from any of the houses or other buildings. This was his favorite spot to enter, where there was no danger of anyone seeing him.

The snow had almost all melted and there were only a few scattered patches to reflect the light.

Stopping at a large evergreen, he took a knee, and she dropped down beside him. He passed her the watch she'd need to keep track of time and a screwdriver with a plastic handle that she'd need later, and he stowed the duffel bag carefully and quietly under a shrub.

Hope looked to him for the signal for her to take off for the power unit.

But he held up a palm for her to wait as he scanned the woods.

Gage's father had been a hunter, or so his mother had told him. His stepfather had been one, too, and used to take him and Claire hunting beyond the gates of Benediction.

In the woods. In the mountains.

This was in his blood. He preferred hunting predators. What he wasn't fond of were his chances tonight.

So, he needed to even the odds.

Movement at his nine and eleven o'clock. Two men spaced

thirty feet apart. They were sweeping the area. In a minute, they'd pass by, headed in the direction of Gage's three o'clock.

Gage signaled her to get down low behind the shrub and to not make a peep.

The four men had probably started in the middle of the woods, estimating where the flares had been shot, and spread out in twos, going in opposite directions.

Them working in pairs made Gage's task harder. If he fired a gun, outdoors in the quiet, sure, he'd kill one, but the other man would hear it. A silencer didn't suppress all sound.

Still, this was better than an urban environment, where that team would've had an even bigger advantage on busy streets with lots of CCTV for them to tap into.

Gage slung the strap of his weapon across his body, leaving his hands free.

Once the men had passed them, Gage held up a palm to Hope, gesturing for her to stay put.

He drew his double-action knife from the sheath at his back and prowled into the woods. If he could've subdued and restrained them, quickly and quietly, then he would've. Even though those men were there to kill him, Gage did not enjoy taking a human life.

But the circumstances dictated his options.

Gage crept up behind one of the armed men, avoiding the patches of snow that would crunch underfoot. He was nearly on him when a twig snapped beneath his boot and gave him away.

The man spun, raising a HP.

Gage stepped in and drove the blade into his side, between the man's ribs, angling it upward at the heart. Moving his left hand, Gage covered the man's mouth before he had a chance to utter a sound.

The man twitched, but the strike had been fatal and there was no struggle.

Bulletproof vests weren't knife resistant. A stab-resistant

vest was made of different kind of fiber and weave. But the sides of a vest were particularly vulnerable. There were two protective panels, one in the front covering the chest, the other covering the back. Gaps along the sides ranged in degree, but they were always there.

Gage lowered the corpse to the ground.

Then he went after the second man, who had altered his course, drawing closer. Gage moved toward the man, head-on. But once the distance between them hit about fifteen feet, Gage ducked behind a large oak. Pressed his back to the trunk. Breathed. Waited. Judged the man's proximity by the subtle sounds the guy made.

The adrenaline moving through his veins quickened.

Branches moved close by. Footsteps through the underbrush shifted from Gage's left to right.

Hold.

Hold.

Gage forced himself not to rush it. To hold still as he coiled with readiness. The knife was tight in his grip.

The man came up alongside the tree.

Gage spun out to face the operative. He knocked the barrel of the assault weapon up with his forearm as he drove the blade of his knife into the man's throat with his other hand, cutting off the yell before it was voiced.

The mercenary gurgled. Clutched at his throat as he fell, dying before he hit the ground.

Gage sheathed his knife and raced back to Hope.

"You got them both?" she whispered.

"Two down. Two to go."

"That was fast, and the way you took out the first guy was…so brutal. And you did that to two of them," she said with an air of awe.

No one had ever him seen him work before—his team didn't count—and it surprised him to hear her sound impressed. "I thought you would've been, I don't know, shocked, horrified."

"That monster Ian shocked and horrified me. You never could."

If he wasn't wearing a ski mask, he would've taken ten seconds and kissed her.

"We're not in the clear yet," Gage said. "Let's go."

Grabbing the bag, he guided her through the woods to the spot where they needed to separate. He checked the path ahead that led to the fence for her, using the NVG monocular. No movement in that direction.

"You're good," he said. "Five minutes. Then you know what to do."

She flicked a glance at the watch on her wrist and nodded.

He handed her the bag. "Sorry that it's heavier than it looks."

Hope held the bag with both hands. "I'll manage." She took off toward the fence in a crouch.

Gage had five minutes to find the next man and eliminate him from the playing field.

He combed through the woods, skulking forward, sweeping 180 degrees.

The other two men would come his way. It was possible that they were both closer to the fence, but they'd want to search near the tree line adjacent to the houses, too.

His internal clock told him the minutes were flying by. At least two, if not more, were already gone. He had to get at least one more before Hope started her part, because his plan wouldn't work if he had to take on two at once.

Gage picked up his pace, keeping his body low. An instant later, he spotted one.

The man stumbled over something but quickly regained his balance.

Gage went all the way to the perimeter, passed the guy and doubled back around to come up behind him.

Time was almost up. Maybe a minute left. He'd have to risk firing his weapon.

Dropping to a knee, Gage slid the weapon off his shoulder, steadied his breathing and raised his MP5K. He lined up the sights through his NVG. A head shot would be quick. Clean. He put his finger on the trigger. Waited for the man to walk around a tree. Back in his sights.

On an exhale, he fired, and the man dropped.

One left.

Chapter Twenty

As Hope had run for the fence, the bulletproof vest had grown heavier, and the bag in her hands weighed her down. Once she'd reached the tree line, saw the fence and the power unit, Goode Lake black and ominous beyond it, she'd dropped by a shrub and caught her breath.

Five minutes passed in a flash.

Time was up. Hope prayed that Gage had had long enough to take out another man.

Standing up from her hiding position, she aimed the gun at the power unit, dead center. She'd never fired a gun before, but she was so close it would be impossible to miss.

To be certain she fried the unit, she pulled the trigger twice.

The unit exploded in a thunderous boom, shooting sparks and sizzling. A plume of smoke wafted into the air.

No wonder everyone was about to make a beeline to her position.

Hope hadn't noticed the hum the power unit had been making until it had stopped.

She lugged the duffel bag over to the fence and dropped it. Panting, she dived into the bag and found the screwdriver. She touched the metal part to the chain link while holding the thick plastic handle.

There was no electric arc or sparks, but she ran the screwdriver back and forth across the fence for a few seconds.

Still, nothing.

Next was the part she was dreading. She had to set the screwdriver and gun down since she needed both hands to use the bolt cutter. Unarmed, with her back to the trees.

The vulnerability and the exposure made her skin prickle.

Holding the bolt cutter, she snipped links close to where

they were intertwined, going in a vertical line from the bottom up. Each strand gave way with an audible snap.

Her spine tingled with the creepy sensation of being watched. But she stopped herself from turning around.

She'd cut three feet high when someone pressed the muzzle of a gun to the back of her head.

GAGE DASHED THROUGH the woods, cutting toward the fence and the promise of a collision with the enemy.

Through the tree line he caught sight of Hope.

A man in all-black tactical gear like the others held Hope by the back of her neck with a gun pointed to her head. Their backs were to the fence, and they faced the woods. The man was waiting for him, to exploit Hope as leverage.

Just as Gage had anticipated. He walked to the tree line with his gun at the ready. Not giving the operative a clear shot, he used the trunk of an oak for cover.

"Drop your weapon and come out with your hands up," the man said. "Do it now and I'll let the woman live."

Even if Gage cooperated, did as he had been told so he could be executed, there was no guarantee that man would let Hope live. Not if the operative suspected Gage had confided in her.

There was an order out on Team Topaz because they knew something, saw something or were simply someone else's loose end. His association with Hope made her unfinished business, as well.

"All right." Gage took a step to the side from behind the tree. "Don't hurt her."

"Come closer and drop your weapon."

Hope's hands were up in the air, high, above her head, the way he'd told her.

The second the man moved the gun from her head to refocus the aim at Gage, then she could act, sending an elbow crashing back and down into the guy and dive to the ground to get out of the line of fire.

Gage edged forward, inching closer, and hoisted his weapon up in the air.

A whispered rustle in the undergrowth to the side betrayed movement.

Years of training, pure instinct had Gage ducking. He dropped and rolled. Bullets bit into bark mere inches were his head had been. More live fire. Dirt spit from the ground beside him.

Adrenaline surged, powering Gage as he raced for cover. A trajectory of gunfire tracked his every move. He scrambled behind a tree, cursing the unexpected fifth man with every ragged, dogged breath.

A fast-moving shadow darted between the trees.

Gage got a glimpse of the fifth man.

White shirt, dark slacks, vest. Must be the team leader, call sign Prime.

Where did he come from?

"Come out!" Prime said. "If you don't, my man will put a bullet in the woman. Hope Fischer. I understand you're concerned about her well-being and don't want anything to happen to her. So, you've got until the count of three."

Gage peeked out and assessed the situation.

The guy in all black had the gun pressed to Hope's skull.

If Gage came out, they'd both have a clear shot at him. He'd only be able to take out one man before the other got him. The scenario might have been different if he had also had his Sig, but it was on the ground behind Hope near the fence.

He glanced at Hope, her gaze meeting his, and the steely courage he saw in her eyes skewered him. She wasn't afraid… because she *trusted* him to get her out of this.

"One," Prime said.

Sweat gathered at the nape of Gage's neck. There was no choice. None. Only one thing he could do.

"Two."

Delayed realization kicked hard at Gage. He loved Hope. Without question, he'd sacrifice himself to protect an innocent. But the fear twisting up his legs and winding along his spine—gut-wrenching fear—was about losing Hope.

Keeping her alive was everything to him.

"Three."

"Sheriff's department, drop your gun! Let the woman go," Ryan Keller called from somewhere in the woods, not too far away.

Gage jumped out from behind the tree, aiming in Prime's direction.

Gage's first bullet smacked into a tree as Prime's line of fire barely missed him.

At the same time, the man in all black shifted Hope like a human shield in front of him, keeping his back to the fence, and fired at the sheriff.

No way Keller would get the shot.

Gage maneuvered forward, closing in on Prime's position. Squeezed off two shots. Took up a new position behind another tree.

A barrage of suppressed fire tore into the trunk, vibrating through Gage. Prime was also on the move, tightening the distance between them, as well. Peppering sound from the steady stream of bullets grew louder as the enemy grew closer.

But the man was almost out of ammo.

Off to the side, the other operative was edging away from the fence, trying to get to the woods with Hope in front of him, but she was dragging her feet, slowing him down.

Two more shots were fired at Gage. *Click. Click.* The sound came, signaling the magazine was empty. Prime would have to reload.

Gage spun around, leaving the coverage of the tree, barrel poised to fire back. But Prime tossed his assault weapon, and two hundred pounds of angry muscle charged into Gage, knocking his gun skyward from his hand and smashing his back into hard bark. Pain ratcheted through him.

Prime was on him. They exchanged kicks and punches. Prime threw a fist to Gage's solar plexus—a meshwork of nerves just below the chest.

It was ridiculously painful, knocking the wind from him in one long whoosh and dropping him to his knees. Doubled over, he blinked through the agony, struggling to regain his bearings and his breath. But another blow hammered his face.

Prime ripped off the NVG monocular and ski mask. Then he grabbed Gage by his hair and tugged back, jerking his head upward. "I want to look you in the eyes as you die." Prime reached for the sidearm on his hip.

Gage couldn't stand. Couldn't fight. He could barely breathe.

But he slipped the knife from the sheath at his back, and with one swift move, he drove the blade into Prime's femoral artery and twisted it.

Anguish exploded on the man's face. The wound was fatal. He'd bleed out within seconds, but the man wasn't dead yet. He drew the gun from the holster, and as he aimed at Gage's head, Gage withdrew the knife and jammed it right up into the portion of his lower belly that was exposed from the vest.

The man's whole body tensed. His face contorted again. The gun slipped from his hand, and he keeled over to the ground.

Gage crawled to his weapon and struggled to his feet to help Hope.

Ten yards away, the man was trying to get her from the fence and into the woods.

But Hope went deadweight, her body going slack, throwing him off balance and leaving him exposed. He tossed her to the side, throwing her into the fence, and shot at the sheriff.

Hope climbed to her hands and knees and picked up the gun. Her fist rose, clenched around the Sig. The barrel flashed, and the man spun in a 180 and hit the ground.

Sweet relief spilled through Gage.

Hope was alive. She was unharmed.

Gage rushed to her, taking her elbow and helping her stand. He pulled her close, her head coming to rest under his chin against his chest.

"Thank God you're all right," the sheriff said, running from the woods toward them.

"It's over," Hope said, holding Gage tighter. "It's over."

"Almost." Gage rubbed a hand up and down her back. "But not yet. The MPs will be here soon."

Hope looked up at him.

"I'm going to have to take you in," Ryan said, pointing the gun at Gage. "You're wanted for something. Those CIA spooks went about it the wrong way, but it doesn't change the fact that you're a fugitive."

"I am wanted." Gage nodded. "But I've committed no crime. I've done nothing wrong."

"I wish I had proof of that," Ryan said.

"Did you see me commit a crime here tonight?"

"No. I didn't."

"Then what am I charged with? Why am I wanted?"

"Those are good questions." Ryan nodded. "Your prints came back with no hits. But those men showed up."

"If you arrest me and take me into custody, it would be like putting a gun to my head and pulling the trigger yourself. The CIA doesn't want me charged. They don't want me on trial. They just want me dead."

Hope went up to Ryan, standing in front of the gun, put her hand on his raised arm and lowered it. "Everything he said is true. Arrest him and you would be killing him. Those men that showed up are proof of that."

Ryan holstered his weapon, but he didn't look convinced.

"Ian McCallister," Hope said, "the head of security at Nexcellogen, killed Faith and made it look like suicide. They were worried about losing a lucrative contract and wanted to keep her quiet."

Ryan shook his head. "About what?"

Hope took off the necklace with the cryptex pendant. "The true test results from her clinical trials. Michelle Lansing, the director here, Neal Underhill and Paul Kudlow all conspired and submitted a false annual report to headquarters. Faith was going to blow the whole thing."

The sheriff's face was a mix of relief and anguish.

Hope put the necklace in Ryan's hands. "Nineteen eight twenty-five. That's the code to open the cryptex. Inside you'll find a thumb drive with all the real data. Nineteen eight twenty-five. Lansing. Underhill. Kudlow. Repeat it."

"Nineteen eight twenty-five. Lansing. Underhill. Kudlow. But what about McCallister? I want the bastard behind bars."

"He's dead. He tried to kill me, too. But Gage stopped him. I owe him my life, again."

Ryan clenched his hands and lowered his head. "First Faith, then almost you."

"There's something else," Hope said. "Faith found out that Paul Kudlow was using the drug she was working on to synthesize Zion."

"What?" Ryan rocked back on his heels, his mouth agape.

"Paul was using someone in the sheriff's department to distribute it," Hope said.

Ryan froze. "Who?"

"Dwight Travers. Paul Kudlow admitted it."

Ryan swore and shook his head in disbelief.

"Go back to Goode," Hope said. "Arrest Dwight. Get a warrant for Kudlow's arrest. Publish the data on that thumb drive through multiple news outlets. Be sure that Nexcellogen headquarters gets a copy, and tell them that Michelle Lansing is a lying parasite."

"I will. You can count on that."

"I never would've found out the truth about who killed Faith and why if weren't for this man." Hope pointed back at Gage. "If you care about me at all, about what Faith would want for me, walk away, Ryan. Tell the MPs you don't know what happened to us."

Ryan rubbed a hand across his chin, deliberating.

"We don't have much time." Gage stepped forward. "Are you going to help us or hurt us?"

Stuffing the cryptex necklace in his pocket, Ryan looked up and said, "I already owed you two apologies. Let's not make it a third. Thank you for finding Faith's murderer. I wanted that more than anything. Justice for the woman I loved." He extended his hand. "Thanks for watching out for Hope, too."

Gage shook it. "If you could buy us ten minutes with the MPs, we'd appreciate it."

"Sure. But then what?"

"I've got that covered."

Ryan nodded and jogged off into the woods.

"Last chance," Gage said. "You can still go back to your life. If that team reported in before they came to Benediction, I'm sure they passed along your name. They'll find you, question you, but if we're no longer together, they'd think you weren't important to me. Just stick to the story that you don't know anything about me."

Hope pressed a hand to his cheek. "But I do know things about you, and I only want to know more. I think we'd be better off together than apart."

He couldn't agree more. "We have to hurry. Did you cut the fence?"

She took his hand and showed him where.

He pulled a portion of the chain link up and ushered her through to the other side. Grabbing the bag, he followed.

Gage unzipped the duffel and took out the box with the inflatable boat. He handed her the pieces for the oars so she could connect them, putting them together while he inflated the two-person boat with the quick-fill hand pump. He'd timed the inflation before and clocked it at three minutes, thirty seconds. The pump filled the boat with air on each up and down stroke, cutting the time to blow it up in half.

His body ached and his limbs were a bit fatigued, but he got the boat inflated in under four minutes. He set the boat in the water, and they climbed in.

Gage put the bag in the middle between him. Then he rowed with all his might. He pushed aside all thoughts of exhaustion, Captain Finley and the MPs headed down to the fence, Claire, Jason, Benediction. The oars dipped into the water and skimmed the surface. Picking up the pace, he powered through each stroke. He found a demanding rhythm and dug deep for strength.

Once he reached the middle of the lake, far from the shore of Benediction, he took a break and caught his breath.

"Where are we going?"

"A town on the other side." He panted. "Called Riverton. I have another car stashed."

"I meant beyond that. You said that being on the run was like flying in a tin can that could crash and burn."

Good memory, but the imagery was chilling. "I have a parachute. But using it means that wherever we land, we might have to stay for good."

"I don't understand. Will we be together?"

"Yes."

"Wherever we *land*, will it be safe?"

"Yes."

"Then use it."

Gage dug deep in the duffel bag and fished out his satellite phone. He dialed the emergency number that he knew by heart. Onetime use. The line trilled.

Someone picked up. "Parachute."

Per protocol, Gage had to give the correct response to the challenge for authentication. "Rip cord."

The person on the other line gave him a set of coordinates.

Gage repeated them in his head, committed them to memory.

"Do you have them?" The voice was Hunter Wright's.

"Yes."

"A man wearing a blue hat will meet you there. He'll ask you about the weather. You tell him you hate hurricanes. Do you understand?"

"Yes."

The line disconnected.

Gage threw the phone into the lake. The one sanctuary he'd fought to find and keep was gone. He'd pulled the rip cord on the only parachute that he'd ever have. He should've been on edge, or at the very least upset.

But sitting across from Hope, staring at her beautiful face, all he could do was smile. This extraordinary, smart, sexy woman had decided to take the plunge into the unknown with him. That made him the luckiest man on the planet.

Epilogue

Three weeks later

Hope sat beside Gage on another boat. This one was little more than a motorized dinghy.

After they'd left Virginia, a man with a blue hat had met them at a port in Wilmington, North Carolina. He'd gotten them passage on a cargo ship bound for South America. The crew had asked them no questions, and no one had requested to see their passports. They were given a cabin. The quarters were cramped, but they'd made it cozy, savoring the time to decompress and connect in more ways than one. They'd shared everything with each other, including their clean bills of health, and made love with nothing between them.

The world could be cold, dark and treacherous, but with each other they'd both found a warm place of light, where they were safe.

Before the ship had docked, a woman also wearing a blue hat picked them up, off the coast of Venezuela, in the small, motorized boat they were in now.

The sun was warm on their faces, and the water was an enchanting light green. "Like the color of your eyes," Gage had said to her.

The woman took them to a small island and let them off at a dock.

Gage climbed out first and helped Hope up. Wrapping an arm around her shoulder, he carried the duffel bag as they walked down the long dock toward a house.

"Why were you in Benediction when you could've been here in paradise?" Hope asked.

"After my team realized that the CIA wanted us dead, we knew we'd be safer apart and scattered. Together we're a bigger target and easier to find. We all had sat phones that the Agency didn't know about. Hunter told us to only call his phone if we were in a jam, something serious, with our backs up against the wall. He'd give us a parachute. But the more of us that pull that rip cord, the more dangerous paradise will become."

A man came out onto the porch and down the steps to greet them. He was around six-two, all solid muscle, and, though a straw hat covered his hair and sunglasses hid his eyes, he was handsome as sin.

Gage dropped the bag on the powdery sand, and the two men hugged like longtime friends. Like family.

"Good to see you, despite the circumstances," Gage said.

"I told you that if you ever needed me, I'd be there for you. For all of you."

Gage stepped back next to her. "Hunter Wright, this is Hope Fischer. It's a long story as to why I brought her."

Hunter extended his hand. "Welcome, Ms. Fischer."

She shook it. He had a strong, firm grip. "Please, call me Hope."

"I look forward to hearing the story. If I had to guess, it's a dramatic tale fraught with danger, probably a little gunfire, but it has a happy ending."

"You would be right," Hope said, smiling. "You must be psychic."

"When you've been doing this long enough, you have to be. Come on inside." Hunter led them up the porch and into the house. The place was light and airy. The furniture modest, but comfortable. "Take a seat." He gestured to the sofa.

A phone rang in another room.

Hunter sighed. "No rest for the weary or the wicked. Please excuse me a minute."

Hope wandered to one of the open windows and stared out at the golden beach and the calm water. "This is gorgeous."

Gage came up beside her and brought her into his arms.

He lowered his mouth to hers and kissed her softly, then deeply, tasting her until her stomach fluttered with hunger for more from just one kiss.

Pulling back, he gazed down at her and smiled.

There went those butterflies again.

Hope had lost her sister and, in her pursuit to find a murderer, she'd also found faith in another. Something precious and rare and worth fighting for.

He'd pulled a rip cord, and she'd taken the leap with him. No matter what happened in the days ahead, she'd never regret choosing Gage.

Hope tightened her arms around him and kissed him once more.

Hunter came back into the room. The smile and humor on his face were gone. "That was Zenobia. She's in trouble, too. We'll see her soon if she survives."

* * * * *

K-9 PATROL

JULIE MILLER

For all the first responders and caregivers who gave so much to help us get through 2020. Thank you.

With special thanks for my readers who helped me with my research: Jennifer Lorenz Mewes, Mary Birchwood Lawson and Danelle Koch!

And a special thank-you to the real director of the KCPD Crime Lab, Kevin Winer, who answered all my questions and sparked some ideas. I appreciate that he allowed me to take some liberties with my fictional story. Any mistakes are mine.

Chapter One

"Me?"

Criminalist Lexi Callahan pressed her lips together, just to make sure her mouth wasn't gaping open as she looked across the hallway to her boss, Mac Taylor, who ran the Kansas City Police Department Crime Laboratory. When he'd stopped her on the way to the break room near the end of her shift, she'd assumed he was asking for a favor or following up on her most recent crime scene analysis report—not that he was going to offer her a promotion.

Mac adjusted his glasses over his scarred face and smiled. "Don't sound so surprised. You've earned the job. I think Supervisor Lexi Callahan has a nice ring to it. True, you'll be stuck on the night shift sometimes, but you'd be running your own squad in the CSIU, reporting directly to Captain Stockman, sitting in on a meeting with me every now and then so I know what's going on at the front lines."

The boss of her own team. Coordinating the jobs of gathering evidence and funneling it to the seven divisions and seventy or so experts who worked on everything from digital evidence to weapons identification, from bloodstain spatter analysis to microchemistry, DNA and more.

Lexi leaned back against the steel railing that ran the length of the windows lining the long hallway and common areas that connected the individual labs and crime lab offices on the west side of the building complex to the Seventh Precinct offices of KCPD on the east. She needed to sit, and she wasn't going to make it to a chair in the memorial lounge, where she and her colleagues often met to decompress from the stresses of the day. "Dennis is okay with this?" Her current B squad supervisor might be a stellar investigator, but he had been reprimanded, fined and ordered to attend sensitivity training to break his habit of calling the women on his team *honey* and *sweetie*, and finding subtle ways to *accidentally* make unnecessary contact with them.

"Dennis doesn't get a say in this. His tenure has left morale fractured around here. He's a liability to this entire department. I can fire him if he doesn't complete the training or picks up his old habits again. Right now, I just need to get him off the front line. There are trust issues that need to be mended around here. I think you're the woman for the job."

No pressure there. Lexi inhaled a steadying breath and nodded.

"Dennis is moving over into an administrative position, opening up the squad supervisor spot sooner than we were expecting." Kick Dennis off investigative work and stick him in an office where he had less chance of offending anyone until he hit retirement in a couple of years? Probably a wise decision for both staff morale and public relations. Putting a woman in charge would no doubt also alleviate some of the concerns from the women on staff. "These days, we're all more specialized than criminalists were when I first started. But you have training in multiple specialties, so I believe that gives you a unique understanding into the challenges each member of the lab faces. There's no one I trust more to bring in what we need from a crime scene. And if you can't get these guys thinking like a team again, I don't know who can."

Lexi tucked a chin-length wave of golden-brown hair behind her ear. "I'm flattered, sir."

"Don't be flattered. Be good." His phone must have vibrated in his pocket, because he held up a finger to pause the conversation a moment while he took it out and read a text.

While Mac answered the summons, Lexi looked to her coworkers in the lounge. Chemists and toxicologists. A nearsighted nerd with crazy mad computer skills. A blood expert who'd lost his legs in a war zone and now sat in a wheelchair. He was playing chess with a man whose prematurely graying hair made him seem older than she knew him to be. There was an ogre-sized sharps expert standing off to himself who'd said maybe ten words to her outside of a case and had yet to meet a weapon he didn't recognize. The uniformed Black police sergeant who assisted Mac Taylor with administrative duties was chatting with a man who, like him, appeared to be in his midforties. The stranger looked like he could be a cop himself, although he wore a suit and tie beneath his winter coat. She'd seen him on the crime lab campus before, although she'd never met him.

She counted many of them among her friends. Other than the man who looked like a bulldog and was chatting with Sergeant King, they were all her coworkers. "I'd be in charge of them? That's a lot of different personalities to deal with. A couple of them have been here longer than I have. Won't they resent me getting the promotion ahead of them?"

"Some of them don't want the job. They're happier in the lab than out in the field. And not a one of them has your people skills." Mac pocketed his phone and continued the sales pitch. "I'm not going to lie to you—people will need time to adjust to your changing role in their world. And how you deal with certain situations could impact those relationships. But if everyone is mature about it and remembers we're a team and we're here to help KCPD solve crimes, you can still be friends. But now you're also their boss. After the issues with Dennis, my hope is that smart, trustworthy leadership will help this unit gel into a stronger team."

"You believe I can do that?"

Mac's good eye narrowed as he debated whether or not that had been a rhetorical question. "Yes."

Stuff like this didn't happen to her. Nothing much ever happened to Alexis Sedell Callahan. Not since her parents had been murdered during a carjacking her junior year of high school. Her overprotective big brother, who'd stepped up to parent her, had seen to that. Levi Callahan was a six-foot-two Marine with green eyes that matched her own. Lexi adored her brother, who, whether he was stateside or deployed across the world, seemed to find a way to keep his eye on her.

That protective streak had only increased after her college sweetheart had cheated on her shortly after moving in with her. He claimed she'd become a workaholic, with no time for his needs. She'd been holding down a full-time job and attending grad school at the time. Kevin Nelson had wanted them to work in his father's pharmaceutical company together, but she'd opted for public service at the crime lab. She'd been inspired by Mac Taylor himself, after his work at the lab had identified the meth head who had shot her parents. His scientific investigation had helped get the killer sent to prison so he couldn't hurt any more families the way he'd destroyed hers.

Now *she* was the one helping the police, uncovering and

analyzing clues, solidifying cases so KCPD could make arrests and the DA could prosecute the perps and make Kansas City safer. If it were in her power, no one else would suffer the kind of loss she and her brother, Levi, had and not find justice.

The crime lab was where she needed to be, where she wanted to be.

If she could make it even better by taking charge of a small part of it, then she'd do that, too.

She waited until Mac had finished the texting that was making him smile before continuing the conversation. "I thought you were calling me in to ask me to cover someone's shift over the Thanksgiving holiday this week. I know you always have a big, multigenerational family deal, and I'm…alone…this year, so I'm available. I didn't realize the board had finished interviewing the candidates and made their decision so quickly."

"Dennis's actions sped the process."

No doubt. She'd been one of the women who'd filed a grievance against her supervisor. "The science and administrative duties I can handle. It's the team management I have to consider. I thought the interview was more of a learning exercise, building experience for me."

"Then you shouldn't have killed it."

"Well, I didn't mean to do such a good job." Maybe she shouldn't be making sarcastic jokes with the boss. "I mean, thank you, sir."

He chuckled and slipped his fingers through his graying blond hair. "Your brother's still deployed?"

Lexi nodded. "He's based in Afghanistan right now. He gets leave over Christmas. We're going to celebrate all the holidays then. As the newest squad leader, will I be on call over Christmas?"

Mac seemed to understand that she had several things

to consider before giving him a firm answer. "You've got a couple of days to think it over. I'll make sure you get time off at Christmas while your brother is home. But I'd like your first shift as squad supervisor to start on the twenty-seventh."

"Thanksgiving Day," she confirmed.

"That gives you two days to decide."

Lexi pushed herself off the railing. "Thank you for the opportunity, sir. I'll let you know ASAP."

Mac nodded. Then he held up his phone and smiled. Although he was blind in one eye, following an explosion in the city's first crime lab, his good eye sparkled as he mentioned his family. "My wife has informed me that our daughter's basketball tournament is about to tip off, and I am not there. I'd better obey the boss and get over to the high school."

Lexi chuckled. She'd had the pleasure of meeting Mac's wife, Julia, at a few work functions, and her impression of the experienced trauma nurse was that she was a gentle, kind soul who was anything but bossy. And it was clear Mac adored her. Lexi ignored the pang of longing that tried to take hold inside her. After she'd dumped Kevin, and her brother had stepped up to screen out anyone he didn't deem good enough for his little sister, it looked like her hope for finding a similar forever relationship of her own would be taking a back seat to her career indefinitely. Good thing she loved what she was doing and didn't need a man to make her happy. Although, that lonely space around her heart wasn't above wanting someone special in her life in addition to a successful, meaningful career.

Suspecting this conversation had already gone on longer than Mac had intended, Lexi sent him on his way. He didn't need to stand here and wait while she deliberated the pros and cons of accepting this promotion right now. "You'd better get out of here, then. Tell Jules hi."

"Will do." He inclined his head toward the break room. "You'd better check in with your entourage. I think they're curious about what we're discussing out here."

Lexi turned to see several of her coworkers' conversations had stopped and they were looking toward the hallway where she and Mac stood. Although most of them quickly glanced away and feigned a sudden interest in coffee mugs, snacks and whoever was standing or sitting closest to them, she hadn't missed their inquisitive looks. With an embarrassed sigh and a shake of her head, she glanced up at Mac. "Sorry about that."

"Don't be. The only place news travels faster than around the Seventh Precinct/Crime Lab is between my mom and mother-in-law." He arched a golden brow above the rim of his glasses. "Good luck if you're heading in there."

"They probably want to know if anyone else is getting transferred or fired. I'll stop the rumor mill before it starts. Good night, sir."

"Good night, Lexi." He pointed a finger at her, even as he was backing toward his office to grab his winter coat and lock up. "Two days and I'll need that decision."

Two days to change the status quo of her utterly predictable life and take on the burden of safe, trustworthy leadership for all those worried souls in the break room and beyond. Right. No pressure at all.

Lexi exhaled a deep breath before she strolled to the lounge. Jackson Dobbs, who looked more like a defensive lineman for the Kansas City Chiefs than the sharps and ballistics expert he was, filled the doorway. He stepped back as though he'd been ready to leave but hadn't wanted to pass by and interrupt her conversation with their boss.

Lexi moved past him to find her coworkers all staring at her again. "You guys saw me talking to Mac? It's not what you think. No one's getting fired."

"Well, duh." Chelsea O'Brien pushed her glasses up onto the bridge of her freckled nose. "Okay, yes, that's what we were thinking at first. At least, I was. But then, Jackson was standing right by the door, so he heard the actual words and was eavesdropping for us." She paused for a breath. "Now we know. You're taking the job, right?"

Jackson Dobbs, the man who gave *stoic* its definition in the dictionary, had been relaying gossip? She tilted her gaze up to the icy gray eyes of the man who towered above her. "*You* were spying on me?"

He shrugged.

Chelsea got up from the tall table where she'd been working on her laptop and pointed to the hallway just outside the lounge. "You were right there. And, you know, Jackson doesn't miss much."

Khari Thomas's long ebony braids stirred across her shoulders as she adjusted her white lab coat over her pregnant belly. "We made him do it." She crossed the lounge to elbow Jackson's arm and take the sting out of her words. "Although, he was annoyingly short on details. One word. One stinkin' word. *Promotion.* We filled in the rest. Congratulations, Lexi. I'm going to like working for a woman for a change. Especially after Dennis." She cupped her extended belly with both hands. "You'd think with him having a new fiancée, and me carrying this basketball, he'd stop looking at my butt."

Lexi swept her gaze around the room. "You guys all know?"

Grayson Malone spun his wheelchair away from the chess game to face her. "We're some of the smartest people on the planet." The veteran Marine scratched at the dark blond stubble blanketing his angular jawline. "We know Hunt is on his way out. It's not that tricky a mystery to solve. Take the job."

Ethan Wynn was a handsome man despite his prematurely graying hair. Since the two of them had gone through orientation at the same time and worked the CSIU together ever since, she didn't mind when he pulled her in for a quick hug. "Congrats, Lexi. Well deserved."

She smiled up into his brown eyes as she pulled away. "Thanks, Ethan. I know you interviewed for the promotion, too. I'm sure you'll be offered the next spot that opens up."

He shrugged off the compliment. "It's a sensitive time for the lab. I can see why a woman is the smart choice for the job right now. Besides, *you'll* get to deal with the transition hiccups and spike in crimes over the holidays, not me." He winked and grinned before turning back to the table and moving his bishop across the chessboard. "I'm holding out for Taylor's position, anyway. The guy's gotta retire one of these days, doesn't he?"

Not anytime soon, she hoped. She couldn't imagine a better mentor teaching her the ropes if she did agree to the supervisory position.

Lexi opened the insulated mug she'd carried into the break room and went to refill it for the drive home. But the pot was empty. Not one to leave a job unfinished, she opened the machine to dump the used grounds and refill it with fresh beans from the cabinet above her. Not only would the next shift be looking for coffee when they reported for work in about twenty minutes, but she needed the jolt to the brain to help organize all the thoughts running through her head. Once the pot started to fill with the fresh, fragrant brew, she turned to face her friends again. "You all think you can take orders from me?"

Gray moved his king to a safe position on the board. "Are you going to be more like my mother or my drill sergeant?"

Chelsea ran over and linked their elbows, standing shoulder to shoulder with her. "She's going to be like Lexi. The team's going to stick together and it's all going to be fine." Today, Chelsea's hazel eyes were circled by tiny turkeys dancing around the frames of her orange glasses. "Seriously, I thought Mac might be transferring you to a different shift. Breaking up the team."

"I haven't taken the job yet."

Shane Duvall, whose narrow black glasses were more "nerdy professor" than Chelsea's seasonal eyewear, fit the stereotype of a scientist and lab technician better than any of them. Supremely logical, he'd probably already created a pros and cons list inside his head. "Why not? I don't see any downside to you running the show. I appreciated your help with the chemical analysis on the Norwell case. And your suggestion that I submit the formula to the state fire office to add to their database, as well, was spot-on. That sort of interdepartmental teamwork will only continue with you at the helm."

"You guys." She looked from face to face, overwhelmed by their show of support. Of course, this was the grace period. The first time she had to reprimand one of them or stick them with an assignment he or she didn't like, they might rethink their friendship with her. "We have different strengths, work in different departments. And we've been on the same level for a long time. It's going to change the dynamic between us."

Jackson finally spoke from his position at the door. "Why?"

"Jackson's right." Gray seemed to speak a code with the big guy, understanding far more than the words Jackson actually said. "With the exception of one divisive clunker who's tried to undermine several of us, the KCPD Crime Lab is a well-oiled machine. We do good work. Shifting our job assignments a little shouldn't alter that. You pretty much keep us organized and on task already. Now you're getting the pay grade to match."

Rufus King came up on the other side of Lexi and touched her shoulder to get her attention. Then he extended his hand to shake hers. "About time they recognized your talent, Ms. Callahan. Congratulations."

"I haven't said yes yet."

"Robert Buckner." Rufus's friend extended his hand, as well. "Why not? You seem to be the only one hesitating here. Congratulations, by the way."

"Um, thank you?"

Rufus explained the stocky man's presence in the lounge. "Buck was my partner before I transferred to the lab to help run the admin side of things. He left the force about the same time. Now he's got his own private investigation firm—still does some odd jobs for the department."

Odd jobs? What did that mean?

"In return, we help him out when we can." Help? In what way? But before she could ask specifically what had brought Buck to the crime lab, or what his definition of an *odd job* entailed, Rufus nudged his former partner toward the exit. "Come on, Buck. Let's let these young pups stew over the decisions that you and I already know the answers to. Besides, you owe me a dinner. I'm thinking steak, since my wife will be feeding me every incarnation of turkey for the next two weeks."

"Mr. Buckner?" Chelsea stopped the man with the salt-and-pepper hair before he headed out with Rufus. "I've got that file you gave me downloaded onto my computer. I'll work on tracking down the information you asked for in my spare time. Around my duties here at the lab, of course. We won't let it be a cold case forever. I promise."

What kind of quid pro quo was going on here? And what did it have to do with the lab's top computer expert using her skills to help a civilian, even if he was a former cop?

Robert Buckner patted Chelsea's hand where it rested on the sleeve of his wool coat. "Thank you, Miss O'Brien. Any help you can give me, I'd appreciate."

"Sure thing. And it's Chelsea. Or Chels. I answer to both. Any friend of Sergeant King's is a friend of mine. And, you know, I do have spare time. Too much of it, really. That's why I'm online so much instead of hanging out with real people. Except for the folks here. I mean, they're real people, obviously... Um, okay. TMI."

To his credit, the older man focused on everything she was saying until her nerves kicked in and she pulled away to needlessly adjust her glasses again. "Thank you... Chelsea," he responded in a gruff voice. "I'll be in touch."

Chelsea's lips buzzed with a long exhalation as the two older men left the lounge. "That was awkward. Of course it was awkward. *I* was talking. I was rambling."

"Easy, Chels," Lexi teased, knowing enough about Chelsea's people-pleasing personality to suspect it hadn't taken much persuasion to secure her cooperation. Although Lexi was sensitive to her coworker's insecurities, she was also protective of the friend who seemed to be even more alone in the world than she was. Was Robert Buckner taking advantage of the resident computer geek's big heart? "What's with you and the private detective?"

Chelsea's hazel eyes darted to Lexi's. "Oh. I can't say. I promised to be discreet. It's an old case that he needs solved. He's not much for computers, but he thinks I might be able to dig up a connection somebody missed." Her gaze swung back to the men disappearing down the hallway. "He's lost a lot, and he seems so sad with those big puppy dog eyes." Um, *puppy dog* was not the descriptor Lexi had thought of when she'd looked at the stocky man hanging out with Rufus. "I need him to smile. When Sergeant King asked me if I could help his ex-partner do some research, I wanted to."

While Lexi felt this personal request required a little more digging into to make sure that neither the lab nor Chelsea herself was being compromised, the frown line above the brunette's glasses made her think her friend was the sad one here. Lexi dropped a comforting arm around Chelsea's shoulders. "Hey, if it's anything to do with cyberspace, then he's come to the right person."

Chelsea grinned at the praise. "See? That's exactly the kind of thing a good supervisor would say to her team. That makes me feel like I can really help him. You're a natural."

"Yeah, well, whatever you're doing for him—it's not impacting your work for the lab, is it?"

Lexi never got an answer for that one. Chelsea clapped her hands together and gasped with delight. "Speaking of puppy dog eyes… Blue!"

A muscular brown dog with a black face and dark eyes strutted into the lounge. He rubbed past Jackson Dobbs's legs, pushed his nose into Khari Thomas's hand and accepted a pat on the flank from Shane Duvall, before stopping at Grayson Malone's wheelchair for a scratch around his pricked ears. If it wasn't for the brass badge clipped to his collar, a stranger might mistake the Belgian Malinois police officer for some kind of therapy dog because he stopped to greet and be adored by everyone in the room. That was, until Chelsea called his name and his sharp-eyed attention shifted to her. The working dog's tongue lolled out of his mouth as he panted with anticipation and hurried over to them.

Lexi scrubbed her palms against the dog's jowls, smiling at the way he huffed with the excitement he felt at the familiar caress. Petting and playing with the high-energy dog added joy to Lexi's afternoon, too.

But it was Blue's partner, Aiden Murphy, exchanging greetings just outside the lounge, who captured Lexi's attention.

"Murph."

"Sarge. Buck."

Lexi looked straight across the room to meet deep blue eyes focused squarely on her.

One of those blue eyes winked. "Congratulations on your promotion."

The deep-pitched drawl that was colored with a hint of Aiden's Irish ancestors when he hit his *r*'s danced against her eardrums. Although she managed to keep her tongue in her mouth, Lexi's pulse fluttered with a silent echo of the excitement Blue was displaying as he rolled over onto his back to give Chelsea access to his chest and belly. The uniformed officer in the doorway was the real reason she had almost no social life, and why her ex-boyfriend and any other man who might be remotely interested in her barely got the chance to date her, much less get involved enough to hurt her.

Aiden Murphy, KCPD K-9 officer. Six feet of lean muscle put together with the same sinewy athleticism as the well-trained dog who lived and worked with him every day. Blue-black hair cropped close enough on the sides that you could see his scalp. He had a tiny scar on his chin and imperfect features that his easy smile and killer blue eyes transformed into a compellingly masculine face. Her brother's best friend. Substitute big brother whenever Levi was overseas.

The man who would never know how seriously close she'd come to letting him break her heart growing up.

Chapter Two

Aiden didn't question the tension easing from his chest when he saw Lexi's smile and the way she wrestled playfully with his dog. Silky, toffee-colored waves danced around her chin as she shook her head at his dramatic wink. Maybe he'd overreacted by jogging through the gym and common areas connecting the precinct offices with the crime lab to see for himself that she was all right. But he was who he was. He was a protective man by nature and training—and he was majorly protective of all things Callahan.

News traveled fast through the crime lab and precinct offices. Any gossip that included Lexi Callahan's name merited an investigation.

The trouble with gossip was that the story changed from telling to telling. He'd prepared to do battle against the reprimand he'd first erroneously heard about, but his outrage was quickly replaced with a sense of pride when he'd learned that she wasn't in trouble at all. She'd been tapped to head up her own squad at the lab. But his concern had reawakened when someone reported that she was hesitating to take the promotion. Why? Lexi was smart, funny, caring and independent; she made the people in her circle more confident and capable just by being around them. *He* was a better man for knowing her.

They were so talking about this. He'd spent eight years of his life with the Callahans. Eight years in which he had three meals a day, a warm bed, and he didn't have to sleep with his too tight shoes and threadbare coat on in case the night went to hell and he had to run away to a place where the adults weren't yelling or using him as a punching bag. Even though they shared no blood ties, Leroy and Lila Callahan, Levi and Lexi were more family to him than his own father and stepmothers had ever been. And now that Mr. and Mrs. Callahan had tragically been taken from them, and Lexi was on her own stateside, he'd promised her brother, Levi, that she would make smart decisions and lead a safe, successful life while he was away serving his country in the Middle East.

Lexi was family. Sort of like a sister. Certainly a friend. And it was killing him.

Her irritation with his cheesy wink gave way to a teasing laugh as she watched Blue work the room. "I see you brought your better-looking half."

"Ha ha." Aiden strolled into the employee lounge, exchanging a nod with Jackson and Khari. He shook hands with Gray and Ethan, and doffed a salute to Shane, following the same path his partner had taken toward Lexi.

By the time he reached them, Blue was on his back and Chelsea O'Brien was on her knees exchanging sloppy face licks for fingernails scratching his chest and belly. "Hey, Aiden." Chelsea glanced up briefly before a slurp against her jaw swung her attention back to the dog. "It's okay if I pet Blue, isn't it?"

"You bet." Aiden leaned his hip against the counter beside Lexi, wondering who was enjoying themselves more—his partner or the computer genius. "He's off duty right now, and you're on the short list of people he likes. I think Blue's got a thing for the ladies." The Belgian Malinois might be all adrenaline and intensity on the job, but he was a sucker for soft hands and a pretty face. He couldn't blame the pooch, really. What full-blooded male wouldn't want Lexi Callahan putting her hands on him? Lexi wasn't the one with her hands on the dog now, and still his thoughts had gone there. Aiden gripped the counter behind him and looked out the bank of windows into the grayish light of the muted sunset until he could shut down that unbidden thought and remember why he'd come here in the first place. He blinked once, then looked over his shoulder at Lexi. "Why won't you take the job?"

She sank back against the counter beside him. "Not you, too."

"Of course me, too." He matched her stance, crossing his arms over his protective utility vest, where he wore his badge, radio, spare ammo magazines, Taser and other gear. He wore his gun strapped to his thigh. "I feel like I'm part of this lab. Blue and I are the primary protection team assigned to watch your backs out in the field. Maybe you guys don't wear a badge and gun like me, but that doesn't make me any less a part of this team. Take the job."

Lexi leaned a little closer, until her arm brushed against his and she could tilt her cheek against his shoulder and drop her voice to a whisper. "I wouldn't be stepping into an easy situation."

Aiden ignored the scents of milk and honey and some sort of laboratory disinfectant coming off her hair and clothes, and dipped his head to match her whisper. "These are good people. Give 'em a chance."

"I'm not worried about *them*."

He frowned as she straightened away from him. He'd never liked when the overachiever he'd grown up with sold herself short. "You take on more than a normal person should. You overthink your decision until you lose sleep and give yourself a headache. Then you kick butt and do a great job anyway." Aiden shrugged. He wasn't the brains of this relationship, but the logic seemed simple to him. "Just skip to the kick-butt part."

Lexi pushed away from the counter to step in front of him and face him, still whispering. "You think I can do this."

"I know you can."

"Back to work, everybody." Another uniformed officer rapped on the door frame, diverting everyone's attention to his arrival. Captain Brian Stockman was one of the two sworn officers on the crime lab staff. While Rufus King liaised the administrative offices of the lab with KCPD, Captain Stockman ran the CSIU, coordinating the work the criminalists did out in the field with the officers and detectives investigating the cases. Only Mac Taylor was more senior on staff, so if Captain Stockman said to move out, they all fell into line. "Unfortunately, you all are still on the clock until the next shift comes on. We need a field team to roll. We've got a break-in with a DB in one of the hotels downtown."

While Stockman's rank earned him respect, his close-shaved graying hair only added to his air of authority, as far as Aiden was concerned. But the tall, lanky man with the obvious hair plugs compensating for his thinning gray-blond hair who pushed his way past Captain Stockman didn't seem to share that same respect.

Dennis Hunt waltzed into the break room. "I hate to break up this party I wasn't invited to." His dark eyes skirted past Aiden and zeroed in on Lexi. "Callahan. You're with me. Dobbs? You, too."

To Blue's chagrin, Chelsea scrambled to her feet, and grabbed her laptop and backpack. "Gotta go. See ya, Lexi. 'Bye, Aiden."

"Miss O'Brien." Dennis's greeting, laced with a subtle amusement, made Chelsea duck her head and scuttle past him out the door.

Aiden grabbed the dog's collar and ordered Blue into a sit when he would have followed the other woman into the hallway. "Is she okay?"

"She'll be fine," Lexi assured him, but he wasn't sure he believed her. "She's one of us who filed a harassment grievance against him. I hooked her up with the staff counselor to talk about it. Dennis seems to bring out the fight-or-flight instinct in all of us."

Aiden's reaction was the curling-his-fingers-into-a-fist variety. There were a lot of things about Chelsea that reminded him of his early childhood, where trust and security had been an option. But where he'd grown tough, gotten physical and trained to take on the world, her insecurities seemed to have made her skittish and fearful. This guy must have one hell of a lawyer and a ton of tenure to still be employed after the stories he'd heard. Of course, Hunt had never been promoted beyond field supervisor, and never would be, so the man was paying for his unacceptable choices in other ways.

When Hunt crossed the room to pour himself a cup of freshly brewed coffee, Blue followed Aiden's nonverbal cue and positioned himself between Lexi and her soon-to-be ex-boss. Hair-plug man ignored the defensive perimeter and spoke to Lexi. "I know Taylor offered you my position. Bet you've already got plans for redecorating my office. But for two more days, I'm still running this squad and giving out the assignments. So come on, sweetie. Let's move it. You and Jumbo are pulling the long shift with me."

Aiden's instinct to shut Hunt up was cut short by the hand that snaked around his forearm. Lexi's touch silently warned him that she could handle this without his help. As quickly as she had touched him, she pulled away to settle her hand on top of Blue's head. Did she worry the dog was as primed to attack as Aiden was? Or was she letting the dog center her? Cool her temper or buck up her strength?

"Sweetie?" He recognized the snap in that tone. "I take it you haven't started your sensitivity training class. Or do I need to file another complaint against you?"

"Just keep 'em coming, honey. You haven't got rid of me yet."

She crossed her arms in front of her. "Is that a challenge?"

Jackson Dobbs suddenly filled up the space on the other side of her. Although he didn't protest like she did, Aiden assumed the big guy didn't appreciate the nickname, either.

Hunt was smart enough, at least, not to take on all four of them. He put his hand up in an insincere apology. "Sorry. Pseudo-Supervisor Callahan, would you move your…?" He thought better of that choice of word. "Would you please hurry? I have plans with Bertie tonight, and I want to get this dead hooker scene processed ASAP."

Lexi didn't say another word until Hunt had left the room. "Wow. You don't think he's bitter, do you? He destroys his own career and thinks he can blame me?" Her tone was almost as snarky as Hunt's had been. "This is going to be a fun evening."

Jackson gave Lexi's arm a sympathetic squeeze before heading out. "I'll get the van warmed up. Meet you out back. Take the job."

Had Aiden ever heard the weapons expert string so many words together in a single conversation? But while Lexi seemed equally surprised by the big man's vote of confidence, Aiden had a more immediate issue to discuss. Now that the room had cleared except for Lexi, Aiden and his K-9 partner, Aiden blocked Lexi's path to the exit and faced her. "Please say I can punch Hunt in the mouth for the way he talks to you."

"And make me write you up on the report, too? That's the kind of attitude I'm supposed to fix." She stepped around him and headed down the hallway. "Besides, if anybody's punching him, I'm doing it."

"That's my girl." Aiden grinned and tapped his thigh, and Blue fell into step beside him as he followed Lexi into her tiny office. He and Blue waited in the doorway while she pulled her coat and crime scene kit from the closet behind her desk. "Now explain to me why you didn't jump on Mac's offer to take over Hunt's job." She set the kit on her desk and eyed him with a silent question. "News travels fast around this place. Anyone would be an improvement over that guy."

"Gee, thanks."

"You know what I mean. B squad would be lucky to have you running the team." He gestured with his thumb over his shoulder to the hallway where the others had gone back to their labs and offices. "If Big Jack mentioned it, then you know they think so, too."

Lexi shrugged into her insulated coat. "They're being nice because they're my friends."

"They're being nice because they know you've earned the promotion and they believe you can make them feel like they're safe in their own workspace. They respect you in ways they'll never be able to respect Hunt again."

"You're sure this isn't just your big brother instincts kicking in?" He stiffened at the brotherly appellation. "I know you promised Levi you'd keep an eye on me while he's deployed. You pulled my car out of the ditch when I hit that patch of ice. Fixed the leaky faucet in my kitchen. Apparently, that mandate means advising me on career moves, too."

"Lex—"

"I'm a grown-up, Aiden. Hell, I'm thirty years old. I can weigh the pros and cons myself without you or Levi telling me what to do. Supervising Criminalist means better pay. More seniority. More responsibility. I'm sure Levi would see it as a step in the right direction for my career. It means job security in his eyes. *Life* security." She pulled on a black knit stocking cap with the letters *CSI* embroidered on the front. "I'd be on the right track to everything Levi wants for me."

"What do *you* want?"

"I want the job. I want to keep making a difference. I want to erase the memory of everything Dennis has said and done and put my own stamp on this lab. But what if I'm not ready for that? What if I screw it up and make things worse? I already lead a pretty solitary existence." She worked her bottom lip between her teeth and glanced beyond him to the hallway where the others had passed by. "What if I lose the friends I do have in the process?"

"You'll always have me." Her eyes widened at that instinctive reply, and the room was silent for several uncomfortably long seconds. Wow. Did that sound as lovelorn-loser pathetic to Lexi's ears as it did to his own? *Turn it into a joke, Murph. Make her smile.* "And Blue." He reached down to scrub his hand over Blue's head. "As long as you're handing out tummy rubs, you'll never get rid of Blue."

Lexi visibly relaxed. Her teeth released the lip she'd worried, and she gave him that familiar smile as she crossed the room to pet Blue, too. "That's the kind of loyalty I want the staff to have with me. You should have heard them. They think changing supervisors is going to make everything right again. But it's not going to happen in a day. They might not be working one-on-one with

Dennis anymore, but he'll still be around unless he does something else stupid to get himself fired. I'd have to run interference in the meantime. That's a lot of pressure."

Aiden inhaled a deep breath, steeling himself to play the part he'd promised. "I don't have to be a stand-in big brother for my best friend to know this is a great opportunity for you. You'll figure out your management style as you go along. Even Mac still goes out in the field sometimes, so clearly, you're not going to be stuck behind a desk. You'll still get to do the job you love. Work side by side with the people who mean something to you."

Lexi straightened to zip her coat. "I'll just have more job to do. More assignments to organize and prioritize. More people to wrangle. More favors to call in and problems to listen to and egos to soothe."

"Nobody can handle the responsibility better than you. I grew up with you and Levi. I know you." The ends of her hair curled beneath the edge of the stocking cap, and he gave in to the urge to capture a strand that clung to the corner of her mouth and brush it back into place along her jaw. "Your brother may be the Marine, but I know who the real tough guy is in the Callahan family. You're taking the job, Lex. I can already see it in your eyes."

She planted her hands on her hips and tilted her face to his. "Okay, Mr. Know-It-All. What are my eyes saying now?"

He'd memorized every shade of moss, juniper and jade in her pretty green eyes. Knew what almost every nuance of color and expression meant, and he was reading this one loud and clear. He was pushing her too hard when she needed time to process her thoughts.

"That I'm not getting invited over for Thanksgiving dinner?" Even though she snickered at the joke, he wisely retreated into the hallway. "Fine. I get the message. Back off. I'll get Blue geared up and meet you at the crime scene to clear it before you go to work."

She picked up her kit, switched off the light and locked the door behind her.

Aiden turned and walked backward until she caught up to him. "And, hey, stick with Dobbs until I get there. I don't want you spending any time alone with Hunt if you can help it."

"Neither do I." She caught his hand and squeezed his fingers to stop him from turning toward the precinct side of the complex. "And, Aiden? I know Levi calls and checks in with you from time to time. Don't say anything to him about the new job, okay? I want to tell him."

"Roger that."

"Thanks for looking out for me."

"Anytime, Lex. Anytime."

Their fingers tangled together as she aligned her hand with his. But just as quickly as the simple touch of her hand began to feel like something more, she pulled away and hurried toward the garage, where the lab vans were kept.

Aiden could still feel the warmth of her skin against his as he watched her walk away. A familiar pull in his gut followed right along with her. She waved over her shoulder before disappearing through the door and breaking the heated connection he fought to ignore.

Nothing like lusting after forbidden fruit. Levi had entrusted her care to him. *Protect my sister. Make sure she's safe and happy. Don't let any man hurt her.* Not Dennis Hunt. Not a criminal. Not a lover. Aiden had given his word. They'd shaken hands on it.

Aiden was alive today because of the Callahan family. Because of Lexi's parents and her big brother, he wasn't in jail, he wasn't dead, and he hadn't become an alcoholic loser like his abusive father, who hadn't even known that when Aiden wasn't in school he had been living on the streets before Levi found him and took him home. The Callahans had saved him in every way that mattered. He owed them.

If Levi wanted him to look out for Lexi the same way he would if he were stateside, then Aiden would do it.

But that promise was exacting a price from him. He hadn't been able to make a serious relationship with any woman work for a few years now. And he'd dated some nice ones. But it hadn't seemed fair to pretend he could do forever when a piece of his heart belonged to Lexi. Maybe if he'd stuck with Patrick Murphy's neglect and drunken rages—maybe if he'd made it on the streets—he wouldn't feel the guilt warring with the desire inside him. Maybe that was all this was—desire. And if that was the case, then he'd keep his hands off Lexi. But if these were real feelings… Hell. He'd keep his heart to himself, too, because he'd made the damn promise. He'd be whatever Lexi and Levi needed him to be.

Wanting the one woman he'd vowed to be a brother to—and doing nothing about it—might well be the toughest assignment he'd ever tackled. And he'd been a cop for twelve years and had survived Patrick Murphy.

Still, Aiden would get the job done.

Even if that meant protecting Lexi from himself.

He patted the dog beside him. "Come on, Blue. Let's go to work."

Chapter Three

Thanksgiving

"Way to make a difference, Callahan," Lexi teased out loud, deciding to move the Advent calendar from the back of her office door, which she intended to leave open as much as possible, to the closet door, where she'd see it at least twice a day when she hung up or retrieved her coat. She was making some groundbreaking decisions on her first shift as supervisor in the nearly deserted lab complex. She reached into the box on her desk to unpack a colorful arrangement of frosted silk greenery and shiny red balls tucked into a mug painted like a snowman. "Now, where am I going to put this guy?"

The news feed from the mayor's Plaza lighting ceremony that took place every Thanksgiving night played on her phone on her desk, drowning out the echo of crickets chirping in the empty hallways. She'd taken a break from filling out paperwork and reading the policy and procedure manual to decorate her office for the holidays.

She'd wanted this job, right? She'd finally decided that she could be a better friend to Chelsea, Khari, Gray, Ethan and the others by being an advocate rather than just a buddy who shared coffee in the lounge with them and commiserated over inclusive test results, evidence that didn't make sense, or all the steps the department had to go through before giving Dennis Hunt his walking papers. She wanted to be good at her new position, to earn her team's respect. But she was off to an inauspicious start.

While there were four squads of criminalists covering the CSIU 24/7 or were available on call over the holidays, administrators and specialists who worked mostly in the lab itself had the day off. These were the people who ran analysis tests and database searches for ongoing investigations. Lexi had kept herself busy for a few hours, but the loneliness was starting to bounce off the walls and close in on her. Not that she'd have any company at home, either. No family, no pet, no boyfriend—just work and home alone. Seemed like her personal life was about as exciting as work this evening. She needed to meet someone, or join a group or activity where she could make friends outside of the lab. Maybe she should adopt a cat from one of the local shelters.

While she had Levi's arrival just before Christmas to look forward to, it was still a long stretch between Thanksgiving and Christmas. Then he'd be gone again right after the New Year, and she'd be all by herself again in that gorgeous rattletrap of a Craftsman home where she'd grown up.

Not that she'd had big plans for celebrating the holiday today, anyway. When she was younger, her parents had taken her and Levi, and then Aiden, too, down to the Plaza after a big Thanksgiving dinner every year. They'd wait with anticipation in the cold, with thousands of other Kansas Citians and tourists, for some local celebrity or lucky child to throw the switch and turn on over a million colorful lights strung along every storefront, roofline and dome in the historic J. C. Nichols Plaza shopping area south of downtown KC. After the decorations turned the shopping district into Christmas and the crowd cheered, they'd go for ice cream or hot chocolate, depending on the temperature. Then they'd walk around the shops to view their elaborate window displays. It wasn't just a Kansas City holiday tradition—it was a Callahan family tradition.

But then Levi had enlisted after graduation, Aiden had gone to a community college and the police academy, and she'd become a teenager too cool to hang with her parents. And then her parents were gone. After that was college, and more college, and work. She never seemed to find her way back to the Plaza to see the lighting ceremony in person, to feel the excitement in the air, to connect with the rest of the crowd and be inspired to celebrate the holiday season. For a while with her ex, Kevin, she'd thought she was getting back to personal connections and family and meaningful celebrations.

But soon she could see that Kevin didn't want the same things she did. Although they shared similar skill sets, she was a woman with a cause, and he wanted to go into the family pharmaceutical business and make money like his father. Even as they were drifting apart, she was fighting to make their relationship work. He wanted a business partner, or better yet, a trophy wife. She needed to feel more useful than that. She was a lab tech at heart. An investigator who liked piecing together clues and solving mysteries and making a difference—the way her parents had made a difference in the world, the way *she* made a difference here at the crime lab.

And finally, there was Kevin in bed with another woman in their new apartment, a slew of apologies, and a lame-ass marriage proposal complete with an impractical, gaudy diamond she wouldn't be able to wear to work, and promises she could no longer believe. The relationship had ended with the realization that she didn't know Kevin anymore, and maybe he'd never known the real Lexi at all.

So much for a family and a home and the holidays.

The snowman mug found a home on top of the file cabinet just as the countdown started on her phone. She sat on the corner of her desk to watch the live feed of the white, red, green and multicolored lights suddenly illuminating the Plaza landscape. She smiled at the festive beauty of it all, as well as the memories of Thanksgivings and Christmases past.

But just as the crowds started to disperse to visit a bar or restaurant, walk back to nearby hotel rooms or window-shop at the stores—there was no sense returning to their vehicles and driving home just yet, as the Plaza boulevards and side streets would be notoriously jammed with pedestrians and parked cars—the happy trip down memory lane faded and disappeared into the sterile white walls of her office. There might be thousands of people down on the Plaza, but she was alone in her office putting up a handful of Christmas decorations and waiting for something to happen.

Be careful what you wish for, Callahan.

The phone on her desk rang. After hours on a holiday meant only one thing. They'd caught a case. She quickly turned off the news feed on her cell and picked up the receiver. "Lexi Callahan. KCPD Crime Lab."

"Lexi—?" Captain Stockman covered the phone and yelled at someone to turn down the game on the television before returning to the call. "First, happy Thanksgiving."

He seemed to need the greeting to cool his frustration and organize his thoughts. Lexi gave him that time. "Same to you, sir. I hope you and your family are enjoying the day."

"Ate too much. My team's losing. Doing great." She

smiled a moment at the older man's deadpan delivery, but had her pen and notepad ready when he got down to business. "Who's there with you?"

"It's just me on site. But Ethan Wynn and Shane Duvall are on call."

"Good. Call them. We've got a murder down on the Plaza. The Regal Hotel." The prestigious historic brownstone was a name that she recognized. The Regal had played host to mobsters, politicians and celebrities throughout the years. Recently, it had been completely remodeled with every modern amenity, while keeping its historic charm. The pricey hotel had a gated entrance and parking lot, and boasted one of the best views of the city, with its floor-to-ceiling windows on the north side facing Brush Creek and the Plaza district down below. Those rooms didn't come cheaply over the holidays, and they were booked years in advance to ensure a warm, elegant place to hang out while enjoying an unobstructed view of the festivities down below.

Not the sort of place where she'd expect to process such a violent crime. "You're sure it's murder?"

"Well, the maid who discovered the body was pretty hysterical, so we didn't get much from her. But the first officers on the scene described indications of a fight and a ligature around the victim's neck."

"That's the same MO of the scene I processed on Monday." Although, the prostitute with fresh tracks in her arm and the by-the-hour room rental hardly compared to the clientele she'd expect to find at the Regal. "That's curious."

"That's why I want you on the scene. That fleabag in No-Man's-Land and the Regal are two different worlds, so it may just be an unfortunate coincidence. But I want your eyes on it to see if anything else matches up. The last thing the department needs for the holidays is a serial killer."

"Understood. I'll call in my team and get to the scene ASAP."

"The officers who responded to the call have blocked the door, so no one has been in there besides the maid that we know of. One of them will stay with the room, and the other will meet you in the lobby."

"That's good." Lexi jotted down the pertinent information the captain was giving her. "Did anyone at the hotel file a noise complaint about the fight? It might narrow down the time of death."

She heard a cheer from the crowd gathered at the police captain's house. Not only had the team they must be rooting for scored, but it sounded like there were plenty of friends and loved ones to share the excitement with. And while that observation triggered a surge of melancholic longing, Lexi quickly buried the emotion and listened to the rest of Captain Stockman's report. "There are a lot of parties going on in the city tonight. If anyone heard anything, they didn't report it. I've alerted Homicide and the ME's office," he added. "They can do a more thorough canvass of staff and guests. You focus on your job. Find us some clues."

"Yes, sir."

"I'll be out of the office until Monday. But call if you need anything. Good hunting."

"Thanks." Lexi tore off the paper with the information she needed and stuffed it into the pocket of her jeans. Then she grabbed her coat, kit, stocking cap and gloves, locked up her office and hurried down to the garage and CSIU van.

Lexi waved to the officer closing the garage door behind her and turned onto Brooklyn Avenue, heading south toward Thirty-Fifth Street. Before she reached the turn, she had Ethan Wynn on the line. "Hey, Ethan. Sorry to take you away from your girlfriend and the game, but we caught a DB down at the Regal Hotel."

"On the Plaza?"

"Yeah. It's one of the brownstone high-rises south of Brush Creek."

"I know where it is." Ethan seemed to be moving, gathering his gear or pulling on his coat, perhaps, while they talked. "It'll take me a while to get there with all the extra traffic in the area. And where are we going to park? Every spot on the streets for blocks in any direction will be taken."

She'd wondered that, too. "There's a lot behind the hotel."

"That'll be full."

"Well, if you can't get into the circular drive in front of the hotel, or the parking lot, do the best you can." The city road crews had done their job clearing snow off the streets, but since it was one of the busiest nights of the year for tourists and locals to pour into downtown KC, she was already running into a snarl of cars parked along every curb. "I'll call ahead to see if traffic patrol can clear a spot for us."

"Do you want me to drive to the lab and we can take the van together?"

She shook her head, as though he could see her through the phone she'd mounted on the dash. "I'm already en route. I want to get the scene taped off and under our control before the crowd on the Plaza breaks up and guests start coming back to their rooms at the Regal. Who knows what evidence all that extra foot traffic could contaminate for us. Plus, I'd like to at least get pictures of the place undisturbed before the detectives start their walk-through."

"I hear that." A door closed in the background, though whether it was him leaving his house or climbing into his car, she couldn't tell. "My kit's in the trunk. I'll drive straight to the crime scene and meet you there."

"Sounds good. And would you call Shane in, too? Captain Stockman said it's a mess. We can use the extra hands."

"Yes, ma'am. Will do. I'll see you there."

"Ma'am?" Was that sarcasm or a genuine attempt at humor? Was having her give the orders going to be a problem for Ethan? "Watch it, Wynn. You're older than me."

"Not by that much." He laughed. "It's the gray hair. Relax. I know today is your first day as the boss. I'm just practicing what I'm supposed to call you now."

"Well, knock it off. I'm still Lexi. Save your *ma'ams* for your grandmother."

"Yes, ma'am."

"Wise guy." She grinned and shook her head. "Thanks, Ethan. I'll start processing the scene. You and Shane get there as soon as you can."

What should have been about a twelve-minute drive stretched into twenty-five by the time Lexi pulled into the parking lot behind the Regal Hotel. Between KCPD and the hotel management, an area near the back entrance had been cleared for the official vehicles with flashing lights and law enforcement markings to be hidden away from public view to reduce the number of curious onlookers, press and potentially panicked guests who had no idea this luxury boutique hotel was now a crime scene.

There was another ten minutes of introducing herself to homicide detectives Keir Watson and Hud Kramer, who were just arriving on the scene, and listening to an initial report from Officer Olivo, who showed them upstairs to Room 920. She was glad to see the door was closed and yellow crime scene tape had been draped across the entrance to keep everyone out. Olivo's partner, Officer Heming, assured them no one had been in or out of the room since their arrival. Once dismissed, the two officers went to help the hotel's assistant manager move the other ninth-floor guests to a new location for the night.

"Booties, gentlemen." Lexi set her kit on the floor outside the crime scene and opened it up to retrieve foot coverings for the two detectives and herself. Since they had their own sterile gloves, she dropped her coat onto the carpet beside her kit, adjusted the CSI cap on her head and pulled on her gloves. Then she grabbed the flashlight and camera from her kit, reminded the officers not to touch the light switch until she could get it dusted, then swiped the key card and led the way into what had once been a beautifully appointed room.

It was a shambles now. A tabletop Christmas tree had been knocked to the floor, its glass ornaments shattered and strewn among crushed gift-wrapped boxes that had been stomped on or rolled over. There was an overturned chair and lamp. Pillows and bedding on the floor. A spilled bottle of champagne was soaking into the carpet. A dent and torn plaster in the wall that indicated where a fist or someone's head had hit.

A raven-haired woman lay sprawled on the floor in the middle of it all, her sightless eyes staring up at the ceiling. One of the victim's holly-shaped gold earrings, adorned with what Lexi guessed were real rubies, had been torn from her earlobe, and a length of drapery cord was cinched around her bruised neck.

Lexi sensed a lot of anger in this room. Had the victim been waiting for someone to celebrate Thanksgiving on the Plaza with her, but an intruder had broken in? Possibly an ex who was abusive and didn't like her hooking up with someone new? Or did she and her lover have a fight that had gotten out of hand and had ended with her dead on the floor and the room tossed as though there had been a real brawl here?

Detective Kramer, a compact, muscular man, seemed to have a flair for dark humor. "Happy holidays to her. I'm guessing the celebration didn't go the way she'd planned."

Detective Watson, wearing a suit and tie and long wool coat that were a dressy contrast to his partner's casual leather jacket and jeans, agreed. "I think we can safely assume this is a homicide."

After an initial look at the woman, who was probably about Lexi's age, Watson and Kramer asked Lexi to pull the victim's ID from her purse, which sat remarkably untouched on the bedside table. Lexi snapped a photograph of the purse before opening it. Jennifer Li was clearly expecting company, judging by the lacy underwear and silk robe she had on, as well as the expensive perfume still emanating from her skin. The drapes that hung at the bank of tall windows were all open, giving a spectacular view of the holiday lights down below.

Keir was studying the same open expanse. "I'm guessing at this height, none of those thousands of people out there saw anything."

"Unless the witness was flying by in a helicopter." Hud jotted the victim's information into a notebook and tucked it back into his pocket without touching anything in the room. He glanced at the contents of the wallet Lexi showed him, letting him see several credit cards and a stack of hundred-dollar bills. "I doubt this was a robbery if the perp left that much cash here."

Lexi agreed. "I wouldn't state anything conclusive, but I'm guessing we're looking at a crime of passion."

Hud thanked her before she replaced the wallet and

retrieved a bag to drop the entire purse and its contents inside. "We'll back off and let you start processing the scene."

"I'll call my brother," Keir stated, following Hud back to the hallway. Was that code for something? Reading the question in her expression, Keir Watson explained, "My brother, Dr. Niall Watson, is the ME on call this weekend."

"Oh. Of course." Keir was younger than the bespectacled doctor she knew, but she could see the family resemblance now. "I've worked with Niall before."

Although the ME would determine the cause of death and collect any clues left on the body itself, Lexi could see that the woman had been strangled. Even without the cord around her neck, she'd recognized the dots of petechial hemorrhaging in and around Ms. Li's frozen eyes.

Keir was already halfway to the elevator, on his cell phone to his brother. Hud peeled off his booties while Lexi sealed and labeled the evidence bag with the victim's purse. "You'll be okay up here on your own?" he asked.

While Lexi appreciated the protective offer, she nodded. "I've got plenty to process in there."

"We're keeping Olivo downstairs to translate for the maid, and Heming's helping us make sure no one leaves the building until we get names and contact information on everyone. But if you'd feel more comfortable, I can send him back up here to keep an eye on you until the rest of your team arrives."

"I'll be fine on my own. I know you guys are short-staffed tonight, and the hotel is booked solid. Plus, with all the people coming and going with the holiday festivities, you'll need Heming for crowd control. The floor is clear, right?"

Hud nodded. "I'll run a double check myself before I leave you."

Keir ended his call and pushed the button to the elevator doors. "I'll head on down to the lobby to start the prelim interviews. We'll send your men up as soon as they arrive."

"Thanks."

Hud backed down the hallway in the opposite direction, starting his sweep of the ninth floor. "You'll coordinate with the ME and copy us on anything you find?"

"You bet."

She knew another cop and his K-9 partner who shared Hud Kramer's protective instincts. Lexi's thoughts strayed for a few moments, wondering how Aiden was spending his Thanksgiving. Although they saw each other nearly every day at work, they rarely spoke about their social lives. She had little interest in hearing about his latest conquest. Lexi knew Aiden dated—after all, what healthy, red-blooded woman could resist that sleeve of tats sliding over all those muscles, killer blue eyes and Irish charm? Although she would gladly face off against any woman who abused his feelings or took advantage of his generous, caring nature, she'd often wondered why he hadn't turned those charms on her. She supposed the pseudo-sibling bond was too strong between them for him to see her as anything but a little sister. And after her relationship with Kevin Nelson had blown up in her face, Aiden's hypercritical evaluations of anyone she tried to date made him seem more buttinsky brother than jealous lover when she talked about her social plans.

She imagined Aiden and Blue were in front of a televised football game with a pizza and a rawhide chew. She knew Aiden wouldn't be drinking beer and feeling sorry for himself at spending the holiday alone. His father had been an abusive alcoholic who'd married three different women after the death of Aiden's mother when he was just a baby. None of those marriages had lasted once his stepmothers realized they were either glorified babysitters or they became part of Patrick's abuse. Even after his father had lost his parental rights and eventually gone to jail, Aiden never touched alcohol. She didn't necessarily think that he believed the addiction was hereditary, but for as long as she'd known him, Aiden had avoided anything and anyone that could be remotely tied to the nightmarish memories he had of his childhood. He'd severed all ties with Patrick Murphy once her own parents had taken him in, both legally and emotionally.

For a moment, Lexi's heart ached for Aiden, as it always did. Unbidden came the admission that she ached for him in another way. The starving, broken boy she'd once known had grown into a strong, healthy, confident man. They shared such a close bond. And yet they would never share the bond she'd often fantasized about. Their friendship was too precious to risk, his vow to her brother too strong to betray.

All the men out there in the world, and she had to want the one who would never want her.

"Really, Callahan?" Lexi chided herself out loud at the dangerous turn her thoughts had taken. She was the one who was feeling sorry for herself. It happened every time that damn loneliness crept in. "He's probably a lousy kisser and leaves his dirty laundry all over the place. Probably forgets birthdays and anniversaries, too."

She tugged her knit cap tight around her hair and shook her head. She had no proof that any of that was true, but this pity party was only making the holiday and her first day as squad supervisor worse. She had a job to do. She needed to focus on that, and on helping find justice for poor Jennifer Li, not bemoaning her own foolish fantasies.

Lexi tucked a handful of marking labels into one of the pockets of her CSI utility vest and pushed to her feet.

She ducked beneath the crime scene tape and took several pictures of the entire scene, working her way across the room to capture the general details from every angle. She paused at the window, feeling the cold from the air outside permeating the glass. She was glad she'd layered up with boots and a sweater. She could hear muffled bits of traffic noise and music from the world below her. So many lights. So much tradition. So many people.

It wasn't until Lexi turned and faced the room again that she shivered. She was alone with death and destruction while it looked like half the city was down on the Plaza celebrating the start of the Christmas season.

This was the job she was so good at, though, she had to remind herself. This was the work she loved. She was making a difference.

So she buried that crushing lonesomeness deep inside beside those useless feelings for Aiden Murphy and went back to work.

Lexi started at the broken tree and crushed gifts between the tall windows. She laid an evidence marker down beside the debris and snapped several pictures before picking up a package and reading the tag. "'To B, Love, J.'" She took a photo of the tag itself. None of the gifts had full names written on them. "Not particularly helpful, but it's a start." The detectives would need to track down whoever "B" was.

Then Lexi looked beyond the wreckage of a romantic holiday celebration and surveyed the chaos around the hotel suite. She'd better get a complete overview of the scene before she got caught up in the individual details. Steeling herself against the tragic loss of life, she snapped a few pictures of the body, including a close-up of the ligature around the victim's neck. She went back to the windows and searched beside each curtain until she found the one with the missing pull. She took a picture of that, too, and marked the rope for further investigation because it looked as though it had been cut with deliberation rather than torn from the window as a weapon of opportunity. Jackson Dobbs would be able to study the edge of the drapery pull and compare the cut pattern to his vast database of weaponry to determine what knife or other sharp instrument had been used to cut the cord.

Lexi watched her reflection in the window turn into a frown as a curious thought struck her. She slowly turned and scanned the room again. There were no sharp instruments here—no knives, no scissors, not even a letter opener. She turned her gaze to the open door of the adjoining bathroom. Would a pair of manicure scissors be heavy enough and sharp enough to cut the decorative cord? Jennifer Li seemed like a woman who cared enough about her appearance to pack a manicure set. But if manicure scissors were a weapon of opportunity—say the killer had dazed the victim enough to have the time to go cut the rope and then come back to strangle her—then how did he know where those scissors were? That indicated a very personal knowledge of the victim and her belongings. More likely, the killer had brought his own weapon. And that indicated premeditation. Both were significant possibilities that she needed to pass along to Detectives Watson and Kramer to explore further.

There was another possibility to this whole crime scene beyond the ideas of intimate knowledge of the victim or premeditation. It was one explanation for Jennifer Li's death she was hesitant to even give voice to.

Lexi scrolled through the pictures on her camera back to the crime scene she'd processed on Monday. The victim that night had been a prostitute found strangled to death in a rent-by-the-hour hotel over in the seedy No-Man's-Land district of KC, where drugs and street crime were king.

Although the victim, Giselle Byrd, had fresh heroin tracks in her arm rather than gold-and-ruby earrings, and the setting had been nothing like the classy sophistication of the Regal Hotel, there were other details that were the same. The room there had been tossed, indicating evidence of a major struggle. And the victim had been strangled with a length of cord from the curtains there. The setting and victimology didn't match at all. But the MO was the same.

Did they have a serial killer on their hands?

Lexi eased her breath out between pursed lips. No need to panic here. Her job was to collect and process evidence from the scene and present facts to the detectives working the case.

The emotional roller coaster she'd been on today—nerves at starting the new job, worries about changing friendships, forbidden thoughts about Aiden, this whole damn woe-is-me holiday thing that seemed to be hitting her extra hard this year—was affecting her ability to do her job. She was good at this because she *could* detach her emotions and stay focused on the task at hand. Observations about potential motives and crime scenarios were welcome; distractions that got in the way of doing her job were not.

With that resolve firmly in place again, Lexi became the supervising criminalist she was meant to be. She sent quick texts to Ethan and Shane, informing them that she was at the scene and had started processing. She warned them it would probably be a long night. When they got there, she'd divide the suite into grids and put them to work collecting and cataloging the extensive evidence without overwhelming any of them.

She received a quick thumbs-up from Shane and another Yes, ma'am from Ethan with a winking emoji. Lexi snickered at his immature stab at humor and tucked her phone into the back pocket of her jeans.

Just in case she could find a pair of manicure scissors or other sharp object for Jackson to compare to the cut marks on the drapery cord, Lexi moved her assessment into the adjoining bathroom. She mentally swore when she saw that the fight must have continued in here, too.

There were bloody fingerprints on the edge of the porcelain sink and chrome faucet. A larger pool of blood was smeared inside the sink and trickled down the drain. She'd sure like Grayson Malone's opinion here. He'd be able to tell her if this was from the killer cleaning up, or from the victim, trying to doctor her own wounds before she expired. But since Gray wasn't here, Lexi documented it all on her camera, then swabbed several samples and bagged and tagged them for Grayson to analyze in the lab.

Lexi closed the swab she'd taken from the sink trap and was labeling the plastic tube when she heard a whisper of sound from the main room. She paused where she knelt on the cold tile floor and listened for some other indicator that she had company. "Hello?"

When she got no reply, she wondered if the sound had come from the floor above or below her. She tucked the tube inside her kit next to the cubby where she'd stowed her camera and tried to pinpoint the source of the sound. She likened the soft, rustling noise to the sound of someone who was slightly winded—as if they'd just walked up a flight of stairs because the elevator to the ninth floor had been shut down until the medical examiner removed the body and the police cleared the scene.

Lexi released the breath she didn't realize she'd been

holding and opened another swab tube to collect a blood sample from the floor. "Ethan? Shane? I'm in here."

When she still got no response, she stopped working. Her imagination wasn't so fanciful to imagine that Jennifer Li had sat up in the next room. Maybe Detective Watson had sent the uniformed officer back upstairs for some reason. "Officer Heming? Is that you?" No answer. "Detective Watson? Detective Kramer?"

Damn it. Either someone had an extreme case of rudeness, they were playing a practical joke she didn't find particularly funny, or she had an intruder. Even if one of the guests had peeked into the room or, heaven forbid, a reporter had gotten past the police downstairs to take a picture, it was Lexi's responsibility to get rid of that person before they contaminated her crime scene.

Pulling the lanyard with her ID card from inside her vest, she got up and headed into the main room. "I need you to identify yourself. I'm Supervisor Callahan with the Kansas City Police Department Crime Lab. You can't be in here…"

There was no one in the room. No one hovering in the doorway.

But the drapes had been closed.

A chill of fear raised the tiny hairs at the nape of her neck and shuddered down her spine.

A spike of adrenaline followed quickly in its wake.

She had company.

Not wasting another moment, she made a quick sweep of the room. Dead body. Major struggle. Ruined holiday. All the same, except for the damn curtains.

Lexi pulled her phone from her jeans and punched in Ethan Wynn's number as she stepped outside of the room and scanned up and down the hallway. No sign of her team. No Officer Heming. No one.

When that call went to voice mail, she disconnected and called Shane Duvall. She snapped into the phone the moment Shane picked up. "Where are you guys?"

"Well, hello to you, too. I'm stuck in traffic."

"What's your ETA?"

"I'm *stuck*." His tone indicated he wanted to add a "duh" onto the end of that sentence.

But something was off enough that it was giving her the creeps, and she didn't appreciate his sarcasm at the moment. "Did Ethan call you? You know to come to Room 920?"

"Of course. Ethan's not there yet? He's probably stuck in this traffic mess, too."

"Get here as soon as you can, okay?"

"Lexi, is everything—?"

But she had already disconnected and was scrolling through the numbers on her phone. She needed backup.

She went straight to the *A*s and pressed the familiar number.

"Lex!" When Aiden picked up, he launched into a silly, friendly chat. "I know you're calling to invite me to Black Friday dinner since we both pulled shifts on Thanksgiving. I may have the bigger TV to watch football, but you're the better cook. And I know my priorities—"

"Aiden. Stop talking. Something's wrong."

The teasing ended abruptly. "Talk to me." He was all serious. All cop. All the protector she could ever ask for. "Lex?"

She slowly turned 360 degrees, scanning for any sign of movement, any door standing ajar, any sound of labored breathing she might not have imagined. "I'm at the Regal Hotel. Processing a murder in Room 920."

She heard the instant response of the siren on his truck suddenly piercing the sounds of traffic in the background.

She explained the creep factor and feeling she wasn't alone, even though there was no one here but the dead body.

"Get out of there," Aiden ordered. She heard Blue whining in the background, probably picking up on his partner's alertness and the sound and speed of the two of them heading into action. "Tape it off and go back down to the lobby, where there are people. Send the officers up to recheck the scene. Go now. I'll be there in five minutes."

Five minutes? She could do five minutes.

"Move, Lex. Now!"

Lexi couldn't leave her kit unattended now that she'd cataloged evidence. She disconnected the call, hurried back to the bathroom, snapped it shut and ran for the door.

Five minutes would be too late.

The moment she set foot in the hallway again, a fist smashed against her cheekbone, knocking her into the doorjamb. As pain rang through her skull, her kit hit the floor and tumbled into the opposite wall. Before she could even think to fight or run, the leather-gloved hand palmed her face and smacked the back of her head into the steel door frame. She crumpled to the floor, tried to crawl, but her attacker grabbed the collar of her vest and sweater to pull her up and toss her into the room, where she landed hard, stinging her breasts and hip.

She tasted the coppery taint of blood in her mouth. It seemed she could literally hear ball bearings clanging around in her skull. Her stomach churned as she turned her head and got a glimpse of black swirling through her vision. Black pants. Black gloves. Black mask hiding the man's features. It had to be a man, didn't it? To pick her up like that?

Was this Jennifer Li's killer? Returning to the scene of the crime?

Thinking she was down for the count, the attacker

walked past her, intent on reaching something else in the room. Lexi rolled onto her side and kicked out. Her legs tangled with his, tripping him. She pushed herself up and kicked again, connecting with his knee and sending him sprawling. She rolled to her feet and staggered toward escape. But landing a blow only elicited a feral growl from her attacker.

Lexi lurched toward the door. But the man recovered faster. He grabbed a fistful of her hair and smashed her face into the wall until her knees buckled. The ball bearings went silent and the world faded to black.

Chapter Four

"Blue takes point." Aiden raised his fist, halting the contingent of police officers and detectives waiting behind him on the landing of the ninth-floor stairwell. "Come on, boy." He rubbed Blue around the ears and patted the flanks of the black protective vest the dog wore, getting the highly motivated, super focused Malinois vibrating with excitement and fired up to go to work. "You know you want to do this. You know you want to find the bad guy." The moment he felt the fierce tug against his arm, Aiden nodded to the officer who swiped a key card to open the door. Aiden unhooked Blue's leash. "Go get him!"

The muscular dog leaped into the hallway, put his nose to the carpet and systematically touched every doorway, including the elevators. Aiden moved out right behind him with his gun drawn and clasped squarely between both hands. He looked first to the far end of the hallway to ensure there was no one in the passageway itself. "Clear!"

Officers Heming and Olivo, followed by Detectives Watson and Kramer, were all on his hit list right now for leaving Lexi alone at the crime scene, especially when he'd stormed in downstairs, asked if she was all right, and they had no idea what he was talking about. But he was glad to have them at his back now as they split to check each door in the hallway to ensure that it was locked. Blue worked at

twice their pace, sniffing every door and circling back by
the time Aiden reached 920. The door stood slightly ajar
behind the crisscross of yellow crime scene tape, and it was
the only one that Blue paused at. He whined with anticipation, indicating he detected the scent of a human inside.

"I've got a hit," Aiden informed the others. He ordered
Blue into a sit, then leaned in, but saw nothing more than
shadows through the half-inch opening of the door. He quieted his breathing and trained his ears toward any sounds
coming from inside.

There. A soft moan. A grunt of pain? There was definitely someone alive in there. But was it Lexi? Or something he couldn't allow himself to imagine?

"Elevator's still locked out," Watson reported, jogging
up beside him. "Nobody came in that way. Heming? Olivo?
You split up and search the floors above and below. If you
run into anyone who can't prove they're staff or a guest, I
want to meet them downstairs."

"Yes, sir."

"Yes, sir."

"This is your call, Murphy." Watson took up a support
position behind Aiden while Kramer flattened his back
on the wall beside the door.

The open CSI kit that lay overturned and spilled on the
carpet was not a good sign. When Blue dropped his nose
to the vials, brushes and camera, Aiden pulled the dog's
attention back to him. "Leave it."

Blue was panting hard, more from excitement than exertion. This was all a game to him, and he hadn't found
the intruder he was looking for yet. And until he found
the person that his handler wanted him to flush out, the
game wouldn't be over. He wouldn't get Aiden's praise or
the chance to play with his Kong until he won the game.

His dark eyes were focused up on Aiden, waiting, waiting, waiting…

Aiden switched the gun to his left hand and wrapped his fingers around the doorknob. He winked down at Blue. Still waiting… "KCPD! Come out now, or I'm sending a K-9 in," Aiden warned. Silence. "Your choice. I'm sending in the dog." He pushed the door open just enough for the Malinois's shoulders to pass through, and Blue charged. "Find the bad guy!"

A few seconds later, Blue's black muzzle reappeared in the doorway and Aiden pushed the door wide open, knowing it was safe. He wanted to swear at the scene that greeted him. Instead, he wrestled the dog around his face and neck and praised him for completing the job. "Good boy. Good boy, Blue. You da man."

Watson and Kramer streamed in behind them, one checking the bathroom, the other the closet and under the bed. "Clear!"

"Clear!"

Aiden holstered his weapon and pulled out the hard red rubber Kong that Blue adored and tossed it into the hallway. Instead of chasing after his reward, the dog trotted beside Aiden as he hurried to the woman with the short golden-brown hair that clung to her face. Lexi was on the floor at the foot of the bed, trying to get her arms beneath her to push herself up.

"Bwue?" Her eyes were squeezed shut. No, one was nearly swollen shut and the other was squinting against the light as she gingerly plopped onto her back and reached out to touch Blue's chest. "Knew…you'd come." She wrapped her fingers through the dog's collar and tried to pull herself up.

This time Aiden made no apology for swearing as he knelt beside her. "Don't move, Lex." He gently cupped her shoulders and eased her back to the carpet. "We don't know how badly you're hurt. Internal injuries? Your neck?" He pulled off his glove and stroked her staticky hair away from the blood pooling beneath her nose and from the split in her bottom lip. He stroked the cheek beneath her un-bruised eye again, hating the chill he felt there. He turned his head to his shoulder without losing sight of her nar-rowed eyes. "Call a medic. Officer down."

Keir Watson strode out into the hallway, making the call on his phone while Hud Kramer took up space in the doorway, the way someone should have been to keep this assault from happening in the first place. He was making a separate call to his Fourth Precinct office, asking for any available backup at the hotel. Without any command, Blue stretched out on the carpet beside Lexi. She slid her hand along the dog's back, perhaps taking comfort in the dog's presence, perhaps absorbing some of Blue's abun-dant warmth.

"Aiden?" She blinked her good eye open, then squinted as though even the lone light shining in from the bathroom caused her pain.

"Shh, Lex. I'm right here." He shifted his position be-side her to block the light, then reached across her to pet Blue and praise him for remaining surprisingly still at his post. "Help's on the way."

He made a visual assessment of her injuries. He'd been in enough fights growing up to recognize the imprint of a fist on her cheek. Bruises were forming quickly on the thinner skin around her face. The cut that was oozing blood in her hairline was sprinkled with plaster. He made a quick visual sweep around the room and spotted the broken dents and droplets of blood in the wall near the door. Yeah, he'd had those injuries, too. But it was tearing him up inside to see that Lexi had suffered this kind of a beating, to know the pain she was suffering, to understand that helpless feeling of not knowing when the next blow would come.

"Can you tell me what happened?" he asked.

Although she seemed to have a death grip on Blue's vest, her right hand tapped at Aiden's thigh and stomach. Then he realized she was trying to find his hand. He completed the connection for her and felt a tad of relief at the strength of her grip in his. She inhaled a deep breath, probably a good sign that she didn't have any cracked or broken ribs. "I was on my way downstairs, like you said. I didn't see him. In the hallway. One minute he wasn't there, and then he was. He hit me, and... I couldn't fight back. I tried. I couldn't get away. I guess I passed out." Her eyes shut and a tear squeezed out, and that tore him up more than the cuts and scrapes and bruises did. "I tripped him once. Got in a good kick, so he may be limping for a while. But I couldn't get away. The self-defense training you and Levi taught me didn't do me a damn bit of good."

He tugged his other glove off between his teeth and dropped it to the floor beside him, then reached down to gently capture that tear with the pad of his thumb and wipe it away. "It's practically impossible to defend yourself against a blitz attack."

"I don't even know what he wanted." Her grip pulsed around his. "He never said anything."

"A killer returning to the scene of his crime?" He didn't have to spell out the obvious. He'd come back for something, an incriminating piece of evidence, most likely, and had found Lexi here, standing between him and what he wanted. He'd needed her out of commission so he could retrieve whatever he was after.

"Is anything missing?" Lexi suspected the same thing. "I need to look. Help me." She pulled against his hand, trying to sit up despite his warning. Twisting her head around, she surveyed the room, moaning at even that slight movement. "My head feels like a bowling ball, rolling toward the pins."

"I told you not to move." With her visible injuries, and uncertain hidden injuries, Aiden wasn't about to wrestle her back to the floor. Instead, he sat on the carpet, pulling her halfway into his lap so that she could lean back against his chest. It wasn't any kind of defensible position if the perp returned, but if using him as a backboard would keep her relatively still until the paramedics got here, then he'd stay put.

The crown of her head lolled back against his neck, and he wrapped his arm lightly around her waist to anchor her in place. "The whole room is spinning. And it's cold." He released her hand and snugged his arms more tightly around her, trying to share the body heat she needed. She lifted her fingers to her hair, becoming aware of the extent of her injuries. Or not. "Where's my stocking cap?"

Maybe she wanted it for warmth. He surveyed the scene again, looking for the familiar cap that usually hugged her golden-brown waves. "I don't see it. Blue." At his subtle hand gesture, the dog moved in beside her again, resting his muzzle atop her thigh, adding his abundant heat. She rewarded him by stroking his head and jowl. Player. It seemed the beast got more affection from Lexi than he did. But Lexi was a beloved part of the dog's pack, and Blue snuggled up to her without any hesitation, much like they practiced with the dog lying beside Aiden to protect him should he ever be injured in the line of duty.

Lexi tipped her head slowly from side to side, searching the room the best she could with one good eye and punctuating each turn with a hushed little gasp or groan. Although her blood dripped onto the sleeve of his jacket, Aiden kept her anchored against him to minimize her movement and keep her from aggravating her injuries. He turned his gaze to the compact detective in the doorway the moment Hud Kramer ended his call. "Where the hell is her team? Why did you leave her alone?"

Hud squared his shoulders against the accusation. "She said she had this. Entry points were secured. I cleared the floor myself. Trust me, the perp wouldn't have gotten anywhere near her if I'd known he still had access to the floor."

Lexi's fingers tightened around his hand. "Take a breath, Aiden. It's not their fault."

"It sure as hell is somebody's fault."

"What happened to my stocking cap?" She must have taken a good blow to the head to be obsessing about that and not her injuries. "It was probably enough cushion to keep my skull from cracking open, but now I don't see it anywhere."

Aiden dutifully swept the room again, but he still didn't see the knit cap with *CSI* embroidered on the front. He reached up and tugged the black knit cap from his own head. "Here. If you're cold, wear mine."

He released her hand to pull the cap over the top of her head, but she suddenly stiffened against him and knocked his hand away. "Wait! Don't touch anything!" She hunched away from him, as if his chest suddenly scorched her. "Don't touch me."

"Lex—"

"There may be evidence on me." She wobbled, fighting to stay upright without his support.

"Huh?"

"*I'm* a crime scene!"

Aiden pulled his cap down over her hair, hopefully locking in some of his body heat. Then he slipped off his insulated jacket. God, she was shaky and looked so pale. "Right now, you're a crime scene who's going into shock."

"I want to process my clothes. He could have left trace on me."

She made a token effort to fight with him, but even if she was 100 percent, he was stronger, and whether she liked it or not, he was in full-on protector mode. He understood that she was all about the job, but right now, he was all about her. He gently wrapped his jacket around her shoulders and snapped it together at the collar. "My jacket will preserve any evidence that's already on you. You can keep it and process it. I've got a spare in my truck."

With the softest of nods, she seemed to calm at his suggestion. She eyed the sterile gloves covering her hands after she pushed them through the sleeves. "There won't be any scrapings under my nails." She pointed to her foot on the floor beside his. "I kicked him. I may have picked up fibers off his clothes. I need to preserve that…" Her head was still bobbing from side to side, although she was leaning against him again, that burst of protest having expended what was left of her energy. "Where's the bootie I was wearing? He had on gloves. But he might have injured himself. Lots of scrapes in a fight. There has to be trace. I just have to find it." Her thoughts bombarded from one observation to the next, making it difficult to follow her conversation. He hoped this was her detail-oriented brain kicking in, sussing out possible clues, and not some rambling side effect of the blows to her head. She reached back to palm the curve of her hip. "My phone's missing. Why would he take…?" Her frantic, disconnected movements suddenly stopped when her focus landed on the dead body lying a few feet away. "Oh, my God. Jennifer…"

"The victim?"

Aiden felt the fight in Lexi try to reassert itself. His pulse leaped as she braced a hand against his thigh, and she pushed herself toward the body. Digging her fingers into his leg to anchor herself, she stretched out her other arm across Blue, reaching for the dark-haired woman. Lexi's fingers danced around the woman's earlobe without touching the body. "He took her earring. Gold and rubies. And the cord around her throat. The probable murder weapon…" Lexi collapsed between Aiden's legs again, the brief burst of emotional adrenaline giving way to her injuries. "He stole evidence. This whole case has been tainted."

"Don't get yourself so worked up. We've still got the body. Doc Watson is bound to find something."

"*I'm* supposed to find something useful."

"And you will. Just not until we get you checked out." He glanced back at the detective guarding the doorway. "Can we get a cool washcloth out of the john?"

"No." Lexi stopped Kramer before he got two steps into the room. "No one else comes in until my team can assess the damage that guy did."

Aiden bit down on his frustration with her putting the case above her own needs. "Either of you got anything I can stanch this cut with?"

Detective Watson stepped up behind his partner and tossed Aiden a white handkerchief. "Here. Ambulance is downstairs. The assistant manager is unlocking the elevator to send them up. One of your team is on his way up, too."

"Finally." Aiden caught the folded square of cotton and shook it loose from its neat folds to gently press it against Lexi's forehead to keep the blood from running into her swollen eye. "Easy, Lex." When she opened her mouth to protest, he silenced her with some of her own logic. "You don't want to drip blood on your crime scene, do you?" Aiden tucked the wadded cotton underneath the knit cap to hold it in place. "How did the perp get by the guards at the elevator and stairwells?"

Keir Watson pulled back the front of his coat and propped his hands at his waist. "Must have been in a room on another floor. Or a service hallway we don't know about. He was in the building the whole time, hiding out somewhere. He must have been moving ahead of our sweep. He'd need to have a master access key to get through the doors."

Aiden was aware of Lexi still turning, even as she leaned against him, to study the mess around them as he and the detectives tried to make sense of what had happened. "You think someone on staff is responsible for this?" He wasn't talking about the murder, although surely the dead woman and the attack on Lexi were linked.

Watson shook his head. "Not necessarily. The guests' key cards work on the stairwell doors, too."

"Somebody could have swiped one," Hud Kramer added. "So this guy was hiding out, waiting for his chance to get back to the crime scene and remove whatever evidence would have incriminated him."

But Lexi didn't intend to be left out of the conversation. "Guys, I was only alone for maybe thirty minutes."

Aiden checked his watch. "You called me fifteen minutes ago." His gaze zeroed in on the detectives. "That means the attack and theft happened in that narrow time frame."

Hud glanced up at his partner, realization dawning on each of them. "He's still in the building."

Keir pulled out the phone he seemed to live by and called someone for a sit rep. "He couldn't have gotten out. We still have every outside exit blocked."

Blue whined at the sudden alertness surging through Aiden. "Unless this was a diversion to get everyone away from their posts so he *could* get out."

Lexi tugged at Aiden's arm. "He stole evidence. Jennifer Li's investigation has been compromised. You have to find this guy before he can destroy the things he took. The murder weapon."

Keir exchanged a nod with his partner. "Floor-by-floor search. Now."

"We're on it. If we can't find him, then maybe we can find his hiding place." As Hud was backing out, he pointed to Lexi. "You'll stay with her?"

"I'm not going anywhere."

"Keep us posted."

Once Aiden was alone with Lexi and Blue and the body, he thought she'd relax. Instead, he felt her pushing against him again. "If they're searching the building, they need you and Blue. I'll be fine. You go."

"Not gonna happen."

"I'm keeping you from doing your job," she argued.

"Part of our job is to protect the members of the CSIU. You called me for backup, and here I am. I only wish Blue and I had gotten here a few minutes sooner."

After the slightest of nods, she burrowed into his chest again. For a split second the lines between protecting Levi's sister and holding the woman he cared far too much about blurred.

But Lexi never forgot that she'd come here to work. She was staring at the windows, that battered brain of hers still searching for answers. "Why did he close the drapes?"

Aiden glanced out at the night sky, warmed by the glow of lights from the Plaza, even at this height. "They're not closed."

"They were open when I started. Then he closed them. That's how I knew something was wrong."

"Maybe he just didn't want anyone seeing that he'd returned to the scene of the crime."

"But why open them again? There has to be a reason."

She collapsed inside Aiden's jacket, her chin resting on the collar, her grip on his hand weakening. Where were those medics?

Aiden heard another man's voice, exchanging a quick greeting with Watson and Kramer. "Hey, Detective. I got here as soon as I could. Came up the stairs like you said... Oh. Okay. They're in a hurry." The bearded criminalist with the glasses who reminded Aiden of a stodgy college professor appeared in the doorway. "Lexi? What happened?"

"Shane." Lexi sat up and lifted her chin as though the movement wouldn't rattle the ball bearings in her skull. "Thank God."

"You're hurt." His initial surprise seemed to be the extent of his emotional reaction to seeing his coworker bruised and bloody at a murder scene. The criminalist pushed his glasses up onto the bridge of his nose and looked around the room. Like Lexi, Shane Duvall was a stickler for details. He opened his kit and slipped on his booties and gloves out in the hallway before entering the room. "What happened?"

Was everyone going to try his patience here tonight? "Someone assaulted her while she was working the scene. Where have you been?"

Duvall's gaze turned to Aiden as if he hadn't realized there was an armed cop sitting behind Lexi and holding her upright. "My son and I spent the day at my parents' in Lee's Summit with the rest of the family. We were on the way home when Ethan called. I had to turn around and drive him back so they could watch him before I came here. He's only two."

"Then you leave him with his mother."

Lexi's grip pulsed around his. A warning?

"His mother is dead," Duvall stated matter-of-factly.

Aiden was upset about so many people dropping the ball with Lexi's safety, but he didn't mean to be a complete jerk. "Oh, man. I'm sorry."

If Duvall took offense at the insensitive remark, he didn't show it. "I do need to look into hiring someone to be with him full-time when I'm on call. That makes sense."

"Lexi getting hurt doesn't make any sense."

"Hey," Lexi chided, turning halfway around to face Aiden. "Ease up. He's part of my team, not yours." The hand resting against his chest and curling into the edge of his protective vest eased the sting of her reprimand. "Shane does logic-speak. He doesn't have an Irish temper like you. Yelling at him won't help him understand."

Shane carried his kit into the room. "It's okay. I'd be pissy, too, if my girl got hurt. If I had a girlfriend."

Her fingers still clung to him, belying her words. "Oh, I'm not his—"

"Where's the rest of your team?" Aiden interrupted, not wanting to put a name to the emotion flaring inside at hearing how quick Lexi was to deny even the possibility they could be more than friends. "I know it's the holiday, but she could have been killed."

"Aiden!"

He wasn't glossing over the extent of what had happened here. "Honey, you can't see your face the way I can. Your words are slurring from the swelling in your lip. That cut on your head needs stitches. You won't stop working and lie still. Where the hell's that medic?"

She frowned. "Honey?"

Oh, man, he was slipping badly here.

Blue rolled to his paws at the ding of the elevator and hurried footsteps of a man jogging through the hallway. "Lexi! Lexi?"

"Easy, boy," Aiden warned, urging the dog into a sit when he recognized the voice. "In here, Wynn."

Although Ethan Wynn was close to Aiden's age, his graying hair made him seem older. He stopped in the doorway and made a quick sweep of the hotel suite. Then he zeroed in on Lexi in the middle of all of it and let out a low whistle. "The cop at the back door said I needed to get up here pronto. You look like you got hit by a truck."

Lexi stirred against Aiden's chest. "You here to work or pay me compliments?"

"Sarcasm is intact." Wynn grinned at Lexi's barb. "She's going to be okay."

Shane gestured to Ethan to put on his protective gear before entering the room. Then he turned to Lexi. "What do you need from us?"

"Take the drapes and cords with us. There was a ligature around the victim's neck the perp came back for. Maybe we can match fibers or the bruising pattern to the drapery cord." She paused to draw in a deep breath, but Aiden hated what this show of strength was costing her. "The guy who attacked me was wearing gloves, so you won't find prints. But we can check for trace. Fibers. Anything he tracked in."

"On it, boss."

"I've processed the bathroom already. Divide the main room into grids and get through it as quickly as you can. I'll download the preliminary pics from my camera, and we can compare if anything besides the earring and ligature are missing or have been tampered with." She paused to press at the handkerchief wadded against her forehead. "Oh, and see if you can find my phone and stocking cap."

"Roger that." Shane immediately went to work.

Ethan got nudged out of the hallway by two paramedics and the gurney they set up across from the open doorway.

With one bootie on and one yet in his hand, he hopped on one foot, whisking on the other foot covering before stumbling into the room. "Ouch," he joked at having to catch himself on the chair beside the door. He sat down on it to finish his prep. "Lots of casualties here. This room must be jinxed."

Before Aiden could comment on his tactless dark humor, Lexi growled an order. "Get to work, Ethan."

"I'm gettin' there." He pushed to his feet. "Don't you worry about a thing except getting to the hospital. Shane and I can handle this."

"Phone!" Shane announced, holding up the cell he'd pulled from under the bed. He knelt in front of her. "Here."

Lexi snatched her hands back from the offering. "No. Bag it. I don't remember it falling out of my pocket. I want to dust it for prints, just in case he tampered with it."

With a nod, Duvall went to his kit to do her bidding.

When she saw the first EMT duck beneath the tape, she warned them away. "Stay out! I'll come to you." She braced her hand against Aiden's shoulder and struggled to get her feet beneath her and stand. He could tell the room must be spinning. She squeezed her good eye shut and dropped her forehead against his collar. "Too many people in the room. This scene has been contaminated enough already."

"Ma'am, you shouldn't move. Let us do the prelim—"

"No," she muttered under her breath. "I've already screwed this up enough. First damn day in charge..." Enough. Aiden got to his knees and scooped Lexi up into his arms. Her head stayed where it was, nestled against his collar. But her fingers latched on to his neck and shoulder as he lifted her against his chest and stood. "What are you doing?"

"You need to see the medic. If you won't let them come to you, I'm taking you to them."

"You're not the boss of me, Aiden Murphy."

Well, if that line wasn't a blast from their childhood? He smiled. "Tonight, I am. Blue! *Fuss.*" He ordered the dog to follow them into the hallway, out of the way of the criminalists now working the scene. He set Lexi on the gurney, laying her back against the pillow as the lead medic stepped in to check her vitals and pupil reaction. A second medic nudged Aiden aside to cover Lexi with a blanket and hook up an IV. She didn't protest when he peeled off her glove and inserted the needle into the back of her hand. "Hang in there, Lex. Let them do their job."

Shane brought the bagged and tagged phone out to Lexi, and she tucked it into the pocket of the jacket she was still wearing. The female medic with long auburn hair grilled Lexi with several questions while she removed the soiled handkerchief, debrided the wound, then packed it with sterile gauze before sliding the knit cap back into place. Good. Aiden liked that Lexi was surrounded by his cap and jacket since he couldn't get to her right now.

The redhead seemed satisfied with her examination and pulled up the rails on the gurney. "What's the verdict?" Lexi asked.

"Probable concussion." While the second EMT packed their med kit and set it on the foot of the gurney, the redhead checked the IV drip and gently slid an ice pack against the knot on Lexi's scalp. "I don't think anything's broken, but I can't give you anything for the pain until the doctors check you out."

"I don't want anything. I'm already fuzzy enough." His jacket swallowed her up as she huddled beneath the blanket. "Did someone open a window? Why is it so cold?"

"We set up some IV fluids to rebuild your blood volume and keep you from going into shock."

"Here." Aiden was having a hard time standing back

and doing nothing. But he spotted Lexi's own coat on the floor and spread it on top of her. "Better?"

She nodded slightly. But when he moved to step out of the way, she pulled her hand from beneath the layers of warmth and reached for him. Aiden grabbed on and didn't let go as the EMTs rolled the gurney onto the elevator. With Blue at his side, Aiden rode down to the main lobby and walked with them outside to the ambulance. He thought with the bite of cold air, she'd withdraw and snuggle under the covers again. But Lexi's grip never once let up.

Even when they reached the back of the ambulance itself, and the medics gave them a couple of minutes while they stowed their gear, Lexi held his hand. Maybe she needed the reassurance of that connection as much as he did.

"I feel like I've been in a prizefight," she confessed.

He wasn't going to tell her she looked it, too. How was he going to explain this to Levi? He had one job to do while his best friend was deployed, and he'd failed miserably. He wasn't failing again. If he and Blue had to work around the clock, he was going to find out who had hurt Lexi, and he wouldn't let that SOB get anywhere close to her again. Then maybe he could look Levi in the eye and tell him he'd done right by the Callahan family. Then maybe that fist of anger, fear and potential loss that was choking his heart would ease its grip and let him go back to being good ol' Aiden Murphy, annoying big brother and friend.

When he couldn't come up with a *"You'll be fine"*, she started relaying directions for her team again. "Tell Shane and Ethan to check all the doors on the ninth floor. See if any of the locks have been jimmied, or if there's residue from being taped off to keep the security locks from engaging. I need to call Chelsea in to run through the hotel's computer system, see if there were any anomalous key swipes recorded. And someone needs to pack up my kit and bring it to the hospital. I want to bag the clothes I'm wearing before anything happens to them."

"They'll figure it out, Lex. No one on your team is a rookie."

"They need direction. I'm their supervisor."

"Right now, you're a patient. Your brain has already been beat up enough tonight, okay? It needs to rest."

"But—"

"Damn it, Lex. When my dad used to wallop me, the school nurse said I needed to lie still and give my body a chance to heal itself." His breath gusted out into a white cloud in the cold air between them.

When the cloud cleared, he saw the stricken look he'd put on her face. She brushed her fingertips against her split lip and bruised eye. "I'm sorry. Does what happened to me remind you of him? I shouldn't have asked you to come."

"You absolutely should have." Aiden bit down on a curse. Because his emotions were so screwed up, he was causing the very stress in Lexi he was trying to help her avoid. "Patrick Murphy is old history. *Very* old history. I was just a boy then." She knew the kind of training he did. Lifting weights. Sparring in the gym. Running with Blue. "I'd like to see him come after me now."

Her fingers slid up his sleeve to squeeze the muscles in his forearm. "Poor Patrick."

He covered her hand with his where it rested on his arm. "I'm just saying I've got experience with this sort of thing. You need to stop being a criminalist for thirty seconds, and let the medics take care of you. You need to rest."

"Okay." It scared him even more that she capitulated so quickly once he'd made the argument personal. He was used to her challenging him, asserting herself as his equal, not worrying about the old hurts and resentments he'd left in his past. "I'll do what they say. For a little while." The corner of her mouth curved into a weak smile, and he felt even more like a heel for causing her one whit of concern about him. "I'll be fine. Don't you worry about me."

"Blue!" The dog trotted up beside him. Aiden hooked him up to his leash. "I'm going with you to the hospital. I'll drive ahead of you and clear traffic with my truck."

"No, you won't. If KCPD is doing a room-to-room search, they need you and Blue here. They're already short-staffed, and Blue does the work of several men."

"*You're* my priority."

"Because Levi said so?" She pulled away with a weary sigh, tucking her hand back under the blanket. "I know the promise you made to him to take care of me while he's overseas. But I am not going to be a burden to him or you or anybody. You have a job to do. Just like I did. Let's not screw anything else up because of me."

Aiden was struggling between duty and his feelings for her. "Sure, I made a promise to Levi. I want to always do right by the Callahan family." He realized he'd left his gloves up at the crime scene, so he stuffed his fingers into the pockets of his black BDU pants and hunched his shoulders against the cold. "Tonight, I let him down. I let you both down."

"Aiden—"

"I could have lost you tonight. I don't want to let you out of my sight."

"I'll be in an ambulance with the paramedics. Then I'll be in the hospital with hundreds of other people. I won't be alone."

"There are hundreds of people here at this hotel tonight, and you were still alone."

She flinched as though his words had dealt her another

blow. She looked away at the emergency lights swirling through the crowd of onlookers gathering on the far side of the iron fence surrounding the hotel's front drive. When she turned her face back to his, her brave, bruised smile was back in place. "Go. Do your job. One of us needs to. Right now, I have to be the patient, right? So you go be the cop."

"Look at you, being all smart and throwing my words back at me." He touched a short strand of silky hair peeking out from the edge of the cap and stroked it back into place behind her ear. "You're not a burden to me, Lex. Not ever. You're…"

"Family?"

Sure. He'd go with that.

The red-haired EMT interrupted their conversation. "We need to go, sir."

Aiden nodded and pulled away as the medics loaded the gurney into the back of the ambulance. "You'll do what they say?"

"I'll be fine."

"Not what I asked, Callahan."

The ambulance doors started to close. That felt like shutting him out, like no matter what he did, he'd always be on the outside, looking in on Lexi's world.

"Aiden?"

He grabbed the door before it closed, always ready to answer her call.

She had her hand outstretched, reaching for him. And when he climbed into the back to take her hand, the EMT discreetly stepped back so that he could kneel beside her. "What do you need?"

"Forget about Levi and make a promise to me tonight."

"Anything."

"Go. Find this guy. Or find me some evidence so I can

track him down." That promise went without saying. "But when you're done here, could you come by the hospital? No matter how late it is? I'll need a ride home."

He nodded to the uncertainty dulling those beautiful green eyes. She wasn't worried about a ride. She was asking for backup. Even though this one-sided relationship that could never be was eating him up inside, Aiden would never say no if she needed him. He leaned in and brushed a gentle kiss across the least bruised part of her face he could find.

When he pulled back, he winked. "Count on it."

Chapter Five

"Here you go." The blonde nurse set the plastic bag filled with medical supply trash in Lexi's lap. "It's an odd request, but I bagged everything we used on you except for the hypodermic. All the swabs and gauze are there. Sealed and labeled it myself like you said."

"Thank you."

"It felt like we were putting together a rape kit on you, swabbing all your injuries." Her forehead knit together in a gentle frown. "Are you sure you weren't sexually assaulted and want us to do a full kit?"

"Thank you for being concerned, but no." Lexi waved her hand around her face. "I'm certain all the injuries are up here. Thank you for being so thorough."

"Glad I could help. Take it easy until your ride gets here." While Lexi tucked the bag on the hospital bed beside her, the nurse set the call button on her pillow. "Even though we're not admitting you, if you start to feel woozy, you need help getting dressed or anything else, just push that button."

As soon as the nurse left the semiprivate room off the ER where Lexi was supposed to rest until Aiden came to drive her home, Lexi crawled out of bed, pulling the bag the nurse had brought with her. The bloody contents of the package might be a gruesome souvenir to most patients, but she intended to register it at the lab and study every inch of it to see if there was any trace from her attacker left behind. Although her desperate need for answers wanted her to open the bag and start working, she knew how important it was to preserve whatever was there until she was in the pristine environment of the lab. She had the potential evidence in her custody, and right now, that was all that mattered.

Instead, she opened the bag with her personal belongings, knowing she'd have to dress before she could leave. She held her boots up to the light above the head of the bed, checking the soles for any unusual trace. But if tripping her attacker had pulled anything uniquely identifiable off him, the evidence had gone the way of the missing bootie.

Although her stitches tugged at her scalp when she squinted to study her clothing more carefully, and her head throbbed with every footfall, she was intent on locating anything that might prove useful to identifying her attacker and Jennifer Li's killer. Once she was convinced there was nothing she could log as evidence, she pulled her jeans on under the hospital gown she wore. Before she put her sweater and blouse on, she spread them out across the bed to study them. Neither one looked very warm and comforting right now. Blood stained the cuffs and collar of her blouse, and her sweater had been cut off her in the ER, so the staff didn't have to pull it over her head. She moved on to Aiden's jacket and cap from the plastic bag with her belongings and added them to the top of the bed.

Her wounds had been treated. Insurance had been filed. She had a printout of concussion protocols with accepted treatments and warning signs that merited contacting a physician again. She'd been checked from stem to stern, with the resulting report that her only injuries were the blows to her head and some bruising on her body. But if

Nurse Polly thought she was going to "take it easy" without having any answers, then they didn't know her very well. The attack on Lexi had jeopardized solving Jennifer Li's murder, and it might even have compromised KCPD's investigation into a potential serial killer, if it turned out Jennifer Li's death and Giselle Byrd's murder she'd investigated earlier that week were related.

Sitting still and doing nothing had never been her best thing. And when doing nothing might impact the investigation her team and Detectives Watson and Kramer were working on tonight, doing nothing would be impossible. Since the doctor hadn't given her a sedative, and recommended over-the-counter pain meds, she wasn't about to fall asleep with her mind racing with the need to work.

She should have brought her kit with her to the hospital and gathered samples as the ER doctor and trauma staff worked on her. She felt like an amateur looking for evidence this way, but at least she was doing something useful. Still, the nurse had purposefully dimmed the lights in the room so as not to aggravate her concussion. And Lexi needed more light if she was going to focus her one good eye and the slit of vision she had in her left eye on anything useful. So she pushed the switch twice, taking the level of light over the bed from naptime in the shadows to piercing Lexi's brain like a fiery hot poker. With three more quick taps, she adjusted the light to its middle level and leaned over the bed, ignoring the throbbing in her skull as she studied the blouse and sweater piece by piece.

Nothing. Nothing. And more nothing.

She needed an ultraviolet light to look for any transfer that was invisible to the naked eye. Lexi shivered in her hospital gown, not feeling terribly inclined to put her stained clothes back on. Instead, she folded them neatly and told herself she would look more closely at them once she had her kit.

When she got to Aiden's coat, she gathered it into her arms and dipped her nose to the collar. She breathed in the spicy, musky scent that was uniquely his and felt a sense of calm seep through her as she exhaled, taking the edge off her frantic need to find answers. Beyond the security of her parents, and Levi's overprotective nature where she was concerned, Lexi had never felt the kind of security she experienced when Aiden was with her. Bully eliminator in middle school. Flat-tire fixer in high school. Shoulder to cry on when her choice in men blew up in her face. He could make her laugh, he could drive her crazy, but she always felt safe with him. She felt as valued and cared for with Aiden as she did her own brother. Maybe because of their opposite personalities, Aiden seemed to bring balance to her world. If her family had grounded him, he had pushed her out of her comfort zone. Get another specialized degree. Take the promotion. Rappel down that cliff. Dump the guy who made her cry. He was that bolster of support who assured her of her strength, that devil's advocate who helped her clear her thoughts so that she could make informed decisions. He was that solid foundation that gave her the confidence to do and be everything she wanted to be.

But something with Aiden had felt different tonight. The way he and Blue had charged into that hotel room to find her. The way he'd scooped her up in his arms and wrapped his jacket and body around hers to give her the heat and strength she'd lost. The balance between them had felt off-kilter. She knew him well enough to know Aiden had been afraid for her, afraid she was more seriously injured, afraid she might die. But where did that fear come from? Reliving his own childhood trauma? Worry about failing his promise to Levi? Failing her? Was it possible his feelings were something other than friendship?

When he'd been eighteen, and she'd been a lowly freshman in high school, she'd had all kinds of innocent fantasies about Aiden charging to her rescue like he had tonight. There'd be a kiss, and they'd ride off into the sunset in his truck. The teasing conversations they shared would turn to more serious, more heartfelt topics. She'd have even given him her virginity if he'd asked for it—not that Levi would have been thrilled with Aiden taking advantage of her innocent desires, and not that Aiden would have taken advantage of anyone—and she'd be a willing participant. But since none of that had happened, those fantasies had eventually become nothing more than girlish entries in her journal. Her lusty admiration for all things Aiden Murphy had eventually receded as she matured, and her teenage feelings had gone the way of her journal—packed up in a box and stowed away in a dusty corner of the attic.

If she ever put a name to the grown-up version of that teenage crush that crept into her thoughts on nights like this, it would feel like too much, like she'd be risking all that was good and loyal and comforting between them for something that might not be reciprocated in the same way. Something that wouldn't last. Something that would drive a wedge into his friendship with Levi and destroy the precious perfection of the relationship she shared with him now.

He'd be without a family. And she'd be without Aiden.

Maybe she'd misread the vibe Aiden was giving off tonight. Clearly, she hadn't understood Kevin's feelings for her. She hadn't even suspected he wasn't as committed to keeping their relationship going as she'd been. Not until she'd found him in bed with his executive assistant did she realize just how broken their relationship had become.

Apparently, Lexi needed obvious clues she could process, whether it was a crime scene or a relationship. And since Aiden had never once presented any facts for her to evaluate—not one kiss on the lips, no seductive words or love notes, not even an invitation for a date—she couldn't trust her gut that he would ever be interested in something more.

Without any evidence to pursue that line of thinking, Lexi breathed in the scent and warmth that Aiden's jacket represented one more time before shaking it loose and flipping it around her shoulders to slide on like a familiar hug. But when she pulled out the knit cap that had been tucked inside the sleeve, she paused.

Something thin, light-colored, almost translucent, was caught in the nubby weave.

She moved closer to the light over the bed to study it more carefully. Although, *study* was a relative term. "What I wouldn't give for two good eyes and a flashlight right now."

She remembered protesting when Aiden had pulled off his cap and tugged it down over her hair to anchor a rudimentary bandage and keep her from going into shock. But maybe she should be thanking him for preserving this tiny piece of evidence.

Was it a strand of pale hair? Some other fiber that was too fine to study with the naked eye? It was too light-colored to match Aiden's blue-black hair. It was too straight to be one of her own waves. Too long to belong to Blue. While she couldn't rule out that it was a hair or fiber from Aiden's most recent date, she knew that he didn't wear his uniform when he went out. And he hadn't mentioned that he'd been seeing anyone recently, anyway. Was this tiny anomaly in Aiden's cap something she'd picked up in Jennifer Li's hotel room?

Could it be trace from the man who'd attacked her?

Lexi's pulse revved with anticipation. Maybe her contributions tonight wouldn't be a total loss. She could analyze it later in the lab, as long as she preserved the chain of evidence, and find an answer to who had attacked her or where he'd been or something he'd encountered before coming after her. Anything besides this helpless feeling of not knowing who had hurt her and ended another woman's life tonight.

She surveyed the room for something sterile she could use to preserve the evidence. Her gaze landed on the water cup sealed in clear plastic on the rolling tray beside the bed. She peeled the bag open, then used it to pluck the hair or fiber from the knit cap. She dropped it into the cup and folded the bag shut around the cup. Another quick search led her to the marker on the dry-erase board beside the door. She wrote the time and date on the bag, listed the location where she'd found it, and was adding her initials to the bag when the door swung open.

"Lexi?"

She backed away, barely escaping being hit by the door as a tall blond man strode in. He wore a black tuxedo, wool coat and white cashmere scarf with long fringe. She knew she was in trouble before Kevin Nelson swallowed her up in a tight hug that lifted her onto her toes. "Kev?"

"Oh, my God, Lexi." Her ex-boyfriend and would-have-been fiancé set her back on her feet, rubbing his hands up and down her arms as he leaned back to see her injuries. "Look at you. I came as soon as we could get away from Mother and Father's dinner party. What happened?"

"We?" Lexi palmed the middle of his chest and pushed him back a step, all the while clutching her cup-size bag of evidence in a fist to her own chest. "Kevin, what are you doing here?"

With some breathing room between them, she could

look beyond him to see the woman waiting in the doorway behind him. Not the office assistant she'd found Kevin with when they broke up. No, this one was a stunning platinum blonde who wore her silvery evening gown, and what Lexi hoped was a fake fur coat, with the elegant confidence of a woman who belonged in Kevin's privileged world.

"Um…?" Why did she suddenly feel like she'd been hit in the head again? She didn't understand what was happening. "Who…?" She tilted her face up to Kevin's. "Why are you here?"

Kevin stepped to one side to make introductions. "Alexis Callahan. This is Cynthia Sterling."

"His fiancée," Cynthia clarified. She pulled her left hand from the pocket of her ermine-like coat and propped it on her hip in a not-so-subtle show of the diamond cluster on her ring finger.

"Oh." When she felt the weight of Kevin's hand settling at the small of her back, Lexi moved away, pulling Aiden's jacket together at her neck and hugging it around her body. It wasn't fur and it wasn't fake, but she'd take his KCPD jacket any day over Cynthia's showy outfit. "Congratulations."

Instead of helping her make sense of his presence here, Kevin pulled his scarf from his coat and looped it around his fiancée's neck, pulling her toward him in what Lexi supposed was some cutesy form of intimacy. Though after what she'd seen tonight in Jennifer Li's suite at the Regal Hotel, Lexi found the gesture anything but cute. "Cynthia, would you find us some hot coffee? And maybe you'd better have a seat in the waiting room. I'm not certain yet what Lexi needs from me, and I'm sure there's a rule about having too many visitors and upsetting the patient."

"What I need from you?" Lexi echoed. Cynthia looked about as thrilled to be here as Lexi was to have the company.

"Yes. The hospital called me," Kevin finally explained. "I'm still listed as your emergency contact."

"You are?" He'd left his parents' swanky Thanksgiving soiree to come see an old girlfriend because the hospital had gotten his name from her purse? "I forgot to change it. I guess I haven't needed anyone since we broke up."

The double entendre of her words seemed to go right over his head. "Well, you need someone tonight. I'm glad University Hospital called. You and I have too much history for me to leave you alone at a time like this."

Cynthia's sigh echoed throughout the room. She understood Lexi's double meaning. She straightened on her spiky silver heels, and Lexi idly wondered how she'd gotten through the snow in those delicate shoes. "Do what you have to, darling. It's good that you can make the time to help those in need." Lexi wanted to arch an eyebrow at what felt like an insult. Cynthia didn't need to be slinging barbs. She had no interest in staking a claim on the other woman's fiancé. The platinum blonde rested her hand on Kevin's chest a moment before tying the scarf loosely around her neck. "I love that about you. I'll get your coffee and meet you in the waiting area."

"Thank you, darling."

"Nice to meet you, Alexis." Kevin's parents probably loved Cynthia's veneer of impeccable politeness. "I'm sorry it wasn't under better circumstances."

Cynthia's insecurity over Kevin's wandering eyes might be laughable if Lexi didn't know she was smart to be cautious.

But the blonde had nothing to worry about from Lexi. As far as she was concerned, this visit was a paperwork snafu, not a second-chance romance about to happen. She nudged Kevin toward the door. "Go with her. Truly, they're not even keeping me overnight. I'll straighten things out with the hospital."

Kevin planted his feet and faced her. He cupped her elbows and ran his hands up and down her arms. "I want to be here if you need me. I hate that you're alone. I know I screwed things up between us, but that doesn't mean I stopped caring."

"Despite what your fiancée says, I'm hardly a charity case, Kev. And I'm not alone." Although, the emptiness of the room belied that statement.

She had Aiden and Blue. And her friends at the lab. Didn't she?

"Isn't Levi deployed?"

"Yes. But I have other people in my life. I appreciate your concern, but I don't need you." She shrugged off his touch and retreated until her hips hit the bed. "I apologize for the inconvenience, but you should leave."

She wasn't surprised that Kevin followed her into the room to argue his case to square things between them after their messy split or whatever this visit was about. But curiosity pushed aside her annoyance when her gaze zeroed in on a dusting of fibers that clung to the lapel of his black wool dress coat.

Long. Straight. Pale in color and nearly translucent.

Her fingers teased the makeshift evidence bag she'd tucked into her pocket. Unless she compared them under a microscope with a bright light, she couldn't be certain they were a match. But to her bruised, weary eyes in the room's relatively dim light, they looked similar.

Were they fibers from his scarf? Strands of Cynthia's hair? Kevin's hair was combed back and gelled into place. Just how long was his hair?

And was this where her battered brain was taking her? That her ex was a serial killer? Sad to say, but she didn't think Kevin possessed the organizational skills necessary to plot out anyone's demise. But losing his temper? A crime of passion? She remembered him chasing her out into the hallway of their apartment building the afternoon she'd come home early from classes and found him cheating on her. Wearing nothing but a sheet wrapped around his waist, he'd pinned her to the wall and pleaded his case as though it was her fault he'd been naked with his assistant.

What were the odds that she would be the CSI who showed up at the aftermath of his crime? She had a feeling Cynthia would be more cutthroat about killing the other woman. But again, what were the odds that Kevin knew Jennifer Li? His initials hadn't been on those Christmas gift tags.

Unless the attack on her was a separate incident from Jennifer Li's murder?

But why? Kevin had just said he cared about her. In the years they'd been together, her heart and ability to trust might have taken a beating, but Kev had never used his fists. Unless leaving him had brought out a different side to his behavior?

Lexi squeezed her eyes shut. Her mind was racing. Spinning. Her brain was legitimately dizzy and full of far too much wild speculation. She'd conjured up too many possibilities and no concrete answers. She wasn't the detective. She needed those facts, lab analyses, detailed reports to sort out all that had happened tonight.

But with a compromised crime scene, were trustworthy answers even possible?

She was so focused on plucking one of the strands from Kevin's coat that she missed him reaching out to pinch her chin between his thumb and index finger and tilt her face up to his. "Letting you go without a fight was a mistake. Cynthia is everything I thought I wanted in a wife, but there's no fire. I don't love her the way I loved you."

"Ouch!" Lexi slapped his hand away, suddenly wishing she wasn't so good at being independent. What if Kevin meant her harm? And now she was alone with him? "I hope that's not true. If you're going to marry her, you need to love her better than you ever loved me." She slid to one side.

But Kevin followed, keeping her trapped against the bed. "That's not fair, Lexi. We had a lot of good times together. We were a good match. My parents would have come around to the idea of us as a couple, even if you didn't join the company."

"I wasn't involved with them."

"I made one mistake. You're going to throw away everything we could have been because—?"

"Yes!" She shoved at his chest, hating that he was here tonight. "It wasn't right between us, and I doubt it was one time. You didn't want to support me, and I didn't have the energy to support you the way you wanted. It was never going to be."

"Don't say that. We're in a different place now. I'm more mature." Although he gave her the space she demanded, he still reached for her. "I believe coming together like this tonight is kismet, sending me a clear message—"

"Your kismet wouldn't have happened if I hadn't gotten the crap beat out of me tonight."

Yeah, she was betting perfectly posh Cynthia had never uttered a sentence like that.

"But you'll heal. It looks harsh now, but the scarring won't be permanent. You'll be pretty again soon enough. I knew your public service job would eventually come to something like this."

Wow. She really had dodged a bullet by dumping this guy. "Your empathy knows no limit, does it."

"Why are we arguing? I'm here to take care of you."

"It's not your job anymore." Lexi batted his hands away. "You weren't particularly good at it, anyway. I refuse to have this conversation again. If you truly want to help, then leave. I'll change my emergency contact information, so you're not called again."

"I don't mind—"

"That's it, pal. You're done here." A large black gym bag sailed past Kevin's shoulder and landed with a thump on the bed. Aiden followed in its wake, moving in beside Lexi and loosely draping his arm around her shoulders to pull her to his side. His uniform smelled like cold, fresh air, his skin like warm spice. It felt like heaven to have his familiar strength beside her again. "The lady says go, so you're going."

Kevin seemed shocked by the intrusion. "Excuse me, Officer. This is personal."

"Damn right it is. Lex asked you to leave. I'll make sure that happens."

"I'm a close friend of Ms. Callahan's—"

"No, you're not." Lexi curled her fingers into the taut stretch of material between Aiden's flak vest and utility belt. Now she was thanking her good fortune that she'd caught Kev in flagrante delicto and had ended their relationship. "We stopped being close a long time ago."

"Whose fault is that? I won't come groveling to you again." Lexi heard the bite in Kevin's accusation. Aiden heard it, too.

He dropped his arm from her shoulders and took a step toward Kevin. "Nobody asked you to."

"So you've staked your claim on her."

"Staked my claim? She's a grown woman who makes

her own choices. And she's not choosing you. Now beat it, before I have to pull out my badge and do something official to keep you from harassing her."

"Aiden." Lexi latched on to the back of Aiden's belt. Kevin was a couple of inches taller than Aiden, and the padded shoulders of his coat made him appear broader, but Lexi knew which man she'd put her money on in a fight. Not that she was going to let the two men get into any kind of brawl in her hospital room. "Take a breath. Please?"

Thankfully, Aiden listened to her in a way Kevin rarely had. She could still feel the wary tension in the muscles of his back, but he turned his stubbled chin to his shoulder to address her, all without taking his eyes off Kevin. "I stopped by the house on the way here. Thought you might want some fresh clothes. Not sure I got all the right stuff, but it'll get you home."

"Thank you. I don't particularly want to put on blood-stained clothes again."

"You have a key to her house?" Kevin raked his fingers through his hair, shaking his head as though the intimacy implied by this man knowing his way around her things confused him.

Oh, if she could only capture one of those hairs as it drifted down onto his coat. But no, she just wanted him gone.

Then Kevin snapped his fingers. "You're Lexi's brother, aren't you?"

Kevin's smile of relief, dismissing Aiden's close relationship as familial, and therefore something he could ignore, grated on what was left of Lexi's raw nerves. She linked her arm through Aiden's, laced her fingers with his and moved up beside him. "My parents fostered him. But we're not related by blood. He's a better man than you'll ever know how to be, and I trust him more than I ever trusted you."

"So it's kinky like that, huh?"

Aiden's grip tightened around hers, and Lexi realized *she* was the one who was losing her temper.

Another man cleared his throat behind Kevin. As Kevin turned, she saw Mac Taylor and his wife, Jules, in the doorway. "Sounds a little heated for a hospital room," Mac observed, taking in Lexi and her visitors.

Julia Dalton-Taylor was a curvy woman with short blond hair and soft hazel eyes. "How are you feeling?" she asked.

"I'm fine," Lexi assured her.

"You don't look fine." Mac's raspy-voiced observation made her wonder if he was here as her boss or her friend. "Ethan reported what happened. Thought I'd better check in with you."

"I'm sorry, Mac." The confrontation with her ex was temporarily forgotten as she hastened to apologize for failing so miserably her first day heading up her own squad. "I don't know where the guy who attacked me came from. The detectives had cleared the floor. He should have been locked out."

Aiden added his own apology. "If only I'd gotten there a few minutes sooner—this wouldn't have happened, and we'd have the guy in custody. Blue always finds his man."

Mac adjusted his glasses. "Neither of you needs to apologize. I'm just glad you're alive to tell me about it." He turned his sighted eye from Lexi to Aiden. "I appreciate you being there for her."

"Yes, sir."

"Do you mind if I have a look?" Julia linked her arm with Lexi's and pulled her aside to read her chart at the foot of the bed. She pressed her fingers to Lexi's wrist and

studied her watch while Lexi kept glancing back at the
standoff between Aiden and Kevin. The three men were
making introductions, recalling that Kevin had attended a
couple of lab staff gatherings with Lexi, but the conversation was more polite than friendly. "Your blood pressure
is a little elevated," Jules reported.

"I'm a little stressed," Lexi confessed.

Jules made a notation on the electronic chart. "Ross
Muhlbach is a fabulous doctor. Polly Cooper is new, but
I've been impressed with her nursing work thus far. You're
in good hands."

"I'm not stressed about the care I received."

The older woman's soft smile was all soothing caregiver
for a moment before it flatlined. "Mac?"

"What do you need, hon?" The conversation instantly
fell silent as Mac excused himself and draped his arm
around his wife's shoulders. Jules glanced toward Kevin
and Aiden before stretching up on tiptoe to whisper into
Mac's ear. "I'm on it." They squeezed each other's hand
before he completely pulled away to face the younger men.
"Mr. Nelson? You might remember my wife, Julia Dalton-
Taylor. She's the senior trauma nurse on staff here, and
the director of emergency nursing education here at the
university."

Kevin's light blond eyebrows knit together with a frown
at the extensive introduction. Still, he offered Mac's wife
a polite nod. "Mrs. Taylor."

Mac opened the door and gestured toward the waiting
area. "I need you to step outside with me. Ms. Callahan
requires her privacy."

Jules pulled the blood pressure cuff from the cart near
the head of the bed. "Sooner rather than later would be
nice."

Was something wrong with her BP? Lexi sank onto the

edge of the bed at the off-duty nurse's direction. But her gaze crossed the room to meet Aiden's blue eyes. They narrowed in concern. "Ma'am? Is she okay?"

The loud rasp of Julia ripping the Velcro apart on the BP cuff sounded ominous. "Officer Murphy, come sit beside the patient. Keep her calm for me."

"Yes, ma'am."

Lexi's fingers felt cold inside Aiden's warm grip. She toppled against his shoulder as the bed took his weight beside her. She didn't try to move away.

Mac pointed to the hallway beyond the door. "Mr. Nelson?"

Kevin reached the doorway before he turned and planted his feet. "Wait. *He* gets to stay? I know you're her brother's sidekick, but—"

"I *want* him to stay," Lexi insisted. Especially if there was something more seriously wrong with her, Aiden was the one she wanted beside her.

Julia Dalton-Taylor proceeded to put the stethoscope around her neck and push the sleeve of Aiden's jacket up Lexi's arm. "Kevin, is it? The patient has asked you to leave. Dr. Muhlbach's orders say Ms. Callahan needs to have a quiet evening. You're not helping."

Mac had no qualms about stepping into Kevin's space and backing him into the doorway. "That lady outranks all of us here. I suggest you do what she says."

Kevin glanced down at Mac, evaluating the subtle threat in the older man's tone. Then, like the man-size spoiled brat he was being tonight, he pointed to Lexi. "*She's* the one who called me."

"The hospital called you," Lexi reminded him. Releasing Aiden's fingers, moving past the nurse tending to her, she grabbed her purse, dug out her wallet and pulled out the old emergency contact card. Then she tore the card into pieces and stuffed it into Kevin's hand. "It won't happen again."

"Shall we?" Mac's terse invitation wasn't really a request.

Kevin was smart enough to finally realize he had no power in this room. He tossed the shreds of paper onto the floor and backed into the hallway ahead of Mac. She wondered if he knew Cynthia was standing right there, holding two cups of coffee, glaring as she listened to every word he'd no doubt have to make excuses for later. "I still care, Lexi. I thought you'd reached out to me. That you'd forgiven me. You gave me hope that we could be a team again. Were you lying—?"

Aiden happily shut the door to block out the useless protests. Lexi picked up the shredded card and tossed it into the trash before sitting on the bed again. "Clearly, I need to update that."

As she pushed her sleeve back up her arm, she realized Mac's wife was packing away the blood pressure equipment and stethoscope. "You two enjoy your evening. I need to go rescue my husband."

"But I thought…"

Jules reached over to squeeze Lexi's knee. "There's nothing wrong with your blood pressure. It was slightly elevated, but not enough to be alarmed. Considering the trauma you suffered tonight and arguing with your unwanted guest, I wouldn't have been surprised if it was even higher." She tucked the equipment back into the cubby beside the bed. "Now, take a couple of deep breaths, let your friend here take care of you a little bit, and congratulations on that promotion."

Lexi imagined she was frowning, although her face was bruised and swollen enough that she couldn't feel much. "Mac's probably reconsidering choosing me after tonight."

"He has no regrets whatsoever. He was only worried about you getting hurt."

"I'll be okay."

"Yes, you will." The older woman extended her hand to Lexi. Although Mac's wife would never be considered a striking beauty, when her lips curved with that gentle, knowing smile, her beauty and compassion shone through, making it easy to see why her boss was so completely devoted to this woman. "I'll leave you two alone."

Aiden shook hands with her, too, before opening the door for her. "Thank you, Mrs. Taylor."

"Good night."

Aiden closed the door behind her. "That is one clever lady. She defused the tension in the room without ever raising her voice. Thinks on her feet." He faced Lexi again. "Like somebody else I know."

"I don't know how that visit got so out of hand. It was just a fluke that Kevin was here. Right?" She unzipped the gym bag Aiden had brought. Her heart warmed at the odd assortment of clothing and supplies he'd stuffed inside— everything from a pair of running shoes and her fuzzy blue slippers, to an embarrassingly skimpy bra she'd gotten as a joke on a girls' night out and only wore on laundry day, thick hiking socks, her travel toiletry bag, a brush and comb, and a chocolate bar. Lexi avoided the bra that made her blush when she thought of Aiden going through her lingerie drawer, and she pulled out the faded T-shirt and Kansas City Chiefs hoodie he'd packed for her. "Don't you take anything he said to heart. There's nothing kinky about our relationship," she asserted, ignoring the whole flush of heat she'd felt at imagining him touching her intimate apparel. "You and I are not related. If he's jealous because I turned to you instead of him, that's his problem."

Aiden raised his hands in surrender to her argument,

without confirming or denying whether Kevin's insinuations had gotten under his skin the way they had hers. "My opinion of Mr. Revolving Zipper Pants notwithstanding, I am here for you. You can turn to me for anything. Crowd control. Chauffeur service. Body heat. Whatever you need."

Body heat? She must have heard wrong. Or read a double entendre where none was intended. Those dusty old fantasies locked away in her high school diary kept trying to resurrect themselves. Lexi blamed her aching head for not having better control of her hormones tonight. "I could use a couple of ibuprofen and a ride home."

"Done. I'll catch Mrs. Taylor and tell her your headache isn't going away. Then I'll pull my truck around front while you get changed." He paused with his hand on the door. "By the way, I've got your CSI kit locked up in my truck with Blue. Duvall says it looks like everything inside is accounted for."

Lexi's mood lifted. "That's better news than if you'd brought me a dozen roses and a get-well card. Thank you."

"I know you're not the roses type." He winked and opened the door.

But her happy relief was short-lived as fatigue, self-doubts and fear rushed in. "Aiden?"

Always attuned to her, he heard even that soft whisper. He pushed the door shut and came back to her. "Do I need to call the nurse?" When she couldn't immediately give voice to the thoughts that were bothering her, he touched his fingers to the lock of hair curving over her cheek and smoothed it behind her ear. "Lex? Hey. You know you can tell me anything."

She needed to touch him. She needed a connection, the secure foundation he'd always given her. Lexi reached up and straightened the collar of his uniform shirt and the turtleneck beneath it. Her fingertips might have grazed the ticklish stubble of his dark beard, might have lingered against his warm skin. Her gaze might have zeroed in on the angular line of his jaw and the firm, slightly crooked tilt of his mouth.

His hands slipped beneath the jacket that was long on her and curled around her waist. She was vividly aware of the imprint of ten fingers against her jeans and the bare skin above her waistband. "Hell. You're not wearing anything underneath."

"Too much blood" was all she answered.

And when he would have pulled away, she dropped her hands to grab his wrists to maintain the connection. "No. Don't let go."

His chest expanded with a deep breath he held for several seconds before it seemed as if something inside him let go and he exhaled again. His hands slid against her waist once more, the tips of his fingers settling over the flare of her hips. "Not to be thickheaded, but maybe you'd better explain what's going on here."

"I was scared tonight," she confessed, drifting half a step closer. She curled her fingers into his shirt above his vest, wrinkling the material she'd smoothed a few moments earlier. "I'm an independent woman. I am the home front of a military family. I have three college degrees. I know how to be on my own. Tonight felt different. I was all alone, and I didn't think help was coming in time, and everything you and Levi taught me, it didn't do me a bit of good. And now with Kevin? For a minute, I was scared again. Not just annoyed with him. I don't know who hurt me. What if it was him? What man am I supposed to trust now? I don't like it when I can't figure things out. And I don't like to be scared—"

"You trust *me*. Always." He released her to frame her

jaw between his hands, turning her face up to his. "Don't
feel guilty about being scared. You're human, aren't you?
Being scared is what makes you run or fight. What you
have to remember is that you survived. That bastard
meant you harm. Maybe he meant to kill you like that
poor woman. It's damn near impossible to protect yourself
against a blitz attack. A slightly built man or a woman or
even a softy like Nelson can overpower you if he or she
gets in that first punch." He traced his thumb across her
bruised cheek and gentled his tone. "But you didn't give
up. You fought back. You got the help you needed. I know
you're brave and smart and did everything we taught you
to defend yourself. And it worked."

Not very well. "He got away. He stole evidence. Probably ruined the investigation. At least, he made it a lot
harder to solve."

"But you survived to still be a key part of that investigation. You *survived*. Never discount how much that means."
He paused in his vehement defense of her. He searched her
face. For what, she couldn't be sure. And then he dipped
his head and pressed a kiss to the corner of her mouth. He
lingered long enough for her to feel the soft scrape of his
stubble against her skin, long enough for every dormant
wish to awaken, long enough for the desire to turn his
touch into a real kiss to rush to the spot and tremble beneath his lips. Her pulse was pounding in her ears when he
pulled away. "I promise you, help will always come when
you need it. *I* will be there when you need me."

Her panties got a little damp at that powerfully evoca-
tive promise.

But there were no panties involved with Aiden Murphy.
No sexy bras. No bare skin touching. No kissing. There
couldn't be. Her willpower was in short supply tonight. If
her lip didn't feel the size of a golf ball, she'd be pulling

his mouth down to hers and obeying the crazy urge to turn that buss on the corner of her mouth into a real kiss. But Kevin had already filled the room with awkwardness by calling Aiden her brother. She needed to lighten things up so he could go back to being the Aiden who made her feel physically and emotionally safe again. "Just you? What about Blue?"

That lightened the mood a bit. She did her best to smile, and he chuckled. "Yeah. The dog, too. We're a package deal."

He started to pull away, but she stopped him. Lexi rose on tiptoe and hugged her arms around Aiden's neck, sliding her cheek against his. Her breasts flattened against the hard shell of his protective vest. But the nerve endings in her skin danced in awareness of his ticklish beard stubble and the heat of his thighs crowding against hers. She breathed in his masculine scent and reveled in his unyielding strength.

To hell with awkwardness. Had anything ever felt so good as having Aiden wrapping his strong arms around her?

"Hey."

"Would you stay for a few minutes and just hold me?"

His arms tightened, securing her against him. His breath eased out of his chest and she settled even more closely against him. He gently palmed the back of her head and tucked her beneath his chin. "Anytime, Lex. Anytime."

of the Craftsman cottage and the snow-dusted around the brown and

Chapter Six

"You wanted snow for Thanksgiving, Levi? Here's your snow." Lexi left the illumination of her porch light and turned her computer notebook toward the snow-dusted hedge in front of the bay window of her Craftsman cottage. She made a slow sweep with the computer to capture the layers of smooth white snow that covered her front yard like a blanket of cotton beset with sequins that sparkled in the light from the streetlamp. "Is it too dark to see it? Aiden? A little help?"

Aiden dutifully turned his flashlight to the pretty drifts that had gathered around the evergreen bushes. An online video chat at one in the morning wasn't his first choice as to how this night would end. He'd rather Lexi be inside the house, where it was both warmer and more secure than her front yard. And he refused to acknowledge the inner voice that had had a very clear idea about where he wanted the night to end earlier tonight at the hospital. Whether it was his bed or hers, he'd wanted them to stay just as close as they'd been when she'd insisted on him holding her. But getting close like that—staying close—was dangerous territory.

And so he was holding a flashlight and walking a dog and tromping through the snow, pretending that things were normal and this was enough.

He didn't really begrudge her this Thanksgiving video chat with her brother. She needed the boost in spirit by sharing a little time with her only surviving family after everything she'd been through. She was determined to give Levi this taste of home while he was surrounded by sand and heat.

Aiden glanced over her shoulder to ostensibly be part of the online family gathering. "How's that?"

"Looks like you got snow there early this year," Levi commented.

"And a lot of it."

With Aiden holding Blue on his leash in the other hand, the three of them had taken a walk around the block. He had originally intended to do a quick sweep of the neighborhood to ease his own edgy concerns and give Blue a bit of exercise before turning in. But to Blue's delight, Lexi was bundled up and leading the way out the door before he could get his own coat zipped. Despite every argument to the contrary, he hadn't been able to convince her to postpone the call or to make it from inside the house. She'd claimed the cold air felt invigorating so that she wasn't tired, and the darkness of the night didn't aggravate her headache the way the artificial lights inside the house did. He suspected that the perfectionist in her didn't want to let anything like a blown crime scene, the assault on her or harassment by her ex-boyfriend spoil the plans she had made to celebrate the holiday long-distance with Levi via their biweekly video chat.

She puffed out a steamy breath to make a cloud in the air. "Can you see how cold it is? You'll be able to feel it yourself soon enough."

"It gets cold here, too, you know." Levi plucked at the neckline of his khaki sweater beneath his desert fatigues.

She scooped up a handful of snow and let it float

through her gloved fingers. "But you don't get this. You're in the desert, not the mountains there."

"Sis, you don't have to indulge me," Levi chided, laughing at her childish enthusiasm. "You look exhausted."

Lexi shook her head at the rugged, familiar face on the computer screen. "Gee, thanks. It *is* one a.m. our time. I've had a long day."

Even though she said she'd taken a nap this afternoon to help her body adjust to working the late shift, Aiden had a feeling she was running on adrenaline. Excitement at seeing her brother, anxiety about the murder investigation, and probably some lingering fear about going to bed and reliving the assault once she succumbed to the vulnerability of sleep must all be fueling her late-night fun and games. He had a feeling she was going to crash hard sooner than she expected.

But Aiden intended to keep an eye on her and be there to back her up when she needed him—whether she'd admit that need or not. She'd practically melted into him during that never-ending hug at the hospital tonight, as if she couldn't stand on her own two feet a moment longer. Another couple of minutes, and he'd have had to step away from her to keep her from realizing how that cheek-to-thigh press of her curves against his hungry body had affected him. Fortunately, she'd gotten whatever she needed from him to find the strength to pull away and send him out to get her ibuprofen and his truck before his desire for Lexi embarrassed them both.

"I'm the one in a war zone. But you look like you've been through hell. You sure you don't need to be in the hospital?" Levi asked, his face set in a worried frown. "Or at least inside the house? Put Aiden on."

"Oh, fine." She sighed dramatically. "Here. Indulge your bro code."

She took Blue's leash and handed Aiden the computer. He sat on the top step of the porch, keeping Lexi in sight as she took Blue around the yard for another chance to do his business.

"Give me the real scoop, Murph." Levi sounded like the sergeant who ran his own unit and was used to getting things done. "Does she need to be in the hospital?"

Aiden shook his head. "Injury-wise, no. Stitches. Concussion. Cuts and bruises that will eventually heal themselves. As long as she takes it easy for a couple of days, the doctor didn't see any reason for her to take up a hospital bed."

"How is playing in the snow taking it easy?"

"Good luck convincing her to take care of herself. She insisted on being awake for your call since it was a holiday." He scrubbed at his jaw that needed a shave, unafraid to show his own fatigue. "She's also determined that you enjoy your break from soldiering. So work with me here, and keep her stress to a minimum?" He scanned the tent wall and tables and electronic equipment behind Levi. "Looks like you're back at HQ. Did you get to have a Thanksgiving?"

"We're talking about unicorns and rainbows so she doesn't think I'm worried about her?" Levi shook his head and played along. "Food is one thing they do pretty well here. The mess served us everything from turkey to prime rib yesterday. Leftovers in about every dish you can imagine for breakfast and lunch today. Nothing as good as Mom's pecan pie, though."

"Nobody could bake like your mom. I swear I gained ten pounds just that first week I lived with you from all the cookies and fresh bread and welcome cake she made."

Levi nodded, but the two of them could only handle so many unicorns and rainbows, even if it was for his sister's sake. "Enough with the trip down memory lane. Get Lexi inside the house."

A ball of snow sailed over the computer screen and splatted across the middle of Aiden's chest. "Hey!"

"You two are not the boss of me. I was enjoying the fresh air." Lexi had been eavesdropping on their conversation, just as Aiden had suspected. She sat on the step beside him, pulling Blue into a sit between her legs so that the three of them were framed in the camera. "Besides, you know with the time difference that one of us has to make the call really early or really late. I have a three-day weekend coming, so I wanted to take the late call so you wouldn't lose any sleep."

"You have a three-day weekend because you got hurt," Levi insisted. "You should be in bed. Healing."

"And you should be home. Not in harm's way."

"This is my job, kiddo."

"And I was doing mine." Aiden glanced over his shoulder, catching a glimpse of the determination stamped on her bruised face. Yes, she was a scientist who had an eye for detail, ran analyses and wrote reports in jargon he didn't always understand. But she was also a member of law enforcement. She might not wear a gun or make arrests, but that didn't mean she wasn't key to solving crimes and keeping their city safe.

He leaned over and pressed a kiss to the bright red Kansas City Chiefs stocking cap she wore. "I'm sorry, Lex."

She looked genuinely puzzled when she looked up at him. "For what?"

"For going Neanderthal on you tonight. You were doing your job. It was more dangerous than I liked. But I needed the reminder that you're trained to do your job just like Levi and I are, and it's wrong to try to wrap you up in a little package and keep you hidden away where you can't do that job, just so you'll never get hurt." He brushed a wheat colored wave off her cheek and tucked it inside the cuff of her red knit cap. "I have no doubt you're going to get the guy who attacked you."

"Thank you for saying that."

"You never know when I'm going to have an epiphany."

"Did it hurt much?" Lexi laughed with him as they turned the heavy moment into something lighter and more familiar. Then she touched her fingers to her lips and pressed a kiss to the screen as she stood. "You catch up with Aiden for a couple of minutes. I've got one more Thanksgiving treat to share with you before we hang up. Remember what we used to do after we saw the lights on the Plaza?"

After she'd gone into the house with Blue dancing along beside her in anticipation of a treat, Aiden got up, as well. "Now what is she up to?"

"Um, is there something you want to tell me, Murph?" Levi asked.

"About what?"

The weatherworn sergeant audibly groaned. "About you and Lexi."

Like what? Had he revealed something he shouldn't? *I want to do more than kiss your sister's hat? I want to date your sister? I want to sleep with your sister? I'm in love with her?*

None of those answers came out of his mouth. Instead, he opened the storm door and carried Levi's image inside. "Let's just say after tonight, I have a newfound respect for the work she does. She's out on the front lines like you and me."

Levi seemed to recognize his avoidance of the question and let it slide. "Maybe. But she isn't armed and dangerous."

"No. But Blue and I are." Once inside the door, he

shucked his coat and gloves and hung them on the hall tree. "Nobody is hurting her again."

They spent a couple of minutes going over the report of tonight's assault, the clue Lexi had found on the cap she'd been wearing that she hoped could be traced back to her attacker, and strategies for beefing up the security around her house, car and work. He and Levi shared a curse at the snafu that had put her ex and his fiancée in her hospital room. They even ran through a list of coworkers Lexi could rely on to go out on a call with if Aiden and Blue couldn't be there, as well as a list of people they wouldn't want her alone in a room with—like the man she replaced, Dennis Hunt. Levi knew that Lexi was one of the women who had filed a complaint against Hunt for using sexist, degrading language and subjecting the women under his former command to other forms of harassment. Aiden assured Levi that the only reason Hunt was still employed at the crime lab was that he had a good lawyer who was ensuring his client received every step in the penalty process he was entitled to—first, removing him from the complainants and then remediating his behavior. But there weren't many ways he could mess up again that even his lawyer could defend.

Aiden carried the computer into the living room and set it on the coffee table to free up his hands. He sat in front of his friend, his elbows braced on his knees, reiterating a solemn promise. "Trust me, if I have doubts about anyone in Lexi's circle, I'll step in and take care of it. I owe this family that much and more."

Levi cooled his jets, no doubt feeling the same helplessness Aiden had felt when she'd called to say she was in danger. "It's not your fault that someone put his fists on her. It's just—"

"You're thousands of miles away and used to taking care of Baby Sister."

Lexi cleared her throat with a loud bit of drama as she reentered the front room. Blue trotted in ahead of her, carrying a rawhide chew in his mouth, while she carried a tray with three steaming mugs that had mountains of whipped cream squirted on top. "Excuse me? *Baby* Sister is thirty years old, can hear every word you two are saying, and she doesn't appreciate being called that anymore. I don't know that I ever liked it."

Aiden scooted over to make room for her on the couch as she set the tray down within the camera shot. "Well, I didn't think you'd appreciate being called PITA, either."

"Aiden Royal Murphy," she chided, setting aside the mug she was sipping from and picking up another. "Just for that remark, you can't have this hot chocolate." She took a swallow from that mug, too, leaving a mustache of whipped cream on her top lip. Aiden reached for the third mug, but she snatched that away, too, and hastily drank from it. "Not that one, either." She set it back on the tray, oblivious to the dollop of cream on the tip of her nose. "This one is for Levi."

"Cocoa hog," Aiden teased.

She turned to the screen. "I'm re-creating Thanksgiving night for you. Giving you a jump start on your holiday. Aiden isn't cooperating."

Levi laughed. "Murph, you got it worse than me, bro. You get to deal with her in person."

"I don't mind." Aiden barely heard the teasing. He was transfixed by the whipped cream on her mouth and the gut-punch of desire to kiss it off her. He wanted to kiss her, period. He could be gentle since she was injured. But more than that full-body hug at the hospital, he remembered pressing his lips to the corner of her mouth. Even with that casual touch, her lips had trembled beneath his. A reaction like that to a simple touch was potent stuff for a man who was fighting a losing battle to maintain the kind of relationship she needed from him.

His body humming with anticipation, Aiden picked up one of the holiday napkins she'd set beneath each mug on the tray and reached over to dab at the corner of her mouth he'd kissed earlier. Despite the swelling and bruising, her pretty green eyes were tilted up and locked on to his, silently asking a question he wanted to answer. Or maybe that was just the question he wanted to read there.

Yeah. He remembered what her lips had felt like beneath his. And yeah, he wanted to kiss her again.

He was marginally aware of Levi throwing his hands up on the computer screen. "Seriously? Do you two really not see—?"

"What's that?" Aiden snapped out of his lusty trance.

"Huh?" Lexi caught sight of herself in the corner image that reflected what Levi could see. "Oh, gosh. Give me that." Her cheeks warmed to a self-conscious pink, and she snatched the paper napkin from Aiden's fingers to hastily wipe away the glob of whipped cream on her nose.

Aiden must have been too distracted to know what Levi was going on about. "Did you two have a fight, and you're pretending everything is all right for my benefit?"

"Fight?" Aiden frowned. "No, we didn't fight."

"He's been pretty bossy tonight," Lexi pointed out, patting Aiden's knee. "But I think his heart is in the right place. He's protective of me. I just argue back when he comes on too strong."

"I have to sometimes to get you to listen. You get stuck in your head and don't seem to notice the rest of the world going on around you."

"I wish I could order you two to make sense," Levi groused. "Why are things so awkward between you tonight?"

"Awkward?" Lexi scooted the tray of hot chocolate off to the side and pulled the computer closer to the edge of the table. "Aiden's a goofball and I keep him in line. Same old, same old."

"She's stubborn."

"So are you."

"Never mind." Levi put his hands together in a T for time-out, stopping the escalating argument. "I'm too far away to fix anything. You're grown-ups. You'll figure it out." Levi checked his watch and nodded to someone behind his computer screen, probably the next Marine waiting for his or her chance to call home for Thanksgiving. "I need to wrap things up," he explained. "Are you certain this assault is a onetime hazard? Is she safe on the job?"

"I've got this under control." Aiden had already chatted with his supervisor in the K-9 unit, Jedediah Burke, about making him and Blue, or another K-9 team, available for every crime lab call until they were certain the lab staff wasn't being targeted. Especially if this strangler struck again, since he'd already proved he wasn't above assaulting an unarmed criminalist to cover up the clues to his crime.

Lexi pushed into the camera shot. "*We've* got this under control. Don't worry about the home front, Levi. You keep yourself safe."

"Keep your head down, buddy. Blue and I will keep an eye on things here."

Levi considered both their assurances, then nodded. "Well, I trust the dog, at least. Good boy, Blue." The dog raised his head at his name and trotted over to nuzzle the screen. They all laughed when he cocked his head in response to Levi's voice. "You keep an eye on those two, fur face. Give him a tummy rub from me."

Aiden patted Blue's flank while Lexi scratched the dog around the ears. "Will do."

"I love you, sis."

"I love you, big brother. Can't wait till you're home for Christmas."

"Me, either. Murph? You keep her safe."

"Always."

"Kandahar out."

Once the video chat ended, Lexi and Aiden fell into an awkward silence, punctuated only by Blue's panting and a mournful whine that had the desired effect. Lexi patted the sofa, and Blue, needing no more invitation than that, jumped up between them, stretching his legs and body out to fill up all the available space, plus a little more, reminding Aiden of a toddler climbing into bed with his parents.

Now that the camera was off and she wasn't putting a happy holiday spin on everything for her brother's sake, Lexi closed the computer and sank into the back of the couch with a weary sigh. She accepted Blue's paws across her lap and stroked his exposed chest and tummy. "You didn't have to tell Levi everything that happened tonight, did you? I was trying to keep things light and nostalgic. He'll worry."

"He's a big brother. He's going to worry whether you tell him or not." Aiden was concerned about the utter fatigue in her posture and wished she'd let him take care of her the way she insisted on spoiling Blue. "I told him the facts so he wouldn't imagine anything worse."

"I suppose you're right." She waved her hand in front of her face. "It's not like I can hide this from him."

"Think about how you'd feel if you knew Levi had been wounded or his unit ran into an IED and you heard there were casualties." He ran his fingers across Blue's shoulders until he could capture her hand on the dog's chest.

"You'd think the worst, wouldn't you? Until you knew the facts and could process them through that beautiful brain of yours?"

"I hate that you're right. That's a scenario I never want to imagine." Lexi turned her hand and laced her fingers together with his. "Not the Thanksgiving I was hoping for."

Aiden shrugged. "Christmas will be better."

That earned him a glimpse of a smile. "I hope so. Sorry about the hot chocolate. I'll make you another mug."

Before she could push herself up, he picked up one of the mugs she'd sipped out of. "I'm not afraid of sharing a few germs. This one will do." He handed another mug to her and raised his in a toast. "To Levi."

She clinked her mug against his. "To Levi."

They shared several sips of the creamy, chocolaty brew before he realized they were both sagging back against the couch pillows, with the length of a sideways Belgian Malinois stretched between them like a furry chaperone. He heard a soft chuckle. "I'm glad he feels at home here. I hope you do, too."

"I spent more time growing up in this place than I did in my own house. I always feel at home."

"Maybe you'd better get going as soon as you finish your cocoa. It's already late."

Aiden shook his head. "Blue and me are sacking out on your couch tonight."

"But—"

"Nonnegotiable, Lex. You need a good night's sleep, and you won't get that trying to watch your back while you mentally relive every moment of what happened tonight. I've got an overnight bag in my truck. We're staying."

"I—"

"I know you." He sat forward to put his mug on the tray. The moment he straightened, Blue popped up into a

sit, ready to move with him. "Easy, boy." He smoothed his
hand over Blue's head and looked past him to Lexi. "Mac
said you weren't supposed to report back to the lab until
Monday. But you've got a mystery to solve, and you aren't
going to truly rest until you figure out the who and the
why and the how. At least, I can relieve you of the burden
of worrying if he's coming back and not feeling safe. You
use that brain and do the science. Blue and me? We're the
muscle. We'll protect."

After a moment of looking between him and the dog
and evaluating his argument, she nodded. She pointed her
thumb over her shoulder. "There are four bedrooms in this
house. You don't have to sleep on the couch."

"My old room?"

"I changed the decor, but yeah. There's still a bed in
there for you." She leaned over the dog to squeeze his
knee. "Thank you. And FYI, it's not all those muscles that
make me feel safe." Every nerve in his body rushed to that
simple touch. Something warmed inside him at her cryp-
tic words. Maybe she was talking about trusting him. Or
the familiarity of shared history. Maybe she was talking
about the gun and badge he wore. Maybe she was talking
about Blue. Didn't matter. He made her feel safe. He was
getting the job done. He hadn't failed her after all. The reassurance washed over him, taking the edge off his emotions that had been all over the place tonight. Her faith in
him was both daunting and soothing, and made his heart
swell with the connection they shared. All that because of
a simple touch and some soft words. No wonder the dog
leaned into her when she hugged the pooch around the
neck. They both had a thing for Lexi Callahan. "Thank
you, too, good boy. Does he need a blanket?"

"Nah. He'll probably sleep at the foot of the bed with
me. If that's okay?"

"You can sleep anywhere you want, Blue." She kissed the top of the dog's head and pushed to her feet. She picked up the tray of mugs and headed to the kitchen, the fatigue of the day evident in every shuffling step. "I'll put out a bowl of water for the dog."

"Put out two bowls. I always keep a bag of kibble in the truck. I'll feed him after I settle in."

Aiden bundled up and walked Blue one last time, scanning the neighborhood and giving the outside of the house a good look to ensure everything was secure before he grabbed his go bag from his truck and headed back inside.

Lexi's door was already closed by the time Aiden flipped on the light in the bedroom where he'd lived for eight years. The space was more generic now, painted a taupe color with navy blue curtains. But he recognized Lexi's favorite color in the shots of turquoise in the quilt and the knobs on the dresser. It was a lot more sophisticated than the glow-in-the-dark stars on the ceiling and movie posters that had once decorated the walls.

He changed out of his uniform into jeans and a T-shirt, pulled on a pair of cotton socks and secured his gun in the lockbox at the bottom of his bag. Instead of going straight to bed, he and Blue wandered down the hallway as he reacquainted himself with the house, checking security at each door and window. After his late dinner, Blue padded along with him. Lexi had taken over the master suite her parents had once occupied, turned her old bedroom into a home office and given Levi's a new coat of paint, although the Kansas City Chiefs helmet lamp Levi had gotten for Christmas one year was still on the table beside the bed.

Aiden hadn't been lying when he'd said he felt at home here. A lot had changed since he'd moved out and gotten his own apartment. But those changes were superficial. This Craftsman-style home might have been updated over the past few years, but at its core, it was solidly built. It represented the family who had lived here and taken him in. It was warm, full of color and life. There were homey smells and familiar sounds—the creak of the hardwood floors, and the hiss and pop of the radiators as they heated with steam from the furnace downstairs. He didn't need to turn on the lights to find his way, partly because of the moonlight and illumination from the streetlamp out front reflecting off the snow through the living room's wide bay window, but mostly because he'd walked these paths so many times.

The first twelve years of his life, he didn't know if he'd have a house or apartment to go home to, much less his own bed to sleep in. If Patrick Murphy had his drinking buddies over, they'd pass out on whatever flat surface was convenient. Each of his stepmothers had tried to create a home. But a drunk Patrick Murphy couldn't keep a job to pay the rent or put food on the table. And when the current wife tried to make changes or couldn't live up to his "sainted Gail's" memory, things got nasty. The cops would come, and the stepmothers would leave. Sometimes, he'd be taken to a shelter, but more often he'd be left alone with the dad who blamed him for his mother's death. His choices had been to endure his father's wrath and wait for him to pass out, or to run away.

He'd survived until Levi had invited him to come home to dinner with him one night.

And then he'd lived. He'd healed. He'd thrived.

A clean house filled with happy sounds. A full belly and kind words, healthy family role models and a safe place to call home had changed him. Saved him.

The refrigerator light was almost piercingly bright in the twilight of the kitchen when he opened it to pull out a bottle of water. But his eyes adjusted quickly after he closed the door and headed out to the front room. He stopped at the mantel to look at familiar pictures and felt lucky to be included in the display of graduation photographs, a shot of Levi earning a commendation at Camp Pendleton and a church directory photo of Lila and Leroy Callahan taken shortly before their deaths.

"Thank you," he whispered, caressing the corner of the picture frame as he almost always did when he came to the house. "I'll do right by your daughter," he promised before turning away and crossing to the bay window.

Blue braced his paws up on the bench seat in front of the window, mimicking Aiden's watchful stare out into the night. A few houses on the block still had lights on and extra vehicles in the driveway, indicating family and friends were still up late celebrating Thanksgiving, or maybe getting an early start gathering for their Black Friday shopping. But other than the streetlamp in front of Lexi's house, her side of the street seemed to be dark, quiet. This weekend all that would change, he guessed, when the neighbors started putting up their Christmas trees and holiday lights. He suspected Lexi had plans to go all out with the festive decor herself since Levi would be here for Christmas. He wondered if she still kept the artificial tree and multiple boxes of lights and ornaments up in the attic—and if she planned on pulling down the attic stairs and going up there herself to carry them all down here.

He'd add that to his to-do list. Watch over Lexi. Do whatever he could to lighten her responsibilities so that she could rest and recover. He wasn't much of a cook without his barbecue grill, but he could do a lot of other stuff for her while he was here at the house. If tonight's video chat with Levi was any indication, he doubted she'd slow down enough to take care of herself. Although he admired her drive and determination, those traits made Lexi her own

worst enemy. Maybe that was the best way he could help
over the next few weeks. It sounded like an oxymoron,
but he could force her to relax a little and let him do more
around here. Let her surrender a little of her control and
rest up for the next few days—allow the sanctuary of this
house to heal her the way it had once healed him.

Aiden swallowed another long drink of water before
capping the bottle and heading back to the couch. Blue
curled up on the seat beside him as he leaned back into the
cushions and stretched out to put his feet up on the coffee
table. No shoes, nothing breakable—as long as he set the
bottle on a tray or coaster, Mrs. Callahan would have allowed it. He needed some time to let the thoughts racing
through his mind settle. For Lexi's sake, and maybe his
own well-being, he needed to have a plan in mind on how
he was going to move forward—not just taking care of
her this weekend, but how he was going to handle the 24/7
watch he intended to keep until her attacker was caught.

How could he have dropped the ball so royally tonight
and let Lexi get beaten like that? True, like every other
available cop, he'd pulled extra duty tonight, and had to
be called off working the Plaza crowd to assist the CSIU
at the Regal Hotel. And how the hell was he was going to
keep his hands and heart to himself since guard duty required sharing close quarters, driving to and from work
together, and shadowing her at crime scenes? At least until
Levi came home, and *he* could keep an eye on his head-
strong sister.

And once this guy was caught, what was Aiden going
to do? How long did he put his life on hold, wanting a
woman, waiting for a relationship that probably shouldn't
happen? Nope. Not probably. Even though Kevin Nelson
was a self-entitled ass, he'd been right about one thing.
Lusting after Lexi, falling in love with her, all felt a little

kinky. And not in the good way. Was he strong enough to walk away from the best thing that had ever happened to him? Or was he doomed to suffer these confusing, unrequited feelings?

Or, hell, did he take the risk and tell her the truth?

Yo, Lex. I know the world thinks of me as your second big brother, but, um, you are an incredible woman. Pretty. Brave. Funny. Strong. Sexy. Smart. From the time I was twelve years old, you made me feel I was worth something. And I'm in love with you.

Would the truth destroy the bond between them? Would simply mentioning his feelings suddenly make it all awkward between them?

Were those his choices? Irreparably damage their friendship by betraying his promise to Levi and Leroy and Lila Callahan? Or sacrifice his heart and walk away to preserve his pride and Lexi's trust?

Didn't sound like there was a winning side to that debate.

He heard the soft click of a door opening, and a few seconds later, he heard Lexi's voice at the entrance to the hallway. "Looks like I'm not the only one who can't sleep."

He set down his water bottle and turned to find her leaning against the wall, wrapped up in a teal-and-turquoise afghan over her pajamas. A dozen thoughts crossed Aiden's mind—how adorably rumpled her hair looked after tossing and turning on her pillow, the trip down memory lane to the Christmas when Lila Callahan had crocheted afghans for the three teenagers in her house. His was royal blue and gold and draped over his couch at his apartment, whereas Levi's had been bright red and gold, like his beloved Chiefs football team. Was Lexi cold? Had he worried her with his restless prowling? Did it feel different to have someone else in the house where she lived alone unless Levi was home on leave? Was she worried about him? Thinking about the case? Had a nightmare wakened her? Did she have any clue how much she meant to him?

Every thought whisked by in a matter of seconds, and Aiden reached out, too tired to fight them both at this hour. He scooted Blue off the couch and held out his hand. "Come here."

That she didn't hesitate to join him was both soul-soothing and a torpedo to any chance that he could keep things platonic between them. He draped his arm around her shoulders, and she cuddled close to his side. "Blue's spot is still warm. You're warm." He felt her relax, sinking into him until he could feel the swell of a small, perfect breast caught between them. "I feel like I can breathe again."

Aiden nodded. Holding her like this was pure torture. Perfect contentment.

"What are you doing, sitting out here alone in the dark?" she asked, drawing mindless shapes across the front of his shirt with her fingers. "Penny for your thoughts?"

He stilled her wandering hand against his chest. "I don't think we can afford what I'm thinking."

Her chin stretched with a big yawn. "What does that mean?"

"Go to sleep, Lex."

"I will if you will." She kicked off her fuzzy slippers, curled her legs up beside her and snuggled in. "I like it when you hold me. More than I should. Doesn't feel kinky." She yawned again. "Feels good."

"Yeah." He couldn't argue the facts. "It does."

"I wish…" She sounded so drowsy, but her fingers had started their curious exploration again.

"Yeah?"

Her hand stopped and splayed over his heart. "Whatever happens…you're not my brother." The tips of her fingers dug into his pectoral muscle, and parts of his tired body perked up at the unintended caress. "A friend, yes, but…" She pulled her hand back to trace the roses inked above his elbow that represented her parents, and the Celtic knot for his Irish heritage, and then followed the winding scroll of the Serenity Prayer that circled his forearm. "Sexy man. Big heart. Loyal to a fault. Good with dogs… Someday I want to find out if you're a lousy kisser."

"Excuse me?"

"I seriously doubt you would be. But it might help."

Help what? Between the yawns and the mumbling, she wasn't making much sense. "Lex, did you take any kind of medication that the doctor gave you?"

She shook her head. "Wrote in my high school diary about you… Lots of kissing… One day…" Maybe she was already falling asleep, and she was babbling whatever dream or odd thought was going through her head.

Still…she wanted him to kiss her?

Not that he understood what the *lousy* part was about, but she'd imagined *lots of kissing*?

Was this what Levi had picked up on from three thousand miles away? Some sort of sexual tension simmering between him and Lex? The gut-deep emotions that had been stripped away by the possibility of losing her tonight? Did Levi suspect he was tired of playing big brother to Lexi? And if Lexi was changing the rules of their relationship, seeking out his embrace, talking about kissing, then he wasn't sure he could maintain the status quo on his own. How was he going to keep his word to Levi and stuff these feelings back into Pandora's box when Lexi was taunting him—perhaps subconsciously—to break those rules? When she was rested and feeling better, she might not even remember the things she'd said to him tonight.

But he couldn't forget them.

One day...

Words of hope? Or an injured, weary mind reliving some teenage fantasy?

A few minutes later, when she was snoring gently against his chest, Aiden stretched out along the sofa, settling Lexi on top of him. Despite the layers of flannel and denim between them, the guilt and confusion inside him eased as her legs tangled with his, linking them in the most intimate of ways. Her tranquil sigh vibrated through him, her soft weight growing slightly heavier as she relaxed. Aiden pulled the afghan over them both. "Blue." He softly called the dog up on the couch to lie beside them and add his warmth and the protection Aiden trusted without question. If he dozed off, Blue would keep watch.

He might not have forever with Lexi in his arms.

But he had tonight.

Chapter Seven

"You really don't understand the concept of a day off, do you." Aiden strode into the living room, carrying the long plastic tub with the family's artificial spruce tree inside. He winked as Lexi looked up from the couch while Chelsea O'Brien read a list of names over the phone at Lexi's ear. "This is the last of them marked Christmas. Do you want me to start putting this together? Don't suppose you found the tree skirt yet, did you?"

Lexi briefly took the phone from between her shoulder and ear and pointed to the braided rug in front of the bay window. Then she got up to retrieve the Christmas tree skirt from the tub she'd opened and tossed it to him, hoping he understood he was in charge of assembling the tree while she paced past Blue gnawing on his rawhide treat. While she appreciated Aiden using his muscle and a better sense of balance than she was sporting this weekend to haul the holiday decorations down from the attic, she was anxious about letting so much time pass between her attack and getting to the office tomorrow morning. If she was feeling well enough to put up Christmas decorations, then she was well enough to start gathering information about Giselle Byrd's and Jennifer Li's killer.

Besides, it seemed a lot smarter to focus on her current investigation than on how quickly she'd become accustomed to having Aiden in the house with her. They'd shared meals, watched a couple of their favorite Christmas movies—singing along with one and quoting their favorite lines from the other. He'd doctored her injuries, taken Blue on routine patrols around the house and neighborhood. Despite her wish that he had some bad habits that might make him less attractive, he neatly folded his clothes, and he helped clean up the kitchen after meals.

She was still holding out for him being a lousy kisser. That might be the one thing that could curtail these feelings he resurrected in her.

But then there was the dangerous habit of falling asleep on the couch she'd developed the past few nights. Well, not exactly on the couch. She'd fallen asleep on Aiden. She'd snuggled up to the furnace of his body, feeling sheltered and content, with his hard body to lean against and his arm draped across the back of the couch behind her shoulders. But she'd awakened to find herself shamelessly sprawled across his chest, the tips of her breasts clutched into tight points where they rubbed against him, the crown of her hair tucked perfectly beneath his chin. This morning, her thigh had been wedged between his legs and she'd felt the evidence of his arousal pushing against her hip. They'd been fully clothed—she in her pajamas and Aiden in jeans and a T-shirt. But it hadn't made a bit of difference to her body's hungry female response to the lure of his masculine contours. Before she was fully awake and aware she was doing it, she'd squeezed her legs around his muscular thigh and rolled her hips, subconsciously trying to ease the liquid pressure pooling at the seam of her legs. That was when she felt the warm hand clamp over her bottom to keep her from rubbing herself against the delicious heat.

"Lex." Her name had come out husky and sharp from

Aiden's lips, waking her completely from her semiconscious wantonness.

"Oh. Um. Sorry? I... Sorry." Lexi had set a record for scrambling off the couch and hurrying into the bathroom to get into the shower. Even turning the water to a cooler temperature couldn't seem to wash away the heat lingering on her skin. Each drop of water pricked her like a tantalizing caress, reminding every nerve ending how it had responded to the feel of Aiden's body pressed beneath hers.

And when she finally turned off the chilly spray, wrapped herself in a towel and stepped out into the adjoining bedroom, Aiden was standing there in the doorway to the hall, his sexy, stubbled, stupidly caring face lined with concern. "Everything okay? You were in there almost twenty minutes. I'm sorry if I startled you or made you self-conscious. Nothing happened. You weren't doing anything you shouldn't, and I was holding myself still so I wouldn't wake you up. I'm sorry if I embarrassed you. A guy's body does what it wants to, sometimes."

Apparently, a woman's body did, too. "I'm sorry if I embarrassed *you*. These past two nights have been the best sleep I've had in ages. Thank you." She clutched the towel around her breasts and raked her fingers through her wet hair, sprinkling water on her bare shoulders and into the rug beneath her feet. With the swelling in her face having receded, she could feel her cheeks coloring with heat. "What would Levi say if he'd come in and found me basically dry-humping you?"

Those blue eyes bored into hers. "I'd tell him to mind his own business."

"Aiden..." She'd been joking, trying to make light of their unintentionally intimate sleeping arrangements. "I just meant that he'd probably give us both some grief."

"I don't care who he is or what promise I made. He doesn't get to upset you."

Aiden sounded...serious. Protective of her subliminal desires. As if her need to wrap her body around his hadn't embarrassed him at all. As if he might be a little mad that *she'd* been embarrassed by it. As if he was struggling with whatever was happening between them every bit as much as she was, and he didn't want her to think she was in the fight alone.

He blinked and the possessive timbre of his voice disappeared. "Now get some clothes on, woman. I need to put a fresh bandage on your stitches and then we've got a house to decorate for Christmas."

Why did everything about that man have to be a turn-on for her? From the fascinatingly complex tats on his warm skin to his sexy voice and sense of humor, his protective, caring nature to those wonderfully strong arms that chased away every fear, every stressor, every thought except security and peace when they closed around her.

"Lexi?"

That wasn't Aiden's voice calling to her. It was a woman's voice. On her phone.

Two hours later and she was still replaying that run-in in her bedroom with the towel and the eyes and the... Oh, damn. Not only was she ignoring her phone call with Chelsea, but she was staring at Aiden kneeling on the rug, sorting out the pieces of the tree. She was measuring out the width of his shoulders, the tapering down to his waist, the deliciously firm curve of muscle in the back of his jeans. She was still reliving the feeling of him holding her, the feeling of being sandwiched between his palm and his body's obvious interest in her, the feeling that he would go to bat for her—against an attacker, against her big brother, against her own self-doubts—if that was what it took to protect her.

No wonder she'd sent him up to the attic and had spent most of the morning on the phone with Chelsea. She'd had to dive into work to keep her thoughts off the man she was falling in love with. Not some high school crush. Grown-up love. Real love.

Love that his overdeveloped sense of responsibility would never allow them to share. Love that was way more complicated than simply obeying what the heart wanted.

"Lex?" Aiden talking. Here. Now. He'd turned around and those blue eyes were staring at her, narrowed with concern. "Everything all right?"

Snap out of it!

Blinking away her thoughts and dreams and despair, Lexi turned away and focused on the phone call. She wasn't the only one from the lab working off the clock on a Sunday afternoon. "Sorry, Chelsea. Say that again. Aiden was distracting me."

"I should be so lucky," Chelsea teased, although Lexi doubted her friend understood the depths of her distraction with Aiden Murphy. "Tell him hi. And give Blue a tummy rub for me." Since the working dog and his handler were inseparable, Chelsea knew that if Aiden was at the house, then Blue would be, too.

"I will. The key card?" she prompted.

"Right." She imagined Chelsea adjusting her glasses on her nose and reading the information off her computer screen. "I've identified the Regal Hotel master key card that was used to access both of the ninth-floor landing doors, the victim's room and Room 921 directly across the hall—all within the time frame when the ME says Jennifer Li was killed. The card was used again on the landing and in the utility closet on the eighth floor and the first-floor stairwell within the hour that you were attacked."

So that was how the perp had eluded the police and their search of the ninth floor. He'd simply hidden out where they weren't looking. And then he'd waltzed out and joined the guests being held in the lobby and restaurant, probably changing his clothes and blending in with the crowd without raising anyone's suspicions before he left the building.

"The card number belongs to one of the assistant managers," Chelsea went on. "I've got his name, but he's not our guy. He broke his foot at work on Wednesday and has been in St. Luke's Hospital since then. Apparently, a cart loaded with supplies overturned on him. It would be a breach of confidentiality with the hotel, but I suppose he could have loaned the card to somebody."

"Or someone stole it." Lexi thought about the chaos that could ensue with a public workplace accident. There'd been enough EMTs, police, guests and hotel staff on the premises when she'd been hurt at the Regal. It'd be easy enough to lose track of a key card. Hell, she'd lost evidence and her hat—a small rectangle of plastic would be easy enough for someone to pick up. She wondered if his accident could have been staged on purpose, just so the perp could get a hold of that master key. "Let's get his name to the detectives so they can ask him about it."

"Will do."

"Can you find out who was staying in Room 921?"

She heard Chelsea's fingers tapping over the keyboard. "Let's see… Paul and Margaret Montgomery."

"Do you have a picture of them?" Could Paul Montgomery be their killer? Or had they been down on the Plaza watching the lighting ceremony while the mystery guest with the key card had sneaked in to wait in their empty room? "What are the camera angles on the ninth floor? Any shots of someone coming and going out of rooms 920 and 921? Or using the master key elsewhere? Did they come into contact with Jennifer Li anywhere else in the hotel?"

"Um…" Why was Chelsea hesitating? "I'd need a court order to look at their camera system to see who was actually using the key card. I mean, I can hack into it if you want me to, but if you want to use anything I find in court…"

Right. Although the lab could process the video, it needed to be collected through investigative channels to be usable as evidence. "Request the court order."

"Me?"

"I don't want to wait any longer than necessary. If our perp has full access to the hotel, then he could get into the security office and erase any evidence of him moving through the hotel. Maybe he already has. Even then, we could track the missing footage. Firm up our time frame."

"Sure, I could do all that. But you know who approves the paperwork for that now, right?"

"Dennis Hunt." Lexi paused. She hadn't been picking up the tentative cues in Chelsea's voice. She'd lovingly describe the other woman as quirky or eccentric. And though she tended to be shy in social situations, when it came to work, Chelsea was a clever go-getter who loved to be challenged. "Is there something wrong, Chels? I know Dennis is a first-class jackass, but this is just a matter of typing up the form and getting him to sign off on it, so we can take it to a judge."

"What if I type up all the info, and you present it to him?" she countered.

"Chelsea?" Lexi hugged an arm around her waist, feeling a real concern for her friend's odd behavior. "Did something happen Friday while I was gone?"

"Nope. Not at all." She answered so fast that Lexi suspected it was a lie. And lying was one of the few things Chelsea didn't have a talent for. "I'm sorry. I know I should be braver, but Dennis gives me the creeps."

"What aren't you telling me? Did he say something to you in slimy Dennis-speak?" That question got Aiden's attention. He came over to sit on the arm of the sofa near where Lexi stood to listen in more closely.

"I haven't seen him since Tuesday of this week. And I'd like to keep it that way."

Lexi sought out the questioning look in Aiden's eyes and shrugged. "I know there's more to this story, and you're going to tell me about it when you're ready, okay? You know you can count on me."

Chelsea huffed a short laugh. "I know. When I'm ready."

Now they were really going to have to talk when she got back to the office. "All right. Get the request together, and I'll deal with Dennis."

"Now I feel like I'm letting you down."

"Uh-uh. Don't go there." Lexi paced back and forth, gesturing as though Chelsea could see her in person. "I'm the boss, aren't I? Ultimately, if it needs to get done, it's my responsibility. But I also intend to protect my team. Send it to my email and I can print it off here. I'll get a hold of Dennis and have Aiden run me in to the lab. And then to whatever judge we can rustle up on Thanksgiving weekend." He met her gaze and gave a reluctant nod. "Will you be there tomorrow morning to work your computer magic?"

"Whenever you need me. I can come in twenty-four seven." Chelsea's sigh of relief was audible. "I'll spell out what we need from the hotel and get that to you ASAP."

"Good woman. And, Chels? Are you sure you're all right?"

"I am now. Thanks for understanding."

Only, Lexi wasn't sure she did understand as they ended the call. She sank onto the couch beside Aiden and opened her laptop to type up notes from the call.

"Is Chelsea okay?" Aiden asked.

"She says yes, but I don't believe her." Lexi tilted her chin to look up at him. "Something's got her spooked. Something to do with Dennis Hunt. I wonder if she's just more sensitive than the rest of us about the things he says and does. She grew up in the foster system. Dennis might not be the first jerk like that she's run across."

"She lives on her own, right?" Aiden pushed to his feet and went back to hooking together the last limbs of the tree.

"Except for the cats. Peanut Butter and Jelly."

"Please don't tell me she's turning into a crazy cat lady."

"More like a penchant for taking in strays. She has a couple of senior poodles she's fostering from the shelter, too."

"Do you think Hunt has threatened her? To get her to drop her harassment complaint?" Aiden slipped the last branch onto the tree. "Would she feel better if Blue and I went and checked out her place? At least she can feel safe at home."

"I'm not sure how well the cats would take to Blue." The dog raised his head at the mention of his name, and Lexi reached down to pet him. The muscles in his shoulders quivered in anticipation at the opportunity to go to work. "But I think *I'd* feel better if we looked in on her."

He surveyed the tubs scattered across the living room and the stacks of ornament boxes she'd unpacked on the coffee table. "You're not putting all this stuff out, are you? We'll be here all day and night."

"No. But I'm not sure what's in each box beyond the tree. I figured I'd take advantage of the time off to consolidate and organize the decorations. Put out Levi's favorite ornaments. Pack the sentimental stuff in its own box. Move stuff I don't use on to the homeless shelter." She glanced up from her laptop. "I should separate the outside lights from the ones that go on the tree, too."

"And when do you intend to sleep?" he asked. "It sounds like we're going into the office today, too. Meeting Hunt? Calling up judges and stopping by Chelsea's?" Aiden shook his head. "Didn't Dr. Muhlbach and Mac's wife say you were supposed to take it easy?"

"I need to take care of this paperwork to keep the case moving forward."

"And while we're at the lab, you might as well run some tests on that foreign hair or fiber you found on you at the hospital?"

Lexi snapped her fingers. "Good idea."

Grinning, he shook his head. "I'm guessing that was already on your to-do list." He picked up the empty tub and carried it toward the attic stairs. "All right. I can swing by my apartment while we're out and get some extra changes of clothing. We'll finish putting up the decorations to-night."

Lexi saved her work and closed her laptop. "You don't have to drive me everywhere, Aiden. I won't be going anyplace but the lab and a judge's house. Well, Dennis's, if he won't meet me at the office. At some point I need to get my car from work, anyway. You don't have to chauffeur me around."

"Uh-uh." He halted in his tracks and pointed a stern finger at her. "Already had that conversation. I'm with you twenty-four seven until Blue and I have a shift, and then I've made arrangements with Sergeant Burke—" the director of KCPD's K-9 Corps and Aiden's boss "—to have someone else on the team shadow you if you get called to a crime scene and I can't be there. And while you're at the lab, we'll rely on Captain Stockman and Sergeant King to keep an eye on you."

Lexi wondered if focusing the security details on her would leave other members of her team at risk. But she doubted she'd be able to argue Aiden out of his protective streak until her stitches came out and the bruises faded from her face.

At least he was more than willing to make the trip to Chelsea's small home in the KC suburb of Independence. Her friend greeted them both with hugs and invited Blue up onto the couch for a thorough petting, scattering the cats into hiding. Blue exchanged some sniffs with the senior poodles, but one was blind, and the other stuck right by his side in the bed at Chelsea's feet. They were more curious than concerned about the big, furry visitor.

Blue enjoyed running through the snow in the huge fenced-in yard after he and Aiden checked windows and doors and the separate garage to make sure Chelsea had nothing to worry about security-wise. That gave Lexi a little time alone with Chelsea to share a cup of tea and press her on why her friend's pale skin was shadowed beneath her glasses. Chelsea dismissed it as a lack of sleep rather than explaining anything to Lexi's satisfaction. Not for the first time, she wondered if Robert Buckner, the former KCPD cop turned private investigator, was taking advantage of her kindhearted friend's willingness to help him, making her feel obligated to burn the candle at both ends. Or were her friend's overly cheerful smiles covering up something else? Like the reason she was so reluctant to have anything to do with Dennis Hunt?

Lexi was pleased to see Aiden slip Chelsea his card with his numbers on it as they headed out the door, in case something came up and she needed a cop or a friend...or a visit from Blue. Chelsea had nearly burst into tears at the offer and rose up on tiptoe to hug Aiden tightly around the neck. *"Keep this guy,"* she mouthed to Lexi before catching her in a tight hug, too. "You two are the best. Thanks."

Then they left her there with only her pets and computers and secrets for company. Lexi resigned herself to biding her time until Chelsea chose to confide in her, either as her friend or her subordinate. But when Chelsea was ready, Lexi would do whatever she could to erase that wary fatigue from her friend's eyes.

Once they were at the crime lab with the proper microscopic equipment, Lexi had no problem identifying the fiber that had come off her as a hair. It was impossible to identify the age or even the sex of her attacker simply by looking at the hair. But she was able to extract a tiny bit of connected tissue from the sample where she had pulled it from her attacker's scalp. Although Khari Thomas was the lab's DNA expert, Lexi was able to run a stain chromatin test on the nuclei of the tissue cells to reveal a male-indicative Y body. Confirming that her attacker was a man was no surprise, considering the strength he'd used against her.

It would take another three to five days to put together a DNA profile and possibly longer to run that profile through all of Chelsea's databases to find a match—assuming their killer was in the system. Lexi sent an email to Khari, asking her to work up the results, compare the profile to the potential DNA samples taken from the prostitute's murder scene and any other DNA evidence from Jennifer Li's crime scene, and get back to her as soon as possible. Lexi promised to reassign one of the newly hired chemists to assist her on Monday if she needed help processing the evidence.

While Aiden brewed them something hot to drink in the lounge, Lexi also discovered an unusual substance within the hair follicle. But with only one hair to work with, there wasn't a large enough sample to run both DNA and a substance analysis. She knew the DNA would put her closer to identifying her attacker than learning whatever dye or hair product or even environmental or medical by-product might have been absorbed into the hair.

Besides, Dennis chose that moment to stroll into the lab. He crossed the sterile, brightly lit room, letting out a long whistle as he leaned across the stainless steel table where she was working to study her. "Somebody did a number on you, didn't they? Must have hurt. You sure you should be back to work already?"

"Dennis," she acknowledged without answering the rhetorical question. She suspected the sudden headache coiling between her eyes had less to do with the aftereffects of her concussion and more to do with sharing breathing space with Dennis. "Thank you for coming in."

He pulled off his stocking cap and ran his fingers through his hair, fluffing the short strands to fill in around the marks from his hair plugs. "You're the boss now. I'm the one on probation. You say jump, and I say... Well, you know the rest."

An exasperated sigh buzzed through Lexi's lips as she secured the sample and waited for the printout of her results. "If you're going to keep messing with your hair, I'm going to need you to put on a hairnet. The lab can't afford to have any stray hairs coming off you and getting into our samples."

"You're not wearing a hairnet."

"I'm not flicking my new-grown hair into our workspace. Surely you haven't forgotten protocols after a couple of days behind a desk?"

Dennis scoffed at the criticism and slipped his hands

into his pockets. "I was surprised to get your call. Thought you'd be out of commission longer than you were."

Tucking the printout into the pocket of her lab coat, Lexi headed to the door. "Sorry to disappoint you."

"Oh, I'm not disappointed." He chuckled as he followed her out. "I'm amused. Everyone thinks you're this golden girl who's going to restore balance to the universe. I got results when I was in charge and you know it." Yes, but at too high a cost for staff morale. "Looks like you can't do this job without me." His subtle digs and smug smile reminded her why she and others had filed the harassment complaints.

"I can't do it without your *signature*," she clarified. She waited for him to exit and locked the lab door behind him. "I've got the paperwork for you to approve in my office." She found the words to be a professional, although thanking him for anything felt like she was conceding to the superiority he craved. "Having the court order ready will enable us to hit the ground running tomorrow morning."

Inside her office, she gestured to a chair, which he refused. So she skipped to handing him the court order request for him to read. He picked up a pen, but his hand hovered above the document, hesitating. "Going to intrude on other innocent people's lives the way you've butted into mine?"

"I know it's hard for you to comprehend, but this isn't about you, Dennis. We used to be a team, remember? And our team helped KCPD solve murders." Lexi took off her lab coat and hung it on the outside hook of her closet, her gaze idly skimming over the Advent calendar she'd start opening in a couple of days. She came back to her chair behind the desk but refused to sit and give him any advantage over her. "I know your career has gone sideways, but we still need you to be a part of that team if you can be. Sign off on the court order and help us solve a murder."

"Nice speech. You been practicing that one?"

Lexi was done forcing herself to be nice to the man. "Are you signing the request? Or do I have to go over your head and bother Mac with it?"

"Doesn't this request show bias?" Dennis taunted, unfazed by her threat. He kept right on nitpicking her ability to do her job. "I don't see any court order for video footage from Giselle Byrd's murder scene."

"Gee. I wish I'd thought of that," she responded, letting plenty of sarcasm leak into her voice. "As I recall, you checked it yourself. That hotel didn't have any security cameras outside of the office. Different clientele in No-Man's-Land."

Dennis shrugged, conceding her point. He scratched his name across the bottom of the document and tossed both it and the pen onto her desk. "Chelsea was afraid to talk to me?" Lexi hadn't mentioned her friend's name at all, but she supposed the requests on the document pointed to their tech expert. For a moment, she considered asking Dennis about the tension between him and Chels. But that felt like betraying a friend's confidence. Dennis tugged on his stocking cap and pulled his gloves from his coat pocket. "But you're not afraid?"

"I'm not afraid to do my job, if that's what you mean. You're a smart man. And you *are* a good criminalist. But your actions undermined the rest of the team."

"Maybe the rest of the team needed to step up their game."

"Maybe you needed to be a better leader."

Dennis threw out his hands in a mock ta-da. "There's the golden girl again, trying to make everything all rosy and right. So I said a few things the wrong way. At least

I got the job done. You've been at this, what—four days? You're already pulling overtime to compensate for the mistakes you made at the Regal Hotel."

"Mistakes? I was assaulted."

"And you lost evidence. Do you think that perp would have risked coming back to the crime scene if you were a man?"

"My God, Dennis—what century were you born in? What woman warped you so badly that you think…?"

There. He was smirking. Laughing. He'd pushed her hot button, and she'd taken the bait and lashed out. She was no better at managing people than he was. Lexi raked her fingers through her hair and let it fall in a messy disarray as she tempered her outburst. "I'm sorry. I shouldn't have said—"

"I always figured when they kicked me upstairs that they'd promote Wynn to take my job. He's been here the longest and has the most experience. He was hungry for it, too. He was ready. Instead, Mac promoted the cheerleader."

"Are you saying Mac should have promoted Ethan because he's a man?"

Chapter Eight

Lexi's mouth opened, ready to argue her qualifications for this job, when she heard the rapid clicking of toenails on the hallway tile. Seconds later, Blue trotted into the office. The dog paused to sniff Dennis's boots before trotting around the desk to Lexi. Dennis watched Blue prop his front paws up on Lexi's desk to sniff at the front pocket of her jeans where she sometimes kept treats. But to anyone who didn't know about the secret stash, it looked like the dog was positioning himself between Lexi and her suddenly unwelcome guest.

She reached out to scrub her hand around Blue's ears, thanking him for distracting her from the rant she'd been about to unleash. It wouldn't have made any difference to Dennis, and probably would have gotten her into trouble. "Who's my favorite boy?"

Dennis grumbled beneath his breath. "Of course, you've got your very own bodyguards. Where's Murphy?"

"Right here." Aiden strode in, carrying two insulated paper cups steaming with the scent of fresh coffee. He walked past Dennis to hand one to Lexi. "I brought the caffeine you ordered."

She gratefully wrapped her fingers around the warm cup and dipped her nose to inhale its reviving aroma. She needed the diversion to keep herself from sinking to Dennis's level. "Thank you."

Aiden propped his hip on the corner of her desk and faced Dennis. Unlike the dog, there was no mistaking that he was purposefully positioning himself between Lexi and her guest. "Didn't know if you'd be staying, Hunt, or I'd have brought you a cup, too."

Dennis's ego kept him from being intimidated. "You don't have to be polite, Murph. I'll have my day in front of the ethics board and prove these accusations have no merit. Then I'll be right back where I'm supposed to be. *This* office." He paused in the doorway and doffed Lexi a mock salute. "Supervisor Callahan."

The moment he was gone, Lexi sank into her chair, closing her eyes and absently resting her hand on Blue's head as exhaustion—both physical and mental—claimed her.

"You sure I can't punch him for being rude, crude and unlikable?" She heard the shift of Aiden's weight off her desk. Her eyes fluttered open when she felt him pluck the insulated paper cup from her hand. He set both coffees on the desk and turned her chair to the side to kneel in front of her. He brushed a couple of loose tendrils of hair away from her bruised eye and bandaged stitches and tucked them behind her ear. He rested his palm at the side of her neck and jaw, his blue eyes studying her face and frowning. "You're pale. Forget the caffeine. I think you've pushed hard enough today."

"It's Dennis who exhausts me. He's right. I blew my first assignment as supervisor."

He stroked his thumb along the line of her jaw in a rough caress. "You didn't blow anything. You were a victim of a crime. No different than Jennifer Li, except you survived. You weren't attacked because you failed. You were attacked because you were doing your damn job, and that was a threat to that creep. Hunt's just trying to get under your skin and make you feel inadequate so he doesn't feel lonely because he's such a loser." His warm, calloused thumb stopped beneath the point of her chin, tilting her face ever so slightly to his. His nostrils flared as he gentled his vehement defense of her from his tone. "Call your judge and let's go home. We'll worry about your car tomorrow."

The warmth of his touch, his caring, his utter faith in her abilities surged through her, giving her a boost of strength. "You always say the right thing to me. Thank you."

She framed his jaw between her hands, leaned forward and pressed her lips to his. She felt a riot of sensations— the rasp of his stubble beneath her palms, the pinch of her healing lip, the coffee-scented warmth of his startled breath caressing her face in the split second before her lips softened against his. It wasn't a sisterly kiss, but it was chaste, full of gratitude, full of want, full of all the unsatisfied what-ifs she wanted to explore with this man but held in check.

A moment later, Aiden tilted his head slightly, his lips settling between hers like interlocking pieces of a puzzle snapping into place. His response to the contact was equally chaste. But his lips vibrated against hers like the pulse she felt hammering beneath her fingertips at the side of his neck. His breathing grew rapid and gusted against her cheek as he feathered his fingers into her hair and cradled her head to hold her mouth against his for several precious seconds. This kiss wasn't anything like what she wanted to share with Aiden. It wasn't wild or passionate or free-spirited. This kiss was an exercise in self-control, and it felt inordinately hot to sense that any moment now they were both about to fail. They were priming a charge for a detonation. And the payoff would be explosive.

Then his shoulders lifted with a resolute sigh and he pulled away, tugging her bottom lip between his like a tantalizing morsel. It gently snapped back, breaking contact, but arrowing a shaft of heat straight to her womb.

With his fingers still clutched against her scalp, he touched his forehead to hers. Those blue eyes opened right above her, and it was like looking up and losing herself in the fathomless depths of the twilight sky. Oh, man, she had it bad, thinking in metaphors she might have used in the ramblings of her teenage journal.

His eyes, though, were anchored on her mouth. "Your lip is feeling better? It doesn't hurt anymore?"

"Not much."

Was that why he'd held back? Was he afraid of hurting her? He pressed the pad of his thumb to the pout of her bottom lip, and she thought, for just one moment, that he was going to throw that sensual restraint out the window and kiss her.

"Lex…"

Suddenly, a long black snout and lolling pink tongue thrust up between them, forcing them apart. Blue slurped at Aiden's face, stealing the kiss Lexi had wanted.

"And there's the chaperone." When the cold, wet nose turned to Lexi, Aiden pushed the dog down. "Easy, boy." He wrestled the dog onto his back and rubbed his flanks.

Lexi leaned over and added her petting to what was apparently a long-overdue tummy rub. "This explains the sorry state of my love life," she teased. "Too many big brothers. Even the furry one thinks he knows what's best for me."

When she realized she was the only one laughing, Lexi turned her chair away and stood. Maybe she hadn't really meant it as a joke. Aiden wasn't stupid. He had to know how she felt about him—how she suspected he felt about her. But if he was determined to ignore both the chemistry and history they shared, she had to give him his space and let him define the parameters of their relationship. What good was pushing him to share his feelings if he didn't choose to love her? She understood. She'd pined after him for years in one way or another but had chosen not to act on her feelings.

But she could have died the other night. She could have lived her whole life denying herself the chance to love and be loved by Aiden. Lexi wasn't sure how much longer she could pretend the status quo between them was okay, that it wasn't twisting something inside her every day she denied how much she loved this man, how much she needed him to love her.

Aiden nudged Blue to his feet and stood, ordering the dog to follow as he retrieved their coats from the seat of one of her guest chairs. "Let's get you home. I'm not doing a very good job of protecting you if I let you work to the point of exhaustion."

While she slipped on her coat and bundled up for the cold weather outside, Lexi wondered whether Aiden would have dropped that knight-in-shining-armor vow of celibacy—or whatever was holding him back—if she'd taken the initiative and deepened the kiss herself? She knew he'd been through hell while growing up, with the relationships he was supposed to be able to trust. Being fostered by her family had given him his best friend, wonderful role models and the security every child should be able to enjoy. It probably made sense that he was reluctant to change the status quo and risk losing the only reliable family he'd ever known.

But how could she make him believe that loving her wouldn't be a risk? Was she supposed to be the strong one and force him out of his comfort zone? Or was she being unfair to hope, to insist, that they could be something more?

By the time she had her court order signed by Judge Whitman, and a plan of attack for her team to pursue the investigation tomorrow, the sun had set. Lexi and Aiden had shared a simple meal, then tackled putting up the decorations on the Christmas tree and around the house. She got out all her Mannheim Steamroller CDs and blasted the jazzy Christmas music throughout the house while they worked, curtailing the need for much conversation beyond where to hang this ornament or where she stored the batteries to light up the Victorian holiday village she set up along the bench of the bay window.

By ten o'clock, the lights from the Christmas tree and the Victorian village offered the only illumination in the front room. The hallway light was on behind her because Aiden was up in the attic, stowing the storage tubs. While Blue snoozed on the cushion behind her, Lexi sat on the braided rug between the couch and coffee table, repacking the ornament boxes in the last tub for Aiden to carry upstairs. Cocooned by shadows, the gentle glow of the decorated tree and front window filled the room with a calming sense of peace and enough nostalgia that she felt like she was surrounded by her missing family.

It had been a long weekend, full of physical demands and emotional ups and downs. Lexi was having a hard time keeping her chin up and not dozing off. But she refused to go put on her pajamas, brush her teeth and head to bed, partly because she knew Aiden would insist on finishing whatever work remained to be done himself and partly because she'd quickly gotten into the habit of falling asleep on him. As frustrating as this protective non-relationship with him had become, a foolish part of her desperately hoped that he'd sit down with her for a quiet chat, and offer a sturdy shoulder to lean on and a haven of warmth and strength where she could fall asleep in his arms again.

Her head had tipped back onto the couch and her eyes had drifted shut when Aiden's voice startled her. "Is that last one ready to go up?"

Lexi snapped her head up. "What?"

"Whoa. Sorry." Aiden flipped on the lamp beside the couch and shut off the CD player. "You know, you can shove that beast off the couch and lie down if you're tired." He shooed Blue off the sofa and held out a hand to help Lexi to her feet. "He may be a lean, mean, feisty machine, but he likes you. He'll do what you say."

"I know he will." Lexi sank onto the cushion, stifling a yawn with her hand. But just as quickly, she pushed to her feet. The last thing she needed was to drift off in the place she would forever associate with sleeping with Aiden. Things were already too complicated between them to risk mumbling in her sleep or, worse, discovering she couldn't sleep through the night without his arms around her. Pretending she suddenly had all the energy in the world, she snapped the lid onto the tub. "It's ready to go. I think we've got everything up except for these three sentimental cuties I found."

She picked up one of the three homemade ornaments she'd laid on the coffee table. Two decades old and built out of foam balls, glue, yarn, cloth, pins and children's imaginations, these had been a craft project her mother had come up with one snow day to keep Lexi and the boys busy.

She handed Aiden the one he'd made. Although one of the construction paper eyes was missing, the plastic cup that had been cut to resemble a helmet was still wedged into place on the figure's head. "Mom was pleased with our imaginations. Not one of us made a snowman out of them."

He snickered at his age twelve handiwork. "Nothing says Christmas like an astronaut."

"That's what you wanted to be when you were growing up."

"I think I just wanted to escape. The planet wasn't very kind to me early on." He hung it on a branch, then paused to study the entire tree. "That was the first Christmas I ever had a tree. I remember seeing presents with my name on them underneath, and I didn't think they were real. The first one I opened was a package of socks. But they were new, and they were mine, and lame as they were, I thought it was the coolest thing ever. Your dad got me a bike, and I didn't know how to ride it. Made your mom cry. But he taught me how."

"Which made her cry again." Lexi remembered how quickly Aiden had gone from novice to daredevil, skinning knees and elbows and, ultimately, cutting open his chin, which warranted a trip to the ER. She glanced up, seeing the faint evidence of that scar through the dark stubble of his late-night beard.

"Your parents taught me a lot of things." He tapped the rudimentary astronaut, making it swing back and forth on its branch. "After a while, I realized I didn't want to go anywhere else. I wanted to stay grounded and make this world as safe a place as your mom and dad made it for me."

Tears stung the corners of Lexi's eyes, and she quickly swiped them away. "You'd better take that tub upstairs and close the attic before I haul off and hug you."

But Aiden didn't smile back. He simply nodded, picked up the tub and headed down the hallway.

How did even those teasing threats of affection become so awkward between them? Did he think he was going to lose those memories, that tenuous link to the only family he'd ever known, by developing a more intimate relationship with her? How could she make him see that the bond between them would only grow stronger, deeper? He wouldn't betray her parents or Levi by wanting her. Together, they could expand the family, make new memories, honor her parents by loving each other the same way they had loved.

But that wasn't something she could tell Aiden and make him believe. He'd have to discover the power of that kind of love on his own.

She listened for the creaking of the folding stairs beneath Aiden's feet before turning back to the tree. Bless Levi's heart—he'd always known he'd wanted to go into the military from the time he was a little boy. His ornament was covered in camouflage material and he'd glued the plastic cap from one of his GI action figures on top of its head. Lexi hung his ornament next to Aiden's, then picked up the angel she'd made with its pipe cleaner halo and hung it on a nearby branch.

She needed to focus on work. And healing. She needed to piece together the clues to two murders and her assault. She might be ready to take her relationship with Aiden to the next level, but he wasn't. She needed to respect that and concentrate on the things she could control—like making sure everything at the house was perfect for Levi's arrival on Christmas Eve.

Inhaling a deep breath to clear her head and shut down her heart, Lexi circled around the tree, adjusting the string of lights, moving an ornament to an empty branch, stretching up on tiptoe to nudge the star on top into a straighter position. She was pleased that the tree reflected the colors of the season, and that the whole front room had a special glow that would welcome Santa and remind Levi how much it meant to be home for the holiday.

Lexi was on her knees, smoothing out the wrinkles in

the tree skirt, when she caught a blur of movement in the window behind her. What was that? A bird flying through the light from the streetlamp across the street? What kind of bird was out at this time of night on the cusp of winter? Was it some funky sweep of headlights moving the shadows of her porch and the row of evergreen bushes in front of the house?

Feeling a vague sense of unease at not being able to identify the source of the movement, she pushed to her feet and turned to study the night beyond the panes of glass. But before she could discern one shadow from another, Blue barked and charged at the window. "Blue!"

The Malinois jumped onto the bench, knocking her carefully placed houses askew. One teetered over the edge and crashed to the floor.

But it wasn't the shattered decoration that turned her blood to ice. "Aiden!"

It was the hooded figure in black, right outside the window. Faceless black mask. Dark eyes. Black gloves. He gave her a mocking salute before swinging his leg over the porch railing. Snarling a vicious alarm, Blue lunged against the glass and the window bowed. "Blue!"

The figure, startled by the dog's attack, lost his footing and tumbled into the evergreen bushes. He knocked the snow off the bushes as he pushed them aside and scrambled to his feet.

She was suddenly aware of the hard footsteps racing up behind her a split second before strong hands grasped her shoulders. "Lex!" She yelped and turned as Aiden pulled her away from the window. "Blue! Get down! *Hier!*"

He ordered Blue to his side and the dog obeyed, knocking over another ceramic house as he leaped down and dashed to Aiden's side.

Lexi braced her hands on Aiden's chest as he pulled her

to the interior wall of the foyer. "Did you see him? Just like at the crime scene. All in black. Watching me. He's running now. Blue scared him off."

"Stay put." Aiden hurried past the coats hanging on the hall tree and pulled his gun.

He unlocked the dead bolt and a blast of cold air swept in as he inched the door open, peering one way, then the other, making sure his path was clear before he gave chase. No! He wasn't facing that intruder alone.

He'd attacked before.

He'd killed before.

Lexi tugged on the sleeve of Aiden's sweater. "Take Blue with you!"

The door slammed shut and Aiden was pushing her back against the wall. His shoulders blocked the world from view, his midnight blue eyes boring into hers. "He stays here. If anyone gets past me, they'll have to deal with him before they get to you."

"If that's the guy, he's not afraid to hurt anyone. He's not afraid to kill—"

Aiden's free hand slipped around the back of her neck and he brought his mouth down in a hard stamp of a kiss that shocked the argument out of her. Not chaste. Not lousy. Lexi's lips parted and Aiden's tongue claimed what she willingly offered. Her fingers dug into his shoulders, hanging on to every precious millisecond. This kiss was a warning. A promise. An unguarded moment when everything they felt for each other sneaked through.

It ended as suddenly as it had begun. With his fingers still tangled in the hair at her nape, Aiden pulled away. "Lock the door behind me. Stay away from the window. Stay safe. Please. For me." He kissed her again before releasing her and swinging open the door. When the dog would have charged out ahead of him, he gave a new command. "Blue! *Pass auf!*"

Guard the place.

Guard Lexi.

The slam of the front door went through her like an electric jolt. Her heart might be filled with a million questions about that kiss and who the intruder might be, but she obeyed Aiden's command. She turned the dead bolt, sent up a silent prayer for Aiden's safety, then grabbed Blue by the collar and hurried through the house with him to make sure the back door in the kitchen was also locked and the latch on every window in the house was secured.

She fought the urge to peek through the windows to track Aiden and make sure he was all right. Because she had no doubt that a confrontation with her attacker would turn violent. Instead of making herself a visible target at the windows, she returned to the foyer, leaning against the wall and sinking down onto her haunches in the very spot where Aiden had kissed her with all that raw emotion.

Blue followed her command and sat right beside her, dutifully watching over her in his partner's absence. She hugged her arms around the dog's neck, counting off the seconds until Aiden returned. The minutes dragged on interminably until she heard the sharp knock at the door. "Lex, it's me. Open up."

She raced Blue to the door. The moment she unlocked it, Aiden pushed his way in, pushed her back from the opening, and threw the dead bolt behind him before holstering his weapon and opening his arms, welcoming both Blue and Lexi. She gave a small laugh as Blue nearly pushed her aside to prop his paws up on Aiden's chest. She was content to wind her arms around Aiden's waist and lean her head on his shoulder and snuggle against his strength. His sweater was frosty with the cold, damp air outside, but she didn't mind the cool moisture against her cheek. "Are you all right? Did you see who it was? What did he want?"

He wrapped his arm around her shoulders, praising Blue and releasing him from the guard command. As the dog dropped down to the floor, Aiden reached around her to dig Blue's Kong out of his jacket and tossed it down the hallway for the dog to chase and play with. "You da man, Blue. Good boy."

Then both arms came around her, his lips settled at her temple, and he exhaled a heavy sigh that stirred through her hair. Something was wrong. He had bad news.

"You didn't see anyone?" Lexi asked, her arms tightening around him. "I didn't imagine him. He was right there on the porch. Blue saw him, too."

"I don't doubt either of you. There are footprints in the snow leading up to the house he tried to cover up. But his escape path was easy to track. They led through your neighbor's yard and out to the street behind us where the snow has been cleared. I'm guessing he had a vehicle waiting and drove off. Without Blue, I have no idea which way he went."

"I knew you should have taken Blue."

"And have that guy double around and come in the back door while I was checking the front?"

She didn't realize how tense she'd become, how isolated she'd felt without Aiden beside her. But she'd had Blue with her, and there wasn't a finer guard dog in all of KCPD. Aiden had been alone. "But if anything had happened to you…"

"Hey. I'm okay." He pulled back just enough to frame her face. His hands were cold on her skin, but his touch short-circuited the downward spiral of her thoughts. "I'm a cop, remember? Routine patrol. I'm just doing my job." He pressed his cool lips to her forehead and pulled her arms from his waist. "Now I need you to do yours. Bundle up and get your kit."

"Good idea." She appreciated the reminder that she was more than a victim here. In fact, she was vital to finding the answers they needed and capturing this freak. She jogged back to her bedroom closet to retrieve her kit and set it on the bench of the hall tree to open it. "I can take pictures and measurements of the footprints. We can match his size against the size of whatever we find on the hotel video."

Aiden put on his insulated jacket and pulled Blue's leash out of the pocket. The dog danced around his legs in anticipation before Aiden ordered him to sit. He put on his harness and attached the leash while Lexi zipped up her coat and tugged on a pair of sterile gloves.

"Wait here." He unlocked the door. "Let me go out first with Blue."

"Why? Is there something else?" Dread sank in the pit of her stomach. "Please, not another dead body."

Aiden squeezed her shoulder, frowning some sort of apology. "There's a present on your front porch."

"From a delivery service?" Lexi huffed a sigh of relief. Why would that be such dire news? "It's probably one of the gifts I ordered for Levi or Chelsea. This time of year, companies deliver on Sundays."

"I think it's from the man who attacked you."

She pushed past him to look at it. "Why do you say that?"

"Lex." He tried to hold her back, but the dog got in between them, and she got out to the porch before his hand clamped around her arm and pulled her back.

But she'd already seen it. At the edge of the porch. It truly was a gift—not in any kind of plain brown or white shipping package, but a Christmas present wrapped in green-and-red paper and tied up with a speckled beige drapery cord. Speckled pink with faded blood. Beige because all the dye had been leached out of it. The box inside was dented at one end, as if it had been through a brawl. And the tag looked eerily familiar.

"It's from the crime scene, isn't it?" Aiden speculated.

"Looks like it." Her breath gusted out in a cloud between them. "Let Blue do his thing. I'll get my camera."

Lexi scrolled through her photos from Jennifer Li's hotel room and found an image with the exact package. Her attacker had taken this, too. But why return it?

Blue's reaction gave her a reason why.

The dog sniffed at the gift, whined and jerked back. He trotted down to the step below it to sniff it from that angle and had the same reaction, as if something pungent was tickling his sensitive nose. "Probably not a bomb," Aiden guessed, drawing Blue back to his side and giving Lex the okay to snap several photographs. "He's not specifically trained to detect explosives, but he wouldn't shy away from the scent like that. I can call Sergeant Burke if you want. His K-9, Gunny, is trained in explosives detection."

"That won't be necessary." Lexi knelt to take a closer look. She didn't need a dog's nose to detect the heavy use of bleach on the package. That explained the pinkish bloodstains, tainted by the chemical and useless for lab analysis now. This was a taunt, a little gaslighting to undermine Lexi's ability to do her job. A threat meant to assert his superiority over her. The man had physically bested her, and now he thought he could defeat her mentally, too. "This isn't a bomb."

Although her fingers were getting stiff from the cold air, she kept working. She snapped a picture of the gift tag. The *B* in Jennifer Li's handwriting had been scratched out, and a new message had been written in its place.

Try to solve your murder now.

The perp was flaunting the tainted evidence. He was mocking her.

"I think this is the ligature that was around Jennifer Li's neck. The one he took from the crime scene." She untied the cord and carefully set it inside an evidence bag. She opened the box inside and let out an audible moan.

Aiden saw it, too. "Is that...?"

"My stocking cap." It was faded from bleach, but the specks of blood on the embroidered *CSI* letters made her certain it was the one he'd taken from the crime scene. He'd tucked another note inside with her cap.

Be a good girl and give up now. I'll take more than your hat next time.

Lexi tried to remain clinical, despite the chill that was seeping into her very bones. "Why would the killer risk this? Even if he's compromised the evidence, why would he return it to me? There might be something in here we could use. DNA isn't the only clue we can analyze."

"Because he's a creep. He's toying with you. Because he clearly gets off on upsetting you. And hell if I'll let this happen, but he could be setting you up as his next target."

Lexi shook her head. "That doesn't fit his MO. I'm not a hooker or the other woman. I'm not having an affair. And there were no signs that he stalked the first two victims like this." Now she was really shivering, and it wasn't entirely due to the wintry night air.

"Lex..." She was marginally aware of Aiden and Blue on the steps below her, standing guard between her and the rest of the world. "Bag that stuff and bring it into the house. I feel like we've got eyes on us."

"Still?" Lexi glanced up to see Aiden swiveling his head back and forth, surveying the street. She quickly sealed the contents inside an evidence bag and pushed to her feet. Once she was inside, she held open the door and urged Aiden and Blue to follow.

He closed and bolted the door behind them before sending Blue after his toy and pulling his cell phone from the pocket of his jeans. "Gifting you with a murder weapon is bad. But that's not the part that concerns me."

"What are you talking about?"

"Finding you at a murder scene he's familiar with is one thing…" He paused as his call picked up. "Yes, ma'am. This is Officer Aiden Murphy. Sorry to call at home, but is Detective Watson available? I have a development in a case he's working. I'll hold."

He reached for her, pulling her shivering body against his chest, hugging her close to his warmth, his strength, his protection.

She understood the point he was making. And it terrified her. "How does this guy know where I live?"

Chapter Nine

Lexi spent the next three weeks fully recovering from her injuries, putting out fires at work, counting the days until her brother came home for Christmas and pretending the domestic bliss she was sharing with Aiden and Blue at her house was somehow real.

Oh, the kisses were certainly real. And Aiden hadn't just made a mockery of her list of items that could make her rethink falling in love with him; the man was a neat freak, he helped around the house, he shared interests with her, and his dog was an adorable sponge for her affection when he was off duty. Plus, Aiden Murphy was in no way, shape or form a lousy kisser—his kisses were exquisite, from the tender, warm touch of his lips on her forehead when he bade her good-night, to the quick press of his mouth against hers when he and Blue were called to duty and he had to leave her at work or at home with one of his buddies from the K-9 corps watching over her house. Lexi had met several of them by now—Sergeant Jedediah Burke and Gunny, Harry Lockhart and Onyx, Albert Logan and Niko, and Enzo Moretti and Blitz didn't seem to mind pulling the extra duty, and they assured her Aiden and Blue had done the same for them and more when asked. She liked his friends, liked that he made regular trips to Chelsea's place to make sure she was feeling secure, liked that he seemed to be having fun prepping for Christmas—sampling the cookies she baked, doing some shopping with her.

When they were away from the specter of Jennifer Li's killer leaving evidence on her front porch and destroying her murder investigation, it almost felt like they were in a real relationship. Like the two of them could really be a couple, and not just friends.

And when Aiden dropped his guard—when he'd had a particularly bad day at work, or one late night when she'd bumped into him coming out of the shower with the towel wrapped low around his hips and his steaming skin leaving little to her imagination—Aiden Murphy most definitely knew how to kiss. Deeply, slowly, thoroughly, until her whole body was a puddle of gooey need and her logical brain couldn't think straight. Or hard and fast and full of promise, demanding an equally frantic response.

But then he'd pull back. Something always seemed to hold him back from crossing the line into being with her. He'd mention her parents or Levi and how much he owed them. Or he'd ask about one of the cases she was investigating and divert her focus to that. He'd made a promise, and keeping that promise meant more to him than his attraction to her did. She could live with that. Damn the man and his code of honor. She loved him, completely, and that was one of the reasons why.

On top of all that frustrated desire, she was a sleep-deprived mess. She'd given up on falling asleep on the couch with him. If she started to nod off during a movie or one of their late-night conversations, she got up and went to bed out of respect for his desire to resist the relationship she wanted with him—that she suspected he wanted, too. But then she'd toss and turn. She'd be cold or she'd hear a noise that made her wonder if the figure in black had returned.

She worried that she'd forgotten something in her plans to make Levi's holiday a perfect homecoming for him. Or she'd start thinking about her cases and wonder what she could do differently. How could she make her team work more cohesively? What had she overlooked? Alone, she couldn't shut off all that speculation the way a few drowsy assurances and the haven of Aiden's arms could.

That was why she was sitting in her office right now, rubbing at the weary tension headache coiling between her eyes, watching Ethan Wynn pace and listening to him vent about the lab's newest hire compromising one of his experiments and jeopardizing a case. "First, she brought me the wrong sample to do the eosin stain on. Started the stain test at her own workstation before I caught the mix-up. Once I got that all straightened out, I asked her to deliver my photomicrographs to Malone to compare to his blood analysis." He huffed in frustration, spun and paced some more. "She was gone twenty minutes. Twenty minutes! I could have had a coffee and taken a sauna by the time she got back to the chem lab."

"Did she say why it took her so long?" Lexi felt compelled to contribute something to turn this from a rant into a conversation.

Ethan stopped and threw up his hands. "She got lost. She had to ask for directions to find Malone's office. She probably went to Daddy to ask for help."

Yep. Lexi's newest hire was Zoe Stockman, Captain Stockman's daughter. If she'd gone all the way to the CSIU office to ask for directions, she really had gotten lost. But Lexi had made her decision carefully, based on Zoe's expertise. Since Zoe was a newly graduated criminalist, Lexi had filled the position with a qualified candidate and saved the department a little money.

But right now, she needed to appease the most experienced member of her team. If he'd been *hungry* for promotion as Dennis Hunt had claimed, then Ethan was probably already nursing a bit of frustration. Having a bad day in his own lab wasn't helping. "Look, I'll advise her to respect your space. But I want to encourage you to handle things a little more diplomatically. Or come to me."

"I've come to you now." He sat in the chair across from her and tapped his finger on the desk before pointing it at her. "You know she only got the job because she's Captain Stockman's daughter. You can't fix incompetence."

"*I'm* the one who interviewed and hired her. On Mac and Dennis's approval. The captain had nothing to do with it." Lexi propped her elbows on the desk and leaned forward, reaching out with a conciliatory gesture. "Zoe's not incompetent. She's new. How many weeks did it take you to learn what was in every storage cabinet and where every division was located? Give her a break. She's a good hire. We need her ready to pick up the workload when Khari goes on maternity leave next month, so we don't get backlogged. Maybe you could be the nice guy and apologize by giving her a more specific orientation tour."

Ethan crossed his arms over his chest and leaned back in his chair. "Not my job. *You're* the boss."

Lexi bit her tongue at the defiant retort. She swept aside the papers on her desk and jotted a note on her calendar. "Fine. I'll talk to her tomorrow. If we invade your personal space again while we're on the tour, it's because *you* asked for it. I don't want to hear any complaints."

Ethan stood, straightened the front of his lab coat and smoothed his hand over his gray hair. "You get the job done? I won't complain."

He nearly collided with the gray-haired police officer who'd just arrived to knock on Lexi's open door. Ethan retreated into the room, waiting expectantly for Brian Stockman's announcement. "Captain."

"Wynn." Brian Stockman gave him a curt nod.

Lexi stood behind her desk, a zing of adrenaline pumping through her veins and pushing aside her headache. Had he overheard Ethan complaining about his daughter? "Captain?"

"How's my daughter doing? First week on the job." Maybe he hadn't heard the complaints.

Although she spotted the printout for a new case in his hand, Lexi took the time to answer his question, hopefully protecting Ethan from any backlash. "She's learning something new every day, sir. I assigned her to my most experienced criminalist for orientation."

"Good to hear." His proud, paternal smile encompassed both Ethan and Lexi before he held up the assignment sheet. "We've got another DB. Same hotel where Giselle Byrd was found. The detective who called says the MO is similar. Signs of a fight. Strangulation." He rested his hands on his utility belt and pursed his mouth in a grim frown. "I hope to hell we don't have a serial killer for Christmas."

"Let's not jump to conclusions." Lexi shed her lab coat and hung it on the closet door behind her. "We'll get the facts first. No-Man's-Land is a pretty rough part of town. Anything could happen there."

"Officers have secured the scene and will remain on site while you work." Captain Stockman came into the room and set the printout with the address and other pertinent information on her desk. "I'm not having another Regal Hotel incident."

Lexi almost didn't hear him at first. Her attention was diverted to the Advent calendar hanging on the door. Over half the colorful windows had been opened, one for every day, counting down to Christmas Eve. But for some reason, she'd skipped a number. Instead of today's date, she'd opened tomorrow's window.

Only, since Ethan had been waiting for her to have this meeting first thing when she'd walked in this morning, she didn't remember opening any window on the calendar at all. Not yet. A vague sense of unease washed over her, leaving a trail of goose bumps in its wake. Why did she feel like this mistake was a coded message that was just beyond her ability to understand? Probably because Khari hadn't been able to get any usable DNA off the hair sample from her attacker or from the bleached curtain cord and stocking cap he'd brought to her house. There were too many unanswered questions swirling around inside her head. She'd been the supervising criminalist for nearly a month now, and she was no closer to identifying the killer than she'd been the night she'd been attacked. She didn't need any more mysteries in her life. She needed solid and reliable. She needed her world to make sense.

"Lexi?" the captain prompted.

"Sorry. Got stuck on a thought." She grabbed her coat and smiled at his concern for his people. "We'll be fine, Captain. Thanks." She spared a moment to open today's date and smile at the fun holiday fact behind the door. Then she pushed the door shut on tomorrow's date and put on her coat as he left her office. She picked up the printout and skimmed the information.

"Thanks for not ratting me out to Daddy," Ethan said, his tone apologetic.

"Just doing my job."

He nodded. "Should I gather the team?"

"Please. I want Dobbs there to secure the murder weapon. You. Me." She looked up to meet Ethan's brown eyes. "And Zoe. She needs the field experience."

"Bad call, Lexi. She's not ready."

"She never will be if we don't give her the chance. Besides, I'm the boss. It's *my* call." She looped her bag over her shoulder and nodded toward the door. "Get the team together and meet me in the garage. You can drive."

With a groan that indicated both compliance and displeasure, Ethan jogged down the hallway to alert the others and retrieve his own gear.

Lexi locked the door behind her and pulled out her phone to text Aiden that she was leaving with the team and gave him the address, simply because she'd promised to let him know if she left the lab.

Not to worry. I won't be alone. See you at home. Your turn to cook. :)

His reply made her laugh.

Do you want Chinese takeout or pizza?

Lexi's answer was brief.

Surprise me.

He sent the reply she'd expected. As soon as Blue and I are done with this locker sweep at Central Prep High School, we'll swing by. Don't like you in that part of town.

Where WOULD you like me? She typed the flirty response, but then backspaced to delete it. Just because they'd been acting like a couple lately didn't mean they really were together. Her heart ached for the boy who hadn't been protected from violence and neglect. She hated that he felt taking care of her was a debt of honor he had to repay her family, but she wouldn't push him into anything he didn't consciously choose to pursue for himself. I'll see you at the hotel or at home. Be safe.

You, too.

THE DOUBLE TIME HOTEL had once been a Kansas City jazz hot spot back in the 1920s. Now, like the rest of the decayed downtown neighborhood, sadly dubbed No-Man's-Land by the members of KCPD who had to deal with the homelessness, gangs, drug use and other crimes in that part of the city that had yet to be reclaimed by a nostalgic younger generation of civic-minded investors, the Double Time had become a hot spot of a different kind. With bars at each of its first-floor windows, it resembled a pawnshop more than a hotel. Most of its Art Deco architecture had either been vandalized or covered up with a corrugated metal sign. And the sad interior hadn't survived the years in any better shape. Mosaic tile floors had been carpeted over, probably in the sixties or seventies, judging by the tiny clouds of dust that marked their footprints as the team carried their gear from the alley where they'd parked across the lobby to the elevator.

Jackson Dobbs wasn't certain the rickety elevator behind the sliding cage door would hold a man of his size, and when he suggested he would take the stairs up to the crime scene on the fourth floor, Lexi and the rest of the team fell into step right behind him. The peach-colored paint in the stairwell was chipped and faded, or covered in graffiti, but at least the steel-and-concrete stairs felt secure beneath their feet.

When they reached the hotel room, Detective Hudson Kramer was there outside the door, waiting for Keir Watson's older brother, Dr. Niall Watson, to finish his preliminary examination of the body.

"Ma'am. Dobbs. Wynn." Lexi shook hands with Hud and introduced him to Zoe Stockman. Then Hud opened his notepad and reported what they knew thus far. "Keir is down in the hotel office with the victim's friend who discovered the body—also in the same business as our vic—trying to get what information he can out of her. Can't tell yet if she's hysterical over finding her friend, or if she's tweaking on meth or some other drug."

"Probably some combination of both." Lexi peered beyond the yellow crime scene tape that crisscrossed the open doorway to see an eerily familiar scene, albeit much less posh than the one she'd processed at the Regal Hotel.

Dr. Watson shifted slightly beside the flame-haired woman's body on the floor, eavesdropping on their conversation as he gathered his instruments. "She's got no ID on her. Blunt force trauma, defensive wounds. Preliminary cause of death is asphyxiation caused by strangulation. The ligature around her neck looks like a section of the curtain cord." The ME pushed his glasses up on the bridge of his nose and stood, diverting Lexi's focus away from the dusty beige drapes at the window. "Based on lividity and liver temp, she's been dead since late last night. I'd say between ten p.m. and midnight." Dr. Watson looked to Lexi. "If you want to come in and get your pictures now, I'm ready to bag her and take her in for a more thorough exam."

Lexi nodded as she gave her team their assignments. "Jackson, you take the bathroom. Ethan and Zoe, you start with the bed and perimeter of the room. I'll be with the vic." Once everyone had gloves and booties on, they ducked beneath the tape and went to work. Detective Kramer stayed with her as the ME stepped out to prepare his gurney and body bag. Lexi snapped general pictures of the room with her camera before zeroing in on the specifics of the crime. "Curtain cord around her neck. Trashed room. Even the position of the body at the foot of the bed is a repeat of Jennifer Li's crime scene."

And she couldn't help but notice that the curtains were open. She took a picture to confirm the observation in case someone tried to play mind games with her later. Because she had a sick feeling that this crime scene was about more than the dead woman. It was about *her*.

Detective Kramer's fingers lightly grazed her elbow, startling her from her thoughts. "Having déjà vu?"

"More than a little." She knelt to take some pictures of the body itself. "If this is a serial killer, there's no pattern in victimology. Giselle Byrd was a Black woman, Jennifer Li was of Thai descent, and this is a Caucasian woman with dyed red hair."

Hud glanced in his notebook. "Her friend called her TNT. Don't know if those are her initials or her personality. Probably a street nickname. The room was rented out by a Paul and Margaret Montgomery. I'm guessing that's not Margaret."

Lexi looked up at the stocky detective. "Montgomery? You're sure that's the name she and her customer used?"

"Yep. Just like the room across the hall at the Regal." He tucked his notepad inside his leather jacket. "We may also have a lead on 'B.'"

"The initials on the gift tags in Jennifer Li's hotel room?"

Hud nodded. "Jennifer was an interior designer. Keir found out that Barton Rutledge III hired her to remodel a lake property he owns. They've worked together for almost two years. A lot longer than it should take to rebuild a deck and put up wallpaper."

"Barton Rutledge, the land developer?" As in thrice-married billionaire businessman? "You think he was having an affair with Jennifer?"

"We intend to find out. His wife alibis him for the night of the murder, but she probably has a billion reasons to lie for him. Rutledge and his attorney are coming in to the Fourth Precinct offices tomorrow for an interview. You want to be there to observe?"

"Yeah." Since some of her key evidence from the Li murder had been stolen, she was both excited and relieved to hear that the detectives had made progress on their end of the investigation. "Maybe there'll be something about him I can connect to the crime scene." She could judge Rutledge's size and build against the man who'd attacked her. Check the color of his hair. And though she expected the real estate mogul had showered and put on cologne between now and the night her attacker had shown up at her house, maybe she could even get close enough to find out if he smelled like bleach. "Text me the time, and I'll be there."

"Will do." The detective eyed the members of her team working around the room, going in and out with gear from their kits or to retrieve what they needed from the van. The ME and another officer were out in the hallway. "I need to join Keir downstairs. You okay if I leave you here? I can't lock out the floor here." He gave her a wry smile. "Not that it did much good the last time."

Lexi pushed to her feet. "That's not on you. Our perp had a passkey and knew where he could hide. It'd be like trying to stop a ghost."

"That's generous of you. My wife had attempts made on her life after she witnessed a murder a year and a half ago. If I was Murphy, I'd be pissed that someone hurt you like that, and I wasn't there to protect you."

She was familiar with the sentiment. "Wow. I'm sorry to hear that. Is she okay?"

"Gigi's great." The detective's expression softened with

a smile when he talked about his wife. "It got a jerk out of her life, and her into mine. Sort of an opposites-attract thing, I guess."

"Congratulations."

Could she and Aiden have a happily-ever-after like that once these murders were solved and the threat to her had passed? Would he move out and insist they remain just friends? Or would he be able to drop the alpha protector routine and allow himself to love her?

Hud headed to the door. "I want you in contact with somebody at all times. With your buddies here or one of us. Stay connected to your team. Especially in this neighborhood."

"We will."

With a sharp nod and a promise to let her know about Rutledge's interview, Hud slid out of the way to let Niall Watson in with his body bag.

Lexi assisted, processing what she could without removing anything from the victim herself. But when she moved out of the way to let Dr. Watson and Jackson lift the body, the victim's hair fell away from her face and neck, and a tiny flash of gold caught Lexi's eye. "Wait a minute." She put out a hand to stop them, then gently brushed aside the hair that pooled against the woman's ear. "Oh, my God."

Shaking with the chill that went through her, Lexi steadied her camera and took a photograph. Then she zoomed in and took another of TNT's multipierced ear. Among the diamond chip studs and silver bands dangled a small gold earring, shaped like a sprig of holly leaves with three rubies.

She'd need to get on her computer to make the identification stick in a court of law, but she had no doubt in her mind. "That's the earring Jennifer Li was wearing before I was attacked."

The killer had taken evidence from that crime scene.

He'd added evidence to this one.

What kind of game was he playing with her?

"You okay, boss?" Jackson asked.

She looked up into the big man's eyes, blinked away her confusion and nodded. "I'm fine." She stood back as they zipped up the body bag and strapped it onto the gurney. Niall Watson was watching her, too, although she couldn't read whether he was concerned by her reaction or annoyed by the interruption. "You two go ahead. Jackson, you'll help the ME with the body?" She thanked Dr. Watson for his patience. "I want that earring bagged and sent to my office when you're done."

The ME nodded. Lexi turned to check Ethan and Zoe's progress and found the man who had been ragging on the newbie just that morning leaning in beside her and explaining the merits of one dusting powder over another for picking up latent prints off different surfaces.

"You two okay in here for a few minutes?" She pulled her phone from her pocket. "I need to make a call to Chelsea. Get her started on some research."

With a nod, the reluctant mentor and student went back to work and Lexi headed into the hallway. Once she'd peeled off her sterile gloves and booties and locked them inside her kit, she walked to the relative quiet at the end of the hallway, as far as she could get from the banging and clanking of the old elevator.

"Hey, Chels," she greeted her friend when she picked up. "You at your computer?"

"Where else would I be?" It was good to hear the friendly eagerness in her friend's voice again. "What do you need?"

"I've got a list."

"No problem. My tea is hot and I'm ready to do your bidding."

"First…" She startled when she heard a screeching whine, followed by a piercing alarm, at the opposite end of the hallway, and a round of male cursing. Poor Jackson. Between the gurney, the ME, his gear and the officer escorting them, they'd probably surpassed the elevator's weight limit and the door had stuck. Using brute force and maybe a tad of claustrophobia-fueled adrenaline, Jackson shoved the door open and stepped out. "Hold on a second." Since the three men seemed aggravated by the stalled elevator rather than being in any real danger, Lexi pushed open the stairwell door at her end of the hallway. When she closed it, it shut out most of the noise behind her. "That's better. Now I can hear you and think."

"Is everything okay?" Some of the good humor had seeped from Chelsea's tone.

For a moment, Lexi considered Hud's warning about her team staying in contact with someone at all times. Well, Jackson was with the ME—besides, who would dare pick on a man that size? Ethan and Zoe were together. And she was connected to Chelsea via telephone. Plus, Aiden had promised he and Blue were on their way. There wasn't any promise in the world that could make her feel safer than that.

"Just some technical glitches. The elevator isn't working and we're on the fourth floor. I found a quiet spot." Lexi breathed in her calm logic and exhaled her momentary concern. She strolled across the concrete landing to peer out the cracked window with a stunning view of the brick wall across the alley. But with the wintry air whistling through the crack and eroding seams around the frame, she shivered and came back to stand near the railing, where the air was a little warmer. "First, I need you to run a search for any known prostitutes with the initials or nickname of TNT."

It was a quick search. "Oh, yeah." Chelsea read the information off her screen. "Mildred Moss, aka Millie Martin, aka TNT. She's been arrested several times for solicitation, possession of drug paraphernalia, public indecency."

"Does she have red hair? Multiple piercings?"

"In one of these pictures, she's a redhead. Yes, to the piercings."

Lexi nodded at having at least one mystery solved. "Then that's our vic. Would you forward that information to the ME's office?"

Tap, tap, tap. Chelsea and her computers were a thing of efficient beauty. "Sent. What else?"

Lexi walked down a couple of stairs and sat on the edge of the landing. "I need you to dig deep into Paul and Margaret Montgomery. I'm guessing that's an alias for someone who's stepping out on his wife or girlfriend—possibly with each of these women." It was a classic ruse for a man to register himself and his girlfriend at a hotel, masquerading as a married couple. "I'd really like to identify who was with these women."

"Okay. Looking…looking…" Chelsea gasped with excitement that quickly dissipated. "I've got a Paul Montgomery, deceased. Almost twenty years ago. Looks like an old-money guy. Do you want me to expand my search outside of Kansas City?"

"Not yet." This guy knew his way around KC. He'd been intimately acquainted with the layout of the Regal Hotel, and he knew enough about the Double Time to leave a body where no one would discover it until the following day. And he'd found Lexi's home and knew the residential area well enough to have planned an escape route. "I think our guy's local." The breeze from the window was raising goose bumps beneath Lexi's sweater and CSI vest. She got up to pace the landing, hoping the movement would warm her up enough to finish this phone call. "This may sound like it's coming out of left field, but see if there's any connection between Paul Montgomery and Barton Rutledge III."

"The real estate guy?"

"That's the one."

Lexi hugged her arm around her waist and continued to pace while Chelsea searched. "Um, you're one smart lady. The late Paul Montgomery was Barton Rutledge's father-in-law. Is that significant?"

"You're kidding."

"From his first wife. Paul's daughter was Margaret. Married Barton before he was somebody. She died of cancer six years into their marriage." Clearly, Chelsea was reading again. "Gossip sheet says Rutledge was heartbroken and dated a bunch of women. Moving up in society, drowning his sorrows in the opposite sex. Looks like a different woman at every social event, in just these few pictures that pop up from the newspaper."

Lexi knew she was onto something here. "I suspect he was seeing some of those women outside of social events, too." Jennifer Li, a beautiful, successful businesswoman who had her own reputation to protect, would make an ideal mistress for a man like Rutledge. They shared the same social circles, the same need for discretion. But why kill her? Did he have a history of violence? And how did the two prostitutes fit in? He wouldn't want either of their pictures in the paper with him.

"There's more." Chelsea interrupted Lexi's speculation. "Looks like Paul Montgomery didn't approve of the philandering, threatened to block the inheritance from his daughter's estate. So Rutledge settled down and married wife number two. That lasted about a year before Rutledge started hitting the gossip columns again. Divorced two years later. The rumor mill quieted down a few years ago when he married his current wife, Mandy."

Lexi didn't believe it. "I wonder how long he's been cheating on her, too."

"I doubt a man with that track record could be faithful," Chelsea agreed. "Do you think he's the killer and the man who attacked you? Maybe he got rid of Ms. Li to keep his wife from finding out."

"Or Mrs. Rutledge did know, and she gave him an ultimatum. Pick her or the mistress." Maybe all of this mess was Barton Rutledge cleaning up his affairs to keep his wife happy.

"Although, ew. That's kind of gross to use a father-daughter alias to hide your affairs."

"He's probably thumbing his nose at his father-in-law by cheating under his name." Lexi resumed her pacing. "Be sure you forward all this to Detectives Kramer and Watson. They're interviewing Rutledge tomorrow."

"I'll put it all in a neat and tidy report for them. Anything else?"

"One last thing." Lexi literally crossed her fingers that she was on the verge of finding their murder suspect. "I need you to get into the Double Time Hotel's records from a month ago and tell me if Paul Montgomery rented the room where Giselle Byrd was killed."

Chelsea typed. She waited.

"No."

"Barton Rutledge?"

"Neither." Chelsea sounded apologetic. "Giselle Byrd rented the room."

Not the answer she'd been hoping for. Frowning, Lexi paused at the top of the stairs. "I thought I was onto something. If we could identify this Paul Montgomery, confirm that it's Barton Rutledge or someone else, we'd have a suspect to connect to all three murders. Why use Giselle's...?"

Lexi heard the door creak open and turned a split second before a man in a black hoodie and stocking mask charged across the landing and gave her a hard shove.

She screamed. But that split second gave her enough time to snatch at the railing. Her phone flew from her hand and clattered down the stairs. Her arm jerked in its socket before she lost her grip, but she'd altered her momentum enough to shorten her flying crash. Winding her arms around her head, she hit her hip hard about halfway down before somersaulting to the bottom of the stairs. She landed with a painful jolt on her hands and knees. Nothing broken. No blood this time. But she was too dizzy and bruised to get to her feet.

"Lexi!"

She heard Chelsea shouting her name over the phone. Her connection. *Stay connected to your team.*

"Lexi! Are you okay? Answer me."

Lexi crawled toward her friend's voice. She found her cell in the far corner of the midpoint landing and picked it up, rolling over onto her bottom and leaning against the back wall. Air rushed back into her chest with a painful gasp. She tilted her head up to watch the eerily familiar figure in black at the top of the stairs looking down on her. He reached into the pocket of his loose black trousers and pulled out a long coil of thin rope. Lexi swallowed hard. Curtain cord, if she wasn't mistaken.

The moment he took a step toward her, she raised the phone to her ear. "Call Aiden. *He's* here."

"Oh, my God! I'm dialing him now." She heard the frantic, garbled sound of Chelsea talking on another line.

The black figure took another step. He tugged the cord between his hands, then pulled it into a loose slipknot. "Find Hud and Detective Watson. Jackson. Ethan. Anybody. I need help."

Where was her team? Didn't anyone hear her scream? How thickly insulated were these walls? Lexi flattened her back against the cinder block wall, getting the leverage she needed to push herself to her unsteady feet. Getting her face smashed into drywall plaster had been painful enough. If he got his hands on her again, there would be a far different outcome if her head hit any of this concrete or steel.

And she could already imagine that cord constricting around her throat.

"He's already in the building." Chelsea sounded breathless but succinct as she shifted from one call to the other. "Where are you?"

Another step. She slid along the wall, wondering if she was steady enough to beat him down to the next landing and out onto the third floor. "West stairwell. Tell him to hurry."

The hooded figure just kept coming, one slow step at a time. He was enjoying his advantage, savoring her stress, probably reliving her fear and helplessness from his first attack.

And then a door slammed open somewhere below her. "Lex!"

Aiden.

"Up here!" she shouted back. "Between the third and fourth floors!"

She heard footsteps charging up the stairs, men harping out logistical orders and agreements as they approached.

The figure in black hesitated.

Aiden was talking to Blue the whole way, pumping up the dog's formidable energy. "KCPD! I'm sending a dog up."

Her would-be attacker's body language changed. He stuffed the cord back into his pocket. His dark eyes glanced up, glanced down, looked at her. *Not so tough when it isn't just you and a lone woman, are you, buddy.*

She recognized the scrabble of Blue's claws as the dog bolted up the stairs ahead of the running footsteps.

Adrenaline surged through her, chasing away the aches and fears long enough for her to meet those dark eyes behind the stocking mask. She shook her head. "You don't want to meet my friends."

Blue was close enough to hear him panting with excitement now.

Cursing on a voiceless huff of breath, the man hurried up the steps and slipped out into the hallway just before Blue came charging around the corner of the landing below her. Aiden and Hud were a flight of stairs behind the dog, taking them two at a time.

"Lex!" Aiden shouted when he saw her. "You okay?"

Nodding, she sank onto the top step and waved them on, indicating she was all right.

Aiden stopped, cupped her jaw and tilted her face up as Hud raced past. His nostrils flaring with each breath, he stroked his thumb across her lips. "Did he put his hands on you?"

She wound her fingers around his wrist, briefly linking them together. "He pushed me down the stairs. But it wasn't a free fall. I'll be fine." She remembered the image of the man preparing the cord to strangle her, too. Her fingertips dug into the muscles of his forearm. "I'm glad you came when you did."

"Murph!" Hud Kramer waited at the door above them. Blue was scratching like mad at the landing door. "Do I let him out to go after the guy?"

"Wait." Lexi tugged against Aiden's arm and stood. "I have people up there. Don't let Blue hurt them."

Aiden whistled. "Blue! *Hier!*" Blue whined, reluctantly leaving the door and trotting down the stairs. Aiden hooked Blue's leash to his harness and shouted up to the detective. "Go! Find that bastard. We'll be right behind you." He holstered his weapon and slipped his arm around Lexi's waist, drawing her to his side. "Can you walk?"

Lexi nodded, clinging to his belt as they went up the steps. Although she felt the bruises as his hip pressed against hers, she was glad to have his strength and sure balance to cling to. "I want to check on my team. I need to finish processing the scene. I need to find answers."

"What did I say about being alone?" he chided, pressing a quick kiss to her temple as they climbed to the fourth-floor landing.

Lexi's eyes widened as she remembered the phone in her hand. "I wasn't alone." She put it up to her ear. "Chels, you still there?"

"I'm still here. Are you okay?"

She turned her cheek to Aiden's shoulder. "I am now. Thank you."

Aiden leaned in to share his thanks, too. "I owe you one, Chels."

"You two are bad for my blood pressure. Just kiss and be happy. I'm hanging up."

After the call disconnected, Aiden paused with his hand on the doorknob. Blue danced around their feet, probably wondering why they'd given up the chase.

Lexi tilted her face to Aiden's. *Just kiss and be happy.* "If only it were that simple."

"I know." He brushed a wavy tendril off her cheek and tucked it behind her ear. By the time he'd dipped his lips to hers, she was stretching up to meet his kiss. It was quick. It was perfect. They shared comfort and passion and even a little frustration, and then it was over. Aiden palmed her hip and moved her behind him as he released her to pull his gun again. "Stay behind me until I give the all clear."

Lexi braced her hand against the back of his protective vest and moved right with him as he and Blue entered the hallway. He quickly checked every access point before moving down the hallway.

They hadn't passed three doors when Hud came out of the opposite stairwell beside the elevator. He grumbled a curse as he holstered his weapon. "I lost him. Kicked in every door on this floor when no one answered." He strode down the threadbare carpet, meeting them in front of the crime scene tape. "I've got two uniforms clearing the stairwell all the way to the roof and down to the lobby. This guy's a chameleon. Either he can blend in with a crowd or he's got multiple escape routes mapped out before he does anything."

"Or both," Aiden conceded, holstering his weapon. "Maybe blending in *is* his escape plan."

"Then what does he do with all those black clothes?" Lexi wondered.

Aiden pulled her up beside him. "A loose jacket with big pockets? A bag stashed close by?"

"Can Blue sniff out something like that?"

"If he had a relatively fresh scent sample to compare it with."

Lexi ducked beneath the crime scene tape. "Ethan? Zoe?"

"Boss lady." Ethan hurried across the room and swallowed her in an unexpected hug that pinched her sore shoulder. His breath gusted in her hair, and she realized he was breathing hard.

"Are you okay?" she asked as she pulled back.

Zoe stepped in beside Ethan, looking equally concerned. "When I heard you scream, I thought the worst. I was never so glad to see Ethan walk back through that door."

Lexi looked up into Ethan's dark eyes. "You left her?"

He raked his fingers through his gray hair, leaving it in a mess. "We needed a bigger evidence bag for the drapes. I never made it down to the van. I heard your scream, too. I thought it was Zoe. I've never run that fast before." That explained the heavy breathing and frantic concern.

Aiden walked up behind Lexi. "Neither of you saw anything?"

Ethan shook his head. "The hallway was empty when I got up here. I had her lock the door behind me. I figured she'd be safer that way."

Zoe nodded. "I didn't unlock it until he pounded on the door."

Aiden turned to Hud Kramer, who hovered in the hallway just outside the room, updating his partner on his cell phone. "You said there were guests—tenants?—in some of these rooms?"

Hud ended the call and gave a curt nod. "I'll get names and contact information and run them against the guests in the rooms next to Jennifer Li's at the Regal Hotel. I'll keep my eye open for any sort of go bag or dump site. Maybe our chameleon is hiding in plain sight as an innocent bystander."

Blue was sniffing the floor, circling around one way and then the other, his nose touching every surface his short leash allowed him to reach. Agitated by something, he probably was picking up the scent of the man on the stairs here in the room where he'd killed TNT.

Blue was warm to the touch as Lexi reached down to pet him. "We'd better get him out of here before he contaminates anything."

Aiden wrapped his hand around Lexi's upper arm, urging her to come with them. Out in the hallway, he gently turned her arm, pointing out the red-and-violet bruise already forming on her wrist. "Damn it, Lex. Your job is not supposed to be the dangerous one." He trailed his fingers down the sleeve of her sweater to capture her hand. "But these crime scenes—it isn't about murder. Not anymore."

She knew what he was going to say. Knew it in her bones. And it terrified her. "It's about me."

Chapter Ten

Aiden pulled his truck into Lexi's driveway and parked. While he was glad to see the Christmas lights he'd installed with a timer had come on as planned, illuminating her entire front porch and some of the front yard, and adding another level of security to the place, he wasn't thrilled to look across the cab of the truck to find Lexi sagging against the seat, staring out the side window into the night.

At first, he thought she'd fallen asleep on the ride home from the lab, since those had been about the quietest twenty minutes he'd ever spent with her in his life. But the lights from the dashboard provided enough ambient light in the truck that he could see her reflection in the passenger-side window. Her pretty green eyes were open, staring through the glass at nothing in particular. That meant she was deep in thought. Either she was processing all the information she and her team and Detectives Kramer and Watson had gathered on the three murders and multiple assaults on her—searching for answers, trying to make logical sense out of a senseless situation—or she was assigning blame, to herself, most likely, for missing a clue that could have captured the killer before he'd had the chance to strike again. What could she have done differently to find the killer, prevent more murders, and keep her and her team safe when they went out to investigate the crimes?

The Lexi he knew had always been hard on herself. She wanted people and cases to line up in a neat sort of organization, so that she could predict outcomes and know who and what she could rely on.

This killer in black who'd come after her three times now had changed the rules, made things personal and far less predictable. She understood that Levi's job was a dangerous one, but she coped by making the world he was coming home to as familiar and predictable as possible. She understood that the feelings she had for Aiden were reciprocated, but she accepted that he wasn't ready to act on those feelings. She was probably feeling a little out of control, a little helpless, because she was used to fixing things and finding answers and speaking truths—and nothing about this past month, from her promotion to tonight, with her attacker coming after her and eluding them yet again, gave her the logic, predictability and security she craved.

Every cell in Aiden's body wanted to reach across the truck and pull her into his lap. He wanted to kiss her until her turbulent thoughts were focused solely on him, and bury himself so deep inside her that the only promise that mattered was the one made between two bodies, two hearts that loved each other.

Just kiss and be happy.

Could the answer really be that simple? What about his promise to Levi and his debt to Leroy and Lila? Thus far, he'd done a lousy job of keeping Lexi safe. He always seemed to be a step behind, as if the killer was closer to Lexi than even he was. How did he get ahead of this creep without taking leave from his own duties to be with her 24/7? And would Lexi really put up with that? What about the friendships he treasured with Levi and Lexi?

Could he trade one kind of happiness for another without the consequences of ruining both?

Her soft sigh filled the quiet truck. "Only one of us gets to brood at a time." She turned to face him. "What are you thinking over there?"

"That I need to get you into the house ASAP. Put a hot meal in you and get you to bed."

Her eyes flashed at the double meaning in those last words. "Don't get a girl's hopes up."

Yeah, a clever and flirty remark like that didn't help his resolve. Although, when he'd seen the blood on Lexi's face Thanksgiving night, and the bruises on her arms this afternoon, he had a hard time remembering what that resolve was. The thought of losing Lexi hurt a hell of a lot worse than losing his relationship with the Callahan family. After all, what was the point of them saving his life if she lost hers?

He had to tear his gaze from the concerned questions that filled hers more the longer he waited to speak. Instead, he made a quick visual sweep of the yard. No new footprints in the snow, no extra shadows lurking near the house. "I think you're mentally and physically exhausted."

"I am a little tired," she admitted, which was a huge concession that probably meant she was dead on her feet. "It took us a while to log in all that evidence, get it into storage and write up the processing assignments for tomorrow's staff meeting."

"That could have waited until tomorrow morning. Or you could have delegated making the assignments," he suggested.

She pushed herself away from the headrest to pick up her bag and loop it over her shoulder. She glanced back at the dog sitting in the cage behind them. "I'll delegate my responsibilities when you delegate Blue's training."

Aiden chuckled. Infallible logic, as always. "Fair enough." He flipped the collar of his jacket up around his ears and climbed out. He retrieved Blue and met her at the hood of the truck. Since her steps were dragging, he slipped his arm around her waist and urged her to lean against him as they walked up onto the porch and unlocked the front door. "Why don't you take a hot shower and put on your pj's while I give Blue an outing and start a late dinner for us."

She dropped her bag on the bench of the hall tree and shrugged out of her coat. "I'm not hungry. But help yourself to whatever you want." She patted her chest to encourage Blue to prop his paws up on her while she stroked his head and flanks. "Don't forget to feed this guy. He gets an extra treat for chasing the bad guy away today."

"Lex..."

She pushed Blue back to all fours and reached over to pat Aiden's chest, petting him like the damn dog. He supposed the more he kept insisting a relationship with him was a bad idea, the less she was going to try to change his mind. "Maybe I will take some hot soup. Or an omelet. Something simple. I like your idea of the hot shower."

Thirty minutes later, Blue was noshing on a rawhide on the rug in the living room. Aiden had had time to put away his gun and protective vest and change into jeans and a sweater. He'd chopped the veggies and set out everything he'd need to throw together an omelet as soon as Lexi joined him.

But the water in the shower was still running. Thirty minutes? The water had to be cold by now. A vague sense of unease put his senses on alert. He knew Lexi had been exhausted. Had she fallen asleep in there? Had she made it to bed but forgotten to turn off the water?

Aiden set down the forks and plates he'd gathered. When Blue picked up on his tension, he ordered the dog into his kennel, giving his partner the unspoken signal that he was off duty for now. If Lexi was asleep, she didn't need an excitable dog jumping on the bed to see if she was okay.

But Aiden was damn well going to check it out. He hurried through the house to Lexi's bedroom and knocked on the door. When there was no answer, he nudged it open to find the lamps on, her flannel pajama pants and long-sleeve T-shirt folded neatly atop the quilt, and the bed undisturbed. "Lex?" he called out. "Everything okay?"

Maybe she couldn't hear him over the running water. He went to the bathroom door and knocked. "Lex?" No answer. The tiny hairs at the back of his neck prickled to attention. "I'm coming in."

The closed-in room was foggy with steam, and the scent of milk and honey shampoo that meant Lexi to him filled his sinuses before the steam dissipated into the bedroom and he was left with a sudden chill. "Lex? You know I worry when you don't answer me."

The water continued to run. Aiden inched toward the ivy-patterned shower curtain. As he moved closer, he heard another sound. A sniffle. A shuddering gasp.

"Ah, hell." Aiden pulled the curtain back to find Lexi hugging her arms around herself, leaning against the white tile as the cold water splashed over her. She was crying. Shivering beneath the cold water and crying. "Anything but that, baby. Anything but that."

He reached into the shower and shut off the water, not caring that his clothes got wet. "Lex? Do you hear me?" Was she in shock? Was this some kind of emotional breakdown? Exhaustion claiming her mind and body? "I'm going to touch you, okay?" He grabbed the towel off the rack beside the tub and stepped into the pooling water. He wrapped the towel around her slim, naked body and pulled her away from the wall. "I've got you, baby. I've got you."

She caught the corners of the towel and crossed them in

front of her, turning into his chest with a loud sob, pressing her face into the juncture of his neck and shoulder. "That woman today is dead because of me." Her voiced sounded raw, and he wondered how long she'd been in here crying.

He tightened his arms around her, rubbing his hands up and down the towel, willing his body heat and the raspy friction of the terry cloth to warm her skin and chase away the chill. "That's not on you," he assured her, turning his cheek into the fragrant waves of her dripping hair. "This guy has fixated on you. But he's the only one responsible for anyone getting hurt." He spied the purplish bruise on her pale shoulder, probably from today's fall, and lowered his head to gently rest his lips against the injury. "We'll get this bastard. You'll figure it out. Blue and I will take him down. No one else is getting hurt."

"How am I going to figure it out? He steals evidence. He destroys it. He adds things that don't belong to throw us off track and show that he's smarter than us." The only warm thing about her were the tears that trickled from her skin onto his. He pulled her impossibly closer, his sweater and T-shirt wet enough to feel the soft swells and frigid points of her breasts pushing against his chest. "He's trying to gaslight me—closing curtains that should be open, disappearing into thin air—and I'm worried he's succeeding. I pride myself on being smart, on thinking logically. But with him... I can't."

Lexi shivered violently against him and Aiden shifted their positions to hook his hand behind her knees and lift her into his arms. He stepped out of the tub and carried her into the bedroom, where he set her down beside the bed briefly enough to pull back the covers, toss aside his sodden sweater and shirt, and toe off his squishy shoes. Then he lifted her onto the bed and crawled in beside her, pulling the sheet, blanket and quilt up over them both. He wrapped his body around hers and pulled her to him like a second skin, and they lay together like they had those first few nights they slept on the sofa.

"You're going to be okay, Lex. You're just having a bad day. You'll come out stronger on the other side."

The shivering gradually subsided, and she shifted her position slightly, finding the sweet spot on top of him where the crown of her hair nestled beneath his chin and her legs tangled with his. "You always say the right thing. Except…"

His body responded as it always did to her clingy softness and sweet scent. How close could a man get to everything he always wanted and still deny himself? He knew what Lexi wanted to hear, and he knew how badly he wanted to say it. But he'd promised Levi.

Stay close to Lexi. Keep an eye on her. Help her out even when she thinks she can do it herself.

You be what she needs when I can't be there for her.

He'd shaken Levi's hand. They'd slapped each other's backs in a bro hug. He'd vowed to always be there when Lexi needed him.

What about what Aiden needed?

After several minutes of blissful torture, as the temperature between their bodies beneath the covers rose and encompassed them in a feverish heat that sped his pulse and made his jeans uncomfortably tight with want, Aiden thought Lexi had drifted off to sleep. But the moment he tried to shift to a less intimate position, her palms flattened against his shoulders. "Don't leave me." She dragged herself up his body until her face hovered above his. The lamps were still on, giving him a clear view of the puffy skin around her red-rimmed eyes. But those beautiful eyes themselves were dark with desire. "I know my love isn't what you want. I know that what we already share is precious, and that changing that is a risk. But I need you right now. To stay with me. To be with me "

Aiden tunneled his fingers into her damp hair and pulled her lips down to his, claiming them in a reckless kiss. He tongued the seam of her lips and urged her to open for him. And when that sexy little moan of desire hummed in her throat, he speared his tongue into her mouth and tasted her answering heat. She welcomed him with passion and tenderness, sliding her tongue against his, angling her mouth to give him access to every supple curve, every mysterious hollow. As they feasted on each other's mouths, her fingertips dug into his shoulders, clinging to him like a lifeline.

He slid his hands over her bare back and the flare of her hip. And when he ran into the barrier of the wet towel, he tugged it from under the covers and tossed it aside before bringing his hand back to squeeze the perfect curve of her bottom and anchor her moist heat firmly against the zipper of his jeans. Lexi squirmed against him, pushing her knees apart and dropping them on either side of his thighs, aligning them perfectly together.

This time, Aiden was the one who moaned, and Lexi's lips traveled across the angle of his jaw in search of the source of that guttural sound of frustrated need. Her teeth grazed across his chin and Adam's apple, eliciting tremors of excitement deep within him. He arched his throat, giving her access to taste and torment him, while he skimmed his hands up and down her back, learning every inch of soft skin, of sleek muscle. He played with the tendrils of damp hair that curled around his fingers at her nape, spanned the width of her slim waist. He palmed her butt and hooked his thumbs into the creases of her thighs, sliding against her skin until he found the slick heat of her desire. He pressed his thumb against that sweet bundle of nerves, and she buried her face against his neck, her knees squeezing his thighs.

"Aiden," she gasped. "I want… Can you…? Can we…?"

God, how he wanted her. She was generous and beautiful, a sexy mix of strength and vulnerability. His need for her was potent. How could he deny her anything? How could this be wrong when being with Lexi made it feel like everything that had ever been missing in his life was right here in his arms?

He rolled her over onto her back and recaptured her mouth with his. He slid his thigh between hers and her back arched, her body answering every touch he offered, his body craving every eager response. Her breath gusted against his cheek as she pulled away from his kiss to focus on unhooking his belt buckle and finding the snap to his jeans. "One of us has on too many clothes."

Desire surged through him like a freight train, and he caught her wrists before the choice in what happened next was taken from him. His chest heaving in deep breaths against hers, he stretched her arms above her head and wrapped her fingers around the top edge of her pillow. He planted a quick kiss on her softly swollen lips and then another, until he could control his body enough to speak.

"How do I come back from this?" He brushed aside a lock of hair that had dried against her cheek. "What if this isn't who we're supposed to be?"

Her green eyes looked up into his as she sighed beneath him. She released the pillow to stroke her fingertips across his lips, both soothing his doubts and arousing his hope. "What if this *is* who we're supposed to be? Who we could be? I know I'm stronger, surer of myself and the rest of the world, when I'm with you. And I think you feel more grounded, more secure, when you're with me."

He nodded. "I don't want to lose that."

She stroked her palms across the stubble on his jaw and held his face between them. "I will always be here when you need me." She echoed the words he'd often said to her. "No matter what happens tonight."

Suddenly, Aiden knew there was no turning back. Their friendship had become something more a long time ago. Being with Lexi now, like this, was merely the expression of the bond they shared. He touched her hair again. "Promise me you'll have no regrets?"

"With you? Never."

And then there were no more words. Aiden shed the rest of his clothes and rolled on the condom from his wallet. Her arms wrapped around his neck and her hands skimmed against his hair as he settled between her legs and pushed inside her. Because of her bruises and emotional catharsis, he moved slowly and tenderly with her. Then, because she was Lexi, because she wasn't afraid to demand what she needed from him, because he could no more deny her than he could stop breathing—he claimed her mouth. He kissed her breasts. She wrapped her legs around his waist and lifted herself into his driving thrusts until she cried out his name and arched against him. He could still feel the aftershocks of her release pulsing around him as he came inside her.

After disposing of the condom and splitting an energy bar and glass of milk to compensate for missing dinner, Aiden snugged his arms around Lexi and pulled her on top of him again, where he knew she'd fall asleep and get the rest she needed.

"Thank you for giving me tonight," she whispered drowsily against his chest.

"Not a hardship for me, Lex," he assured her, stroking his fingers through her hair. "I wanted it, too."

"I love you, Aiden Murphy."

With that burden weighing on his mind, he tucked the covers securely around them and lay awake in the darkness long after she drifted off to sleep.

LEXI WOULD HAVE thought having Aiden with her 24/7 would be a good thing.

But having moody, brooding Aiden with her was a little like having a damaged tooth throbbing in her mouth. With the right kind of attention, and some TLC, the tooth could be fixed, and the pain would go away. Why couldn't that man choose to be happy? She'd always thought she was the brainiac in this relationship, who spent far too much time inside her head. But he could work a problem for hours, days, years, maybe—until he'd assessed all the possible outcomes and made the right choice. But whose idea of what was right was he searching for? Had he lost too much to believe that he'd lose her, too, if he let himself care too deeply? Because she knew he did care.

The man who'd saved her from her own minibreakdown last night cared.

The man who'd made such glorious love to her last night cared.

The man who kept her demons at bay and held her throughout the night cared.

He could fix a mean breakfast and drive her to work and brood and stand guard, all with that sexy, crooked smile of his. He'd risk his life for her and kiss her until her toes curled and give her everything she needed.

But he wasn't ready to take that leap of faith with her. He wasn't ready to say this was love.

He might never be.

But she would take their unique version of a relationship over whatever twisted thing was going on between Barton Rutledge III and his wife, Mandy.

Lexi had taken Hud up on his invitation to observe him and his partner, Keir Watson, interviewing the real estate mogul and his wife, who had to be at least three decades younger than her white-haired husband. The husband and wife sat with their attorney across the table from Hud and Keir, facing the observation window in the next room, where Lexi stood with her arms crossed, taking in every detail of the couple's interaction as though it was a crime scene.

Mandy Rutledge applied her lipstick in her compact mirror again, dabbing a tissue against the already perfect arc of matte pink. Then she reached over to wipe away the tear that ran down the billionaire's gaunt cheek before tucking the tissue into his misshapen arthritic hand where it rested on copies of Lexi's crime scene photos.

"Your questions are upsetting my husband, Detective Watson," Mrs. Rutledge said.

Keir was unfazed by the accusation. "I only asked if he knew the woman in the photograph."

"Of course he knew her. We hired her to revamp several lake properties for us."

"Shut up, woman. I can speak for myself."

"Don't say too much," his attorney warned.

"Both of you, stop," he ordered, his aging voice still indicating that he was the boss. He raised a gnarled knuckle to wipe away his own tears. Then he lowered his hand to touch one of the gruesome photos of the lifeless woman. "Yes, I knew Jennifer. We met through the lake project, but we became…more."

"You were having an affair with her?" Keir prompted.

He glanced over at his wife, who quickly turned away. "Yes. I've been seeing her for some time."

"Looks like you were planning to see her on Thanksgiving night. The night she was killed."

Hud pointed to a different picture. "She bought a bunch of presents for you, big guy. She was looking forward to seeing you."

Rutledge eyed Hud with contempt, as though being spoken to by the only man in the room not wearing a suit and tie was an insult. He turned to Keir to answer. "I was looking forward to seeing her, too. Jen was such a light. She was so smart, such a good listener. She made me laugh."

Aiden walked up to the window beside her, propping his hands at his waist. "If he says she was good in the sack while his wife is sitting there, I'm leaving."

Lexi couldn't help but grin. "I don't think he cares much about what his wife thinks. Chelsea's research says Mr. Rutledge has a long history of affairs. He marries for money or status. Then, after a while, he steps out, looking for the love he doesn't find at home because that's not what the marriage is about for him."

"Hell. Sounds like my dad." When she glanced up in concern, Aiden shrugged off the bad memories. "On a much cheaper, drunker scale, of course. Patrick Murphy married for a sex partner, a paycheck or a babysitter. I used to hope that he at least loved my mother. But maybe he just didn't have it in him to love."

Lexi reached out to rub his arm, since this wasn't exactly the place to offer a kiss or hug of comfort. Not that she was sure Aiden wanted anything like that from her today. "You're not like your father. You know how to love better than any man I've known. You're too good at taking care of people—of your friends, of Blue, of me—to not have love inside you."

He reached over to briefly cover her hand where it rested on the sleeve of his uniform when the fireworks started in the interview room.

"I loved Jennifer!" Rutledge insisted, shoving the photographs across the table. "Why do you think these pictures upset me? I can't stand seeing her like this."

"Did she threaten to break it off with you?" Hud pushed.

"Had she become a liability you needed to get rid of?" Keir pushed harder.

Rutledge's chair slammed against the back wall as he stood up. "I did not kill her!"

Aiden braced his hands at his waist again. "He's mad enough to throw a punch, isn't he?"

Lexi's gaze went to the man's bony knuckles and twisted fingers. She flinched as she relived the fist coming out of nowhere and cracking her cheek Thanksgiving night.

"He's not our man," she murmured under her breath.

Hud and Keir were on their feet, too.

"Sit down, Mr. Rutledge." That was Hud, circling the table to muscle the suspect back into his chair if he had to.

"Where were you Thanksgiving night?" Keir asked. "In the hotel room across from Jennifer, staying under the assumed name of Paul Montgomery?"

"What? No. I canceled that reservation…"

"Barton." His attorney urged him to sit and be silent.

By the time Rutledge had resumed his seat, he looked more like a confused old man than a powerful business mogul. The old man shook his head. "I was at home with my wife."

Hud remained standing while Keir sat. "Why the change of plans?"

Barton glanced at his wife. Now she was primping her flawlessly styled blond hair into place. "Family gathering. For the holiday. It was last-minute. Mandy arranged it. Typically, she flies home to her family. But I guess, with the snow, her flight was delayed, and so she wanted to surprise me." He glanced back at Keir. "I called Jennifer, told her I'd be late. Or it might even be the next morning before I could get away."

Mandy's compact tumbled onto the table. "You planned to see her anyway?" She snatched it up and tucked it into her purse. "You couldn't give me a whole weekend of your time? After I went to so much trouble?" She stood and headed for the door. "I'm sorry. I find this all terribly upsetting." When she got to the locked door, she spun around to lambaste her husband until Hud could get it open for her. "You never were going to give me a chance, were you? Jennifer. Jennifer. Jennifer."

When Barton didn't even look up at her, she stormed out.

Lexi shook her head, sorting out the answers that would have this all make sense. "Barton Rutledge didn't kill Jennifer Li."

Aiden didn't see it yet. "His heartbreak and anger could be an act."

"Look at his hands."

Aiden curled his own fingers into fists the older man could never make. "He's not our killer."

Lexi squeezed one of those fists and hurried to the door. "I know you're not a detective, but will you follow my lead? Play along with me?" She nodded to the interview room. "Get Hud or Keir to come along after a couple of minutes, too."

"What are you...?"

But Lexi was already out the door, hurrying over to Mandy Rutledge as the blonde stepped out of the interview room.

"Mrs. Rutledge?" Lexi fixed a sympathetic look on her face and extended her hand. "I'm Lexi Callahan from the crime lab. I was watching that interview. Would you like a cup of coffee? Some tea? A chance to sit someplace that's a little quieter?"

The other woman never took Lexi's hand, but she hugged her clutch to her chest and exhaled a grateful sigh. "Yes. A cup of tea would be nice. This whole sordid business and the detectives' veiled accusations have me quite distraught. And no telling what the stress is doing to Barton's heart."

Not to mention the stress of being married to a calculating wife, if what Lexi suspected was true.

Lexi escorted her to the break room down the hall. It wasn't the expansive modern space they enjoyed in the crime lab's memorial lounge. But the yellow brick walls and black vinyl sofa of the Fourth Precinct's third-floor lounge, especially with its glass front wall, should do the trick.

Mandy perched on the edge of the sofa while Lexi opened a tea bag and dropped it into steaming water. "Cream or sugar?" Lexi asked.

Once she'd doctored the tea to Mandy's liking and handed her the insulated paper cup, Lexi poured herself a cup of coffee and sat at the small round table across from her.

"Thank you." Mandy graciously accepted the tea and played with the tea bag before taking a sip. "I know it's the detectives' job to ask questions. But it's just so humiliating to hear my husband spell out that he's been unfaithful to me."

"I can't imagine what that's like," Lexi sympathized. "Sometimes those police officers barrel into a situation and ask questions later. They're hardwired to take action. Me, on the other hand? I like to tiptoe around the crime scene after the fact. Have some quiet time to myself to process and understand what has happened before I start to look for answers." She smiled. "More observing and less action."

"Thank you for saying that. Yes, a little more delicacy would be appreciated in how they handle suspects." Aiden strode in between the two women and poured himself a cup of coffee. Then he went back to the entrance and leaned against the door frame, casually crossing one booted foot over the other, clearly not going anywhere. Mandy set her tea on the table beside her, not too sure about Aiden lingering close enough to eavesdrop on them. "I thought this was a private room."

Lexi smiled at her hero. "He's my armed guard. I've worked three murder scenes this month. I was attacked while I was processing Jennifer Li's murder scene."

"Attacked?"

Aiden held out his coffee cup and pointed to her, catching on to Lexi's informal Q&A session. "You were attacked at the third murder, too. Don't forget that."

Mandy's skin went pale beneath her makeup. "Third murder?" She glanced from Aiden over to Lexi. "I thought we were here because of Ms. Li."

"We are." Lexi chatted on, as if they were discussing Chiefs football or the weather. "There were three murders with the same MO. There was a struggle. The victim was subdued with a blow to the head, then strangled. Or, possibly, the struggle was staged afterward. Three women knocked unconscious or incapacitated. Three women strangled with cord cut from the draperies."

"No, there were only two women." Mandy scooted to the edge of the couch, then erased the contention from her tone and sat back. "I mean, that's what I read in the paper."

"Trust me, I have the bruises to prove there was a third."

Mandy moved to the edge of the couch again. "Barton didn't do it. He didn't kill anyone."

Lexi rose to pour the coffee she hadn't tasted into the sink. "I know he didn't. I saw his hands. He couldn't hold a rope, much less pull it tight enough to choke someone to death. Punching me with a fist would have been unbearably painful. And my attacker didn't cry out. He never said a thing."

"Barton was home with me. All day Thanksgiving. All night."

Hud, Keir, Barton and his attorney were gathered at the door behind Aiden now. "Your husband might have come home on Thanksgiving, Mrs. Rutledge. But were you there?" Lexi asked. "Are you alibiing him just so you have an alibi for yourself?"

"You weren't there when I got home, Mandy," Barton admitted. "You said you were running errands on your way home from the airport, then got stuck in traffic. I was home by myself for three hours—long enough to watch a football game—before you got there." He glanced at his attorney. "When we heard about Jennifer on the news, Mandy offered to cover for me. She said the police were bound to find the connection between me and my mistress."

Mandy shot to her feet. "Why are you being honest now, you idiot?"

"Did you kill Jennifer?"

She shook her head, blaming her husband. "You cheating son of a bitch." Then she turned to Lexi, as if being the only other woman in the room meant she would understand. "He said that he was in love with her and that he was going to leave me. I was going to lose everything. It's one thing to cheat on me." She whirled around to her husband again. "It's another thing to cast me aside like you're trading me in for a new model."

"And the two prostitutes?" Keir asked.

"I'm telling you, there weren't two!" Mandy must have

finally realized that she'd already confessed to too much. "I hired Miss Byrd. Told her she was a birthday present for my husband. I was waiting for her when she checked in. I wanted to practice, to make sure I could do it and cover my tracks. Throw the police off, too—have them think they were looking for a serial killer. I was so certain I'd taken care of everything, staged it so it couldn't be solved. How...?"

Lexi looked to Aiden, then to Mandy. "Someone came along after you left and tampered with your crime scene."

A complication she hadn't anticipated. Mandy's shoulders sagged in her Chanel suit. "I want to talk to my lawyer now."

The attorney stepped into the room and took her by the elbow. "That would be wise, Mandy. Remember, you were Mirandized along with Barton when we went into that interview room. I'll do what troubleshooting I can, but for now, just keep your mouth shut."

Mandy walked out the door with him but turned to Lexi one last time. "I didn't kill *three* women."

Hud gestured to the interview room they'd vacated. "Well, let's talk about the two you did."

"She didn't kill three women," Lexi agreed after they left with the detectives. "After Jennifer Li, she had no need to."

Aiden crossed the room to rub his hand up and down her arm. "What about her accomplice? The man who attacked you?"

"There was no accomplice."

Aiden tossed his cup, then came back to stand in front of her. "You're going to explain this to me, right?"

"We agree that TNT was murdered to get me to that crime scene?"

"Yeah. And?"

"Who would know all the details of the first two murders and be able to stage that scene to look just like the first two deaths? Especially to a trained eye like mine?"

"Another criminalist." He'd been trying to protect her from a stranger, an unknown subject who liked to hurt women. If he could keep the danger away from her home, away from her work, she'd be fine. But the threat was already part of her world. "We've been investigating this like there was one perp. We've got two separate crimes."

The enemy was one of her own.

Chapter Eleven

"Thank you, Mac."

Lexi's boss was shaking her hand in the middle of the crime lab lounge, with most of her friends and coworkers gathered around for their lunch break. "Thank you for proving my faith in you was justified. Two murders solved, and you've barely been running your part of this place for a month."

He released her as several of the others came up to congratulate her. Grayson Malone rolled up in his wheelchair. "Can I tell you how much faster work gets done around here? People aren't looking over their shoulders and second-guessing themselves. You don't give us orders we can't carry out." He squeezed her hand. "Very military-like of you."

High praise indeed.

Khari Thomas was right behind him. She leaned in for as close a hug as her nearly full-term pregnancy allowed. "You're the best, sister. I hardly remember Dennis What's-His-Face anymore."

Lexi smiled. "Thanks for putting the rush on that DNA comparison. Detectives Watson and Kramer are very happy to have the science to back up Mandy Rutledge's confession."

"Just doing my job." Khari grinned. "Not having to worry about anything else while I'm doing it is a pleasure."

Jackson Dobbs patted her shoulder. "Nice job, boss."

Brian Stockman reached in to shake her hand, too. "You resolved the dispute between Ethan and Zoe, which I appreciate. Next thing you know, those two will be dating. Not sure how I feel about a man who looks my age being sweet on my daughter."

Lexi laughed and sought out Ethan and Zoe sitting at a table together with their sack lunches. Zoe's back was to her, but Ethan sat up straight and gave her a thumbs-up.

But as the congratulators began to disperse and the crime lab staff went about fixing their lunches, setting up chess games and joining conversations, a stocky figure wearing a suit and loosely knotted tie appeared at the lounge door and gestured to get her attention. Why was Robert Buckner waving her over? Beyond their introduction a month ago, she hadn't traded more than a polite greeting with the private investigator.

Still, his square face had a stern set to it. Something was wrong. Something to do with Chelsea? Lexi quickly glanced around the lounge. Where was her friend, anyway?

Lexi excused herself from her colleagues and crossed to the door. "Are you looking for Rufus?" she asked about his former partner, just in case she'd misunderstood that he wanted to talk specifically to her.

"No." He closed his hand around her arm above her elbow and pulled her into the hallway. "Could I see you in your office?"

"Sure." He released her when she fell into step beside him. "Is this about an investigation?"

"No." His voice turned gruff with some tightly controlled emotion. "But I need you to handle this. I don't think I'm the right person to do it. Your boss might not appreciate how I'd deal with it."

Now *she* was concerned. "What are you talking about?"

They'd reached her office. She'd left the door open when she'd gone to meet Aiden for lunch in the lounge. He was running late after he and Blue had been called to help with a drug-related traffic stop. And then Mac had come in for a bottle of water and the embarrassing adulation had started.

But now her door stood slightly ajar. She glanced up at Mr. Buckner, and he inclined his head, indicating she enter first.

Lexi pushed open the door and Chelsea vaulted out of her chair and threw her arms around Lexi's neck. "Oh, gosh, Lexi, I screwed up."

"*You* didn't do anything wrong," Buck grumbled from the doorway.

Chelsea shook in her arms, crying. There were no tears, only dry sobs, clueing her in that her friend had been at this crying jag for some time. She mouthed a question over Chelsea's shoulder to the older man. *"What?"*

"Oh. Buck. I'm sorry." She held out a soiled navy blue bandanna that she'd been wringing between her fists. "Here."

He gently pushed the bandanna back into her fingers. "You keep it."

Chelsea hiccuped a laugh. "Right. It's gross. I'll wash it."

She stepped forward as if she wanted to hug him. Buck's arms came out. And then there was an awkward pat on his chest and a squeeze on her shoulder, and the hug never happened.

Chelsea sniffed and tipped her chin up and smiled. "Thank you."

Buck nodded. Then looked beyond her to Lexi. "Take care of her for me."

Lexi nodded as the older man closed the door. After a

slight hesitation, Chelsea turned and reached for Lexi's hand. "We need to talk."

"Okay." Lexi settled into the chair beside her friend because she seemed to need the tight clasp of their hands. "What's with you and Buck? That's what I'm supposed to call him, right?"

Chelsea nodded. "I couldn't take it anymore. Dennis came by my computer lab this morning. And when Buck picked me up for lunch, I just...broke down. He gave me his handkerchief, and I blubbered all over the front of his suit."

"Dennis?" Lexi sat up straight, suddenly feeling every bit of grim tension Buck had displayed. "Go back, Chelsea." What did Robert Buckner know that she didn't? "Tell me about Dennis."

Chelsea pulled her hands back to her lap and worked the bandanna between her hands until she could speak. "Dennis has been blackmailing me."

"What?"

"I know he's in trouble for harassing several of us here." But this was something more. Lexi let her friend tell the story the way she needed to, although she was already composing the text to Aiden, warning him that he might have to handcuff her to keep her from committing violence. "But one of my foster home placements..." Lexi frowned as the story took a turn into left field. "It wasn't a good situation. Dennis... A few months ago, he had me in his office." Lexi could already imagine where this scenario was leading, what must have happened to make a relative stranger, yet one who was a former cop, like Robert Buckner, get involved. The tears threatened to start again. "Dennis cornered me. He had his hand up my skirt, and it triggered a flashback from the foster home."

Lexi carefully schooled all the rage from her tone. "What happened?"

"I attacked him."

"You fought back. You defended yourself."

"I assaulted him. I stabbed him in the shoulder with a letter opener, sliced open his hand."

Lexi remembered the unexpected four-day weekend Dennis had taken. She'd had to cover for him and pull extra duty shifts. When he got back, he explained away his bandaged hand and limp arm by some outrageous excuse about his fiancée scratching him during sex—then claiming to have had an accident when he'd been working on fixing up her house to sell it before they moved into his place together.

While she abstractly prayed that Bertie would get a clue and dump him, Lexi stayed focused on the big problem at hand. "He threatened to report you if you don't withdraw your complaint against him?"

"He took pictures. Put the letter opener in an evidence locker. He's going to claim to be the victim and turn it around at his hearing to say we're the ones harassing him. Making up lies about him."

She didn't know Buck well, but she could imagine how an old-school man like that would handle this extreme form of sexual harassment. She'd like to be there if that ever happened.

But she was new-school. And her way would be no less effective. As Chelsea's supervisor and best friend, it was her responsibility to deal with this.

"You have to report him, Chels. He's the one who assaulted you. You had to defend yourself."

"But he's the one with the evidence."

Lexi knew plenty about false, corrupt evidence. "I don't

mean to the review board. I mean to the police. Dennis committed a crime. Attempted rape."

Chelsea shook her head. "I can't talk to the police about this."

"Could you talk to Aiden?" She already had her phone out, prepping the text as Chelsea considered it. "I'll be right there with you. If you want me."

Chelsea dabbed her nose with the bandanna and gave one last sniff. "Okay."

Lexi sent the text. She had no doubt the cavalry would be on its way soon.

"You're a good friend, Lexi. Buck said I should come to you. Of course, I couldn't stop crying. He probably just wanted to get rid of me."

"No, I think he was concerned. I still worry about you moonlighting for him, but I think he's a friend. I'm glad he brought you here." She squeezed Chelsea's hand and stood. "I'm glad you talked to me. I promise you—Dennis won't be here tomorrow." She pulled her friend in for one more hug. "Take a few minutes to splash some cool water on your face and regroup. Take however long you need." Lexi headed out the door.

"Where are you going?"

"I'm going to go be your boss right now."

Her confrontation with Dennis Hunt proved to be short and immensely satisfying. She'd already contacted Mac and knew Aiden was on his way. Once she'd laid out how the police were going to be investigating him for attempted rape, witness intimidation and extortion, he'd come up out of his chair.

"What is your problem, Callahan?" She backed out of his office as quickly as she could. But he grabbed her arm and slammed her against the wall, spitting in her face as he cursed her. "You witches are all out to destroy me."

Lexi heard a low growl. The most beautiful sound in the world.

Lexi's words were as succinct as she could make them. "You touch? You go."

Dennis wisely released her, but he didn't immediately back away. He glanced to the left to see Mac, Khari, Jackson, Rufus King, Gray Malone and other witnesses at one end of the hallway. Then he glanced to the right to see Aiden in full protective gear, fighting to hold a lunging, snarling Blue in check. He only had to say one thing to convince Dennis to surrender.

"I can let go of the leash."

BY THE TIME December 23 rolled around, Lexi had begun to relax. She was getting the hang of this supervisor stuff. She still had friends at the lab, and she still had Aiden living at her house, if not sleeping in her bed. They shared meals. They watched old movies and laughed. Aiden was still the model houseguest.

But they couldn't seem to recapture the closeness they'd shared that night she'd been shoved down the stairs at the Double Time Hotel. Confessing her love had pushed her knight in shining armor back into his celibate vow, putting duty and protection before affairs of the heart.

Lexi thought she could handle his decision not to pursue a romantic relationship as long as he was with her. Maybe she had enough love for both of them.

But it whittled a little bit away from her heart each day. It made her sad that Aiden didn't seem to believe they could be both best friends and soul mates—that he'd rather close off his heart than make a mistake that might hurt her or cost him the family he needed so much.

Until they could confirm that Dennis was behind the assaults on her—an accusation that he denied as vehemently as he denied the other charges against him—Aiden had vowed to remain her round-the-clock protector. But since there had been no other incidents, the timing seemed to indicate that the man with the grudge against women was her attacker and had murdered TNT to lure her to the crime scene. Lexi's team hadn't been called to any other homicides, and the lab was getting the chance to catch up on and clear backlogged cases they were working for KCPD, the state police and the Cass, Clay, Platte and Jackson County sheriff's offices.

Meanwhile, Mandy Rutledge had been indicted on two counts of homicide. Dennis was in jail awaiting trial, no longer a cancer impacting so many lives at the lab. Chelsea was smiling again. The crime lab team was gelling in a way that made it a place where everyone looked forward to going to work again. A fresh new fall of snow had made the city pretty again, ready to celebrate Christmas.

Tonight, the lab was running on a skeleton on-call crew like during Thanksgiving, in deference to the upcoming holiday. Lexi was on duty as supervisor and it had been a quiet evening, giving her plenty of time to catch up on paperwork and wrap a couple of presents on her breaks.

Since it had been such a quiet night, she was startled when her phone rang. Captain Stockman was off duty, calling from home to give her the assignment. "Sorry to do this to you, Lexi," he apologized. "Don't know why the criminals don't hole up and stay home like the rest of us when it's cold and snowy like this."

She had her pen and notepad at the ready. "What have we got?"

"Another trip to No-Man's-Land to visit the Double Time again." Lexi chuckled and jotted down the information. "Homicide in Room 519. You be careful."

"It's okay, Captain. I'll have Aiden with me."

"He's a good man."

"Yes, he is." Lexi was already up to get her coat from the closet. "Okay. We'll roll in Aiden's truck and I'll call the team in to meet me there."

"Be safe. And merry Christmas."

"Merry Christmas."

She texted Aiden. Got a call. Homicide. Can I bum a ride with you and Blue?

On my way.

Twenty minutes later, they were pulling into the alley beside the Double Time. Aiden killed the siren, but left his lights flashing—for the illumination as much as for the official presence of law enforcement. Lexi frowned as she peered beyond the trash bins and garbage bags into the shadows. With Blue locked in his cage behind them, panting with excitement at the opportunity to go to work, she had to look in the side-view mirror to see the street behind them. There were plenty of parked cars and music and lights from the bar across the street. But the recent winter storm had driven almost everyone inside. The sidewalk was empty except for the trio of men smoking out on the bar's front stoop. There was some traffic moving along the street, but not much. It was cold. The streets were slick, and the hour was late.

"Where's the CSIU van?" They'd had to spare a few minutes to give Blue the chance to relieve himself and put his protective vest on him. "I figured they'd be here before us."

She pulled out her phone to text Ethan, Shane and Zoe, and ask them what their twenty was. She looked across the truck to Aiden in his KCPD jacket, gloves and stocking cap. He was surveying their surroundings, too. But where she'd been curious, his blue eyes were narrowed in suspicion.

"What is it?" she asked. His wariness filled the cab's warm air and put her on alert, too.

"Where are the black-and-whites to secure the scene? Who called it in?" He reached across the seat to squeeze her hand. "Stay put. I'm going to check things out."

He opened the door. A blast of chilled air rushed in as Aiden left her.

And then the nightmare began.

She heard a soft impact sound, like leather gloves clapping together. Then Aiden swatted his thigh. If it wasn't zero degrees out, she'd think he'd been stung by a wasp. Then she heard the jolt of electricity buzzing through the air and Aiden cursed. By the time he was shaking and collapsing to the asphalt, Lexi had unhooked her seat belt and was crawling across the center console. "Aiden!"

She'd processed enough of the barbs that delivered a powerful electric jolt to know that he'd been tased. Blue barked wildly behind her, seeing his partner pass out and fall like that.

But Lexi never made it out of the truck. She never got the chance to see if Aiden was hurt. If he'd hit his head on the truck or the pavement or worse. Just as she was stepping out the door, a black-gloved hand pointed the Taser at her. She sank back onto the driver's seat, feeling the chill of the wintry air and something even colder deep beneath her skin.

The figure in black. Hooded. Faceless behind his mask. Always one step ahead of her. But someone she knew. Someone she trusted. She knew that now. She quickly scanned through her memory, lining up body shape and height of the people she knew to this man. Two working legs, so not Grayson. Not big enough to be Jackson. Average height. Average build. Average in every way except for the weapon he held in his hand. He switched the Taser to his left hand, keeping it trained on her as he stooped down to unholster Aiden's Glock. He pointed the gun at her, too.

He made his first mistake. This time he spoke.

"Get out of the truck and come with me. Or I'll shoot the dog." Blue was going nuts behind her, shaking the truck as he jumped against the walls of his cage. Would anyone in this part of town respond when they heard a dog bark like that? Or would they duck their heads and shy away from the obvious threat he represented?

Second mistake. He'd threatened Blue.

When Lexi didn't immediately move, he aimed the gun at Aiden's head. "How about I shoot the boyfriend?"

Third mistake. He'd threatened the man she loved.

The enemy in her midst.

"Hello, Ethan."

Chapter Twelve

By the time Ethan had unlocked the door to Room 519, Lexi knew he'd rerouted the rest of the team to a different address and planned to meet them there within a reasonable time frame. They were all on call, coming in from different locations, dates and family events. Just like after the murder at the Regal Hotel, no one would question them arriving separately at different times. Only Captain Stockman had this address and knew where Lexi had been dispatched. But with Ethan calling the shots, there'd be some confusion and miscommunication before he figured out that Lexi was missing.

By the time he unlocked the door, she also knew he intended to kill her.

Ethan closed the door behind him and nudged her toward the foot of the bed with the barrel of Aiden's gun. "As much as I want you to suffer, I have a plan and a schedule to keep."

Lexi turned to face him and the gun. "What about Aiden? That Taser won't render him unconscious forever."

"I gave him the maximum voltage. He'll be out anywhere from ten to thirty minutes." He pulled a length of cord from the pocket of his black pants, which she now realized fit so loosely to hide the khaki trousers he wore underneath. That explained his ability to disappear into a crowd, or even reappear at a crime scene without anyone ever noticing. A quick-change artist. Those pants probably doubled as a bag to wrap the rest of his black gear in. Drop it inside a CSI kit or large evidence bag, and no one would be the wiser. "My goal wasn't to kill him." He was careful to keep his hood and stocking mask in place as he circled around her. Smart. That way he wouldn't accidentally leave a stray hair behind. Other than the one she'd raked off him at the Regal Hotel when she fought with him. "I want Aiden to find you. Dead, of course. The two of you are just too precious, pretending to be friends when I'm sure you're shagging each other, living together the way you do. The hypocrisy makes my stomach churn."

Lexi mentally tried to visualize how many minutes it had taken them to ride up the hotel's rickety elevator and get to 519. Five? Ten? What if Aiden came to sooner than Ethan expected and found her alive? If she could stall him long enough, it would give Aiden enough time to rescue her. If she could figure out how to get that gun and Taser away from Ethan, it would give her more than a fighting chance to survive this vendetta against her.

She realized Ethan had his CSI kit in the room. Everything had already been staged like the other crime scenes. Furniture tipped over, a dent in the wall—all signs of a violent fight. He reached into his kit and pulled out a long narrow bag with a knifelike object in it.

"What's that?" Lexi asked, sitting on the edge of the broken-down mattress. With everything else topsy-turvy in the room, she doubted wrinkling the bedspread would make any difference.

"Dennis Hunt's DNA." He pulled the bloodstained item out of the bag. A letter opener. Was that the weapon Chelsea had used to defend herself against Dennis? "Thanks to you, he's already a suspect in everyone's mind. He makes the perfect patsy to take the fall for me."

"Why, Ethan? I know you didn't kill those first two women. Why did you attack me at Jennifer Li's murder?"

"Because I was pissed off!" He whirled around, stabbing the letter opener into the mattress beside her. When she jumped out of the way, he pushed her onto the bed and put the blade to her throat. She felt the burn of its sharp edge nicking her skin. The gun ground into her stomach. "You got everything I wanted. Everything I deserved."

She shook her head, afraid to antagonize him, but knowing she needed time for help to come. *I will always come when you need me.* Aiden's voice echoed through her brain, calming her fear, allowing her to think.

As she tried to avoid both the gun and the knife, her breathing was shallow, so her words came out in a breathless gasp. "You've already screwed up, Ethan. There were no knives at any of the crime scenes. None of the victims were cut."

He laughed, tossed the letter opener into the corner beside the dresser and jerked her to her feet. He shoved her hard, and she stumbled backward until she hit the wall. "No, but the victims all fought back. They all had defensive wounds. This time, the victim grabbed the letter opener to fight off her attacker. He wrested it from her, and she died anyway. You don't know everything, boss lady."

"There were no guns, either. How are you going to explain Aiden's gun being here?"

He took slow steps toward her, and with every step, she moved to the side, keeping what distance she could between them. "Are you kidding? In this neighborhood? Stolen guns show up around here every day. I'll drop it in a dumpster or give it to some homeless guy."

How many minutes had it been? Fifteen? Twenty?

Keep him talking. He thought he was invincible. Smarter than her. *Play to that ego.*

She inched closer to the door. "What do I have that you feel you deserve, Ethan? How have I hurt you?"

"Cut the 'I'm your friend, let me help you' act." He tucked the gun into the back of his pants and picked up the drapery cord from the bed. He wrapped an end around each gloved hand and snapped it taut. He hadn't touched her yet, and she could already feel her throat constrict. *Get to the door.* "Dennis was right. You act like you're some kind of golden girl who can't do anything wrong. You know what's wrong? You getting the job I should have. You're going to be running the whole lab one day, and I'm just going to be that guy who keeps getting passed over, time and again."

Her shaking fingers curled around the doorknob behind her. "I asked you if you were okay with me being your boss. You wished me luck."

Once step closer. "*I'm* supposed to be running the show. I've worked there longer and harder than you, and Mac never seemed to notice. He kept putting 'needs to work on' memos in my file, even recommended me for a psych eval once. Said I didn't always react appropriately to stressors." *You think?* Her fingers found the lock above the knob. "Dennis was going to recommend me for promotion. And then pretty little Lexi comes along and charms her way in with the top brass." One step closer. Another step. She could hear the excited pattern of his breathing now. "I want you to understand that you're not that smart. You're not gifted. You're lucky. You don't deserve what you've got. You lost evidence at one crime scene. Incompetent! You rattle on about curtains opening and closing like you're crazy."

"You wanted to undermine my authority. You set me up to look bad and to doubt my abilities."

"And it was working. You weren't going to last until the New Year." He was close enough that she could feel the heat coming off his body. "And then you solved those murders. You got Dennis fired. You got him arrested. I was never going to be liked the way you are. I was never going to be golden." Was that the elevator she heard whining and creaking in the distance? That wretched, ancient noise was the sound of hope. "I just wanted you to know it was me before I killed you and put me out of my misery. After a few weeks of mourning, Mac will be looking for a new supervisor to run the lab. The team will be looking for leadership. With you gone, they'll look to me. You didn't save the lab. You couldn't even save yourself."

How many minutes had passed? Her grip tightened around the lock. Ethan could torment her. He could even try to kill her. But he wasn't going to win.

"You really are a dumb criminal, Ethan. Telling me everything. I know what you've done. I know you killed TNT to lure me here and plant the tainted evidence. I know your motive. I will make one hell of a witness when I testify against you."

He laughed. "Who's a dead woman going to tell?"

"You were a decent criminalist, but a lousy criminal. Any first-year CSI will figure out what you've done here."

The instant he heard the door unlock behind her, Ethan lunged. She kicked at the door, but instead of freedom, he threw her to the floor. Before she could scramble to her feet, he looped the cord around her neck and dragged her back into the middle of the room.

Lexi clawed at his hands, twisted her body like a fish caught on a line. But the cord only grew tighter. Her breath locked up in her chest. She gasped for air, but nothing happened. She couldn't scream. Tighter and tighter. Her eyes seemed to swell from the pressure. The beiges of the room faded into murky shadows. She was choking. Dying.

She never saw the door swing open. But she heard the bam of the knob striking the wall. She heard the crunch of fist on bone.

And suddenly she was free.

Lexi collapsed to her knees, clawing at the ligature around her neck. Suddenly, there were other hands there, unwinding the rope from where it had embedded into her skin. She dragged in a noisy gasp of air, whimpering at the pain in her neck, rejoicing as her lungs filled with oxygen again.

"Blue! *Pass!* Guard the bad guy."

As oxygen returned to her brain, she blinked the world back into focus. She was surrounded in warmth, sitting in Aiden's lap on the edge of the bed. His fingers gently inspected what she expected was a pretty nasty mark around her neck. She caught his hand, found his blue eyes and smiled. "I'm okay. I knew you'd come if I gave you enough time. You said you'd always be there for me."

Aiden nodded, pressed a hard kiss to her lips, then hugged her tightly against him. "I'm just glad I finally got to punch somebody."

She glanced down at Aiden's feet. Ethan lay on the floor, his hood down, his mask gone, his broken nose bleeding. Sucker punch. Blitz attack. Whatever it was called, Aiden hadn't needed his weapon to lay Ethan out flat and free her. Ethan's moaning elicited no sympathy from her. He'd done the same to her and worse. He'd killed an innocent woman, attacked Aiden, threatened Blue and had tried to kill her more than once. With his hands zip-tied behind his back, he wouldn't hurt anyone again.

Not that he was going anywhere. Blue lay on the floor,

only a few inches from his face. If Ethan so much as twitched, Blue would take a chunk out of him just as enthusiastically as he went after his Kong.

ONCE THEY'D BEEN cleared by EMTs, the rest of her team had shown up to process the right crime scene, and Ethan had been put in the back of a police car by their new friends Hud and Keir, Lexi and Aiden had driven home and fallen into bed together. They slept in each other's arms for several hours. Then they got up to shower and eat an early breakfast and went back to bed. This time, they made love, celebrating their survival, exploring the unshakable trust they shared, loving and protecting each other in the most beautiful way.

Afterward, sleep claimed them again. Lexi wasn't sure if it was a matter of minutes or hours that she'd slept on top of Aiden's chest, tucked against him with their hearts beating together, in the most secure place she'd ever known, when she heard Blue barking an alarm. Someone was at the house. The front door was opening.

Aiden must have already heard someone jimmying the door, or a key turning in the lock, because by the time she had slipped from beneath the covers to grab her clothes, Aiden already had his jeans on and his gun drawn and was racing down the hallway.

"Oh, hell!" She heard Aiden curse. "Blue! *Sitz!*"

Sit. Not attack. Not a threat.

"Haven't you ever heard of knocking?" Aiden accused.

"I did. Nobody answered. I remembered the key hidden in the mailbox and decided to let myself in."

She knew that voice. Joy surged through her as Lexi tugged down her pajama shirt and ran through the house to greet her big brother. "Levi!"

Her brother opened his arms and she launched herself into his embrace. "Hey, kiddo."

"Welcome home! Oh, it's so good to see you. Merry Christmas. Welcome home!"

Her toes hit the floor as he set her down. "You said that already." He frowned at the mark on her neck. "Hey, what happened here?"

"It's work stuff. Aiden saved my life. We caught the bad guy. It's all good." She waved aside his concern and turned his face down to hers. She pushed off his khaki stocking cap and inspected him from his buzz cut of hair down to the snow still clinging to his Marines-issue boots. He looked good. Tired, but fit. His tan was darker, his eyes lined a little more deeply, but it felt wonderful to finally have him home. "You've already walked through the snow, haven't you?"

He nodded. "I love the cold air. Feel like I can breathe here." They were still gathered in the hallway. Levi in his digitized camo uniform, Lexi in her jammies, and Aiden in...

Oh, no. Her cheeks heated with embarrassment.

Levi grinned, seeing the exact moment when she realized that she and Aiden looked like they'd just made love. He flicked at the tag at the back of her neck. "Your shirt's on inside out, sis." Then he inclined his head toward Aiden. "And you, my friend, have no shirt on at all."

Aiden tucked the gun into the back of his jeans. "I can explain. It's been an interesting month. Things have changed."

Levi arched an eyebrow. "Seriously? You think I care that you've been in bed with my sister? Now, some other guy—"

"There is no other guy." Lexi stood beside Aiden, linking her arm with his, wondering if this was the moment that Aiden backed away from the closeness they shared. Because he owed something to her family, and he didn't believe that loyalty and nobility and love could all go hand in hand.

"I know that. Do you?" Levi stooped down to pet Blue, giving the dog a thorough wrestle and tummy rub. "Get a clue, you two. I've been throwing you together from three thousand miles away every way I could think of—telling you he needs a square meal at least once a week, telling you she needs someone to rotate her tires, shovel snow, look after her?" Levi pushed to his feet and winked at Aiden. "You've had the hots for her ever since she sprouted breasts—"

"Levi—!"

"And there's no man I'd trust to love her any better than I know you can."

He cupped Lexi's cheek in his big hand and smiled. "There's not a better man in the world, Lex. Have you two figured it out yet?"

"I have. I'm in love with Aiden." She tilted her gaze up to Aiden's. "I've been in love with you for a long time. The evidence is in my journals upstairs. I know you didn't want me to love you. That you just wanted us to be friends. But we're both. I'm closer to you than anyone else in the world, Aiden. You're my best friend and the man I love."

Levi crossed his arms over his chest and dared Aiden to better that speech. "You?"

"I kind of wanted to tell her how I felt first." He brushed a lock of hair off her cheek and tucked it behind her ear. "I love you, Lexi Callahan. I've never loved anybody else. I just didn't think I was the best man for you—"

"Shut up." Lexi rose up on her toes and wound her arms around Aiden's neck and kissed him. "I've never loved anyone else, either. You're the best man—the only man—for me."

Levi chuckled behind them. And when she turned to face him, her big brother was grinning from ear to ear. "My work here is done." He pulled his cap back on and lifted his duffel bag onto his shoulder.

"Where are you going?" Lexi stopped him at the door. "You just got home. Tomorrow is Christmas."

"Hotel. Don't worry. I'll be back for the festivities tomorrow morning. But I think you two have some celebrating you need to do tonight."

"I love you, Levi."

He leaned down to kiss her cheek. "Love you, too, kiddo."

He dropped the bag to shake hands with Aiden and pull him in for a quick hug. "Love you, bro."

"Love you."

"Densest couple I ever met." Levi headed out the door to his rental car, grumbling as the door closed behind him. "The Marine's always got to come in and save the day."

Once he was gone, Aiden and Lexi faced each other. Aiden loved her. Nothing seemed impossible to her now. "I think the K-9 Patrol saved the day just fine, without any help from the Marines."

"I had a lot of help from the crime lab."

She tangled her fingers together with his and backed toward the couch, pulling him along with her. "I had such a crush on you growing up. After Mom and Dad died, I was lost in grief and anger and pain. I needed you to be my friend. And you were. Then I went off to college and life happened, and we never got the chance to be something more."

"After your folks were killed, I was just lost. Patrick and my stepmoms weren't family to me—you and Levi were. I couldn't lose that." He set his gun on the table beside the sofa and recaptured her hand, tugging her to him. "It took nearly losing you to admit how deep my feelings go, how I never want to lose you again."

"For a cop and a criminalist—"

"Senior criminalist," he corrected, kissing her smile.

"We weren't very bright." She glanced at the door as they heard Levi driving away. "I can't believe that thick-headed Marine was playing matchmaker all along."

"I see the light now. I'm not losing my foster family. I'm gaining a family of my own."

"You're not going to lose me, Aiden Murphy. I love you."

"I love you, Lex. I need you. You're the only Christmas present I ever truly wanted."

"So I can take back those gifts under the tree?"

"You know what I want under the tree?" He scooped her up in his arms, then sat with her on the couch. A few minutes later, they were on the rug, kissing beneath the tree.

"Tell me one thing." He paused and lifted his head, looking far too serious as he waited for her to speak. "Did you really notice when I sprouted breasts?"

He laughed, palmed said breast and proceeded to make love to her. "Oh, yeah. I most certainly did."

* * * * *

COMING SOON!

We really hope you enjoyed reading this book.
If you're looking for more romance, be sure to
head to the shops when new books are
available on

Thursday 11ᵗʰ November

To see which titles are coming soon, please visit

millsandboon.co.uk/nextmonth

MILLS & BOON

MILLS & BOON

THE HEART OF ROMANCE

A ROMANCE FOR EVERY READER

MODERN

Prepare to be swept off your feet by sophisticated, sexy and seductive heroes, in some of the world's most glamourous and romantic locations, where power and passion collide.

HISTORICAL

Escape with historical heroes from time gone by. Whether your passion is for wicked Regency Rakes, muscled Vikings or rugged Highlanders, awaken the romance of the past.

MEDICAL

Set your pulse racing with dedicated, delectable doctors in the high-pressure world of medicine, where emotions run high and passion, comfort and love are the best medicine.

True Love

Celebrate true love with tender stories of heartfelt romance, from the rush of falling in love to the joy a new baby can bring, and a focus on the emotional heart of a relationship.

Desire

Indulge in secrets and scandal, intense drama and plenty of sizzling hot action with powerful and passionate heroes who have it all: wealth, status, good looks…everything but the right woman.

HEROES

Experience all the excitement of a gripping thriller, with an intense romance at its heart. Resourceful, true-to-life women and strong, fearless men face danger and desire - a killer combination!

To see which titles are coming soon, please visit

millsandboon.co.uk/nextmonth

LET'S TALK
Romance

For exclusive extracts, competitions
and special offers, find us online:

f facebook.com/millsandboon

y @MillsandBoon

◎ @MillsandBoonUK

Get in touch on 01413 063232

For all the latest titles coming soon, visit
millsandboon.co.uk/nextmonth

JOIN US ON SOCIAL MEDIA!

Stay up to date with our latest releases, author
news and gossip, special offers and discounts, and
all the behind-the-scenes action
from Mills & Boon...

 millsandboon

 millsandboonuk

 millsandboon

It might just be true love...